# Ghosts & Gravity

## ANTHOLOGY BENEFITING
## VETSPORTS

### foreword by
### RANDY THARP

BT URRUELA AND ANNE MALCOM - I KNEW IT WAS LOVE
SHANI STRUTHERS - THE GUARDIAN
BECCA VRY - CHRYSALIDE
AI TRAN - THE MAN IN WHITE
A.S. ORTON - THE BLACKEST CROW
SUSAN K. SWORDS - HARRY NILSSON WAS RIGHT
KRIS BABE - A SUMMER OF LOVE
CHRISTOPHER WINKS - THE SOJOURN
D.L. HARTMAN - BELLALOKI
RUMOR HAVEN - GHOSTED
MORGAN & JENNIFER LOCKLEAR - ROBERT

Front Cover Design: Krys Janae
Interior and Back Cover Design: Lindsey Gray
Published by Locklear Books

This book is a work of fiction. Names, characters, places, and incidents are the product of the authors' imaginations and are used fictitiously. Any resemblance of actual events, locales, or persons, living or dead, is coincidental.

ISBN:

Locklear Books

LocklearBooks

www.locklearbooks.com
info@locklearbooks.com.

All proceeds of this collection are to benefit VETSports:
https://vetsports.org/

# Table of Contents

# Acknowledgments

Locklear Books would like to thank all Veterans for their service and sacrifice.

The following people volunteered their time on this project:

Jocqueline M. Protho and the production crew at The Audio Flow: Daniele Lanzarotta, Margaret Gorski, Amy Deuchler, Jillian Cole.

Voice actors: Aaron Shedlock, Amy Landon, Teri Clark Linden, Andrea Emmes, James R. Cheatham, Michael Wolfe, Noya Einhorn, Amy Deuchler, Deanna Anthony, Marnye Young, Krys Janae, Zachary Johnson, Hillary Huber, Lydia Palmer, Jocqueline M. Protho.

Krys Janae, front cover design.

Lindsey Gray, back cover and interior design, all formatting.

Marla Esposito at Proofing Style, copy editing.

The authors who all worked to intertwine elements of their stories.

Thanks to everyone for supporting VETSports with the purchase of this unique anthology in any of its three formats, digital, print, and audio.

-Morgan and Jennifer Locklear

# Foreword by Randy Tharp

President and Co-founder of VETSports

War, the ugliest and most brutal act of violence mankind can possibly bring upon itself. The devastation, heartache, and bloodshed that comes with it leaves in its wake much more than the rubble of a building's past or tombstones carefully placed in perfect rows upon a beautiful green field. It leaves behind an emptiness, a void in a soldier's heart when they reintroduce themselves with the world they once knew. A world that was once a familiar place is now something they will never relate to the same way again.

Heroes live silently around us, carrying the burden of war in their memories and nightmares as they watch their society thrive around them. The ugly truth is that many will never find comfort or peace again. Society forgets about the more than 3.3 Million brave men and women who donned the uniform to serve in Iraq and Afghanistan on their behalf as they go about their busy lives. And that is okay, that is expected, and that is the goal of a successful war campaign, is it not. To live free. To live in a place where our family doesn't have to worry about war?

For my co-founders and I, we were not going to be silent nor forget about our fellow soldiers. Our individual journeys to find comfort at home led us to the same place, VETSports. We were in separate units, deployed to Iraq at separate times, and fought tirelessly in battles from the desert to city streets. While never crossing paths on the front lines, our paths at home brought us to the same fork in the road. Alone, despite being surrounded by family and friends. Sad, though on paper happiness should have been abundant. Empty, as though nothing could ever fill it.

All of us were looking for something and there was nothing available. As prior athletes, we sought a healthy and active life and found a synergy between belonging to a team that resembled both military and team sports. We saw ourselves as competitors and strived to push boundaries despite mental or physical injuries and wanted an avenue to prove that we could be competitive. We sought comradery, friendship, and struggle which can be found on the friendly fields of strife. We wanted to belong and improve our communities, not just sit idly by. With a shared vision and passion, the seeds of VETSports were planted.

VETSports was founded ten years ago, with the goal of being able to provide a platform for Veterans across the country. A home where courage, teamwork, and resilience are valued and shared. VETSports members belong and earn their jerseys. They are not just encouraged to participate through sports every week, but to volunteer and help other organizations bettering the community around them. Our approach was simple, lean, and scalable. VETSports has seen significant growth as Veterans returning home look for an opportunity to lead, belong, and thrive through sports, physical activity, and community involvement. Our Veterans are part of a team, held accountable, and are counted on to show up and participate. They find a social network where they naturally belong, share stories, and heal without even knowing how much they are growing in a world where they may have felt lost in before.

In 2020, VETSports served over Veterans across thirty-four different chapters around the United States and Japan. We are the only organization that provides league uniforms, registration fees, travel, meals, scholarships, and financial assistance as we focus on the whole health of our Veterans, and not just one aspect of it. We have partnered with the Department of Veterans Affairs by participating in their adaptive sports program and have even supported athletes pursue goals of major league baseball and even para bobsledding through our sponsored athlete program.

During 2020-2021, VETSports along with the country fought to find a new normal through the COVID-19 Pandemic. Unable to host large fundraisers, we relied upon the good will of individuals who knew the benefits of our organization and knew that Veterans needed our support. As other businesses and outlets shut down, Veterans sought our support to get active and get outside. Our membership grew to over ten thousand members as we fought hard to find the funding to keep our programs and chapters going to be the resource they needed. We are hopeful the pandemic has slowed, which we know will lead to increased participation with more indoor sports.

Our growth and ability to sustain and support our Veterans is only possible with the help of generous people like you. By supporting this anthology, you are supporting over ten thousand Veterans stay active and belong in a world instead of being a part of the twenty-two Veterans that leave us each day to suicide. Thank you for acknowledging the sacrifices they have made and thank you from the bottom of our hearts for putting your trust in us.

Randy Tharp
President and Co-founder
VETSports

BT Urruela
VP and Co-founder
VETSports

# I KNEW IT WAS LOVE
## BT URRUELA & ANNE MALCOM

# Chapter One
## Eddie Mac

It's a funny thing to spend years in a place but still feel like a stranger. The world ebbs and flows around you, moving and weaving in all directions, as you stand motionless in the center, frozen. Unable to join in or move freely on your own. You're the porch light of which the bugs gather, turned on and off at the whim of another, unable to act on your own. Unable to buzz freely into the night like the bugs that surround you.

It was how I felt growing up in the South Bronx, and how it had been since I moved to San Francisco nearly five years before in pursuit of a music career, and to escape the life I led before it. In my youth, it was my shyness that precluded me from making friends, that kept me on the outskirts of social circles. It was my disjointed and often violent home life where I placed the blame then. As an adult, with New York City and all the ugliness of my youth in the rearview, it was my straight edge nature that carried the blame. I had turned down drugs of all varieties many times over the five years that I spent in San Francisco, struggling to find my way as a musician in a city full of prodigious, doped up hippies. I tried hash just once and felt as if my soul was caving in on itself, like I couldn't remember how to breathe. The drink, I always shied away from, worried it would turn me into my father, or worse yet, into my father's father. I managed one hit song when I first arrived in San Francisco, when I still possessed some semblance of aspiration and hope. "I Knew it was Love" was a lousy record, all things considered. And it paled in comparison to what I had written before and after it, at least in my humble opinion. However, the poppy, saccharine sweet mess of a song stuck with listeners, and then it stuck to me like aged honey. I couldn't shake it. Couldn't break free from its strangling embrace. Couldn't write another hit record if my life depended on it. I felt washed up already, and I was only in my late twenties. How ironic it was that a man who had never known love based his whole career around a song about it, his whole fucking identity.

Despite all of that, I was filled with sadness on my last day in San Francisco, my eyes trailing the wooden cladding of the dilapidated stick style house that I had called home for several years. It was a sadness fueled by the five roommates inside who couldn't bother seeing me off, and by my own inability to get to know them over the course of my stay. The cool bay breeze rushed past me, smelling of salt and scum. People passed by too. Some with arms interlocked and wide smiles on their faces. Others engaged in raucous conversations and boisterous laughter and they made me feel that much more alone.

At my feet sat all of my worldly possessions: a crate of my favorite vinyl records, my acoustic guitar in its tattered case, my father's military A bag filled with my white tees and Levi jeans, and a tackle box filled with all of the letters my mother had sent me over the years; many of them left unopened. They would soon be loaded onto the tattered seats of my rusted, powder blue '63 Buick Riviera, and driven back to New York City, to the place I left behind all those years ago, to the place that still held all my pain, and my secrets, and my mother now six feet underground, beside the father I never quite knew. The man who left us both as damaged as two people could possibly be.

# Chapter Two
## Alice

"I had the dream again."

I wrung my hands together on my lap, twisting at the smooth skin, inspecting my fresh manicure.

There was a chip. Small. Miniscule. But it was there. A ragged edge on the otherwise perfect pale pink polish. There was no such thing as perfect. Always decay.

But focusing on that small chip in my perfect manicure kept my mind off other things. Uglier things. Like the way a body looked twisted on the sidewalk. Lifeless. How it somehow didn't look human. Except the eyes. Staring with a sadness that a corpse shouldn't have.

A clock ticked in the quiet room. It was louder than a clock should sound. It echoed against the beige walls, covered in carefully chosen impersonal art. It wasn't loud enough to drown out the sickening thoughts inside my head, though.

"The same dream?" Harris asked.

I glanced up at her. She was gazing at me through spectacles that were too big for her face. Made her look like she was a kid trying on her mom's glasses. Dorothy Harris was hard to find. She was a highly regarded female therapist who graduated from an Ivy League school. One of very few women in her graduating class. One of very few women in the city with her own practice in an industry dominated by men. Then again, every industry was an industry dominated by men. But that would change. It had to change.

I called her Harris in my own head. Didn't quite know why. But Dorothy didn't suit the woman with the tight low bun, the severe cheekbones, the expensive blouse and the skirt that was too long to be fashionable or flattering. Harris was better.

I sighed, eyes flickering from her glasses and small, childlike face with thick eyebrows and small lips to the degree on her wall.

"The same dream," I said finally. "The exact same dream. Of that day."

"Your mind experienced a trauma, Alice," Harris said. Her pen scratched on the pad that had been resting in her lap. "Something like that leaves a mark. A stain. Dreams are our subconscious trying to deal with things that we avoid in our waking hours. You're trying to forget what you went through, Alice. And you can't forget. Not until you've dealt with it."

My fingernails dug into my palms, and I gritted my teeth against the fury that bubbled in the back of my throat.

"I'm dealing with it," I gritted out. "That's why I'm sitting here, isn't it? That's what I'm paying you for, to fix."

Harris put down her notebook and pen, pushed her glasses back up to the ridge of her nose and smiled at me without teeth. Her lips thinned with the expression.

"You cannot be fixed, Alice, because you aren't broken," she said. "Sitting here for forty-five minutes once a week isn't going to erase what happened. It certainly isn't going to change it. I'm here to listen. To make sure that you don't try to forget this, pretend it didn't happen, that you acknowledge it so it doesn't crop up later in life in other ways." Her hazel eyes held mine.

I hated her. Which didn't make a lot of sense. Harris was an intelligent, accomplished woman who was good at her job and was trying to help me. But still, I hated her. For not giving me a pill. A magic solution. An eraser of some sort to scrub my mind of that moment and all the moments that came after it.

But no.

She asked about my family. My past. My childhood. My relationships. Asked why I wasn't married, despite closing in on my thirtieth birthday. Despite the fact that she was older than me—even though she didn't look it, she looked a decade younger and I'd bet she still got carded whenever she went to buy her nightly bottle of Chardonnay—her left ring finger was also naked.

Though she wasn't asking the question for the same reason everyone else asked it, wondering what was wrong with me, what hid underneath the carefully styled hair, the tight, fashionable clothes, the conventional beauty that made it so a man didn't want to marry me.

Even though we were supposed to be moving past all that, a woman still had to be broken or difficult or crazy to be single. It couldn't be she didn't want to be a wife. She wanted to be something more.

Harris wasn't asking this particular question for the conventional reason. She was asking it because she wanted to pick me apart, wanted to dissect my insides so she could use it to help me, sure. But maybe also in case she could find something juicy, something rotten that might land her a spot in some medical journal or be a chapter in her book someday.

Despite her youthful, petite appearance, I could see the sharpness in her eyes, the hunger. I saw it in my own icy blue irises. The need to be something more than a woman. To make it in what was still a man's world.

Which was why I was here. Sitting in the chair, talking about this thing that happened. Because I'd tried to forget. Tried to be strong, then I had somewhat of an ... episode at work.

Which was what people called it in hushed tones, either behind my back or if you were an asshole, like my boss, Harold, to my face.

*"Now we can give this assignment to someone else, we don't want you having another ... breakdown."*

I was already on his shit list because I happened to have a vagina and did not automatically bow to him because he happened to have a dick. But that was the way of the world. I was lucky that he moved on from me when I became too complicated. When it became obvious that I wouldn't be fucking him. Not if my life or my job depended on it. Nonetheless, I was lucky to have my own job, a good income, a great apartment, and be in charge of my own life.

Everyone I'd gone to school with were married with about three kids by now, married long enough for their husbands to develop a paunch, start balding, and only vaguely resemble the handsome teenager he'd been when they'd married. Long enough to see those husbands take up mistresses, younger and leaner than the wives they left at home with the kids. Beyond that, they were still in some dead-end job, drinking or gambling away the family money, so the fridge was always bare.

I knew that life because that was the way of the world in the South Bronx. Because that was how I grew up, how my friends grew up. It's all we'd ever known.

Until I got out.

"Alice?"

I jerked, staring at Harris. I had not heard a word she'd said. But you could bet your ass I'd be paying for it anyway.

"Our time is up," she said with her probing eyes still focused uncomfortably tight on me.

I snatched my purse.

"Same time next week?"

I nodded through gritted teeth and escaped before she could prod at anything that I wouldn't be able to tuck safely back into the corners of my life before work.

New York magazine was relatively new on the scene in 1972. It was controversial, brash, and the New Yorker's trailer trash cousin. Which is how I got the job as fashion editor in the first place.

Well, Gloria Steinem was the reason I had a job as a fashion editor. She was the one who convinced the powers that be to do a *Ms.* issue which was only in its infancy and the reason I was a fashion editor and not a secretary like I had been only last year. A well-paid secretary to be sure, but only because I actually did the work of about four men that would've been paid double what I made.

"Hi, Alice," Betty, the receptionist, chirped as I walked past her.

Chirped.

She was perpetually happy, her hair always set, sprayed and firmly in the 1950s. Betty was only here until Trip—who worked on *Wall Street*, you know—popped the question.

I nodded and smiled tightly because that was all I was capable of right now. I was coiled with tension, with that teeth grinding feeling that I hadn't been able to shake since *that day.*

Luckily, today was the day I could shut myself in my office—I was pretty sure they converted a broom closet—and work on a piece for the next issue. I stayed at the office as long as I could, much longer than I used to. That was only partly due to the piece I was working on. Mostly, it was because I was afraid to go home. Afraid of the memories that haunted me there.

# Chapter Three
## Eddie Mac

I stayed the night in a seedy motel room in the South Bronx, exhausted from the two-day drive from San Francisco with stops in Salt Lake City and Chicago along the way, unaffected by the stiff mattress and the periodic rattling like an earthquake caused by the subway passing overhead. After grabbing a quick bite to eat, I made my way down the sidewalk along the streets where I spent my youth, though, nothing looked as it once did. The Bronx had always been sketchy, but the area carried with it now a looming sense of danger and dread. The street was dotted with the remnants of buildings tattooed with char from fires that had burned throughout the city on a regular basis.

I found the lawyer's office situated between a bodega and a hair salon. The office smelled of mothballs and musk, and pictures and diplomas were perched askew on the walls. I sat idly by in a faux leather chair, a desk across from me strewn with papers and folders and stained with old coffee rings. An ashtray was situated among the mess, crammed full of cigarette butts. The opening door behind me drew my attention, and I turned back to see the man I was meeting with waddling his way through, out of breath and with a fresh cup of coffee in his hand. He looked worse for the wear from the last time I saw him, and a good hundred pounds heavier than all those years ago when he first befriended my mother and father.

He paused momentarily as he took me in, a goofy smile on his face, a bushy mustache straddling his upper lip. He nodded before proceeding to his chair across from me. As he took a seat, he said, "Edward McArthur, my Lord, you're all grown up! What's it been, ten, fifteen years?"

"Something like that," I replied. "How you been? I'm surprised to see you still out here in the South Bronx. This place has turned into a real shit hole. It looks like a war zone out here."

He nodded his head in agreement. Shrugged. "Yeah, it has. Piece of shit residents can't stop burning their own shit down. Trying to mooch off the system. But the South Bronx has my heart. Always has. Always will. Can't give up on it so easily. It'll come around once we get the trash out of here. As for how I've been, well ..." He motioned to his gut. "The pizza and donuts have taken their toll." He then motioned to the strands of gray hair combed over his bald scalp. "And father time has as well." He let out a belly laugh and took a noisy sip of coffee before setting the mug down onto the desktop. "What about you? Have you been keeping at the music thing? Your mother told me you had become a rock star. She played me that song of yours. Good stuff," he said, unconvincingly.

"It was garbage, you can say it," I responded through a grin.

"Well, not my cup of tea, but an achievement, nonetheless. Better than that disco garbage that's all over the damn place now. Gotta be pretty neat to hear your own song on the radio, at least."

I shrugged, wishing we were talking about anything else. The Yankees, the traffic, the weather … anything other than the song I just couldn't shake or replicate. "It was far out the first few times, I guess. Can't seem to get another one to stick though."

"You'll get there, I'm sure." His eyebrows raised. "Amazing you managed to avoid the draft. What are you twenty-five, twenty-six years old now?"

"Twenty-eight."

"Twenty-eight … prime war fighting age," he muttered. "Hm … you didn't burn your draft card like the rest of them pussy hippies and fairies out there in San Fran, now did ya?" He smirked, but his tone was snarky.

"I would never. If my country called upon me to serve, I would serve. But I can't blame those people you speak of for wanting no part of it. Hard to find the desire to serve a country that hates you. And fighting for all the wrong reasons, at that."

He eyed me curiously as he pulled a pack of Embassy Gold cigarettes from his breast pocket and tapped one out. He lit it and took a puff, releasing the smoke into the small room in little circles. "I imagine just as hard for a country to care about people who hate it and who disrespect it at every goddamn turn."

"Is it disrespect, or is it simply asking the country to stop sending our young people halfway around the world to die for some bullshit cause? Asking for the same freedoms allotted to others? I don't see senators' kids shipping off to 'Nam. I don't see gay people being given the same rights as straight people. If they can't marry, why should they be forced to serve?"

"Your father served this country, you know. And proudly. Fought the Japs *and* the krauts. He's probably rolling over in his grave right now hearing this."

"I know full well that my father served. And he brought the war back home with him in spades. I don't wish that upon the youth of today. On the kids and wives of the lucky ones who don't come home in a body bag. The ones who bear the brunt of the war at home."

He took a long drag of his cigarette, annoyed eyes peering at me through the smoke. "Well, I wish we were meeting under better circumstances. I assumed our meeting would've occurred sooner, though. Like, soon after we discussed everything on the phone. Thought you might've come out for your mother's funeral, at least. It was only me and a few of her old coworkers from the library there. Even her dirtbag ex-husband showed up. But not you."

I was struck by shock as I hadn't known that she remarried. It was most likely told to me in one of those unopened letters in my tackle box. "I don't think she noticed my absence. And I had matters to settle back in San Francisco before I made the trip."

"You didn't know she remarried, did you? I can tell by the look on your face." He shook his head judgmentally. "He was a real piece of work. Treated your mother terribly. Took her a while to get rid of him, though I had been telling her she needed to for years." He pursed his lips, eyeing me peculiarly over the top of his horn-rimmed glasses. "Help me understand something, Edward—"

"Eddie."

"I'm sorry?"

"I go by Eddie now."

"That's right … Eddie Mac, musician extraordinaire," he corrected himself, a frown growing on his face. "Help me to understand. What is it your mother ever did to you to deserve this treatment? You take off to the other side of the country. Leaving your mother behind and never visiting her. Never ringing her. Never responding to her letters. She told me all about it, you know. She was lonely. Had to deal with the loss of her job at the library after bullshit budget cuts. Had to deal with that miserable ex of hers. Divorce. Had to spend her last few years without family to care for her. I can't help but think things would've gone differently if you were here to support her. Maybe, she'd still be alive today. Didn't she deserve at least that for bringing you up?"

"I'm not here to talk hypotheticals with you. I'm also not here to be lectured by you. So, how about we get to the business at hand, huh?" I crossed my arms and bobbed my foot. I wasn't too keen on being disrespectful, especially toward an old family friend, but that man didn't know me.

He knew my parents, and he didn't know enough about them—about what happened behind closed doors—to be telling me how things were.

He hesitated, peering at me, his thick mustache twitching. He dabbed his cigarette out in the crowded ashtray. "As you wish. As I mentioned when we spoke on the phone, your mother left you everything. Her apartment at the Wellraven Apartment Complex in Manhattan, as well as everything in it, and what remained in her checking and savings account. A great deal of what was left in those accounts was used to pay back taxes, and my fees, of course, but there is several thousand left. Which isn't gonna last you very long with the crazy tax rate out there. Hope you can shit out another hit song before you run out of funds." He chuckled, rifling through papers on his desk, and he located a manila envelope. He handed it over to me. "You'll find the apartment information—deed, and all that—as well as keys to her apartment, the complex itself, and her letterbox in there, and also her account information at Chase Bank. You'll just need to sign a few forms and we'll have you on your way." He hesitated a moment before continuing, "It was her dream to live in a skyrise in Manhattan, you know? She finally made it happen with insurance money from your father's death. It's too bad she only had a few short years to enjoy it. It's too bad she spent those few short years alone."

"Too bad, indeed." I nodded. "Too bad she didn't have a friend of twenty-plus years close by who could've checked in on her every now and then. Made sure she was doing okay. You dig?"

The relatively mild morning temperatures gave way to a balmy midday. The concrete walkways and towering buildings of Manhattan seemed to suck up all the heat and trap it, and I could feel the heat radiating through the soles of my boots, making the walk to Wellraven from where I parked my car a mile away that much worse. I had spent the better part of the morning after my meeting battling traffic and then simply looking for a place to park, and it was a nice reminder of just how much I hated that part of New York City. As were the filthy streets and the ever-present smell of piss that lingered in the air. I left my A bag with all of my clothes along with the tackle box in the trunk of my car to retrieve later, but I didn't dare leave my records and guitar in the car in an area like Manhattan, with the dodgiest of people around every corner.

It wasn't difficult to spot the Wellraven building off of Seventieth Street. It was painted a gaudy orange like some monstrous traffic cone towering into the clouds. The colors of the 70s were something I had never quite gotten used to. I held on to that fifties James Dean mentality— conservative, muted tones—as the world shifted to technicolor around me. I was Levis and motorcycle boots in a world of bell bottoms and platform shoes.

22

As I approached the building and scanned it from the tip-top down to the stained, mucky sidewalk at my feet, my stomach went queasy. My skin went cold and lined with goose bumps. I stood for a moment there, the guitar case and milk crate of records weighing heavy in my hands as I waited for the feeling to pass.

I stood in front of apartment 1402 for some time, apprehensive about entering into a world I left long ago, worried about opening old wounds and developing new ones. Fact of the matter was I was madder at myself than I was toward my mother's old lawyer friend because, for the most part, he spoke the truth. My mother was never the one to lay a hand on me, she never had a coarse word for me, she loved me as best she could. It was my father and all the painful memories associated with him that I tried to escape from. The anger I carried toward my mother spilled over from that, along with her inability to get us out of that situation, away from my father's spectacular rage. I wanted her to care about me more than him, more about our own emotional well-being than some hope of him ever getting better. But she stayed, and I became the focal point of my father's hatred for everything and everyone after the war, and in turn, I became a shell of a man in my adult years, unable to cope with my own emotions, unable to form a lasting relationship with anyone. And now here I was, forced to reconcile with my past, and made to accept that I was a party to the death of my own mother.

I slipped the key into the lock and opened the door slowly. I slid the milk crate full of records in through the doorframe with my foot and followed in after it. I shut the door behind me and set my guitar case against it. The air in the apartment was stale and hazy. Everything was covered in a layer of dust. The walls of the entryway were adorned with photos of my mother and her family and friends, a few were of me, and I stopped at the photo of my father in his military uniform. My stomach turned as my eyes traced the outline of his young face, his thin frown, his deep-set, chestnut eyes. I removed the frame, turned it around, and set it on the floor, leaning it against the wall. Continuing into the apartment, I couldn't help but feel as if I was entering some massive time capsule. The furniture was all the same as I grew up with in the old brownstone in the South Bronx. There was the antique percolator on the kitchen counter, my Aunt Jean's hand stitched afghan laying across the back of the old rocker my mother used to nurse me in, and even the old Admiral television in the cabinet beside her RCA record player in the living room. I worked my way to the cabinet and pulled open the record drawer, sifting through the vinyls until I located Frank Sinatra's *In the Wee Small Hours*—my mother's favorite—and I put it on the record player and started it up.

As Frank crooned away, I took a moment of pause. I wasn't ready to enter her room just yet, to feel her presence to that degree. I breathed in deep. The smell was reminiscent of the days of my youth—lavender, which my mother always kept in the house, and the Avon hand cream she adored. I passed through the living room slowly and lingered in the first room I came upon. The room was

24

filled wall to wall, floor to ceiling, with bookcases, hundreds of books lining the shelves. Faulkner, Fitzgerald, London, and Hemingway, to name a few—many of them with tattered bindings, well-worn from the hands of a true bibliophile. I trailed a finger down a row of books and landed on *The Bell Jar* by Sylvia Plath. I removed it from the shelf, as if not by my own hand but orchestrated by some omnipresent being. I turned it over and skimmed the back, and then I took it with me to my mother's room. When I walked in, I felt overwhelmed, as if her presence surrounded me, embraced me. An eerie chill trailed my skin.

Her four-poster bed took up much of the room, the same bed she once shared with my father. A picture of Jesus hanged just above it. Her vanity sat on the far wall, but I couldn't bear to look at myself in the mirror. I felt that if I did, I might see her staring back at me, her hollow eyes pleading for me to save her, her wrinkled hands reaching out to me. I opened the door leading to the balcony and a rush of air met me from the other side. I sucked in a breath as I made my way to the railing. When I looked over it and down toward the concrete below, I imagined my mother in this very spot, looking down at the sidewalk, her tears rolling down her wrinkled cheeks before making their descent toward the pavement. A descent she would make herself, before meeting the hard concrete in a violent collision, her body crumpling against the surface in a pile of blood, bones, and viscera. I wondered what she might have been thinking about in those few moments before she decided to jump. I wondered if regret hit her on her way down. I wanted to cry, wanted to unleash the guilt and the turmoil I had pent up inside, but I just couldn't. I couldn't seem to feel a thing.

I woke up some time later from the chair on the balcony with *The Bell Jar* open and resting on my chest. The sun had slipped behind the surrounding buildings, and the temperature had lowered substantially. I headed to the bathroom to splash water on my face in an effort to wake myself up. After doing so, I lingered there in front of the porcelain washbowl, my fingers gripping the ledge. The water rolled down my tired face, collecting in my five o'clock shadow. The mirror cruelly reflected my sense of self-hatred in the various imperfections dotting my skin, and the sunken eyes of a man who could only sleep when he shouldn't be, and who never slept when he should, when the world turned off, and the sheep reached the thousands. Out of curiosity, I opened the mirror, exposing the medicine cabinet. I wondered if I would find my mother's old friends in there. They surely would help me sleep when the time came.

I did find the Seconals in the medicine cabinet, the ones I had OD-ed on so long ago, when I was a sad young man with seemingly no other means of escape from a father I despised, and a life that was swallowing me whole. I didn't know what they were for back then, not even after they were pumped from my stomach. I just knew my mother seemed to love the little red pills more than she loved me, and that a bottle full in my empty stomach should've done the trick and put me out of my misery. If it weren't for my mother coming home early and discovering me convulsing on the bathroom floor, they would have. It wasn't until I read *Valley of the Dolls* years later that I was able to understand what my mother was doing. Why she seemed to have a pill for every occasion. Beside the Seconal bottle were bottles of Obetrol, six in total. I recognized the pills as those that Andy Warhol used for stimulation. A fleeting thought swept through my mind that perhaps the pills would be helpful in locating my own genius just as they had done for Andy. Perhaps, they could block my apprehension and self-doubt and allow me to make music freely for once. I fought the temptation and grabbed one of the packs of Lucky Strike that lined the bottom shelf of the medicine cabinet instead, and I closed the cabinet door. Though I wasn't too keen on Lucky Strike cigarettes, I had run out of my Marlboros that morning and was in desperate need of a nicotine fix. I opened the pack and tapped one out, lighting it with a matchbook from the back of the toilet, before making my way out of the apartment, first, to grab the rest of my stuff from the car, and then, to check my mother's mailbox, which was likely overflowing.

"Edward McArthur!"

The voice caught me off guard. I had been preoccupied with collecting up the pile of mail from my mother's letterbox and stuffing it into the tackle box resting at my feet that I hadn't noticed someone else come along. By the name they used, I knew it must've been someone from my past, and not someone who had simply known me from my one and only Johnny Carson appearance from what seemed like a lifetime ago. Despite my very short stint of success, I was still recognized for that appearance from time to time. I reluctantly looked over, taking in an incredibly beautiful woman standing next to me, a wide smile on her face as she tended to her own letterbox. There was a familiarity to her, but I couldn't quite place it.

"That's me," I said sheepishly. I forced a timid smile. "Though, I go by Eddie these days."

"You don't remember me, do you?" she asked, and slipped a hand to her hip. Her tone was slightly teasing, familiar.

"I want to say I do, but I'm coming up short. My memory is shit."

"Alice Freeman," she replied, and immediately I realized who she was. "Bobby Freeman's sister. It's been a while. I don't blame you for not remembering."

I closed and locked the mailbox door and pocketed the keys. "Of course! Sorry for my momentary forgetfulness. You just look so … different. All grown up."

Grown up for sure. She'd been a beautiful girl then. Smokin'. There was a constant layer of grime that covered my memories of the South Bronx, but Alice Freeman was one of the few clean, stark images I could recall. She was always dressed up, even then. In clothes with sparkles, colors, and sheens that didn't belong in the Bronx.

She was wearing all black that day. Molding over the curves that the years had perfected. Tiny waist. Hips. Tits that it took all my willpower not to stare at. But her face. Rosebud mouth. Delicate features. Eyes that were sharp, piercing, strong. A gaze that I felt in my dick. Her hair wasn't teased up like most of the girls did those days. It was pulled back, slick off her face in a way that should've looked severe but only made her more beautiful. Back in high school, her chocolate brown hair was unruly, thick, and shiny. I'd always wanted to run my fingers through it. Sometimes I'd get close enough to smell the raspberry shampoo she used. Usually, if I was that close, she was giving me shit about something.

I was suddenly pissed off at her. Fury crawled up my throat. I hated her for smiling warmly at me with those plump lips, tilting her head ever so slightly to the left so I could see the smooth column of her neck.

"You do too," she said, nodding, unaware of my anger toward her. Unaware of the impact she'd had on me. "You sure aren't that shy little fifteen-year-old anymore."

29

I shrugged, doing my best to shrug off that anger. "Well, the shy bit is unfortunately still there, but, no, I'm not the little runt you once knew. How's Bobby doing by the way? It's been ages."

"He's doing really well. A stockbroker now, if you can believe it." She smiled proudly, speaking warmly of the brother she'd tormented back in school.

"No way!" I genuinely couldn't believe my mischievous childhood best friend—the guy who introduced me to cigarettes, graffiti, and shoplifting—now worked on Wall Street. "Bobby freakin' Freeman a stockbroker? How did he manage that?"

"He finally grew up." She chuckled. The sound was throaty and feminine at the same time. "How about you, mister rock star? I love that song of yours, by the way. 'I knew it was love in that moment between us, when time tick-tocked and stopped from the feel of your touch,'" she sang, her smile growing wider, her perfectly aligned, porcelain teeth gleaming under the dull light above. "What a writer you became! How is the career going?"

I gritted my teeth, forcing the smile to stay plastered on my face. "Stalled out after that song, sadly. Haven't been able to break out with anything else since."

Alice barely blinked at the well-rehearsed line that still came out like razor blades. She motioned around the lobby. "Well, you live in Wellraven. You must be doing all right. Did you just move in? I haven't seen you around before."

"Yeah, yeah I did." I didn't elaborate. Couldn't. Wouldn't. "And you? Have you been here long?"

"A couple of years now. It's close to work and the neighbors are nice."

I nodded like I cared. Like I had any intention of staying long enough to know *nice* neighbors. I would sell what I could of my mother's possessions, throw away what I couldn't, and unload the apartment to someone who actually wanted it. The sooner, the better. Maybe,\ I'd go back to San Francisco. Maybe I'd fuck off to Mexico, and waste away on a beach with tacos and tequila. "Where are you working these days?"

"*New York Magazine.* It's a gas!" She adjusted the purse on her shoulder. I didn't know much about purses, but it looked expensive. "Been writing for them for about five years now. Since I finished with my masters at NYU."

"Impressive! I always knew you'd become something great." And by that, I meant, she was the toughest woman I'd ever known, and not in the best of ways sometimes. She gave me more shit than any guy friend ever had. Bullying would be an understatement. Her reputation at Morris High School carried on long after she graduated. And as her brother's best friend in high school—terribly shy with an ugly past that everyone knew all about—I bore the brunt of it. I wondered at that moment if she even remembered just how hard on me that she was back then, back when I still had a chance. I wondered if she remembered the stories that went around the school like a

31

plague, the stories of the sad boy who nearly killed himself.

She smiled openly at me, without memory or visible regret. No, that pretty girl turned stunning woman wouldn't hold on to any of that shit like I had. To her, it was likely just a little innocent shit-giving to pass the time. For me, in conjunction with all the other shit I received in a school and a town of people who could never understand me, it was damaging. She lived in Manhattan, wrote for some fancy magazine, looked like she could walk down a runway at any moment. Looked like she'd shed every scrap of her past. Her memories of me weren't stark, carved out of muck. They were vague, soft and blurry around the edges, like some dusty old photograph. It was a miracle she even remembered my name.

The silence between us had lasted a few moments too long, I realized. It had gone from being a natural, comfortable pause between sentences to something thicker, more awkward, harder to penetrate. I cleared my throat, suddenly that uncomfortable teenage boy again. "Well, I should probably ..." I trailed off because I had nothing to do. Nowhere to go. The prospect of heading back up to that museum of my mother's suffering, artifacts of my failures as a son, was suffocating—like a noose around my neck.

"Yeah," Alice said, saving me from having to pull together a lame lie. "I should probably," she pointed upward with a pink fingernail, "too." She smiled, clutching her mail to her chest.

*Don't stare at her tits*, I reminded myself. *You hated this woman. You still do. Always will.*

Her blue eyes kept me ensnared. "It was really good to see you, Eddie," she said softly. "Maybe we could grab some coffee one day and catch up?"

I nodded. "Absolutely."

*Not a fucking chance.*

# Chapter Four
## Alice

I dropped my mail on the credenza in my entryway, mind still on the conversation with Edward McArthur—*he goes by Eddie now*, I reminded myself.

Eddie.

It suited him. Just like that onyx-colored hair that was swept up on his head except for one strand curling down toward his eye. Effortlessly cool, something he hadn't been in high school. I had to mentally squint to call up what he'd looked like back then. Gangly. All arms and legs. Awkward. Unsure of himself. Uncomfortable in his own skin.

Sad eyes that flit in all directions, avoiding contact with others.

He still had those sad eyes now, edged with maturity, with a little sparkle that I was sure made the girls go wild. He had the musician look down pat. Leather boots, good quality but worn. Jeans, the same. Plain white tee, crisp, without wrinkles or stains, rolled up at his biceps, showing off lean and muscular arms. My mind was still on those arms as I deposited my purse on my sofa.

The best sofa in the world. Emerald green. Velvet. Cost a bomb. I'd emptied everything in my account to buy this sofa five years ago. But it was *luxury*. It was the kind of luxury I'd never thought I'd own; never thought I'd even be allowed to touch in the store. Buttery soft, elegantly designed, instead of screaming money, it whispered it with class. The natural light from my windows streamed in, illuminating everything else I'd collected over the years to embody the luxury of my green sofa. Vintage rugs. Carefully curated art-prints, of course not originals. Every surface gleaming because I would never live anywhere that was covered in dust and stains again.

My apartment in Wellraven was designed to be everything I never had. Designed to be a testament to my hard work and an oasis.

It hadn't felt like that since that day. Since I barely slept. Since I stood at the window at three in the morning with a generous glass of whiskey, washing it down with a little white pill, aching for that sound to go away.

I wasn't thinking of that now. I was thinking of Eddie and his arms. Those sad eyes. The way his voice was low, husky, and soft.

My fingers dialed. While I wondered about him, I twirled the cord around my finger while I listened to the low thrum of the phone.

"Lizzie," I said when my friend finally answered. The only one I kept in regular contact with from school. The only other one to escape the South Bronx.

"Alice!" she replied. "Where have you been? I've left *a thousand* messages."

My grip tightened around the phone cord. "Work has been crazy busy," I said, not a lie. I didn't pause because I didn't want her to push me. Lizzie knew me too well, and I wasn't ready to talk about that. "You'll never guess who I just saw," I continued quickly, in that hushed tone I knew would get her off the scent. Lizzie was a good friend and she loved me. But she also loved gossip.

"Who?" she asked, mimicking that same hushed tone.

"Edward McArthur."

There was a pause, a faint crackling in the line. "Bobby's friend? The one who ..." she trailed off. "Took all those pills," she said on a whisper, like we were back at school and he was seated at the next table over in the cafeteria.

"Yeah," I replied, feeling faintly sick remembering all of that. It had been the talk of the school and everyone spoke in those whispers, everyone stared at the back of his head and averted their gazes when he made eye contact. I'd been removed from the tragedy of it all, because I was a teenage girl and the world revolved around me. But it hit me harder now than it did back then.

"He goes by Eddie now," I said, snapping myself out of it. "He's a musician. He looks good."

Better than good.

"Oh yeah, he's got that song, 'I knew it was love in that moment between us, when time tick-tocked and stopped from the feel of your touch,'" she sang that line that stuck in your head like gum on a shoe.

"That's the one," I agreed.

"Woah, blast from the past."

I nodded, trying to remember more about him. But the defining and overwhelming memory was *that time he took all those pills* and not much else. "He's living in Wellraven."

"Is he now?" There was something in Lizzie's voice.

I rolled my eyes. "Don't even start with me. He was Bobby's friend. He is not my type." Not a lie either. My type usually wore a suit, had family money, and worked in an office. Someone sensible, reliable, and boring. Someone disposable. I did not need to fall in love. When the time came, if it came, I'd likely marry one of those suits, one of the more progressive ones who didn't want a housewife. I'd marry him, with or without love. Because love was what got my mother pregnant to a deadbeat that smacked her around, stole her youth, made her angry, bitter, and cold. Love kept her children near poverty and chained her to the South Bronx.

I did not want love from an edgy looking musician who had sad, lonely eyes and a hit single.

There was a pregnant pause at the other end of the phone. "But he looks good?"

My mind went to those mesmerizing eyes. "Yeah, real good."

I didn't think about "Eddie" Edward McArthur for a couple of days. Well, except when his song came on the radio. And when I saw a man in a white tee.

Passing thoughts. I kept an eye on the mailboxes, thinking it might be nice to catch up with an old friend of Bobby's. I'd have to tell my brother about seeing him on our next phone call. They were tight in high school. I'm sure Bobby would want to catch up with his old friend, even though life had taken them in vastly different directions. Bobby had left the boy he was in high school in the Bronx. He'd put on a suit, got off the grass, found an apartment on the West Side, and got himself a girlfriend. The suits got nicer; the girlfriend turned into a wife, and the apartment turned into a house in the suburbs. I now had a chubby one-year-old nephew that I adored and enjoyed spoiling rotten.

Yes, Bobby had changed. So had Eddie. So had I. We were all adults now, with adult responsibilities, adult jobs, and childhood traumas we were trying to escape.

Though it was a considerably more recent trauma that I was trying to get away from.

I thought a change of scenery would help.

Plus, if I sat in that apartment for one more second, I might've ripped apart my beautiful emerald sofa with my bare hands.

I didn't change from work; it seemed like too much of a herculean effort, even though my feet were protesting loudly at having been crammed into five-inch heels for ten hours. I gritted my teeth against the pain as they clicked along the sidewalk; I was glad for the distraction.

Sophie's was only a three-minute walk from Wellraven, had good cocktails, decent music, and a relatively quiet crowd. The disco loving party goers went to the East Village or Tribeca, and sometimes, I joined them. There were parties, drugs, men. There was oblivion.

As enticing as oblivion was, I thought it better for some mellow music, enough drinks to take the edge off, and a familiar barstool. As it was, there was not only a familiar barstool, but a familiar tee attached to all too familiar arms sitting in one.

I sat down next to him and he didn't even look up from his book.

"Fancy seeing you here."

Eddie jerked ever so slightly, even though I'd spoken softly. His eyes zeroed in on mine, and I grinned.

"White Russian," I said to the bartender, regretfully taking my eyes from Eddie. "And whatever he's drinking." I nodded my head to the amber liquid in front of Eddie.

The bartender nodded once.

"Whiskey?" I asked, turning back to Eddie. My body relaxed slightly in his presence. That didn't make sense. Or maybe it did. Something familiar from the past, comforting when the present was so prickly and dangerous. Something else to focus on other than that awful day that lived on forever in my mind.

Yes, it had to be that.

"Ginger ale," Eddie said, voice gravelly and low.

I raised my brow. "Ginger ale?" I repeated.

He nodded, dog-earring his book and placing it on the bar. *The Bell Jar.*

"*The Bell Jar* and ginger ale," I said, crossing my legs—I didn't miss the way Eddie's eyes flickered downward as I did so. Heat traveled up my legs with his gaze. I swallowed roughly. "Sylvia Plath? Not exactly what I'd expect from a rock star."

Something moved in his face. Tightened. "I'm not a rock star." His voice was sharper now. "I'm a one-hit wonder."

Sore spot.

"Okay, not a rock star," I agreed. "But a young man who isn't too hard on the eyes, sitting alone at a quiet bar drinking ginger ale and reading Sylvia Plath. You're not like most men."

"No," he agreed. "I'm not."

I swallowed thickly at the way his words filtered through the smoky bar, standing up hairs on the back of my neck. My thighs still burned from where his eyes had been.

Two glasses slid in front of us and I jerked out of … whatever the heck that was to find purchase on the cool glass. I needed it.

"So," I said, sipping my drink. "If you don't drink, don't look to be after conversation or company of a young woman … what are you doing at a bar?" I asked.

He shrugged. It was an adolescent gesture, one that belonged on an awkward, gangly teen and not a grown man with a five o'clock shadow and a hit record.

"I like to watch people," he said. He wasn't watching anyone but me when he spoke.

Usually, I was confident around men. "Abrasive" was the word my boss used. Confident women were called abrasive at best. I was used to that in the office. But at bars, clubs, restaurants, I managed to sand the edges off "abrasive" and become endearing. If I did say so myself. I knew I was attractive, knew I was good at flirting, and knew how to capture a man's attention.

I never felt awkward, unsure of myself. Until right then. With little Edward McArthur who was most definitely not little anymore.

"Are you okay with the company now?" I asked, my voice low and thick with suggestion.

# Chapter Five
## Eddie Mac

*I like to watch people* ... My last words rang in my head in a disturbing echo. I realized how weird it must've come across to her. How weird my whole demeanor must seem to the woman from my past who was genuinely just trying to catch up. I didn't want to be so coarse with her, so indifferent, but it was hard for me to forget the girl she was, laughing with her friends at the boy who tried to kill himself. Hard to accept the fact that it wasn't so much the people watching that brought me to bars by myself, as it was a means to ease the burden of my loneliness.

I turned to her, mentally fighting back the sweat from collecting on my brow line. "Company sounds great," I said, forcing a smile.

"And I won't disturb your people watching?" She chuckled, taking a sip of her drink.

"I've been here a while. I've had plenty of time to do so. It helps with the writing, you know. Gets the creative juices flowing."

"Have you been writing much?"

I tried not to laugh. I hadn't written a word in at least a year. Couldn't even seem to put two chords together that I didn't hate, that didn't sound like every other song on the radio. I'd spent the past few days trying to go through my mother's things, trying to figure out what I would sell and what would get thrown away, and I made little progress. I couldn't seem to detach myself from her things, from her dust covered life. I couldn't bear the feelings such things brought out of me. I had come across her diary in the process of cleaning things out, and after reading some of it (I didn't dare read her final entry) I was left with a mental firestorm. She wrote often about me, about her love for me. There wasn't an inkling of anger over my absence, my abandonment. Only pain. I still couldn't cry, couldn't make sense of my feelings, but I wanted to. I wanted to shed the remorse and the guilt that my mother's words brought me. But it was so hard to shed something I couldn't make much sense of in the first place. No, I wasn't writing. I couldn't seem to do much of anything those days.

I nodded. "Yeah, I've been working on a few things," I lied. "I'd like to get back to performing soon."

"Oh, shoot!" She put a hand to my shoulder, and I tried to ignore the warmth that radiated from her touch through my entire body. "You remember Lizzie Jenkins from high school?"

I nodded. "Yeah, I do." I remembered her too well. She was the meanest of the mean girls. It was she who spread word of my overdose through the school like wildfire.

"Her husband owns a club in Tribeca. They have musicians play there all the time. I could talk to her about getting you in, if you want. They'd be thrilled to have you."

I swallowed thickly. The thought of playing in front of people again filled me with immense trepidation. I knew I needed to do something. I needed to start playing again or give it up entirely. There was no in-between. And I wasn't ready to give it up. Music was my life. What the fuck else would I do? Without my voice and my guitar, I was nothing.

"Yeah, yeah, that'd be great. Preferably on a less busy night." I let out a nervous chuckle. "Haven't done a show in a little bit. I'm liable to be pretty rusty."

"Great!" She smiled wide, finishing off her White Russian. "I'll set it up then. Do you have a number I can reach you at, so I can let you know what day and time we come up with?"

I nodded, grabbing a cocktail napkin and pen from the bar top. I wrote my number down—well, my mother's number—and passed it to her.

She folded the napkin and tucked it into her purse. "Maybe, we can set up that coffee date soon too. You do drink coffee, right?" She winked.

"Yeah, coffee is definitely in my wheelhouse. Just let me know." I snatched my pack of cigarettes from the bar top and pulled one out, anything to busy my nerve-racked mind. I lit one up and took a deep inhale.

She hesitated for a moment, as if searching for the right words to say. She cocked her head curiously. "Hey," she said. "Can I ask you something? And you can be honest with me."

I felt heat trail up my spine as I worried about what she might ask. "Shoot."

"Do you really want to grab coffee, or are you just trying to humor me? I don't like to see myself as some self-conscious girl, looking too far into things, but I just get the feeling like I'm bothering you."

"No, no." I waved her off. With some genuineness in my voice, I said, "You don't bother me at all. I'm sorry about my awkwardness. It's hard to explain. It's been a long time since I've been home. It brings with it a lot of different feelings and emotions. Not all of them good. I think it's just throwing me off a little. Has my mind in a bit of a mess. But I would seriously love to grab some coffee sometime. And I can't thank you enough for putting a good word in with Lizzie. It would be so nice to play again."

"Okay, good. Just wanted to make sure." She rose from the stool and pushed it in. She gestured behind her with her thumb. "I better link up with my friends before they get cranky, but I'll call you about the coffee and the gig soon. Sound good?"

"Sounds great." I smiled back.

With that, she was off, meeting up with her friends across the bar, and I couldn't help but miss her presence. Despite what may have occurred in the past, despite what my jaded mind might've conjured up, being with her gave me a sense of ease I hadn't felt in a long time. There was a comfort in our history. I wasn't sure what that meant, or whether it was simply a byproduct of never having a real relationship or any genuine connection with a woman in my entire life. Fact of the matter was I had always managed to avoid them; too worried about the heartbreak such a connection might bring. Love for me was foreign and frightening, and at the same time, it felt as if it could catch me at any moment, especially with a woman like her. More than anything, I wanted to love and to be loved by someone else—to have a best friend to go through life with—but it's hard when you don't love yourself. When inside your mind there exists only self-hate and self-deprecation. When the only kind of relationships you've ever known are the ones filled with pain, suffering, and sorrow.

I wandered slowly back home, my mind wandering along with me. I couldn't help but wonder whether Alice's niceness toward me was a result of things she remembered from our past, awful memories of an overdose and the boy who spent time in inpatient psychiatric care because of it. Did she remember? Did she feel sorry for me? I couldn't bear the thought of that and felt sick over the notion that that messed up little boy may have never quite grown up.

After getting home and shedding my clothes, I laid down on the couch and tried to get some shut-eye, but my brain wouldn't stop turning. An image had implanted in my head since arriving in New York—really, since I received news of her death—of my mother seated alone in this quiet apartment. Tears filled her eyes, and her old, wrinkled hands clutched the rosary her mother gave her, the one I found inside her nightstand just beside her diary.

In this mental image, she cried out to the Lord to rid her of the pain she felt inside, cried out for the son who had abandoned her, cried out for something to fix her broken mind. But she heard nothing back. She received no solace. She realized, just as I had thought a million times before, that this world would not change for her, that her mind would not magically fix itself, that the only true relief from the pain she felt would be a peaceful, everlasting sleep.

I picked up my guitar then, without much expectation, but with hope that the old acoustic could ease my own pain and burdened mind. If only just a little. My hands trembled as I strummed a few chords, and well into the night as my calloused fingers burned, a song began to take shape. Once I was finished playing—emotionally exhausted yet bursting with creativity I hadn't felt in a long time—I was compelled to retrieve my tackle box from the kitchen, and I went through each of those unopened letters from my mother on her living room floor, one by one. I read every line. And before long, the tears began to flow.

# Chapter Six
## Alice

My stomach was a ball of knots as I dialed, clutching a napkin in my sweaty palm. I was worried I'd been too bold with the coffee thing. Eddie was so hard to read. As a teenager, he'd worn everything on his sleeve, so uncertain, so uncomfortable in his own skin. I might not remember a bunch about him from back then, but I remembered that.

Something about him was so … aloof now. Cool in a way that wasn't forced. He intimidated me a little. Sitting in a bar with a book and a ginger ale, watching people with sadness behind his eyes. Because sure, a lot of things might've changed since high school, but some things still remained.

I ached to ask him questions about his sadness, if only to have a vacation from my own. Beyond that, I wanted intimacy with him. He was sensitive and masculine at the same time, distant in a way that made me long to be close to him.

"Hello?"

Shit. He answered. Of course, he answered. Wasn't that what I wanted?

"Eddie," I said, my voice too high and chirpy. "It's Alice. This is kind of a long shot, since you're probably busy writing a kick-ass song or something, but I was wondering if you're free for coffee?" I twirled the phone cord around my finger.

"Right now?" He had a good phone voice. A great phone voice. Deep. Husky.

"You're busy," I said quickly. "Of course, you are. We can go another—"

"No," he interrupted. "I'm not busy. I'd love to get coffee with you."

I grinned, my fingers still tangled in the phone cord, feeling like a gleeful teenager at the prospect of a *coffee date*. I was a New Yorker. A feminist woman. Coffee dates were no big deal. Unless they were with Eddie Mac.

"I can meet you at your apartment," I said.

"No," he replied, voice raising an octave. "I'll be at yours in five, if that works?"

"Yes, that works. I'm apartment 803."

"Okay. I'll see you soon, Alice."

I swallowed thickly as I hung up the phone. I liked the way he spoke on the phone. I very much liked the way he said my name.

Yes, I was in trouble with Eddie Mac.

The walk to the coffee shop was full of nerves, awkward laughs—me—and some accidental hand brushing. Eddie looked good. Great. His hair was James Dean messy; his five o'clock shadow was dark and rough, and I wanted to run my fingers through it.

I refrained, making small talk with him until we'd ordered our coffees and were sitting in front of each other. Small talk was suddenly much too small, even for our compact table in the corner of the coffee house.

"Tell me about your life," he said, sipping his coffee, his eyes holding my gaze.

"My life?" I repeated. "What about it?"

"All of it," he invited. "How you went from the Bronx to a life of nice purses, clothes, and apartments. Articles with your byline."

I raised my brow. "You've read my articles?"

He nodded. "I especially liked the one on teaching your husband about the importance of spicing it up in the bedroom."

I almost choked on my coffee when he spoke, his voice velvet, eyes dark. Heat crept up my neck. "I, um, well," I stuttered, completely unlike myself. When other people mentioned my more controversial articles, I was always proud of talking about female sexuality, making it known that men did not know what they thought they did about it. Most men knew nothing.

Eddie's eyes told me he knew something. A lot.

I shifted in my chair ever so slightly. He watched me do so.

Silence crept in between us. It wasn't uncomfortable. It was something else entirely. It was the sexual tension I felt at the bar, increased tenfold.

"Your life, Alice," Eddie said softly. "You were going to tell me about it."

I cleared my throat, watching his fingers unwrap from his coffee cup before finding his eyes again. Right then, I wanted to tell him about that day. The urge to share it with him, the pain and the horror, was so strong I had to pick up my coffee and sip just for something to do.

Because I couldn't tell him about that day. It was not something you talked about on a first date, even with somebody you already knew. It was the kind of trauma that you kept, swallowed, let grow inside of you and come out in all sorts of unhealthy and destructive ways.

Sharing traumas with men never ended well. They either thought you were crazy or broken. Men liked their women sane and intact, anything else was too much work. So, women were excellent at pretending they were okay, undamaged.

Something about Eddie—the sadness in his eyes—told me he'd be okay with me being broken, because he was broken too.

"Well, after high school, I gathered whatever could fit in a cheap suitcase and ran for my life," I said with a forced lightness to my tone. "Then I found a shitty job that gave me shitty pay and I could afford a shitty apartment. I scratched and clawed to pay my way through school, and to keep my grades up while working forty-plus hours a week. I graduated and found myself a somewhat less shitty, but still significantly shitty job and kind of ... worked my way up from there." I shrugged.

"Not kind of," Eddie said. "You *worked*, Alice. It's terribly impressive."

I smiled. "Thank you," I said shyly. "Now, you need to tell me about your life. Everything."

And he did.

Tell me about his life, that was.

But not everything. Not the broken parts. And those were the ones I wanted. Those were the ones I craved.

"This was nice," I said lamely, fiddling with my keys as we waited for the elevators back at the Wellraven. I hadn't wanted the date to end, if it was a date, and surely it was. There were only so many cups of coffee I could consume without having a heart attack. And Eddie didn't drink.

Plus, as much as I wanted to, I couldn't stay with Eddie forever. We both had lives, and I knew a thing or two about men. They wanted a woman who was harder to get. Which was why I didn't invite Eddie up to my apartment, no matter how much I wanted to. I'd see him again the next evening anyway. He had accepted a gig at Lizzie's husband's club on short notice after another act had to drop out. They were more than excited to get a legitimate, money-making musician in there for once. I reveled in his discomfort when I told him about the gig while we were having coffee. On a Friday, the busiest night in New York City, when people would be drinking their work weeks away. I enjoyed seeing a man who carried so much swagger, so much edge, show just a little bit of trepidation. Especially one who had already accomplished so much. It reminded me that he was still human.

How close he was standing to me—close enough for his hand to brush against my silk skirt—told me he might want to come up to my place too.

"It was very nice," he agreed, moving forward an inch, his gaze moving from my lips to my eyes.

My heart thundered in my throat.

"I would very much like to kiss you, Alice Freeman," Eddie rasped.

My stomach dipped and my thighs clenched. His voice was pure sex. "I don't know what I'll do if you don't, Eddie Mac." I breathed.

Our lips met gently at first. He was being tender, gentlemanly, tentative almost. Then, suddenly, he wasn't. Suddenly, my back was pressed against the wall between the elevators and Eddie was pressed against me, one hand on my neck, the other at my hip. His tongue moved against mine, he tasted like coffee and something else.

The kiss burned hotter, and his hand moved from my hip to my ass, grabbing it with force and pressing my body closer to his.

No one had ever kissed me like that in my life. It was pure, hot-blooded passion. It would've been much more than a kiss, had the elevator not dinged.

We split apart like two kids on the sofa when the parents turned the light on.

Mrs. Henderson and her small dog, Archie, exited the elevator. I waved and smiled, smoothing my hair. She nodded once and looked at Eddie with suspicion.

She walked with devastating slowness, making it clear that she was going to watch this entire thing. She didn't trust men, Mrs. Henderson, having been married to three assholes. She took it upon herself to comment on any and all men she happened to see me with.

Eddie cleared his throat and rubbed the back of his neck. "I should go," he said, his voice rough. I felt it in my panties, that deep tenor.

I nodded, not trusting myself to speak. Not trusting myself not to launch at him, Mrs. Henderson and Archie be damned.

Eddie glanced to his side, where Mrs. Henderson was pretending to look for something in her purse, then back to me. He reached forward and brushed a hair from my face.

"I'll see you tomorrow," he said.

"I can't wait."

# Chapter Seven
## Eddie Mac

I woke up the next morning with the taste of her kiss still lingering on my lips. The smell of her perfume still clinging to my skin. A yearning for her like I'd never felt before stealing my every thought. Was this what love felt like? All-encompassing. All consuming. A desire so strong I could nearly taste it. And it wasn't just sexual, though I'd be kidding myself if I said I didn't want every part of her; to feel her and touch her and taste her. But this wasn't lust. This was something else, something stronger, something that filled me with a clarity and motivation I never felt before. I wanted to spend more time with her. I wanted to know everything about her; the good, the bad, and the ugly. I hoped it wasn't a fleeting feeling. I hoped the feeling would be reciprocated. She seemed to enjoy my company, seemed genuinely interested in getting to know me and spending time with me. But was she feeling what I was feeling? Was she brimming with excitement just like me? Was she rife with anticipation for another evening together, getting lost in each other?

I picked up my guitar again that morning, playing through the pain that remained in my fingertips. And I found myself inspired like I hadn't been since I first moved to San Francisco, with youthful exuberance for what seemed at the time like an attainable dream. I felt alive again. And in the midst of the morning sun that bathed me from the window, I worked out another beautiful melody, and found equally beautiful words to go along with it. The notes and words flowed from the depths of me with ease, without apprehension or overthinking. Pieces of me put into musical form.

Alice and I shared a cab for the ride to Charades Club in Tribeca that evening and I reveled in the way she rested her hand on my knee.

"Are you nervous?" she asked, smiling.

"Am I making it that obvious?" I flashed a nervous smile back. I could feel my palms starting to sweat.

"You're going to do great! They're going to love you."

"I sure hope so. But even if they don't, even if I bomb, at least I'm getting my feet wet. And at least I'll be there with you."

The bar wasn't small, but it looked to be with the amount of people packed inside. Along the left wall there was a large, rounded bar top, every stool occupied, and in the back, there was a stage where a small man played an acoustic guitar and sang into the mic in front of him. The air was hazy with cigarette smoke, and through the haze a jovial man approached us, his arms open wide. A petite woman followed behind him. I recognized him immediately as my old pal Bobby Freeman—Alice's brother—a few pounds heavier than he was when I last saw him with a thick mustache straddling his upper lip.

"Eddie fuckin' Mac!" he said, swallowing me up in a big hug. "It's been way too long, my man."

I looked him up and down. He wore a nice suit, a tie loosened around his neck, and gator boots on his feet. "Way too long," I said. "You look great, man!" I brushed off his shoulder. "Look at you. Like a million bucks!"

He chuckled and shrugged. "Livin' the dream, my friend." He put a hand up toward the petite woman next to him. "This is my old lady Janet." She flashed a sweet smile and put out her hand as Bobby continued. "Janet, this is my best friend from my high school days, Eddie. Or Edward, as we called him back then."

I shook her hand and smiled. "Edward ended right along with high school," I said with a chuckle. "Pleasure to meet you, Janet."

"And you, Eddie." She nodded; the genuine smile still stretched across her face. She was naturally beautiful with just a hint of makeup.

"Alice tells me you've got a little one now," I said.

He nodded. "Yeah, the in-laws are watching him tonight. He's an awesome little man, but we are certainly enjoying the night off. He can be a fuckin' handful." He motioned to the bar. "Can I get you a drink?"

"Yeah, a ginger ale would be great."

He cocked his head curiously, a shit-eating grin on his face. "A ginger ale? What are you, twelve?"

"Hey, you do remember my old man, don't you?"

He passed me a knowing look and nodded. "Ginger ale it is." He wrapped an arm around his sister and led her to the bar. "And you, sis?"

"You know my poison, Bobby boy," she said with a wink.

Bobby leaned over the bar top and ordered the drinks, and I set my guitar case down, leaning it against the bar. He pulled his wallet out and threw some bills down as he looked back toward me. "How is the old man, by the way? Still an ornery old bastard?"

I shrugged. "I'm sure he's in hell giving the devil his due," I said, chuckling.

"Oh no, man. I'm sorry to hear that. When did he go?"

"A good ten years ago now. Got held up by knifepoint down in Manhattan and the stubborn old fool refused to give up his wallet."

"Fuck's sake. This city has really gone downhill fast," Bobby said, shaking his head in disgust. "How's your mom doing?"

"She's gone too."

"Jesus." He put a consolatory hand to my shoulder. "When did that happen?"

"A while ago."

Alice passed me a sympathetic look.

Bobby gave my shoulder a light squeeze. "I'm really sorry, Eddie. She was a stellar woman. Always so sweet to us neighborhood kids. Best damn cook on the street too."

"That, she was." I nodded mindlessly, trying to fight the image of her from my mind and the tears from my eyes.

We spent a good amount of time there at the bar chatting, laughing, and catching up, and it felt like the old days. Not the sad little boy with the shitty home life, but the days in Bobby's basement sneaking his dad's cigarettes and making prank phone calls. Those days when I was given a few hours to ignore the realities of my life and just be a kid. I had nearly forgotten what I was at the club for, too engrossed in conversation and the lingering glances with Alice when her little brother's back was turned. I couldn't wait to kiss her again. Couldn't wait to hold her in my arms and feel the weight of the world lifted off my shoulders. It was amazing to me just how far we had come in so little time.

"Do you remember how much shit you used to give us, sis?" Bobby asked out of the blue, taking a sip of his drink and eyeing his sister peculiarly.

She waved him off. "Oh, please. I wasn't that bad."

I put a finger up. "Uh, you were a nightmare, actually," I said, chuckling.

She faked offense, a hand to her chest. "Who me? No, I was an angel!"

"Selective memory, eh?" I winked at her.

"You ain't kiddin'," Bobby said, letting out a good laugh. "I can't even count how many pairs of underwear you ruined giving me wedgies. And how many of my Roy Rogers figures did you burn?"

"Whatever. That was when I was like ten. I got much better with age."

"Ha!" Bobby responded. "You're in so much denial! You used to turn the lights off on us when we were listening to music or watching TV in the basement and you'd make ghost noises. Scared the daylights out of us. You'd give us wet willies and tell Mom on us when we were prank calling people. And I seem to remember you being in high school when all this was happening. Don't even get me started on when we reached high school ourselves. I seem to remember you telling the whole school that I hooked up with the lunch lady."

"Who, Miss Edna?" Alice said playfully. "I'm pretty sure that little rumor gave you some serious clout around the halls of Morris High."

"People thinkin' I hooked up with a wrinkled old lady in her seventies gave me no clout! I was teased for ages over that."

I burst out in laughter, remembering the rumor coming around to our lunch table one day, and the endless shit Bobby received over it. He never quite lived it down. "You really were quite evil, Alice," I said, mid-laugh.

"I like to think I just hardened you both up. Got you prepared for the real world," she responded, poking a tongue out at us.

"So, what you're saying is we should be thanking you?" I asked, grinning.

"Absolutely!" she said. "I'd go so far as to say you probably wouldn't be a rock star and a stockbroker if it weren't for me. I'll accept another drink as payment for all of your successes." She smiled wide and it caught me like a shot to the heart. What a perfect smile it was. She nodded toward the stage. "Speaking of you, mister rock star, it looks like it's your turn."

I glanced toward the stage and noticed the bar manager waving me over. Turning back toward Alice, I smiled and said, "What did I tell you? It's mister one-hit wonder." I winked at her, still grinning like an idiot, and then I picked up my guitar case and made my way to the stage.

The bar manager took the stage and grabbed ahold of the microphone. "Everybody, please put your hands together for our next act. We are very lucky to have a bona fide star playing for us tonight. You'll know him from his Johnny Carson appearance where he played his hit single, "I Knew it was Love" … Mr. Eddie Mac!" He put a hand out toward me as applause broke out around the room.

He shook my hand and patted my back as I took his place on the stage. I removed my old acoustic from its case, pulled the stool over toward the mic, and took a seat. "Thank you, everyone," I said, my voice unintentionally low. I swallowed thickly, taking a moment to calm my buzzing nerves. "It's a real pleasure to be here. I'm a man of few words, so I'll just let the music do my talking for me."

I began the set with "I Knew it was Love," wanting to get it out of the way, and knowing that was what everyone really wanted to hear. I played a few more lesser-known songs from my first and only album after it and saved the two new ones I worked out the past few days for last. To close out the set, I played a song called "Can You Hear Me Now." It was the song I wrote the night before, with tears streaming down my face, and thoughts of my mother bombarding my brain. I looked to the crowd as I strummed the first few chords, something I never did when performing live. My old manager used to scold me for it. Told me I needed to engage with the audience more, to keep my eyes open, and sing to them, instead of seeming like I was playing alone in my living room like some angsty teen. "You look like goddamn Ray Charles up there," he used to say. "With a frown instead of a smile. Open your goddamn eyes. Move around. Make love to the crowd."

It wasn't the crowd I was worried about during that last song. It wasn't them I was looking toward. It was the gorgeous woman in the back by the bar with the warm smile on her face, with pride beaming from her eyes. And to her, I sang—

*I am a ghost in this place.*
*Tracing your name in the dust with my bones.*
*And with these cracked hands folded,*
*I prayed to not feel so alone.*

*I am a bastion of shame,*
*Aching for something, anything to soothe,*
*my weary heart, my tired soul,*
*Memories that choke like a noose.*

*Was I the fall for you?*
*One day, will I fall too?*

*Can you hear me now?*
*Prayers like whispers in the wind.*
*Drifting off*
*As your cries start drifting in.*
*Can you hear me now?*
*My pride came before the fall.*
*Breaking down,*
*A man with nothing left at all.*

I finished up the melancholy tune, and thanked the crowd, and as they applauded me while I loaded my acoustic back up in its case, I felt a surge of relief, adrenaline, and excitement. It felt like my first time playing for a crowd again all those years ago. It rejuvenated my soul.

# Chapter Eight
## Alice

I never got why women were into musicians. They were usually unshowered with greasy hair, wearing an air of arrogance mingled with desperation. If they were successful, they acted like they'd invented music. If they weren't, they were sure that no one understood their *sound* and were willing to do anything for even a shred of fame or money.

No, musicians held no mystery for me.

Until now.

Until I watched a nervous, uncertain, and slightly green looking Eddie Mac transform. There was no other word for it. The second his fingers started moving, his voice started to filter through the microphone, he captivated me. He captivated the entire audience. The words, the music, the fact that his eyes were on me for the entire song.

The song.

I could barely breathe through the beautiful sorrow of it. People swayed along as if he'd enchanted them. The pain was raw and unadorned, carving through the air and into people's hearts.

His song on the radio was good, catchy, in a way where you'd sing it mindlessly, the words easy to remember.

This was not a song that you'd sing mindlessly. This was a song you listened to while it was raining outside, with a large glass of wine and a heart that hurt. This was a song that gave you company, that told you that you were not alone in your pain. This was a song that did more work in three minutes than the three months of therapy I'd been through.

It was a disappointment when it was over. I felt empty without his words. But I was desperate for something else. Someone else. Him.

I'd been attracted to him from the start, of course. It was impossible to be a living, breathing human woman— or man, for that matter—and not be attracted to Eddie Mac. I'd been very interested in kissing him again, in doing plenty of other things that were a lot more than kissing, but this made me desperate to do a lot more than kissing. Eddie's words were inside of me. Now I needed Eddie inside of me.

He walked off stage with the cheers and adoration of the crowd sitting perfectly on his shoulders. People approached him the second he left the stage. Swarmed him. Girls. Most of them. He obliged them, but his eyes lingered on me.

Something hot and bitter crawled up the back of my throat, an urge to rip those girls away by their hair and write "mine" on Eddie's head in permanent marker.

But I figured that would be unattractive and slightly crazy, so I gripped my White Russian and stared in what I hoped was a casual and endearing way.

It was nice to watch Eddie like this, with people fawning over him in this way, instead of avoiding him, whispering behind his back like they did in high school. It was nice to know Eddie like this.

He eventually extracted himself from the crowd, sauntering over to me with his guitar case in hand. The way he walked told me things, told me he'd be a great freaking lay.

Eddie shed something when he came to stand in front of me, some of that confidence was watered down with my presence, he grinned at me shyly, eyes twinkling. A few strands of hair curled over his forehead, shining in the dull lights of the bar. His face glowed with a thin sheen of sweat, evidence of just how much he'd put into those three minutes.

"So?" he said after a few moments of silence.

I blinked, realizing I hadn't exactly spoken since he approached. I'd just been standing there drooling over him, wondering what his mouth would feel like in between my legs.

Eddie was nervous for my opinion, obviously worried that I hadn't liked it, despite the fact an entire nightclub of people had lost it over him. That meant he liked me. A lot. That gave me the bravery to put my White Russian down on the bar and step forward close enough to smell his leathery cologne mixed with his musky, manly scent.

I wrapped my arms around him, taking him in for a hug, and I whispered in his ear, "That was truly incredible, Eddie. Just beautiful. You should be very proud."

Bobby looked at me inquisitively as I released my hug. He reached his hand out for Eddie, his eyes still on me, his eyebrows scrunched together. He finally looked toward Eddie and said, "Well done, buddy. Well done."

"Those last two, were they new?" Jane asked. "I don't remember them from the album."

Bobby looked toward his wife, surprised. "You never told me you were a fan of his," he said in an accusatory tone.

She shrugged, her eyes remaining on Eddie, a mischievous smile perched on her face. "You don't know everything about me, Robert James."

"Well, I damn well should!" Bobby responded, looking toward Eddie and chuckling. "Those last two were definitely not on the last album. A little depressing, aren't they, buddy? Felt like I needed a good cry after. Or a razorblade to slit my wrists."

"Bobby!" I scolded, slapping the back of my hand against his arm, and he rubbed it out in pain. I looked at Eddie and smiled. "New or not, they were beautiful," I assured him.

"Thanks, Alice," he said bashfully, his eyes flitting away from my own. His nervousness was endearing. "Yeah, Jane, they're pretty new. The old stuff—not that I'm complaining, because they did me some great favors— they weren't quite what I would've written if it weren't for studio influence. I much prefer the mellower stuff. Less pop and more folk."

"Well, I really liked them, even if pop is usually the way I lean," Jane said, smiling.

It was then a man approached. He was wearing a maroon polyester suit, his hair passed his ears and parted down the side, and a pair of large glasses with rose-tinted lenses resting on the ridge of his nose. I recognized him earlier but didn't dare mention that to Eddie. I didn't want his nerves getting the better of him.

"Pardon the interruption," the man said, putting a hand out toward Eddie. "The name's Shelton Briggs."

Eddie shook his hand. "Pleasure to meet you."

"Just wanted to say, I'm a big fan of yours. *Big* fan," he said. "I usually just come here for the cheap drinks, but what a surprise to see *The* Eddie Mac on stage. Really love that tune of yours, 'I Knew it was Love.'" He leaned in, ribbing Eddie with his elbow. "Screwed my wife for the first time to that song," he whispered, though it was loud enough for me to hear, and then he cackled.

"Well, uh, thanks, man. I appreciate the support."

"I'm not here just to puff up your ego. I'm actually an executive over at Electric Lady Studios. We recorded stuff for Hendrix, some other local artists too. We produce mostly rock records, but I gotta say, those last two songs, man. *Groovy*. Very groovy. Very Bob Dylan-esque. As you and everyone else knows, Dylan is a god around these parts, all over the world, really, but especially here in New York City, and we're always looking for singer-songwriters who can capture his essence. Those last two songs, I haven't heard them before. Are they new? They're certainly not on your album, I've listened to that thing front and back, time and time again."

"Uh, yeah, yeah, very new."

"Well, do you think you can write a few more like 'em?"

"For an opportunity to work at Electric Lady? Are you kidding me? You bet your ass I can!" Eddie replied enthusiastically.

Shelton nodded. "Good, good!" He reached into his back pocket and pulled out a card. "Well, give me a call tomorrow and remind me of this conversation, all right? We'll have you over to check out the studio and talk about what working together might look like."

Eddie shook his hand, a beautiful, genuine smile on his face. "That sounds incredible. Thank you so, so much!"

"No, thank you, Mr. Mac. I look forward to speaking with you further." He tipped his imaginary cap toward Jane and me and clicked his teeth. "Ladies," he said, and with that, he was off.

Eddie looked toward the three of us slowly, his eyes wide and mouth gaping. "Holy shit," he muttered.

"Holy shit is right! Electric Lady is the real fuckin' deal, man," Bobby said.

"Congratulations, Eddie," I said and then I leaned in close, just beside his ear. I was unsure of what motivated me to be so forward, but I needed this man's hands on me. I needed to feel his skin against my skin. His tongue against my clit. His pulsing cock inside me. "This may be too forward of me, and let me know if it is," I whispered, low enough so that my brother wouldn't hear, "But I would like to take you back to my apartment and have a lot of sex."

His eyes flared as I spoke, nerves and arousal mixing together in the pit of my stomach. I chewed on my lip as I waited for his answer, the mumblings of people around us turning into a dull roar.

He put his hand at my hip and yanked our bodies to press together. My stomach dipped at the dominance of the gesture, at the hardness of his body pressing against mine. "I would very much like that, Alice Freeman."

There was no fervent making out in the cab. No hand on my thigh moving further and further up my skirt until it brushed the side of my panties. There was no touching at all, apart from the soft brush of our bodies when the cab turned, or we went over a bump. My skin tingled every single time that happened, and I pressed my knees tighter together. We didn't speak, either. The sexual tension thrummed between us, and despite the number of times I'd made out with a guy in a cab, nothing was more arousing than sitting here with Eddie, his leg brushing against mine.

He paid for the cab and grasped my hand to help me out. He didn't let it go once I was standing on the sidewalk outside our building, he pulled me toward the entrance. I let myself be pulled, my heart roaring in my ears and my mind focusing on his firm, dry grip.

There was no one in the lobby, and we stepped into the elevator alone. I don't know who moved first as the door opened, but all that mattered was that our lips met. That he pressed me against the wall of the elevator, boxing me in, caging me in his embrace. His hands were everywhere. His mouth moving over mine in a passionate fury. There was something carnal about the way he was kissing me, utterly masculine and dominant. Something that caused me to lose myself in the kiss so deeply that I didn't notice the doors to the elevator had opened and closed and we were making out—almost having sex—in a public elevator.

"We need to get inside your apartment, so I can take off your dress and taste every inch of you," Eddie murmured against my mouth, his voice rough.

I blinked, licking my lips, tasting him. "We need to do that," I agreed.

Neither of us moved.

Eddie's gaze moved over my face, hand at my ass. "I can't bring myself to let you go."

I swallowed. "Once we get inside, you don't have to."

I was right.

Eddie was a man that liked going down on a woman. A lot. We'd stumbled into my apartment after I'd had to

71

attempt unlocking my door three times, my hand was shaking that badly. It was only with Eddie's fingers threaded through mine that I got it the fourth time.

Once the door was closed, my purse and my keys clattered to the ground, my lips plastered to Eddie's once more. The kiss was deeper, dirtier, and much more intense than the one in the elevator had been. My legs were wrapped around his waist, his hands on my ass in an instant. He growled in the back of his throat as my dress made it possible for my thin panties to rub against him. He was rock-hard. My body cried out with the friction, needing more but also on the edge of climax just with rubbing myself against his cock, still inside his jeans.

But somehow, Eddie had found his way to my bedroom while I was moving against him like a sex starved teenager. He threw me on my bed. Threw. Me. On. My. Bed.

I stared at him through my eyelashes, standing above me, breathing heavily, eyes dark, and hardness visible against his jeans.

"Pull up your dress," he said, voice so husky it was almost a growl. There was no awkward, shy Eddie to be seen.

My hands shaking, I obeyed.

His eyes flared when I showed him my thin, see through, lace panties.

"Panties, off."

Again, I obeyed, feeling vulnerable, exposed, and almost ready to explode.

"Spread your legs," he rasped, still standing above me, fully clothed.

It might've felt wrong, tawdry, and degrading with any other man. But this was not any other man. This was Eddie fucking Mac. So I spread my legs.

He let out a hiss through his teeth. His gaze went from between my legs to my eyes. Slowly. My body shook under the weight of it.

"You've got the prettiest pussy I've ever seen, Alice," he said.

Holy. Shit.

Eddie Mac talked dirty.

Then he wasn't talking. Then he was feasting. On me. On my pretty pussy. I let out a strangled gasp as his tongue moved rhythmically against me, working expertly on my clit. His hands were under my bare ass, lifting me so he could get deeper, drive me crazier.

My hands fisted my comforter as I writhed and exploded against him, shuddering with aftershocks as he slowly lifted his face from between my legs.

While I was recovering from one of the most powerful orgasms of my life, Eddie undressed. I was in such a haze that I didn't watch, didn't revel in his muscular body. His hands brushed up my bare hips as he leaned over me and pulled my dress off. Lifting my arms up was a mission in and of itself, but I managed it.

Eddie leaned down to put his lips around my hard nipple, and my hands gripped the comforter once more.

The man moved like he had all day, lazily, moving his lips up my collarbone, then my neck.

I grasped his head, tilting it up so I could meet his eyes. "Eddie, I need your cock inside me within the next minute."

His eyes flared, and he moved quicker now, up my body, both of us gasping as he pressed against the most sensitive parts of me. Eddie kissed me, and I could taste myself on his lips.

"Condoms," I breathed, almost willing to let him inside me bare.

Almost.

Safe sex was something I practiced religiously, and though Eddie's body on mine was an utterly sinful experience, I wasn't about to throw it all away.

Eddie's face froze and some of that hunger gave way to something resembling panic. "Uh, I don't, uh, have one," he stuttered shyly.

I did not know how a man could manage to mumble so shyly when he was naked on top of me, having had his mouth on my pussy, but Eddie managed it. Somehow, it was not a turnoff. Not at all. It made him infinitely sexier.

"It's okay," I said, moving to reach over to my bedside drawer. "I've got it."

I fumbled with the box of condoms I kept here exactly for these kinds of situations. There were many men who "forgot" the condoms because they were selfish and irresponsible. Eddie "forgot" because he was Eddie, because he obviously didn't make a habit of sleeping with women consistently and because he didn't expect to sleep with me tonight.

"Do you want me to put it on?" I asked, my voice raspy as I grasped the foil package. Eddie's eyes flared. Yeah, he wanted me to put it on.

I used my free hand to push his chest and move him, so he was the one flat on his back and I was straddling him. I loved looking at his face against my pale pink comforter. I loved his smell, his naked skin on mine. I especially loved the way his cock felt underneath me.

Eddie's chest rose and fell rapidly as I ripped open the foil package, never moving my eyes from his, well, until I got to putting the condom on. Then I put my eyes on *him*. And he was magnificent. My breathing was ragged, and I rolled the condom on.

Eddie let out a strangled moan, his body taut underneath me. Now he was the one fisting the comforter. Once the condom was on, I kept my hand circled around the base of him, rubbing once, twice, watching his eyes squeeze closed in arousal.

I would've stayed to watch that for a lot longer had Eddie not spoken.

"Alice, climb on my cock and ride it, this instant," he growled.

*Growled.*

I didn't think men actually did that. Nor did I think it would work on me.

But I climbed on his cock. And rode it. That instant.

We spent the rest of the night tangled up in each other, having the absolute best sex of my life.

And, when I eventually went to sleep—or more aptly, passed out in Eddie's arms—I did not have the dream.

# Chapter Nine
## Eddie Mac

I had perhaps the best two-week period anyone had ever lived in the history of the world. That's hyperbole, of course, but that's what it felt like. Just me and Alice spending time together, getting to know each other, falling for each other. We had corn dogs and Italian ices at Coney Island. We stole kisses at the top of the Empire State Building. We chased ghosts in Sleepy Hollow. We made love each night like it was our last opportunity to do so … freely, sensually, electrifyingly. I made her my "famous" spaghetti and meatballs and played for her the new songs I was working on for my deal with Electric Lady.

The meeting with Shelton and the other executives at Electric Lady went superbly. And after a good chat with the four of them and playing them a few of the songs I was working on, including the two Shelton heard that night at Charades, I left the studio with a deal in place. I was going to be a recording artist again. This time, I would be making the music I always dreamed of creating. I would be pouring my heart and soul into every line. I would be singing my truths and not what I thought the world wanted to hear from me. And this time, I would not be enjoying my successes alone. I had Alice there to cheer me on. To remind me what this life and all its successes were meant for in the first place, to be shared with someone truly special. Someone who understood you. Who didn't fault you for your flaws. Who encouraged you to be better every single day. That's what a woman like Alice does to a man. He only needs to see the way in which she lives her own life, striving for success each and every day, fighting to make a name for herself in this world despite what roadblocks might come.

I was strumming my guitar that morning, working on a new one that wasn't about death, or sorrow, or loneliness like the others, but about love. About *her*. I sang about seeing her again for the first time, like breathing for the first time, like needing for the first time, this love, this perfect love.

Abruptly, a knock at the door brought my eyes open. It startled me. No one knew where I lived, not even Alice. We had spent every night at her place, as I was wary of telling her about my mother, about this apartment, about the ugliness that brought me back to New York City in the first place. I thought perhaps it was one of my mother's old library friends, or perhaps the lawyer friend coming to give me some fresh shit. I set the guitar down on the floor, leaning it against the couch, and rose to my feet. When I opened the door, my heart dropped.

"Alice …" I stood with the door open, frozen still. She held two coffees in her hands and wore a smile on her face that dissipated when she saw the shock written on my own.

"I'm so sorry. I thought this might've been a bad idea. Just popping by like this," she said, and she began to turn.

I put a hand on her shoulder to stop her. "No, no. You know I love seeing that face of yours. And you come bearing gifts." I motioned toward the coffee. "Surprised is all. I didn't think you knew which apartment was mine."

"Yeah, I've known since that day at the mailboxes. I noticed the number when you were locking it up." She sighed heavily. "Which now when I say it sounds super creepy. I just wanted to surprise you, is all." Her bottom lip slipped between her teeth, her eyes averting toward the ground. "Wanted to see you."

"And I, you. Come on in." I took one of the coffees from her and stepped aside to make way.

She reluctantly entered and eyed the photos on the wall, pointing at the one of me as a baby in my mother's arms, my arms and legs like rolls on a pug and she let out a giggle. She continued on, slowly, eyeing the one of my dad in his uniform that I had put back in its rightful place some time ago. Then the one of me in my baseball uniform in high school, a tight frown on my baby face. She stopped abruptly at the one of my mother and her best friend from the library, Shirley. The most recent one. Her mouth gaped. Her hand met her open mouth.

"Oh, my God," she muttered.

"What is it?"

"That woman …" She pointed to the picture. "Is that your mother?"

I nodded. "Yeah, did you know her?"

She shook her head; her face ashen white. "No, I didn't, but I remember her from the papers. I …" Her eyes glistened with fresh tears, her hand trembling as she lowered it to her side. "I was there the day she died. It happened right in front of me."

*Alice*

His mother.

*Eddie's mother.*

She was the one who had hit the pavement in front of me. Whose eyes had stared at me, lifeless and empty, whose eyes I saw in my dreams. The thud of her body hitting the cement was the soundtrack to my nightmares.

But she wasn't just a stain on the sidewalk, she wasn't the reason I'd taken myself to therapy. She was a person. A person with a life, with a past, with a son. Eddie.

My Eddie.

Before he was mine, he was hers.

Eddie was staring at me in shock. Which made sense, since I'd just told him—the man I was sleeping with, the man I was quickly falling in love with—that I'd seen his mother die.

"What?" he stuttered.

I gripped my coffee so hard I feared I might spill the scalding hot liquid all over my hands, though I was tempted for some kind of distraction.

"I, uh, I was running late for work," I said, unable to find a way out of this, beyond turning around, running out the door and avoiding Eddie for the rest of my life. But that was impossible, not just because we were bound to see each other at the mailboxes at some point. But also, because I couldn't fathom my life without him.

Not looking at Eddie, I walked further into the apartment, my eyes running over the clutter. The furniture was exactly what I'd expect from a woman in her sixties. It would almost be considered vintage now, if it wasn't worn and sun bleached.

"I was running late for work," I repeated. "I wasn't thinking about anything, really. Except what was coming in the next issue, the fact I wanted to buy a new pair of shoes."

I bit my lip, standing at the window of the apartment.

"And then she …"

I trailed off. I didn't need to say it out loud. Eddie knew what happened. Eddie, lovely, sensitive, sexy Eddie, lost his mother.

I turned to face him. He was standing in the same spot, holding his coffee, staring at the window, eyes glassy.

He looked smaller than he ever had.

I put my coffee down on the windowsill and crossed the distance between us. "I'm so sorry," I whispered, putting my hands to his neck.

"I …" Eddie cleared his throat. "I hadn't seen her in a long time. We fell out of touch." A tear trailed down his cheek. I wiped it away with my thumb, biting back tears of my own. "Well, I let us fall out of touch. She never stopped trying to reach out. Never stopped telling me how proud she was of me. How much she loved me." More tears then, cascading down his flush cheeks.

"I was dreading coming back here," he continued, voice rough. "Coming back to this city, this apartment full of ghosts. Dreading the regret that I felt over losing her and never giving her a chance. Never being there when she needed me. Then came you." He reached up to grasp my wrist. "Alice, I was drowning in guilt for leaving my mother here, alone, helpless enough to do *that*. I was drowning before you."

He gripped my wrist harder and my heart splintered hearing the agony in his voice, the helpless grief in his eyes.

"My father. He was …" he trailed off again, all of his features scrunching up, his body taut. "A piece of shit," he said finally. "A hero to his country but a villain to his family. He made my life hell. Our lives hell. I got out when I was old enough, I got out. When I was younger, I tried to get out. You, uh, know about that."

My stomach dropped. The pills. The entire school talking about him. The sad and helpless boy looked at me through a man's eyes.

"Even after that, she didn't leave him," Eddie said, his voice shaking ever so slightly. "I was so angry at her. So *fucking* angry. More angry at her than I was at him, even though that doesn't make sense. But she was supposed to protect me. She was my mother. I'd always thought she was weak. Hated her for it. But she was just a person. Struggling. Drowning. And I let her."

His eyes went to the window. My heart broke just a little more.

"Hey," I said.

His eyes remained on the window.

"Hey!" I repeated, louder this time.

His eyes found mine. "This was not your fault, Eddie," I said firmly. "You were trying to survive. To heal. You needed to leave it all behind. This is not your fault."

My eyes roved over his face, trying to think of how I could help him. How we could help each other.

"She brought us together," I said, everything clicking. "You came back here for her. Came here for her."

"But too late," he said. "I was too late."

I smiled at him. "No, you weren't too late, Eddie. I didn't know your mother, she might've made a whole bunch of mistakes, but I'm grateful to her. Because without her, I wouldn't have you. Wouldn't have this."

I went up on my tiptoes and laid my lips on his gently.

"And we've got this," I said against his lips. "You've got me."

Eddie's eyes were molten. "And you've got me."

Then he kissed me. Not gently.

# Chapter Ten
## Eddie Mac

We walked hand in hand through the Long Island National Cemetery. The sunlight glinted off the neat rows of marble headstones that stretched as far as the eye could see. Mighty trees dotted the land beyond the grave markers, their branches twisting like outstretched fingers toward the bright sun. In my free hand, I held a bouquet of pink lilies, my mother's favorite. My heart cinched in my chest. My stomach was tied in knots. Alice squeezed my hand, as if sensing my apprehension, my nervousness. Or, perhaps, she felt a bit of her own.

We finally located their headstones; my mother's fresh, white, clean, the earth around it still showing the freshness of the grave. My father's marker showed a bit of its age. The grass atop his casket grew lush and thick. I dropped to a knee and dusted his headstone off as best I could. The sunlight caught the flecks of gold in the Medal of Honor emblem at the top, just above his name and his rank, and it sparkled. Tears began to well in my eyes as I inched closer to my mother. I set the flowers down on the freshly turned dirt and put my hand to her headstone.

"I'm sorry, Mom. I'm so sorry I wasn't there," I whispered, a tear cascading down my cheek and hitting the dirt. "I love you. I always have. I always will." Alice's hand met my shoulder and she squeezed, and it eased the pain in my heavy heart.

As we walked away, I felt compelled to be perfectly honest with the woman who had stolen my heart and made it whole. For better or worse, the experience over the past few weeks, dealing with the heartbreak of losing my mother and not being here for her in the days leading up to it, as well as the ugly history with my father, showed me the importance of honesty, of getting things off your chest despite what those truths might bring. I stopped mid stride, and she stopped too, looking back at me curiously.

"Alice. I have to tell you something."

She smiled. "Don't look so worried. Whatever it is, it'll be okay."

"I hope that still stands once you've heard what I have to say." I let out a nervous chuckle and took her hand into my own. "Alice, despite the short amount of time we've been reacquainted, despite how crazy it may sound, I have fallen madly, stupidly, ridiculously in love with you. I've loved you since that day at the mailboxes. If I'm being perfectly honest with myself, I've most likely loved you since we were kids and I thought I hated you."

She chuckled, and the sound of that sweet laugh eased my tensions a bit.

"Truth is, despite the fact that I made a name for myself with a song about love, I didn't even know what that word meant before you. I didn't know what it felt like to go to bed every night with someone on your mind, to wake up every morning wishing that that someone was there beside you. To ache when they're away, and to buzz with excitement when they're close. I didn't know what it felt like to envision a future with someone. To want to make a life with someone. To *need* someone. Alice ... I fucking love you. That's what I needed to say." My whole body went flush with the heat of embarrassment. I felt like I said too much, felt like my stupid mouth had just ruined the best thing that ever happened to me.

But then she took my cheek in the palm of her hand, and she kissed me with her impossibly supple lips. When she pulled back, and her ocean blue eyes—glistening in the afternoon sun—met mine, she said, "I fucking love you too, Eddie." She smiled, gripping my hand and squeezing it. "I love you too."

# THE GUARDIAN
## SHANI STRUTHERS

# The Wellraven Building
## Room 802

This apartment is not empty, although they think it is. And I am not a ghost, although some might describe me as that. I do not thud around or thump on the wall at all hours, although some think I do. The man in 801, for example. He… imagines things. On occasion.

But he could never imagine me.

How long have I been here? It seems like forever. Have I always dwelt in this room? 802. I think so. Lurking in the shadows, or sometimes on the edge of vision. Just… waiting.

I appear to be the sole occupant now, but I haven't always been. There was another here too, once, a man. He'd been here a good long while, not quite when this building first evolved from bricks and mortar to living accommodation but soon after. He haunted these rooms, hardly venturing into the outside world, the hustle and the bustle of it, vivid colors so abrasive that they cut right through you, seared the soul. He spent his time within these walls—as solitary a creature as I am.

His name was Richard, and he was tall, he was thin, with hair the same color as the walls, a sort of… beige color, growing longer, more unkempt. In the living room, he would sit on the couch and stare at the walls, occasionally reaching up a hand to adjust spectacles that sat on the bridge of his nose. Other times, though, he would rise from the couch and pad across to the dining

88

room to sit at a table there, on which lay a notepad. He would write on the notepad, one hand leaning on it to keep it in position, the other busy scrawling, scrawling, scrawling. They were letters, ones he never posted. Instead, after completing each one, he would then tear the page from the notebook, screw it into a ball and hurl it at the wall, watch as it floated uselessly to the floor. And there it would stay, others soon joining them, gathering dust, just as everything else in the apartment gathered dust, layer upon thick layer.

Richard wasn't a bad man. But he was very, very sad. He had done something before coming to live here, that something being *why* he'd had to. The Wellraven might be a sanctuary for some, but not him. For him, it was more like a prison. One he'd condemned himself to.

And so, I would sit with the prisoner. For many, many days. Many nights too. I sat with him, and I tried to let him know that he wasn't alone. Because no one ever is. Despite thinking otherwise. There is *always* someone beside you, and although you might not be able to see them, often you can sense them. Your kind are sensitive, you see, even if many of you refuse to acknowledge it. Oh, he was a stubborn man! Stubborn because whomever it was he'd upset, that he was hiding from, he could never bring himself to apologize, not face-to-face or indeed by letter. But he *was* sorry, so sorry. That was the word he would scrawl, sometimes written in small letters, quite neat to look at, sometimes in big capitals that scored the page. *SORRY! SORRY! SORRY!*

Another way in which he was stubborn was that he never admitted I was there. And yet... when he lay on his bed, whimpering, and I lay too, beside him, he would stop for a moment, lift his head and stare straight into the depths of my eyes. Then he would blink, shake his head, and return it to the pillow, continuing to emit such pitiful sounds.

Richard! You were beginning to love misery! To thrive on it. Wanting it to consume you. If only you'd been braver! If only you'd sought to discover whether that person might have been as desperate to hear your apology as you were to say it. Too stubborn for your own damned good! I couldn't change that, though. All I could do was be there. To the end.

If there are thumps and thuds to be heard from other residents on this floor, as I have said before, it is not me who is guilty. Nor was Richard. Although certainly there were thumps and thuds when his desolation finally bore fruit. His feet kicking as his body jerked, as the rope tightened around his neck. A residual sound, but one that can amplify.

Even in death, Richard refused to acknowledge me—his constant companion. Instead, with his head held high, no longer laying at such an extraordinary angle, he left his body dangling there, turned his back on it and me. He walked out of the dining room with its Formica table, pen and notebook, past the living room to the door and opened it, stepping not into the corridor beyond but the light. A great big blinding flash of it.

Gone. In spirit. And I could have followed him. The light is always so tempting. Warm instead of stark. Maybe I will. But not now.

For now, this is my kingdom, my domain, the Wellraven.

A commotion, such as it is, pulls me from the reverie I am prone to. The door to 802 is opening again; someone is walking through it. For a moment, my heart leaps. Has Richard returned? Maybe to say… thank you. For being there. Through the darkest of days, the darkest of actions. For not turning away. It isn't him. It is someone new, a woman, younger than Richard, pretty, her red hair crazy but cool crazy, her green eyes full of… wonder. Yes, that's it. Living with Richard for so long, I'd almost forgotten what wonder looked like; certainly, it was never apparent in his eyes. She looks about her, at beige walls, at beige carpet too, rooms devoid of furniture, and then she opens her mouth and breathes a word.

"Perfect!"

Closing the door behind her, she whirls around and around.

"This is just perfect! I love it. New York, New York. I love *you*."

Her joy is infectious. For so long I've been sitting in a corner, in the dining room, staring at the space where Richard's body had kicked and jerked so violently, where one hand, right at the last minute, had reached up as if trying to loosen the rope, as if he'd had a sudden change of heart. It's as empty as the rest of the apartment now, that space. I would sit there, and I would muse, maybe Richard was brave after all. For surely such an act requires courage? But there is no more time to ponder. Instead, I approach the girl as she continues to dance, to pirouette through the apartment, heading to the bedroom first, peeking into the bathroom en route, doubling back into the living room, then toward the second, smaller bedroom and its bathroom. Again, on nimble feet she returns to the living room, spies the kitchen, sighs in pleasure and then, last but not least, turns toward the dining room.

She freezes. As do I.

Does she know what took place there? Just how long Richard swung for before finally, finally, someone in the outside world noticed his absence, and the cops came calling, breaking down the door, shouting, "NYPD. NYPD. Hands in the air, it's NYPD."

One of the officers entering, young, broad chested, a roughly hewn face, puked when faced with what was actually in the air. And in the hallway, there were those that hovered, shadows too, others that lived here, but the door was closed upon their prying eyes quickly enough.

How long ago was that? I don't know. Time really does mean nothing to me, there is no tick, tick, ticking of the clock. Maybe those who hovered in the hallway, the neighbors, have since moved on. Maybe Richard was the reason they did, believing that at a new address nothing like this could ever happen again. No guarantees, I'm afraid. Cities can be full of despair. Full of those like me, who stand on guard.

Even if she doesn't know about Richard, she senses... Having entered the dining room, some of her shine fades.

"Man," she says, hugging herself. "It's cold in here."

And yet the season is summer, I believe, the dress she is wearing, an orange paisley print upon it, light and loose.

"Whatever, it doesn't matter. This is great, just great. A home. That's what it'll be. I'll make it so. A place where dreams really do come true."

Lucinda, I come to realize, often talks out loud. Richard never used to; he kept it all inside, the words that wanted to spill from his mouth, the reasons why he did what he did—whatever that and they may be. Not Lucinda, though, who did indeed give this apartment a homier feel, who filled it with furniture and flowers and friends.

Lively. That's what it became. And I liked it. It made such a refreshing change. I liked, too, the parties she would throw, always careful to extend invites to the neighbors, although whether any of them attended I wouldn't know. Plenty did, though. Women dressed just like her, in brightly patterned dresses or tiny shorts and cheesecloth blouses, their hair hanging loose. The guys often wore their hair as long as the girls, their jeans wide at the bottom and shirts open rather than the way Richard wore them, buttoned to the neck. They would smoke, they would drink, they would sing along to song after song. *Bye-bye, Miss American Pie...* Have the time of their lives, it seemed. And I would weave in amongst them, I would sway too sometimes in front of someone, trying to match them, movement by movement.

Not that they knew that. Or indeed had reason to.

They weren't here for me. I wasn't here for them.

Only the occupier of the flat.

To watch over them. To be there when the party ended.

Because all parties ended.

Lucinda was an actress, and doing well, by all accounts.

I would listen to conversations between her and her friends when they were here in person but also on the phone.

"I've got the part!" she would squeal. "A speaking part! In *All in the Family*. Oh my God, I can't believe it. I love *All in the Family*!"

She got speaking parts, as she called them, in other shows too—shows that would often blare out from the TV, which she always had on, even when she wasn't watching it, like it was some kind of lucky charm—like it *had* to be on because it was a world within a world, because it *meant* the world. *Bridget Loves Bernie*, she had a speaking part in that.

"You know *Bridget Loves Bernie*?" she squealed yet again. "Can you believe it? It's just for one episode. I play a love interest for Otis, Bernie's best friend. We kind of meet, fall in love, argue and break up, all in one day. It's going to be so great, and you know, it'll all add up, showcase me. It'll lead from New York to LA, to Hollywood!"

So many bit parts. I'd hear her squeal about them all. In top raters, as she called them, each and every one. Most days she'd skip out of the apartment as happy as a bird that sometimes comes to sit on the balcony railing, and I'd watch her go, then head to the balcony too, to join the bird, to watch her as she disappeared into the tumult below. Such crazy streets filled with yellow taxis, their horns constantly blaring, the buzzing of tools too as yet more buildings like the Wellraven erupt into being. People like ants, always rushing, just as she was rushing, hailing a cab, disappearing from view.

And I'd return to the dining room, stare at the space I used to stare at...

She was so excited when she came here, so... alive.

A girl with crazy red hair, green eyes, and bright clothes, celebrating success, day after day, night after night.

When did it change? When did success become failure? Bit parts now described as "parts for losers." When did the TV go so quiet? Gray replacing orange. And when did the bedroom, where often there was a lover in tow, and the kitchen, where she and her lover would create fancy meals, get swapped for the dining room and where he used to sit. Richard.

I admit, I'd been riding high alongside her—that's what I do, swing low or ride high, depending on the mood of the occupant. I don't judge, I *never* judge, that's not my role, just to be there, but I was enjoying the change of tempo. Even if the neighbors cursed her under their breath, I was enjoying the parties too, the swaying from foot to foot, the songs I learned—*Hi, ho, silver lining...* It was all just... fun.

When did her voice become bitter?

She was on the phone again. Lucinda spent a *lot* of time on the phone. Now, though, she was complaining, one hand running through her red hair, as if trying to tame it, to pull tight curls straight.

"Can't go on like this," she was saying, sitting at the dining table, her other hand scrunched, just like Richard used to scrunch his as he sat there. I winced to see it. "This isn't getting me any nearer to the goal."

I edged closer, enough to hear the tinny voice on the other end.

"Come on, Lu, it'll happen. Have faith."

"When, though? When? We keep going for bigger and better, my agent and me, and they keep promising. Time after time, they promise. Sure, they say, she's a perfect fit. Looks great too. Fits the bill. And then nothing! I get just another bit part, a love interest that gets dumped or dies, sometimes within a matter of minutes. It's not fair. It isn't! You don't have long to shine, not in this business. This business is... cruel."

When the tinny voice kept disagreeing, Lucinda grew angrier.

"You know what," she said, finally. "You don't understand. You can't. You don't... burn like I do. You never have."

She ended the call, slammed the cream receiver down onto its base, and sat there seething. More than that... absorbing.

The dining room, she'd barely used it until now. Even when eating those fancy dinners, she and whomever she was with would sit on the sofa in front of the TV, the plates balanced on their laps, laughing at what was on the box, which was sometimes her, kissing another guy. Or laid out on a stretcher, the cops bursting in again, shouting... again.

Richard, Richard, Richard. You may have left the apartment, gone to the light, but feelings, emotions, *despair*, cannot dissipate as quickly. And all it takes to feed from it is a touch of despair in someone new. Like calls to like, and the proverbial calf fattens.

And that is why I cannot leave the apartment. Because of the likelihood of what happened to Richard happening again. That's why I stay. And from being... somewhat lax lately, I have to step up my game.

*I'm here. Always here.*

That's what I say when even the bit parts stop. A cruel business, she'd called it. *Fickle* is another word. The flavor of the week gets replaced, a penchant for sleek brunettes rather than crazy redheads, for blue eyes rather than green, for curvaceous rather than tall and willowy. Everything changes. Everything shifts. Good situations turn bad, hope turns sour, and what was once enough can no longer fill the well. What burned inside her was ambition. Ambition caused by what? A need to be loved?

At the dining table, she would sit and cry, and I would wonder. Did she feel loved growing up? Where were her parents? They never came to visit. Did she have siblings? If so, they didn't either. No family, just friends. Some of whom hung in there, who continued to try to console her, to insist things would get better. And they were right— they would. But her continued denial drove even the valiant from her door.

But not me. Never me.

She'd sit at the dining table, and I'd sit with her. Reach out. Touch her.

Once she flinched, looked around her, eyes wild.

I wouldn't do that again. I'd refrain. My touch can be a little… cold.

She started drinking. Night after night. A clear liquid. Vodka.

"Just so I can sleep," she'd murmur. "Just so I can… forget."

Crazy red hair became greasy, became lank, translucent skin blotchy.

"Go away!" she yelled once. Someone had come to the door to try again.

"Lu! Lu! Come on, open up. What is going on with you?"

"Just leave me be!"

So angry, when she'd been anything but at the beginning. But then, excitement can mask so much. Hope can too.

She'd weep. Into the early hours. Sometimes torture herself too by turning on the TV again, tuning not into TV shows, their canned laughter resounding, but a full-length feature film. Flamboyant productions, all of them, peopled with actors and actresses so beautiful they hurt your eyes to look at. "Award-winning actresses," she'd mutter, those who'd made the grade, who'd soared high about the clouds. Liz Taylor, Audrey Hepburn, Shirley MacLaine, Katharine Hepburn, they compounded the pain. Pain that was surfacing, just like it did with Richard, because pain always did. I'd hoped it'd be different for her, though. I had wanted it to be. I grow fond of them, you see, the occupants. Despite the pain they put me through, that I experience by proxy.

I want only what is best for them.

*You're not alone. And there is always hope.*

I tried hard to lure her from the dining room. If the TV was on, I'd switch the channel. If it wasn't, I'd make it burst into life. I'd knock an ashtray from a surface, cause the sheers to flutter when there was no breeze. Anything to distract her.

But I can only go so far. I can't haunt her as such, frighten her.

Again, not my job. Others exist to do that. In other rooms in this building, perhaps, but not in 802.

"Alone," she'd cry. "I'm so alone."

*You're not!*

"And no one cares. Not anymore."

*They do!*

"Only want you when you're something."

*You are something, Lucinda, you are!*

"When you're down on your luck, they disappear."

*You drove them away!*

"Cruel… this business. This life."

*Don't. Don't do this.*

"I'm never going to make it."

*You might!*

"Not now."

*Lucinda, you might.*

"Dead in the water."

If I had a beating heart, it would have started to thump against my chest. What did she mean by that? Dead in the water?

She rose from the dining table, lurched forward, unable to walk in a straight line thanks to the vodka, her face stained with tears and snot. I padded behind her, as close as I dared, watched as she staggered into the bathroom, popped the plug into place and opened the taps.

*Dead in the water!*

Suddenly, I understood. Understood something else too… my efforts had been in vain.

I liked Richard. I liked Lucinda.

If only they had liked themselves, weren't so hard on themselves.

If only they'd acknowledged someone was there for them, always.

Being the guardian of 802, now *that's* a cruel business at times.

Later, she rose from the bath. Not her body, of course, that lay as she'd described it, cold water as red as her hair. She traipsed out of there, footprints wet behind her, and I followed. Couldn't help myself. Not just because it was my job to be with her, but because when the door opened, I'd see the light again. That tempting, beautiful light.

Step by step, she was being drawn to that other place, that better place, that resting place. There to be healed. I could almost sense it again, her joy, her hope, sadness-tinged, though, but then it would be. As I've said before, emotions linger.

I reached out again. Nudged her when she faltered. Would she flinch? Would she turn around? See me at last?

She didn't. She kept on going. My touch too light, perhaps.

She was passing through the door now, faltering no more.

Should I do it? Should I follow? Elysium meadows, abundant with flowers gently swaying in the breeze, their colors not garish but soft, always soft, held such appeal. And this apartment, because of what had happened in it, not once but twice, may remain empty.

But what if it didn't?

Memories are short.

The truth can be hidden.

What if the next person that lived here could sense me? And if they drew comfort from my presence. What if it helped them should they ever have an hour of need, if when I reached out, they didn't flinch, didn't shake their heads or turn away.

Hope springs eternal.

My hope, at least.

The door is closing. The light fading.

She is gone. She and Richard.

But I will remain. In the bathroom, in the dining room, wandering between the two, backward and forward, backward and forward, remembering, contemplating.

Waiting.

# CHRYSALIDE
BECCA VRY

"Scripts bore me. It's much more exciting not to know what's going to happen."
Andy Warhol


Coming out of a shell. Shedding skin. A butterfly breaking loose from chrysalis to take magnificent flight.

It's the art of a big reveal, allowing our new shape to emerge into a masterpiece of existence. In good times and in bad, how we embrace experiences, the *sunsong* and *stormspeak* and everything in between ... how we unfurl during unscripted moments *matter*. And it especially matters when caught in an inconvenient rainstorm while traversing soaked paths in the high-rise canyons of the Big Apple.

When an urban pedestrian is faced with an unexpected downpour on a summer morning commute, it usually becomes all about avoidance strategy. Some burrow under an awning, back drenched yet resolved to be patient, while others crowd into building lobbies, praying for a tolerant doorman. Some hail a cab, the high fare a barter for dry space. Some are not tamed easily, and don't avoid the rain at all—*They embrace it.* They take off their shoes and enjoy splashing barefoot on their journey, without fear of dirty sidewalks or judgment from perplexed side-eyers and head-shakers as their free-spiritedness is mimicked by the downpour.

On the receiving end of those perplexed glances now was Amy Rooney.

Relishing the sensation of the water splashing against her bare calves, she giggled like a little girl as she dashed through and jumped into the puddle at Madison Avenue and Seventy-Seventh. A high heel dangling in each forefinger, she waited for the light to turn green. Lifting her chin into the sky, rain slicked her long blond hair against her scalp, and she giggled at the sensation of the *rainspeak* tickling a trail down her spine.

Amy savored the refreshing sensations as the cityscape began telling its own story in a way that always mesmerized her. At the moment, New York was clearly drunk on what nature was pouring, as even the sewer drain near her feet slurred its speech.

Inspired by the rainspeak around her, Amy appreciated the personification of what it was like to live in such an amazing place. It's what she loved about residing on the Upper East Side. Life was never scripted or dull, and every step, rain or shine, had something to say, even if the conversation soaked her through.

Luckily, she kept a few outfits at her burgeoning new hair salon, Upper East Dyed. Living and working in a city that never sleeps required pragmatism, many fashion options stored under desks and at the back of work closets or file cabinets for the unexpected ... and *unexpected* was something New Yorkers were fluent in. *Unexpected* was something Amy learned to embrace after years spent in a small Iowa town with eleven stop signs. A breeze-through, carefree kind of place with dirt roads and corn-topped miles between neighbors, a broad expanse of sky allowing a storm to speak a different language entirely.

It was a fact that made Amy smile, an appreciation for where she'd come from, and where she and her husband Jay finally landed a year ago.

Embracing extremes was something they were good at, and nothing was more extreme than moving from a farmhouse with fifteen rooms set on twenty acres of land, to a three-room apartment perched on the eighth floor of the Wellraven mid-rise on Seventy-First and Lex. That move from the Bread Basket to the Upper East Side had been a decision based on a once-in-a lifetime career opportunity for her husband to travel the world as a musical talent scout for RCA's A&R Division.

A year after taking their daring first bite out of the Big Apple, Amy and Jay never regretted their impetuous decision. Now, it was as if the rain even understood, answering with an impetuosity all its own, an erratic flood of joyful vehemence quintessential of the New York they'd grown to love.

As rainfall reduced to a trickle, she danced through the biggest puddles. Her childlike exuberance was so infectious that even a few strangers joined in the splashing as they passed her on the sidewalk.

The window pane of the pale-colored gray stone she stood across the street from groaned open. A familiar face edged into view, his smiling, coal-lined eyes greeting hers as he yelled, "Are you crazy? Being barefoot in that street-sludge!"

She chuckled and shook her head. "Yes, crazy with *happiness*. Wanna join me, Boom?"

Boom had black-dyed hair teased so high that he would have to enact a complicated yoga pose just to maneuver his head outside. His prosthetic arm was the only part of him exposed to the gentle fall of remnant drops, the clouds above having their last say.

At nearly seven feet tall, Boom cut an imposing figure in anyone's mind, made even more striking by the height of his back-combed hairstyle, which added another ten inches onto his imposing form, wild fringes framing his facial features. His signature hairstyle was well-known around town, a look gaining popularity in the punk movements slowly taking the world by storm.

Boom and his wife Tanya were famous personalities in the edgy New York punk rock scene. They were often mentioned in gossip columns as frequent guests at Warhol's Factory, and both worked as assistants to Leo Castelli, the world-renowned art dealer and owner of the famous gallery window pane that Boom was sheltering in and shouting out of now.

Shaking his head and smiling, his thumb aimed itself at his long black hair, which was back-combed to gravity defying perfection. "And mess up this masterpiece? But ..." His smile bloomed with the gentle reverence of a friend who understood her verve for enjoying every moment—that of someone who'd also faced the Reaper eye to eye, and won.

And did he ever. It was a tragic lesson earned from a mortar in the Vietnam War, an impact claiming one side of his body's limbs as collateral.

When first meeting Boom, Jay and Amy asked about his unique nickname—he admitted that it was easier for him to make light of something rather than hold on to the resentment and pain that accompanied his injuries. He'd made the decision to *own* it, personally claiming the sound of the blast that took his limbs as his own. He refused to shy away from it. The fact that *Boom* had turned into his calling card, earning him a small amount of fame in the cultured and edgy social circles he and Tanya moved within, only added to the appeal of his obvious inner-strength. It also helped to get them into all the coolest places in town, earning him respect steeped in his authenticity and steel of resolve. He was a masterpiece all his own.

Boom flourished despite his life-altering war injury. He was disarming, something many appreciated when meeting him for the first time ... or the fiftieth. The fact that he chose to be known by the sound of the explosion that claimed his right arm and leg, owning the experience in a very unapologetic way, said a lot about who he was.

Working at the world-famous Castelli Gallery accentuated that this towering, complex human also resembled a work of art, hard-won grit and perseverance honed into a persona that was unique and larger than life. He was the embodiment of a New Yorker in the flesh, his newly acquired East Coast accent shining through as he continued, "… That's one hell of a way to start a dreary Friday morning, Sunshine."

Amy loved the nickname Boom and his wife, Tanya, bestowed on her when she and Jay arrived in the neighborhood a year ago. It was a compliment to her sunny disposition and fit Amy perfectly. No matter the situation, she had a genuinely happy way of looking at life, a gift of finding and holding on to the positive. She *was* a ray of light in even the darkest place. Amy's light blond hair made the nickname even more fitting.

Surviving a near-death experience with a severe form of childhood diabetes had taught her to embrace every moment in life as if there might not be a tomorrow. The two missing fingers on her left hand was another reminder of that life lesson. A farming accident while bailing feed as a teenager, the machine sucked her left hand into the knife roller along with the stalks she was pushing through it. After the accident, the doctors warned her that her disease may muddle things, that she might lose her whole hand. It was a miracle she healed as well as she did, without further complications.

These were important experiences about *unscriptedness*, teaching her to adapt and move on. *When it rains, dance in it.* It was a motto she continued to live by.

"Is Ginger still in France?"

Smiling at Boom's nickname of her red-headed husband, Amy was reminded about Jay's recent success and reason for the trip that had kept him away for the last four weeks. "He comes back tomorrow night. How's Tanya's visit with her family been so far?"

At that moment, her best friend Tanya stuck her head out of the opened window to respond, her mocha skin darkened further by the sun she'd soaked up on her trip. "I just got back from Elma last night. Was a really nice visit. Lots of rainfall, stalks more robust than expected, so looking good for yields."

The way that Tanya's accent slid from sassy big city into Midwestern twang as she delivered this news inspired an even broader smile on Amy's face. She was happy to hear this report, as it meant good news for her own family's autumn harvest growing in Spillville, thirty miles away from the small town Tanya had just returned from.

It was truly a small world, a fact Amy and Jay realized the moment they learned that Boom and Tanya had also been Iowa natives, from small towns far enough not to know each other, but close enough to share acquaintances.

Tanya was the first friend Amy made upon moving to the Upper East Side, and soon their husbands became fast friends as well. Initial getting-to-know-you conversations turning into wide-eyed wonderment at how similar their stories had been. Both couples were born and grew up in Iowa. Both made the move to New York City to chase and catch dream careers. Tanya was a decade older than her husband Boom, and Amy was nine years older than Jay, so both couples understood the benefits and challenges of their age-gap romances.

Their commonalities helped them forge a deeper friendship, often doing couple-y things around town. The fact that Tanya and Boom lived in the building across from Wellraven, and they worked a few doors away from Amy's beauty salon, made socializing even more convenient. It was a fact Amy was grateful for, a reminder made even more pertinent when Tanya's loud voice slid across the glistening pavement to land clearly across the street. "Do you have plans for this evening? We brought in a few new pieces and just caught wind of a *happening* tonight. Want to join us?"

The crickety sound of windows opening above and day-sleepers snarling out insults at the noise they were making by conversing over the expanse of the wide street inspired Amy to shout out blanket apologies to the curmudgeons above. Crossing the street to stand just beneath Castelli Gallery's window, smiling as she neared her friends, she lowered her voice to reply, "I'm glad you invited me, it will take my mind off the nervous excitement I have about seeing Jay again after this very long month. I'll walk over after I close up shop for the evening."

Waving at her friends one last time as they closed their window to begin their day, she walked in the direction of her salon, just a few doors down. While she'd enjoyed her time rain-dancing, she was soaked through and had muddy splatters everywhere, so she was happy she didn't have far to travel looking like a drowned rat.

Entering the back of the building so she didn't create a mess in the salon itself, she stripped and showered in the small bathroom at the back of her salon, changed into a new outfit and slicked back her hair in a style she knew would serve her well throughout the day.

Her first appointment of the day would be arriving soon, and Amy made sure to schedule extra time to devote to making him look his best. Keith was a Wellraven neighbor who lived in the apartment beneath their own. An actor constantly going on casting calls, his agent had been hounding the attractive twenty-something to spruce up his image to audition for a recurring role on *All My Children*. She was honored that he'd chosen Upper East Dyed for this task, and that her appointment book was filling up with neighborhood clients who were becoming repeat customers, too. Ruthy, Deb, and Helena were among her favorites, and were also expected in back-to-back appointments that day.

Beautifying her clients and their fun conversations made the hands on the clock move faster.

Many hours and four make-overs later, she locked the front door and went to the back closet to put on the fanciest dress she kept for unscripted happenings—a navy Diane von Furstenberg wrap dress that came to just above her knees. Throwing on a pair of strappy heels to complete her outfit, she grabbed her purse, turned off the lights, locked the front door, and retraced the steps she'd made that rainy morning, greeting the warm humid evening with a smile as she ascended the gallery steps two at a time.

Entering the Castelli Gallery was always like entering the most vibrant dream, the blurred boundaries between the ethereal and reality growing more stark. The gallery space embraced the most outlandish and compelling works of creatives, and Amy became entranced by the new pendant lights hanging above the reception area. They were cocoon-like illuminated forms with odd-shaped appendages poking out in many directions.

"Aren't they extraordinary?" Amy recognized the familiar voice immediately, turning her attention away from the lights to smile at the receptionist who'd come to greet her. Amy had gotten to know Rita through attending many gallery events in the past. She was a beautiful young woman with an entrancing Israeli accent and the contemporary art history knowledge worthy of the esteemed, world famous gallery she worked for. She'd honed her skills at the Louvre Museum, and many other galleries throughout Europe. She had incredible insight about the pieces within Castelli's walls, so she continued softly, "They're Castiglioni Suspension sculptures. We've just acquired these pieces from a collector. Aren't they fascinating?"

Amy nodded in response, replying, "Their organic shapes are really cool, as if something extraordinary and unexpected is about to burst free—" Amy's voice halted as she was struck by how much she loved the sculptural aspect of the pendants above their heads, and how closely she related to the appendages stretching into escape. They resembled a texture of life she'd felt in her soul while dancing in the rain just a few hours ago. The imagery hanging above them engendered a hope she believed in, a truth that penetrated every aspect of her life. It was her *thing*.

A sly smile graced Rita's red lips as she turned her head to look at Amy's clipped response, whispering, "The act of freeing ourselves from constraints and embracing life in a fearless way, it's ..." Amy's eyebrow quirked in curiosity at Rita's slight pause, before her thought continued, "Chrysalide de papillon. Sorry, I slip into French often. Butterfly chrysalis, breaking free and then taking flight. It's something you excel at, isn't it, Amy? We all saw you dancing in the rain this morning. I wish I had the guts to be more like that in life. You shed your hesitations often, I think. It's such an admirable quality."

The blushing Rita cast her eyes downward, afraid she said too much to the almost-stranger. Their interactions had been limited, yet there was a thoughtful, familiar warmth in the way Rita expressed herself. Amy gripped the young woman's hand and smiled, silently thanking her for the kind assessment of her antics that morning. Most New Yorkers would call her *crazy*, so she was grateful the young woman before her spun a more appreciative assessment of her joy rousing.

"Chrysalide. The way you've pronounced it in French is beautiful."

Blushing from the compliment and in a hurry to begin her weekend, Rita turned to lock the front door of the gallery and shut off the lights in the entryway, returning to point to a corridor leading to the new Castelli summer installation.

"Boom and Tanya said they'd join you in a few minutes, just head in. Enjoy your evening!" With one last wave, Rita walked toward the back of the building while Amy headed where she was directed.

Rounding the final corner, she stopped in her tracks to take in the new pieces lining the perimeter of the large room, the white walls allowing the vibrantly colored artwork to shine. She was drawn to the floor-to-ceiling, silk-screened self-portrait of Andy Warhol positioned on the farthest wall. The green background stood in sharp contrast to his bright red-tinted face, his hand hovering over his mouth in an unexpected pose, his gaze peering back at Amy as she walked toward the large portrait.

Eyes fixed on one another. It was as if Warhol was aware of her unapologetic scrutinization. It was the first time she'd seen this particular Warhol portrait in person. The experience confounded her, unexpected questions surfacing as she stood motionless, gazing silently at the composition, face-to-face, as if she'd become a sculptural addition to the Castelli display, too.

"You like that one?" She was startled out of reverie and turned quickly to smile at the tall friend leaning against the wall behind her. Boom's prosthetic leg balanced his weight, his prosthetic arm hanging at his side while the other lifted to touch the studded belt end dangling from his waist. His leather coat and all-black clothing added to the rebel look he'd become famous for, and tonight was no exception. She lifted her shoulders at his question and replied while turning around to look at the picture once again, "I do and I don't. The red face is so blood-like that it's …"

"… Disturbing. I agree." His interruption while she paled and paused was welcomed. She was finding it hard to place the right descriptive while being reminded of that bloody afternoon long ago. Unconsciously looking down at her missing fingers, sunshine dimming beneath the memory of the sounds and phantom sensation of bone crush. It was a dark place she rarely visited, yet the military tactician standing tall next to her knew *that* haunted house inside and out. He'd scoped out shadowed corridors and knew every angle well enough to realize her sudden entrance into the unscripted. That kind of unexpected reaction was something Warhol relished in when creating his art.

Subtle was not Andy's forte—blunt force trauma was more his *thing*. Understanding this, Boom allowed life to imitate art, making use of Amy's silence as he spoke. "Warhol's known for being obsessed with themes of death, especially after the assassination attempt on his life. This portrait was done before he was shot, yet it still bears that morbid tint to it. The color combination is unsettling. I understand why you might be disturbed by it."

Amy measured her response before intrigue overtook caution. "Does it disturb you, Boom?"

Her tone rose slightly in hesitation as she asked his opinion. This topic of discussion seemed like a potential downer on what promised to be a fun evening. Yet there was no pause in his response, an emphatic tone claiming his surety. "No, I like it very much. I *get* it."

Her eyebrow lifted into her forehead in surprise as she considered her own adverse reaction. Warhol had become well-known for his bold public image, as did the imposing man standing beside her. She was certain there were other parallels she had yet to understand about the man on canvas and the hero beside her, although she wasn't certain she'd ever grasp them easily. The artistic types in her life all seemed so worldly and excellent at interpreting even the most obscure pieces of art. She didn't consider herself a country-bumpkin, but deciphering imagery wasn't necessarily her strongpoint, either.

What she *was* good at was appreciating that shared knowledge and embracing the positive perspectives of everyone she met—it was something she valued most about the friend standing next to her now, stoic and in deep thought as he focused on the portrait they were discussing.

Ultimately, the perks of making lemonade out of lemons worked for Boom, yet there were just some things Amy never wanted to dwell on. Her voice reduced to a weary scrape against the pristine ambiance of the white-washed gallery walls surrounding them.

"I have difficulty assuming that same appreciation for this content. I don't … like thinking about death, Boom."

Yet, at that moment, she couldn't help it. Her childhood memories of being a terrified ten-year-old rose to the surface. The frightening sensation of cold, starchy hospital sheets binding her little body to a stiff bed as needles poked her painfully, doctors and nurses scurrying around her prone form as they tried different methods to get her blood sugar under control. She never forgot the moment she overheard the doctors tell her parents that she would've died had they not brought her into the hospital. She'd never forgotten the moment she learned that she had a disease called Diabetes, and that her pancreas was now a dead organ, requiring having to prick herself with insulin-filled needles for the rest of her life.

As one scary memory surfaced, another rose to take its place … The ugly wails of *ohmygod* and the sudden pain of flesh stripping and bones gone. The reminder of the difficulty in having to learn to maneuver the needle and every other aspect of dexterity with fingers forever lost.

Both were life experiences that changed the way she looked at daily tasks. They'd altered the way she viewed everything about life, ultimately happy she could grow up and hopefully live her life anyway. Yet the red color of Warhol's face on the wall before her was too close to the reality of blood for her comfort, her certainty gone brittle. She squirmed in her heels as the bottoms of her soles began to sweat, a sudden need to take them off breaking any elegant gallery protocol she imagined might exist. She doubted Warhol would give a shit, so neither did she.

Boom looked over at his silent friend as she kicked off her shoes with a surprising flourish. They clattered on the floor beneath Warhol's glare, landing a little too close to the gallery's prized possession for his comfort—yet her far-away gaze belied the defiant action, the sloping angle of lines on her face a tell-tale sign of being pulled into uncharacteristic somberness.

"Death *is* scary to face, isn't it, Sunshine? By reconciling ourselves with the inevitable, I think it empowers us to live a more vibrant life *now*. It's about lack of control and fear of what we can't change, too. I get *that*. But out of that fear, we also learn to overcome and transform, and even take a new road that's ultimately taking us in amazing directions."

Amy nodded, realizing that not only was it true in her case, but even more so in Boom's situation.

Spillville Iowa's dust-field rapaciousness had nothing on the jungles of Vietnam. Boom stood tall beside her, a literal giant among men. A warrior hell-bent on adapting and reclaiming what he deserved: a life well-lived. Lingering in negative spaces was his non-negotiable. That would never be his *thing*.

As Amy considered how the positive shift in the air made her feel more at ease, she smiled and turned her attention back to the red-faced Warhol. It was an inspiring thing to realize how the artist, while nearly killed, still trusted in the journey life took him on. Enough to still share his creativity with the world.

"Sunshine, I … I wanted to thank you for earlier."

Her eyebrows knit in confusion, unaware of what he could possibly thank *her* for, if anything, her recent admiration of his tenacity would have her verbally thanking *him* for his sacrifices for their country. Yet Amy waited silently for him to continue. When he did, she was surprised by the sudden gentleness in his voice.

"Most people write me off as unable to do anything much at all, let alone anything *fun*, yet you didn't hesitate in inviting me to puddle-jump with you." His voice cracked with uncharacteristic emotion. "Thank you for being someone who didn't think twice to ask me to join you."

Over the year of knowing Boom, she'd witnessed the eggshell walking others did around him. She wasn't sure if the wide circles others formed around him had something to do with unconscious pity for his limb loss, or that he was often considered aloof and was prone to clamming up around strangers. Yet she knew, at this moment, what a gift he'd just given her by sharing tenderness and gratitude for something as simple as playing in the puddles.

His appreciation touched Amy deeply, her voice warming as she grinned and responded, "I love you and Tanya very much, and would never hesitate to include you, in *anything*. You're both such important parts of our lives." Taking in a deep breath, Amy felt a sense of regret that her other half wasn't present for the conversation.

*How I miss Jay.*

Boom's smile was small, but evident enough.

The look in his eyes turned from gratitude to deeper contemplation as he seemed to have a new thought, turning his head to look at the Warhol portrait again. Aiming his left index finger at the bottom portion of the picture, Amy's gaze followed his direction, their eyes drawn downward to the hand covering Warhol's mouth. Amy couldn't explain why, but even in such an expansive room as the gallery they stood in, this moment between them felt even *larger*. When he began to speak, that truth was realized.

"After I woke up, I was missing half of my body. I wanted to die. Going from a soldier's mindset of showing no weakness, to suddenly being the epitome of weakness and requiring help from everyone, to do every damn thing … dying seemed preferable. I'd considered suicide many times. I was in so much pain, and it's tough to lose something that's intrinsic to your movement, to feeling like a complete and virile man, to … to feel *whole* and …" The last consonants sounded as if articulating them singed the roof of his mouth, his pause allowing more tepid thoughts to soothe the lingering burn.

After a few moments, he swallowed. "And yet being immobile, forced to be still while I healed, gave me a much needed shift in perspective, it …" Drawing in a long breath, his tone dropped to a whispered truth. "… It became time to decide how I'd transition into my future, and taught me some important things about myself, too. It's why the topic of death doesn't faze me anymore."

His eyelids shuttered momentarily beneath the weight of the past churning, before opening and pinning her with a glassy gaze. Tears were threatening, yet refused to be shed.

"It was my place to be silent and still until I was ready to shed the tomb I'd spun for myself out of pain, anger, of self-loathing. Instead, I decided instead to wake up, to chew myself out of the dark place I kept myself prisoner … to emerge, to transform into who I always wished to be, who …"

*Quiescent. Stupefied. Pupafied.*

She turned her head slightly to witness Boom shut his eyes before returning her gaze to the hand covering the mouth of the famous artist on the wall. While she couldn't relate to the severity of Boom's injuries, she could empathize with being forced to alter life to suit unexpected circumstances. Being beholden to the needled vials she relied upon to live also gave her that perspective. From every challenge she faced in life, she learned something new about herself. Unscriptedness was an edifying taskmaster.

When he opened his eyes, he continued, "… who I'm … *we're* brave enough to *be* now."

That he included her in his assessment touched her deeply. Amy angled her shoulders to face him and smiled in understanding, once again appreciating the friend standing beside her.

"I loved serving our country, being surrounded by brave brothers who I knew would have my back in even the deadliest of situations. It was an amazing time in my life, even though it didn't end so great for me. But … didn't it?"

Amy knew the answer to his rhetorical question already, nodding silently in agreement, reminded of the deep love he shared with Tanya and for the fabulous career he'd established for himself, living a life in a city he and his wife adored. They were living their dreams.

"After the impact of that fateful day, I slowly discovered I could choose to foster septic wounds and wither away, or I could accept the circumstances and change how I reacted to them. You understand this, Sunshine, I know that already."

Amy nodded, feeling his truth deep in her gut. Boom never hollowed himself out with bitterness. There was a power in deciding how to accept plot twists, in embracing the perspective that no matter the scenario, no matter how broken, or scared, or suffering … *you* are enough to thrive, no matter what happens along the way.

It was the decision to choose healing over an undertaker.

Amy also refused to live in a sunless world. She believed that joy was like air, that taking in anything polluted with negativity was a detriment to the potential life offered. This revealed and validated so much about the Boom she knew today—the tall-haired rebel who walked through life with an unapologetic confidence and sense of edgy fashion that never played it safe.

"I do the same, Boom. It's why I choose to be happy. My memories are so vivid about learning that my pancreas gave me its walking papers. I'll never forget learning I was so close to dying. Finding joy in experiences is far more enjoyable than constantly looking for what's wrong in life. And I may have only been a teenager when I lost part of my hand, yet I understood the brevity enough to never let go of that initial lesson about embracing life. I know that people probably judge me for being *too* happy, but I like looking at life *this* way."

"I admire that about you, Sunshine. Watching you *carpe diem* in such a fun way this morning, it ... it was fucking awesome to watch. I almost felt like a voyeur, intruding on a joy impossible to be contained. I swear your enjoyment of rain-dancing actually shooed away that storm."

Amy smiled at the thought of a human having the power to clear away nature's voice. The way that Boom and Rita framed her morning experience, and the way he turned their conversation from morbid to insightful, reaffirmed her belief that *anything* was possible, even if it began with something as simple as an altered perspective.

"This conversation is reminding me a lot of my parents."

Amy turned toward him and tilted her head to the side in surprise. Reserved as he was, it was the first time he'd mentioned them.

"They were both artists who created art in many unique ways, but over time, they found a very personal way of looking not only at life, but what resilience meant to them. Dad was interested in entomology and had a huge collection of butterflies and moths. He loved studying and collecting things of beauty."

Amy considered butterflies to be among the most beautiful creatures on earth, so she silently nodded.

"Mom and Dad were also avid historians interested in archaeology, so they used to make beautifully decorative terracotta tiles in their kiln in the barn, paint butterflies on them, sign them, glaze them, and then hide them along their world travels. They've thrown these tiles into the Nile, buried them everywhere from Mt. Rushmore, to the Swiss Alps, to a Beijing park near the Forbidden City. Thousands of pieces of them are left for others to find, long after they're passed on. The impermanence of life drove them to find ways to leave a legacy in a creative, permanent way, but ..."

His decipherable intake of breath was held longer than Amy thought humanly possible, and her attention remained on Boom's face as his eyelids lowered beneath weighty remembrance—the scent of rain-forests, of pungent death among the elephant grass, and gunpowder burning into cinders of final memory of the Ia Drang Valley. The stench of 1965 was unforgettable, the burn left singed to marrow, even if the literal was no longer attached. The pain and sense of loss was unimaginable.

"Then the painful lesson of leaving pieces of myself ..."

Amy's eyes widened, her phantom fingers flexing in response to his admission before Boom drew in a deep breath and hurriedly continued, "When I came home after, I was in the hospital in Davenport for nearly a month. My fiancée, my high school sweetheart, didn't want to be burdened with a cripple, so she called off our engagement and walked away without a backward glance. The fact that two of my siblings were anti-war and refused to visit me … I shut down, feeling even more injured than I'd already been. I was missing two of my limbs, and then my heart broke with that abandonment and rifts in every part of my life."

Amy related to the middle-finger often flashed by life. There were times she still resented her pancreas for its *fuck you*. She made a momentary glare at Boom's upper chest as she contemplated stolen dreams and broken trust, stuck in place and ill-equipped to deal with the trauma of losing both limbs and loved ones at once. How his heart must've ached.

"When I was discharged and moved into my old room, my parents covered my walls with their entire butterfly collection. The Laxtons were life-long neighbors, and their oldest daughter Tanya was always close with my family. Tanya convinced them to remove the drapes from my window, too. She knew what I needed more than I did at the time, refusing to let me stew in darkness, knowing that unavoidable thoughts are often necessary to move on. And being surrounded by the vivid colors of those gorgeous creatures, constant reminders of what *could* be. What the caterpillar calls the end of the world, the master calls a butterfly."

Hearing Richard Bach's famous quote about perspective and persistence pushed the corners of Amy's lips into her cheeks, Boom's demeanor brightening along with his tone. The flight he'd ultimately taken in life displayed beautiful wings.

"Chrysalide." Amy clumsily mimicked Rita's pronunciation, a beautiful sounding word that ended with what sounded like the English equivalent of *lead*. It was fitting to consider one form *leading* into the next—to influence, and advance in a positive direction. Deeply inspiring to Amy, she preferred the French version of the word most. Her rusty pronunciation was barely a whisper, and Boom smiled.

"My dad was obsessed with those imago-moments and I'm grateful he was. Tanya's familiarity as a close family friend made me feel safe to open myself up to life again. She was always around, seemed to know how to best get me to look past my suffering. She and my parents taught me the importance of what must develop within ... that sometimes we find transformation in silence, buried and to be freed *later*, perhaps in a different place, or in a different way. If I lived in seething bitterness, I would never be where I am today, or have opened myself up to the passion and love that found its way in. I'll be right back, I have to do one last thing in the office before we leave for the night."

The baring of one's soul was never easy. Even without military training, Amy knew a tactical retreat when she saw one. The glistening of Booms' eyes in the gallery's lighting barely hid the tears broaching his coal-lined eyelashes. The echoing staccato of wooden-pound to combat boot sole and back again as they hit the wood floorboards while he walked toward the back of the gallery grew softer and softer, as it diminuendos into silence.

Amy recognized that high emotion was often the signal that it was time for a few moments of private time to reclaim zen, a peace-filled cocoon to be spun, created, and be kept warm in, to regroup before *Imago moments*. She was left with the inspiring thought of hikers somewhere in the Alps or excavators in Egypt, unearthing butterfly tiles, and how similar a path their brave son also took. By claiming his deliberately chosen moniker, Boom had embraced something akin to the ultimate empowerment. It was a bravely signed legacy of his own, left for all who knew him. He gave the next leg of life an entirely new and even more stirring meaning.

The marks he left on the world were beautiful, too.

After a few moments of silence, Amy whispered quietly, "You can come out now, Tanya."

She'd smelled her best friend's Diorella long before Tanya made her presence known, long before Boom revealed his parent's story. As heeled soles rounded another wall in the gallery, Amy turned her head to shower an owlish gaze on her friend, who was wearing a guilty expression that belied the coy quirk to her lips. Tanya didn't have a bashful bone in her body, her expression affirming *deal with it*. It was a trait Amy admired in her friend, an unapologetic mantra consistently held into light. Tanya and Boom really were the perfect match.

"I'll admit to eavesdropping because he so rarely opens up like that to anyone. I wanted to give you both privacy. It's touching that he trusts you enough to be *that* exposed to you. He's far from a fragile man, but he can be very vulnerable, when in the right company."

Memories of her husband's fragility flooded Tanya's consciousness as those words passed her lips.

*The way he shut down when his childhood sweetheart returned his engagement ring to him, after learning the severity of his injuries.*

*The way he began opening up to conversation as he listened and comforted Tanya when her messy divorce dragged on through the courts.*

*And the way he celebrated her freedom with a glass of wine on the back porch, more than crops ripening under the summer sun.*

Tanya's smile broadened into her cheeks as she silently reminisced over love and harvest, a gesture mimicked by her best friend as Amy replied, "I'm touched that he chose to share that part of himself with me."

Nodding in agreement, Tanya lifted a red-nailed finger in the air to point at the Warhol Portrait.

"You've been standing in this spot for this entire time. I only caught the tail end of your conversation. What's got you glued to it?"

Amy smiled. "Something that your hubby just said about keeping silent, it … it has me wondering about Warhol's body language of hand over mouth, questioning what he's hiding or suppressing."

Tanya disagreed. She tilted her head a few times toward the picture, silently demanding that Amy *look again*. "Art can be mystifying. By seeing the smaller

129

things, you'll begin to see the even bigger picture. If he were to remove that hand, words breaking free from his silent state, fleeing the envelopment of tight-lipped truss …"

*Imago moments.* Amy imagined Boom's voice saying those two words as she began considering Tanya's point of view, conceptualizing what Warhol's experience might've been. What it would be like to have an assassination attempt on your life, which led to bullets, shell struck, near-death experiences, personal strife, and life-altering circumstances that forced stillness to fixate, contemplate, and extrapolate. To be still long enough to gain hope-affirming clarity, to begin incremental steps toward the future and develop the courage to move on—chrysalide situations that led into wing-stretching newness.

With sudden clarity, Amy gave realization wings, asking the portrait, "What are you about to say?"

Her whispered rhetorical inquiry took flight into the air as Amy looked into the eyes of the icon staring back at her.

Tanya grinned, and a deep, masculine voice added, "Now, if only everyone asked themselves that question, instead of hesitating to share what they think or who they are with the world. Pretty cool, looking at things from the *Leo* perspective, huh, Sunshine?"

Amy's eyebrows wrenched together, unsure if Boom was referring to the owner of the gallery, Zodiac symbol, or hidden imagery within the picture. The arty types she knew always saw things differently, in a deeper context.

Tanya and Boom were no exception. Realizing her puzzlement, he added, "Sorry, I forget not everyone is ex-military, reducing things into acronyms, nicknames, and Boom jargon. Leo. Life. Experience. Opportunities."

The phrase delighted Amy as she laughed and replied, "*Leo* ... I love that!"

"Says the puddle-jumper. Of course you do! Should we head out, beautiful ladies?"

With one last parting glance at the portrait, Amy slid on her shoes and the friends followed Boom out of the gallery, lights flipping to darkness as they made their way toward the front door of the Castelli. Amy pointed at the dimmed objects above their heads as they neared the main doorway.

"I really love these pendant lights. Rita told me a little about them. I'm curious about what transformed creatures might emerge from them."

The corner of Tanya's lip cunningly bit into the apple of her right cheek. "We seem to have established the perfect theme of this evening, no doubt continuing when you meet *Bob*. Let's catch a cab, we don't want to miss any fun."

"Bob?"

Tanya's silent nod gave nothing away, and her steps seemed to take an extra bounce on the now dry sidewalk. The laugh lines on her best friend's face were even more pronounced, so she was clearly up to something. While Amy loved Tanya dearly, she wasn't the biggest fan of surprises.

Changing tactics, Amy turned her head slightly to the silent man slowly descending the graystone's steps. "Another Boomism?"

Boom's responding laughter was so loud that Amy was certain it could be heard across the Hudson. "No, but Bob's a cousin of Leo. You can blame the Warhols of the world for *that* one, long before I came on the scene. You'll understand when we get there."

A twenty-minute cab ride later, *there* they *got*.

Max's Kansas City was a legendary destination where the fabulous chose to constellate. It seemed to have a force field all its own, New York's star-eyed, *fame now* enthusiasts caught in its gravity.

The open-minded zeitgeist of the sixties had thrown the door open for edgier aesthetics to follow in its footsteps, Max's is the embodiment of this shift into *new and now*. Everyone waiting in the Max queue was trying to out-do the other, a kind of counterculture ecosystem thriving on a host of bigger and brighter. It was so New York.

While observing everyone in line, Amy regretted the under-punked blandness of her expensive yet simple dress. The deep voice of the long-haired, large-muscled bouncers Boom greeted as Seza, Adam, and Rick drew Amy out of worrying about the wholesome primness of her attire as they waved them to the front of the line. The photographers and line-waiters belted Boom's name to get his attention as the friends moved toward the front door.

Amy's heart quickened as she stepped inside. She and Jay had been too busy establishing their careers and working overtime to socially venture outside of their Wellraven neighborhood. Plus, Max's Kansas City seemed the one place to be *too* out of reach for almost anyone to get into.

Missy, the jovial hostess, greeted Boom and Tanya, and introduced herself to their guest, taking the lead and escorting them through the front part of the packed bar. Amy noticed the photo-filled walls of the famous and infamous as they walked past. People were sardined into booths, and began shouting their greetings to Boom and Tanya over the boisterous crowd, many high-fiving them as they passed the tables lining the walls.

Recognizing and waving at a couple Wellraven neighbors, they weaved through the crush of people like trout migrating upstream, trying to gain positions at the back of the bar. Only very few were allowed to move back farther, bottle-necking everyone to a standstill while Boom and his hair cast a shadow on the two excited beauties behind him, and everyone else around him, too.

While Missy tried her best to make a path in the crowd, Boom realized they needed a plan B, shouting in the direction of the large man stationed at the back of the room. "Hey, Sylvester! Can we get past this clusterfuck?" Missy wiped the sweat on her brow as she glanced back and smiled, while Amy and Tanya chuckled at their military inspired way-maker. After hearing his name, the brawny man guarding the arched doorway waved in acknowledgment before ordering the immediate area to be cleared.

They were pulled through the archway into a large room, the red hue cast from the florescent crucifix light hanging from the ceiling overpowering every visible surface. It was like peering beyond the gates of Hades, everything bathed in hellfire.

*It was marvelous.*

Taking in her surroundings with wide-eyed wonder, Amy realized she was in the presence of some of the most famous people on the planet. World-renowned artists, fashion tycoons, models, writers, rock stars. Her husband's record company had been wooing one, in particular, for months.

"Jay is going to fucking die when I tell him who I saw tonight."

"The *who* pales in comparison to the *what*. Girl, anything goes in here. Just *wait*." Tanya's knowledge of the world was far more extensive than Amy's. Hearing her friend's announcement as they slid into their designated booth was akin to Satan opening an awards show in which they all had front row seats.

People were stripping off shirts and dancing in the aisles and on top of tables. Many were even pushing tables together to form a perimeter around a makeshift dance floor. It became an atmosphere Amy had only ever seen in movies, yet had never experienced before in real life, and her open-mouthed wonder inspired Tanya to grin, and lean in to say, "Far cry from Spillville, right?"

Noticing her friends staring at the glowing sculpture on the ceiling, Boom pointed at it and yelled over the music, "Bob. Bucket. Of. Blood. Now you understand why many regulars also refer to *Bob* as *The Gallery*, because of Dan Flavin's piece of modern art dangling from the ceiling, casting bloody hues on us all. Just as Warhol is famous for grouping theme variations together in a setting to showcase variety, similarities, and differences, you can see it happening all around us, in the flesh!"

Realization dawned on Amy's face as she nodded and grinned, a red-hued room of debauchery, claret-spiked ... suddenly *Bob* made sense.

Nudists were taking off their clothes, sly smiles and the light from above the only thing they wore. The gory hue painted a hedonistic tableau of revelry over the apple eaters cast in shades of sin. Meeting *Bob* was like entering a naughty fairy tale, where none of the heroes submitted to life goose-stepping with conformists or normality. Bob was glorious. Bob was ridiculously flamboyant. Bob also happened to be well acquainted with *Blow*, who was sprawled akimbo on the table next to the newcomers. Some dancers stopped to snort, while others passed on gaining a pearl-high.

What no one was passing on was *fun.*

Amy's attention was drawn to a group of women gathered on the other side of the room. She recognized a few of them from magazines, but what made her smile was how much they seemed to enjoy each other's company, their laughter drowning out much of the conversation happening around them. Pointing at the group of joy rousing women, Tanya smiled. "It's fun to watch them, isn't it? Those are the Bunker Babes, a group of artsy types that often hang out at Warhol's Factory. They're authors, poets, photographers, fashion designers, actors, artists, culinary geniuses ... That woman in the white latex is Mistress Icy, owner of Snow, in Queens."

"I've heard of that store, it's across Queensboro Bridge, right by Silk City Distillery."

"Yep, best sex shop on the East Coast, and she's now a best-seller of one of the hottest novels to hit the book world. The Bunker Babes definitely know how to enjoy life. And ..."

Tanya's index finger moved to the left, landing on a dapper-looking gentleman wearing an argyle beret. A large group surrounded him, while a huge bottle of Laphroaig sat in the center of their table. "*They* are Sir and The Muses. Have you heard of them?" Amy shook her head, although their name did sound slightly familiar. Boom's voice cut through the noise emanating from the surrounding tables as he took over where his wife left off. "Your Ginger has probably been chomping at the bit to get his teeth into them, too. They're from Toronto and have become famous for mixing Renaissance instrumentals and modern accompaniments, incorporating lyrics inspired by Dante's Inferno into a unique fusion that has a very different sound. They're really hot in the New York Jazz scene right now, a headliner at The Emmerzoom Coral near Emerson Cafe and Gilbert Rossman's Book

Emporium, on Sixty-Ninth. You should check them out the next time you get the chance. I'll introduce you to their manager, Flavia Watson, if we see her tonight. She's someone Jay will definitely want to know by sight."

Amy took the Muses in with heightened interest, noticing they were all wearing plaid designs of some kind. It was a conventional choice for a club setting where people were stripping naked and snorting cocaine on any stationary surface. Amy suddenly understood why some referred to Max's Kansas City as a type of gallery all its own. There weren't enough Boomisms in the world to adequately describe what she was witnessing in Max's Kansas City. It was confounding to see nipples and plaid in one glance, a Bob-tastic reality defying words.

"I didn't think Tartan was a thing." Amy's wry humor made Tanya and Boom chuckle, his response equally buoyant.

"They've made it a *thing*. Argyle is everywhere lately due to their group's popularity."

Amy didn't care for jazz music and did not have her finger on that particular pulse. Yet seeing the beautiful tartan designs worn by this argyle empire inspired her. Amy was instantly convinced that it was time for a remodel. This trend would enhance the vibrant ambiance when clients walked through the door of Upper East Dyed.

Just as Amy was about to express this design idea with her friends, Tanya bounced in her seat and moaned.

Nudging Boom with her elbow, Tanya announced, "Shay and Cillian just walked in!"

Tanya was rubbing her hands together in excitement. Boom winked at Amy, a smirk of wicked knowing forming on his lips, before returning his attention to the doorway. The new couple danced provocatively down the aisle, commanding the attention of the tables they passed.

Shay's legs were bare, her vinyl black dress hugging her ample chest and flaring out at the waist. She swayed her hips to the music as she turned her body to spread eagle against the mirrored wall, palms matched to reflection as her partner smiled deviously, meeting her gaze in the mirror. Throwing the bag he was carrying on the floor, Cillian bent down to unzip it while keeping his other hand pressed on the small of her back. His left hand slowly lifted a shiny object from the bag, a patent leather bundle that appeared to have long strings and rings dangling from it.

"What is *that*?" Amy's inquisitive tone made her best friend smile.

Tanya's crooked smirk grew further when she answered, "An under-bust corset."

Shay accepted the article from her partner, reminding Amy of parishioners accepting the sacrament at Sunday mass. The offering now made in this blood-stained den of sin made Amy's Catholic guilt rise. She imagined her favorite childhood priest, Father Roberto, assigning her three Hail Mary's and an evening of volunteering at his wholesome Raspberry Cordial Bible Study. In sudden need for penance, Amy performed a mental sign of the cross and waved at their waitress, Mandy. She ordered a Chambord and vodka as mea culpa, hoping Father Roberto would understand the substitution for liquid penance.

As Mandy collected their second round of drink orders, Amy watched Shay wrap the corset around her waist, fastening the buckles at the front and slowly turning around. Bending at the waist to lean into the shiny surface in front of her, palms meeting reflection again in what appeared to be an act of submission, Cillian's fingers traced down the back of the corset, pulling the laces tighter on his descent. Amy was shocked at how such a small article of clothing cinched in Shay's waist, showcasing her beautiful curves even more.

Shay's breathing visibly increased as she watched Cillian bend to the floor, his long fingers reaching into the bag once again. This time, he pulled out a thick rope looped into a bundle, and Shay began to pant, her chest rising and falling in a cadence of heightened excitement.

The room couldn't pull away from their spell. As Cillian leaned in to whisper instructions into Shay's ear, she brought her legs together. He began unraveling the bundle in his hands, creating loops in his grip and then cocooning her limbs within intricate knots around her legs and waist.

Pulling the ends of the rope through the metal rings jingling from Shay's corset, Cillian threw the ropes over the pipes high above their heads. Bending one last time, he pulled out a ball gag and fastened it in a knot at the back of her head.

A shocked gasp escaped Amy's throat as Cillian pulled on the ropes to lift his lover into the air, where she hovered high above the pulsing crowd gathering to dance beneath the area she dangled. Her corseted waist angled perpendicular to the floor, knees bent as they held the back of her black vinyl skirt captive. The ankles of her combat boots were knotted to her wrists, her ponytail bound in a knot attached to her spine, her head pulled back and her lips eclipsing the vermilion ball in her teeth's grip.

Shay was clearly in a heightened state of excitement as she squirmed against the delicious bite of the hemp, her teeth baring around the shiny gag, her lips quivering in a smile. She seemed to enjoy the restrained tension, not caring about the dancers and spectators beneath her while she hovered in an erotic trance.

The way the ropes constricted against Shay's skin as she hung in her contorted position in the air conflicted with everything Amy believed to be erotic or sexually appealing. Yet witnessing Shay's responses to the pain and pleasure her position afforded her ... the eroticism of the exhibition was enhanced when she began to quiver within her restraints. This new kind of sexplay inspired Amy to rethink her stance, especially as Cillian lifted his right hand high above his head to trace the front of her corset to finesse where the juncture narrowed between Shay's legs. The pressure he placed against the knot there caused an immediate reaction in Shay, and he smiled knowingly, licking his lips as she arched her back further into her binds. Shoulders rolled back and deeper into her spine near the ceiling, her legs convulsed as her arching tilted the ropes, swiveling her mid-air while she panted into what Amy thought was a climax.

She never thought watching a couple share their erotic secrets with strangers would be so titillating, yet Amy could not deny the raw sensuality she'd just witnessed. This realization was another cog in her racing mind. Being an Iowa girl, she was well familiar with the bite of a rope from a wayward colt or topsy-turvy haystack. She never imagined rope and pleasure sharing the same context.

Amy's mind immediately summoned Spillville's mayor and her husband, Darrelyn and Ken. They also owned the general store and had many varieties of ropes available for purchase. They were known as the local rope experts and could teach even the most complicated knots necessary for various farming purposes. Amy smirked, wondering what they'd think of the current application of ropes in such an erotic way. Then again, given the long Iowa winters stuck indoors, and their often saucy sense of humor, Amy wondered if they'd be right at home in this sexually explosive atmosphere of *tieverse* and *ropesong*.

Dragged out of quixotic Iowa memories by the jarring motions of Cillian lowering Shay's trembling body, Amy was struck by the peaceful look on Shay's face despite the precarious way she'd just been hung from the ceiling. Red marks bloomed under where the ropes had held her tightest. Angling her feet to stand on the floor, Cillian began caressing Shay's corset laces once again. Tanya turned to her mouth-gaping friend. "What ya' think of *that*, Sunshine?"

"It was really cool to watch, but I couldn't imagine getting turned on from being tied up and strung up like she did." Amy's wryness made the couple chuckle.

"If the fibers and the bite of the hemp hit you just right at certain pleasure points, they'll torture you in the most delicious way." The wistful tone in Tanya's admission and the look of longing on Booms' face made Amy's eyes widen, still convinced that erotic rope play was not for her. The corset, however—she couldn't take her eyes off of it as Cillian slowly unraveled his rope masterpiece from Shay's limbs, the path of his handiwork leaving remnants on her pale skin as the rope dropped to the floor. Pulling the string at the back of her head, the ball gag fell into his waiting palm as Shay flexed her jaw and twisted her neck around to look into Cillian's eyes.

With a few deft moves, he unzipped his slacks as she pushed him off of the dance floor and into the nearest empty seat, straddling his lap as the volume of her skirt settled around her spread-wide thighs. Shay gyrated against her lover's lap, the corset pushing her vinyl covered breasts into his chin as she controlled the pace of their new *blendsong*.

"Are they ..." The incredulous tone of Amy's question as her words drifted away in shock made Tanya laugh and nodded.

142

Amy had never witnessed exhibitionists in action like this, the shock on her face clear to her friends. Tanya leaned over to whisper, "Imagine how good that corset feels for her, bound and aware of the effect that's having on him, feeling the tightness of it as she tightens around *him*."

Her best friend's words made Amy's breath catch in her throat as she squirmed in her seat.

This had become an evening of opinion altering eye-openers. Amy always considered the corset a torture device for women of generations long ago—a sexually objectifying, evil garment that confined a woman's movement and restricted them in social, psychological, and physical context. Amy had a hard time reconciling that misconception with the erotic visual of what the room was being exposed to as leather and skin slid *deep, deep, deeper* into *fleshheat* and *givetake*.

The heat in the room was visceral. There was something primal about Cillian's reaction to his lover wearing the corset, as well as the way Shay maneuvered her own constricted torso while she moved. It was one of the sexiest things Amy had ever witnessed.

"*Now* what do you think, Sunshine?"

Reminded once again of all the painful rope burns she'd received on the farm, Amy answered emphatically, "The ropes are a big fat *no* for me, but ..." The way her voice softened into a pregnant pause made Tanya smile. Amy's voice lifted higher as she turned to Tanya and asked, "Have you ever worn ...?"

"Yeah. And Boom loves it on me, just as I love wearing it." Tanya's breathy admission and dancing eyes smoldered with something Amy couldn't place.

"Is it painful to wear?"

"Not at all. It does take a few moments to get used to, but I find that I actually prefer the stiff feel of it, how it supports my back and holds the bazongas up high." Tanya's décolletage was already gorgeous, but Amy was having a hard time imagining what her own rack would look like while wearing a corset. Being a woman in her late thirties, her nipples were beginning to droop south and her tits had definitely seen better days.

The *Bob* reactions seemed instinctively at odds with her own, and Amy suddenly felt more self-conscious about her naivety as the erotic scene continued to unfold before her. She wasn't the type for insecurities or self-doubt, usually never daunted by things that were different or new. Yet Amy's sudden hesitation and inner-monologue surprised her, brows joining at the center of her forehead as she swallowed, trying to choke down the unexpected feelings rising up from deep within. She was also taken aback by the different reactions of others compared to her now. Many revelers around her barely took notice of the couple once the straddle-fucking started, as if it were common to see a couple screw so openly, and in such an erotic way. Clearly, plot twists were their *thing*.

"I just don't know if it's for me …"

Tanya rarely saw this side of her friend. "Say's the don't-give-a-fuck puddle-jumper we witnessed this morning. It's for every woman. And I'm telling you, it's especially for *you*. You're not getting missish on me now, Sunshine." The uncharacteristic brow-pinched look on Amy's face resembled the pickled onion gripping onto the side of Tanya's cocktail, concerning her even more.

"What's *really* wrong, Amy?"

Amy shrugged her shoulders, not quite sure what to think about the darker direction of her thoughts. Pointing at the corseted woman who now sat still and sated in her lover's lap, she asked, "Would *this* be me trying too hard? I never want to feel like I'm having to do something like this to keep Jay's interest." Tanya shook her head. While both women genuinely believed that age was *just a number* and had no bearing on their happy marriages, they'd begun noticing little changes with their bodies lately—small reminders of getting older.

Jay's youthful appearance also added to Amy's surfacing insecurities, a fact Tanya understood all too well, given that her own husband often looked much younger than she did. In private moments, the best friends had discussed some of the difficulties presented with the age gap. Tanya often referred to it as the *love span*. The wilt of once perky breasts. Energy levels waning as Amy worked the long hours to get her salon to a profitable place, or Tanya fighting her way through the cut-throat world of the New York art scene. They were empowered women unafraid to fight for what they wanted, yet neither woman wanted to admit publicly that they were beginning to worry that the ten-year age difference of their younger men was not wearing well on them—that they were slowly being claimed by some arbitrary disadvantages.

"I ..." Gaze sinking to the tabletop, Amy found it hard to voice her thoughts. Instead, she stuck to safe. "I think I've just missed Jay. The distance has been tough this go around. And I'm not sure what my jugs would look like wearing something like *that*. We've talked about this, so you know what I mean. They've become ..."

"Droopy? Gravity is turning into a cunt, isn't she? Trust me, not only would your décolletage balance champagne flutes when wearing that, but Jay would go absolutely fucking wild. Amy, you've got to trust me on this, it's not trying too hard. The only thing hard about this will be *him*. It's just a healthy dose of *Leo*."

Amy's forehead relaxed and her smile grew, her best friend's reassurances buttressing the excitement she'd been feeling prior to her momentary dance with panic. Tanya's reminder about life experience opportunities put all of Amy's hesitations to rest, her self-recrimination getting the ball-gag it deserved.

Boom nodded, pointedly staring at Amy and shouting, "Carpe diem!" before returning his attention to the sated and still exhibitionists, Shay hugging Cillian tenderly in her straddled embrace. The tension that unraveled from the final erotic scene seemed to release its bounds on everyone present, the trio's eyes drifting off to new red-tinged places as Amy considered the fact that Boom had used that exact phrase earlier that evening.

*Watching you carpe diem in such a fun way this morning, it ... it was fucking awesome to watch. I almost felt like a voyeur intruding on a joy impossible to be contained.*

*Voyeur.* While she was a shocked intruder at first, the sensual exhibitionism removed any culpability, wrongness, or even judgment as the couple loved freely beneath the red stain of the gallery the brave couple displayed in. The only restraints that existed were around Shay's waist and the ropes her love had spun from the ceiling.

Amy wasn't sure why she was so willing to be harsh and judgmental of herself, inflicting self-restraint on what sensual possibilities could lie in her own future. It *could* be fun. It *could* be a sensual scenario she spun to ensnare the love of her life, by breaking their rhythm. So why not? Her hesitation and uncertainty untensed and fled her facial features, the *coulds* inspiring the corners of her lips to pull into a tense hyphen separating one emotion from the next.

*Imago-moments, indeed.*

Amy knew she was being silly. Jay was open-minded when it came to their sex life. Intimacy between them had always kept their passion hot, but long absences, late nights getting their careers off the ground, and less frequency fed her current hesitations. Their sexual intimacy seemed to be slightly dull, even by her standards, and parts of her were literally sinking toward her belly button.

*Fucking drooping titty traitors.*

She had a sense Jay would enjoy this new addition to their bedroom antics, especially when it wasn't something he was expecting. While Amy was lost in thought about sagging body parts and thinking of how to best ask her best friend if she could borrow her corset, Tanya smiled as she watched her friend war with the same self-doubt she often felt. Clearly, Sunshine was coming to some promising conclusions, because even in the blood light of the room, the blonde's lips curled into a sly half-smile, and her cheeks were downright puce.

Tanya wasn't the only one to take notice.

Boom and Tanya turned their attention to the aisle and waved at a stunning, smiley brunette wearing a white latex catsuit from neck to toe. The stranger was carrying a long, thin bundle in her perfectly manicured hands. Tanya's friendly tone filled the air as she shouted over the music, "Icy! Nice to see you again. This is our friend, Sunshine. Would you like to join us?"

"I would love to—that was quite a demonstration, wasn't it? That goddess is fierce when she's on display, a sexy, fearless *savage*. I love watching Shay enjoy herself" Icy's open demeanor and posh British accent caused all three friends to smile. Their new companion slipped into Amy's side of the booth, settling next to her as the scent of roses bloomed in the air between them. Her perfume was beautifully refreshing, adding a lightness to the self-inflicted doubt Amy had been silently imposing on herself and her drooping tits.

She felt pinned by the stranger's eyes as the brown-haired beauty asked, "Sunshine, you enjoyed the show, didn't you?" Puce turned into burning fire on Amy's cheeks and chest as she nodded, embarrassed and unsure how this stranger would know how turned on she'd actually become while watching.

When the charming Englishwoman placed the bundle on the table and slid it toward Amy, three sets of eyebrows raised ceiling-ward as Icy smiled. "Even from across the room, I could see how much you were intrigued. I brought a few things with me tonight to deliver to clients, but I'd like you to have this as a gift from me. I have a feeling you're going to enjoy it more than anyone else present tonight."

Amy unrolled and held up the black leather corset in the air, her left hand covering her mouth at the perfectness of the gift. Tanya clapped her hands together wildly and bounced in her seat, shouting, "Yes! She! Will!"

Icy smiled and set her gaze on Boom, asking, "The new exhibit open yet?"

Shaking his head, he replied, "Monday. But if you come by tomorrow afternoon, I'll give you and your friends a private tour, if you're available?"

Slipping out of the booth to stand, Icy replied, "We'll be there at two, if that works for you?" Boom's nod confirmed he'd heard the time over the loud music. As she stepped away from their booth, Icy looked over her shoulder and said, "Nice to meet you, Sunshine. *Enjoy.*"

Amy was only capable of a nod, too surprised by what had just transpired to formulate words. Suddenly reminded of the similar gesture in Warhol's portrait and gallery discussion from a few hours ago, Amy's gaze met the laughing eyes of her friends.

"So, Sunshine … What are *you* about to say?"

A shy grin drew Amy's lips into blushing cheeks as she thought of what she would say as Jay walked through their door after a month away, to discover her new acquisition. *Welcome home. Surprise. I've missed you. Fuck me. Now!*

Her best friend screamed, "He's going to be out of control when he sees you, you're not going to be able to walk for days!"

Amy's blush pushed under the straps of her dress, traveling down her chest. She wasn't going to remain bound by surfacing insecurities, keeping her from trying something so spectacularly new, especially when handed to her by an unexpectedly generous fairy kinkmother on a silver platter. Determination glinting in the steeled gaze she planted on the friends sitting across the table from her, Amy grinned and replied, "I'm counting on it!"

Jay Rooney was restless. His month-long orchestration of potential deals, scouting, and courting new British talent had been hair-pullingly frustrating—another reason he sighed and settled deeper into his plane seat. The remoteness of the Atlantic stretched in infinite blue as his flight traced the path of the sun.

*Chasing sunshine.*

He smiled at how wonderful his life was, with the woman of his dreams casting warmth on him along the way. Theirs was a story of life-long acquaintance. One that deepened after a twist of fate brought them together after years of exploring life outside of Spillville—an idealistic little town filled with all of the best things life could offer. If quiet and a life of farming was one's *thing*.

The Boyers were his parents' nearest neighbors, a half-mile of corn, wheat, soybeans, and one stop sign standing between their homes. Amy Boyer was the oldest of four children, and Jay was the sixth of eight redheaded Rooney's. She'd been close with his oldest sister, Tina, so he'd always seen her around the Rooney Farm until it was time to go off to college—seeds scattering in the wind.

It was while Jay was attending Northwestern University's MBA program that a fortuitous sidewalk rush hour collision changed his life forever, when he literally ran into Amy Boyer while passing over the Chicago river on the Michigan Avenue Bridge. Eyes locked as recognition hit, struck full force by an instant and irrevocable attraction. Their ten-year age difference no longer mattered.

From that collision came their first date over drinks, to long weekends never leaving bed, to their walk down the aisle. Comfort of familiarity added to their progressing romance, and it didn't hurt that two Rooney siblings ended up marrying Boyers, keeping their family bonds tight.

So in the end, and despite hundreds of miles and millions of stop signs apart, Spillville's soil produced lasting, intense romance. That harvest definitely turned out to be their *thing*.

Prompted to step back from reminiscing by Janelle, the friendly stewardess in charge of first class, Jay accepted the dirty martini she'd expertly made for his enjoyment. He leaned forward to pull down his tray, hoping to cover the rise beneath the zipper of his trousers as thoughts of his wife persisted. When one martini didn't suffice, he asked Janelle for another, a stopgap to being crawling-out-of-his-skin excited about holding his wife in his arms once again—his most favorite *thing* of all.

After a fitful night of sleep, Amy tempered her excitement with running errands, hoping any distraction would counter the creeping of the hours until she was reunited with her beloved once again. Waiting for his anticipated return to their home was almost like watching crops grow—yet corn ripened faster than the hands moved on the clock. Nature wasn't the only one being a cunt.

Nearing the entrance to Wellraven, as dusk draped its cloak onto the Upper East Side, Amy pulled out her keys. Deciding against taking the elevator, she harnessed her jittery anticipation by bounding up the winding wooden staircase three steps at a time; the floorboards protesting her anxious exuberance as she climbed floor after floor until she reached the eighth.

Thirty minutes and one exhilarating shower later, adrenaline flooded her veins as she slipped on black lace lingerie. She then laid the white box containing her treasure on the vanity counter, remembering Tanya's words of whispered wisdom during their back seat cab ride home from Max's.

*"Fasten the front and then you can reach around to pull the laces tighter. If you bend over while you pull on the loops, you'll get that delicious constriction. Then unzip it just as you're on the brink of coming, it's the most powerful orgasm I've ever experienced, I can tell you that. I like to think of a corset as a sensual cocoon, one that you encase yourself in or burst free from at the perfect moment of your own choosing. I found sex to be very different after wearing mine. It constricted me in ways that held me in differently. I know it sounds crazy, but I feel as though I'm tighter everywhere when I'm in mine. Other times, I have strong orgasms when I leave it on during climax, enjoying coming out of it long afterward. Closed or open, you'll just have to experiment to see what works for you."*

The memory of that conversation was enough to raise the rose blush on Amy's skin. She also wondered about something else her best friend said leaving the gallery the previous evening.

*"We seem to have established the perfect theme of this evening, no doubt continuing when you meet Bob. Let's catch a cab, we don't want to miss any fun."*

Amy suspected Tanya knew all along that Shay and Cillian would be dropping sensual, corseted shibari bombs onto Bob'ers that evening. If these were the kind of surprises Tanya and Boom had when going out, she'd make it a point to accept their invitations far more often, even if she had to dress her husband up in complicated costumes just to evade rivalries and get him access.

Her introduction to Bob was a sensual surprise she was grateful for, the flavor of the experience delicious enough to take a bite of her own, even if she was currently back to being a nervous wreck, worried that her missing fingers would make it more difficult to adjust the hard-to-reach laces on her own.

*Leo, girl.*

Chuckling at the fact that even her inner monologue sounded like her sassy best friend, Amy shook her head and got back on task. Bending over to lift the lid with shaking hands, she carefully pulled the black leather corset out of the box. The faint smell of lingering perfume drifted upward, putting her at ease.

Amy gulped back nervousness and wrapped the corset around her flank, bringing the base of the zipper below her belly button and slipping the two ends into place. The teeth bit loudly as she pulled the zipper up with resolve, enclosing herself in the cool, tight casing, her fingers momentarily jiggling the two metal rings dangling above each thigh. Amy stood in awe at her reflection in the mirror. Even without the laces along her back pulled taut, the corset did amazing things to her waist and her décolletage.

Hooking her thumbs into the longest loops dangling from the rivets ascending her spine, she pulled the laces outward. The leather slowly cinched her in as far as her ribcage would allow, her body and posture transforming further before her eyes. The patina of woodsy leather cloyed around her, adding to Icy's lingering, subtle rose.

As Amy stood admiring her image in the mirror, she understood. It was not just the scent of leather or of her initial hesitancy, but of sensual seduction. It was an empowering moment she was choosing to claim for herself . It was the scent of a secret blooming under boldness, a scent of a surprise and a new life experience she could share with her beloved, unsuspecting lover.

The provocative mélange of buttery opulence as it warmed against her torso was definitely a scent she could get used to. And her tits *could* balance champagne flutes. Her reflection made her gasp in awe—lace and leather cocooned against her pale skin, she was relieved that gravity was blessedly *not* being a cunt.

As she grew accustomed to the new sensations of constriction, Amy pulled at the knot at her back and drew in a deep breath, helping her to stand up straight, her glances constantly returning to the clock. She knew Jay would be returning any moment, so she slipped on a pair of high heels and clinked her way around their home as she turned on every light in their small apartment. Wellraven was known for residences with character, but definitely not for spacious living, so she didn't have far to roam. She wanted to be certain that reuniting with her husband was not hidden by the dark that cloaked the street outside.

Putting her in clear sight of their front door, she stood in silence, waiting for the key in the door to announce his arrival. She could not wait to witness his reaction.

When the landing in front of their door creaked, a wry curl of bravado lifted the corner of her mouth.

When the handle of their door turned, she held her breath as she tried to calm her inner chaos.

When it swung open to reveal a stunned looking ginger, the thud of his duffel bag onto their hardwood floor matched the gasp taking hold of her lungs, straining to exhale.

"What the ..." Jay's whooshing whisper spilled into the foyer as his gaze took in his wife's surprise. He kicked the bag far enough into the room so that the door could close. The sound of the lock clicking into place cut through the pent-up tension surrounding them.

Jay's gaze wrenched up his wife's appearance. Her brazenness was an unbelievable turn-on, his chest rising and falling visibly as he watched her stalk toward him. She was overcome with the way that he looked at her, suddenly high on the power a lover holds when offerings like this are made.

Her eyes widened further when his tongue beckoned her attention, slowly tracing his plump upper lip. His grin broadened with lust, promises, and wickedness, and his bold stance solidified his undaunted intentions as he took four long strides toward his excited wife. Unsteady breaths and weak-kneed longing fueled resolve as he picked Amy up by her waist, her legs surrounding his flank as he spun them into the nearest wall. Picture frames fell and crashed on the floor as their lips broached the final gap of their month-long separation.

Ignoring the destruction, Jay's hands gripped beneath her thighs, her legs spreading farther apart and knees rising on his waist as she was pressed higher against the wall. He moaned as her hands worked down his chest, pinching his nipples through the soft cashmere under her palms, tilting his head back to gasp as she sighed. "I'm so happy you're home." Her whisper tickled his exposed neck, and she felt his strong, broad chest quiver beneath the slight strokes of her fingertips.

He turned into her neck to lick the shell of her ear, whispering, "I've missed you so much …"

Lifting his left thigh to support the weight of his panting wife, his right hand flew upward to land against the wall behind her head. Chipped paint and plaster fell around them as his palm slid between splintered wall and soft leather, curious digits tracing the laces, molding and playing peek-a-boo with the subtle tract of her spine, around the base of the corset to stop at her belly button, down, down, down. His fingers twitched the moment he discovered the wet heat, slick against the lace between her legs, burning up his fingertips.

Amy's lips traced the sharp angle of his jaw as they made a sultry path toward his ear, whispering, "Do you like your surprise?"

The vibrations of his laughter reverberated through her corset and into her own chest as he slid his fingers against her laced heat, whispering, "You have no idea how much."

She smiled wider as he stuttered and then repeated himself, shaking her head. One eyebrow quirked up curiously on his gorgeous face as she arched off the wall to get even closer to his touch. "You can feel how much I do, and I love wearing it … for *you*."

His grin grew and she brought her lips to the corner of his, her tongue teasing his upper lip until their tongues began to dance, heat emanating from the passion building, her hips beginning to mimic the movement of her tongue.

Thighs strained with their wall dancing, Jay's lips broadened into a mischievous smirk as he decided on a change of position to slow the muscle burn. Without warning, he spun Amy around, dropping her feet to the floor. The table next to them rattled so violently with the motion that a vase of flowers tipped off the side, shattering on their floor along with all the pictures surrounding it. A lamp soon followed, and then the table itself collapsed, the window the only thing left standing along the wall they'd just destroyed. Both chuckling at the mess they'd created, he lifted her over the heap of crushed wood and glass, lowering her to stand in the only space free of broken things.

At that moment, Amy made a decision that would change the direction of their lovemaking forever. Lead him around the destruction to the predictable comfort of their bed, or be bold where they stood?

Emboldened by her lustful audaciousness and reminded by the constriction of the corset that set daringness into motion, she turned quickly to place her hands on the glass, making him an offer that took her shocked husband's breath away. Spreading her legs to easily balance on heels, she leaned forward. The lust filled fog of her breath misted the windowpane, splayed hands silhouetting the cityscape beyond their *welcome home*. She didn't care that the light behind them would show them to the outside world. In fact, it excited her even more, and that shocked her … just not enough to stop the hushed plead of what she hoped would happen next.

Drawing a deep breath, Amy waited while her stunned husband paused behind her, unable to decipher what she was silently asking for. She stood motionless, wondering if his pause could be blamed on jet-lag. She had no way of knowing that Jay was thinking the same thing.

Their lovemaking was far from boring, yet he wasn't accustomed to this level of sexual daredevilry in his wife, no matter how impulsive she often was in unexpected circumstances. As he pulled back to peer around at her face pressed against the glass, her eyes were fixed on what he imagined to be his reflection, backlit by the only lamp left standing in the room.

For one brief moment, Jay pondered why they hadn't broken the one thing that needed to be broken. They'd nicknamed that lamp the White Elephant, an impractical heirloom bestowed on the couple as a joke gift after Jay's siblings claimed the ugly, rusted monstrosity when Aunt Madge died. It blinded everyone who shared a room with it—probably the reason why it was found in her attic, holding court with a leaky roof and wearing a coat of bat shit. Impossible to use without optical damage, yet difficult to part with due to sentimentality, Madge's atrocity had become the family joke passed on to Jay and Amy after announcing their plans to move to the Big Apple, insisting that they'd need a spotlight to deter criminals hell-bent on *breakin*. The Upper East side *did* have a sketchy reputation.

How it was the one thing that survived their wall-fucking was unfortunate.

Until it *wasn't*.

As Jay saw beyond the grinning reflection of his wife, he noticed the woman standing in the window across the street from them, and the people congregating in their windows above and below, too. All the voyeurs were slack jawed and holding their drapes wide open, unabashedly watching as Aunt Madge's blinding monstrosity became an unexpected ally in the cunning coup *d'érotique* his wife had staged.

If the strangers could see them, and if his wife knew *they* knew, and if *he* knew that *she* knew that *they* knew, and didn't care … His rock-hard cock was requiring too much of his blood supply for him to perform mental gymnastics. Yet as the smile on his wife's lips grew in the reflection of the window, jet-lag turned into *fuck-yeah*, realizing her invitation and catching on. *Finally.*

He may have been a small-town boy, but he'd adopted that big city, go big or go home attitude after settling into the Wellraven. Amy's brazenness at turning the White Elephant on before he got home, knowing the blinding light it cast—If his wife was taking an exhibitionist attitude to heart, so would *he*.

Amy knew the moment Jay made his own realization, his motionless freeing into movement. His fingertips scorched her shoulder blade, dragging his touch down her exposed spine to pause at the top of the lacing as his chest heaved in quickening breaths. She felt him trace the grommets and the laces, lamb skin slipping under the determined pads of his fingers, pursuing the knot and lacing on a tactile descent. The sensation was divine, an indescribable flood of satisfaction at having the control of having him pant as he caressed her surprise like a second skin.

Jay was determined to slow down and take in every facet of the moment. It was a moment he intended to savor.

Slowly, deliberately, he stepped back and leaned forward, the cashmere of his sweater teasing the lace of her panties, feeling his breath on her exposed back as his kisses began near her tailbone and ascended her spine, dragging his tongue up and around the peek-a-boo skin beneath leather and laces, until his chin was resting on her left shoulder. His closeness allowed her to feel even more of him as hardness scraped lace, arching her back so that slickness gained even more friction.

Amy sighed, the sensual angle of her posture filling her with *want-more-now* as his saliva cooled on her spine. After witnessing Bob's erotic show the previous night, the fantasy of wearing a leather corset for Jay had been provocative enough. Seeing his actual reaction to it was fucking breathtaking. His gaze meeting hers in the reflection of the window pane said all she thought she needed to know. That was until he whispered, "Your curves are made even more tantalizing, rounded and begging for what I'm about to give you. I don't know what's gotten into you to act this way, but now it's gonna be *me*."

His meaning overflowing with promise, Amy sighed loudly, the pace of her breath increasing with every motion. Excited by the fact that she was turning him on in such a bold way, she reached higher on the glass as she pushed back, his large erection twitching against the back of her thigh, his left hand slipping between her legs to drag his fingers against her soaking heat. He pushed the material into her slit; the lace dragging against her most sensitive skin. Her response was to buck against him and scream in frustration, wanting that fabric to be him.

Jay's breaths were uneven, his wildly erratic heartbeat detectable through the leather against her back as she turned to look over her shoulder in silent inquiry, wondering what he'd do next. His hands moved to her hips, where he brushed against the metal rivet and O-ring on each hip, the sound of rattling metal overshadowing their labored breathing. He gripped the rings with his index fingers, pulling her hips back into the juncture of his thighs.

He used his thumbs to push her forcefully away from his hips, only to use the rings to bring her quickly back again, his hardness pushing into the flesh of her ass. They both moaned at the contact, but Amy was done with the teasing and slower pace. A month had been long enough.

She leaned back with her hips; the corset pushing her lace-clad breasts against the glass as she tried to right herself in her heels, her legs still spread wide to support their precarious position against the window. Reaching her left hand backward to snake between their bodies, she gripped his length through the fabric of his pants. His hiss made her bones ache in anticipation, a breathless groan so wanton yet drowned out by the sound of the teeth of his zipper, finally freeing him against the back of her thigh.

Palms and cheek against glass, heat against dripping heat, he pushed into her with an unexpected slowness, considering all the things that lay broken around them. Tenuously inching forward until he thought he could go no deeper, he paused, his hands poised over the leather at her stomach that constricted her in a way that also gripped him tighter than ever. It was heaven. Instead of uncomfortable pressure, she felt sensually embraced. Instead of focusing on restricted breathing, she found herself enraptured by the idea of self-control to manage that restriction. It was a heady mix of lust and restraint.

And luckily, restraint was something her husband no longer possessed.

Jay rounded his hips as they began to sway, the sound of the rivets clinking against the metal rings near Jay's fingers begging to be held on to. Amy thought it was impossible for him to get any deeper until he wound his fingers through and pulled the rings toward his hips and up, instigating a connection she thought might short-circuit her sanity. Her entire perception of his depth was transformed in that moment. Her waist constricted and her insides packed tight, the fire within asphyxiating her already tenuous control. He pushed and pulled on the rings, driving into her with precision and out of her with the desperate need for friction, the *in-out, in-out.* *yessssssss* growing with every thrust.

He used the strength of his forearms to drag the rings toward the ceiling, lifting her hips up and her heels off the floor, his thrusts pushing into a spot inside that sent her uncontrollably onward, the building, the pounding *there* sending her chest against cool glass as she melted into his thrusts, his thighs and forearms trembling with the exertion and then they were spinning, ecstatic, slipping free of the tension of release, quivering from the aftershocks gripping them both.

Still deep inside his wife, Jay noticed that Amy's chest was heaving against the glass, the corseted pressure on her diaphragm preventing her from regaining her breath. Her mouth opened wide, trying to gasp for much-needed air as her eyes closed. Unexpectedly, her open mouth set in a wide smile, her screams renewing as a second orgasm ripped through her body, violently gripping him so tightly that he felt pulled in even deeper as she still *craved*.

He moved his hips, trying to draw out Amy's sensations until she came down from her second high and settled against the steamed window pane, her outline dragging down night-kissed glass. Her chest heaved against it as Jay pulled at the knotted bow at the base of her corset, the laces freeing easily up and down her spine, giving her leeway to regain her breath. He reached around her breasts and found the top of the zipper, pulling it down quickly, the teeth chafing and releasing loudly with the alleviated tension. Unwrapping the leather from around her torso, it dropped to the floor, the large rings on the leather jingling against the rousing melody of her breathy pants as it landed amongst the ruins.

Jay's fingers immediately traveled to the red indentations, remnants of the laces and the leather casing on her perfect flesh. He bent down, pulling out of her slowly as his lips began kissing the reddened proof of the garment now splayed next to the piles of destruction littering their living room.

Amy's face remained against the cool glass, mouth agape in disbelief at how powerful her orgasms had been, and how much the constriction of Icy's gift had led to a sexual awakening she never dreamed possible. It was one thing to witness strangers get off in such an explicit way, yet there is a huge learning curve between seeing and *doing* for yourself. There was a new sense of power in knowing that the same kind of passion could actually be experienced, and so intensely; it was eye-opening in the very best sense.

Amy had always enjoyed the passionate moments with her husband, yet this experience felt like a metamorphosis, unfurling wings spreading into a whole new intimacy, a new kind of connection after so long apart. That sensation of refreshing newness made her long to really *look* at him after missing his presence for so long, so she mustered the energy to pry herself from the cool glass, turning slowly to face him, grabbing the back of his hair to draw his mouth to her own.

Soft, lingering kisses grew more intense as she sighed when his fingertips began tracing her nipples beneath her black lace bra. At nearly forty years old, she'd felt her sexual appetite waning, self-conscious issues playing a bigger role in her recent reticence to instigate intimacy, or enjoy it to the level they'd just experienced. Perhaps it was because of this that her mind began racing with the possibilities that she'd finally freed herself from the hesitancy she'd spun herself with threads of self-doubt. Her mind raced with the realization that not only Mother Nature was not a cunt, but her own was aiming for a trifecta and that the reputation of a virile younger man held true, given that her husband was hard as a rock so soon after the welcome home he'd just given her.

She swayed her hips to pull away from her husband's grasp, pushing him in the direction she wanted them to go. Jay's calves hit the soft cushion of their couch and he sat down, his wife straddling his thighs, his teeth pulling down lace and mouth enveloping a nipple, dragging it between his teeth as her senses heightened, slamming onto him, sliding him to the hilt.

"Yes, Jay! Ahh ..."

Amy's passionate howls echoed off of the apartment walls, pushing him forward into her willing body as she quivered against him. Her screams of release melted into fading edges as her vision flanged to a narrow tunnel of stars and fading sounds, silky strands of darkness enveloping her. Her husband's stuttering, breathy sigh brought her back from the black sea she was happily swimming in, blinking her eyes until the colored lights ushered in her vision quick enough to recognize his own come face. It was a sight to behold after missing him for so long.

As he came down from his own high, Jay remained boneless, amazed at the experience they'd just shared. He always thought it was impossible for his wife to be any more perfect, yet she surprised him at every turn.

As their breathing evened out and they settled into sated euphoria, the unexpected sound of loud clapping and catcalling could be heard through their closed windows. Lifting themselves off of the couch enough to look out their windows, in the direction of the buildings across the street, many neighbors were hanging out of their windows and applauding in their direction and animatedly waving.

With broad, prideful smiles taking over the coy expressions after realization struck, Amy summoned enough energy to halfheartedly wave back. Jay offered an exaggerated thumbs-up in response, before lowering his head to rest on her breastbone once again, whispering, "I'm too high from this mind-blowing experience to give a shit."

Amy's chuckle suffused with amusement, nodding as she wiped the sweat from her husband's brow before leaning forward to rest her own head on top of his. Her thoughts continued to race with the realization that not only did she *not* give a shit, but she was ready to do it again in the future, knowing they might have an audience.

It was a realization that illustrated how empowering and incandescent the experience had been, unexpected complexity emerging, opening wings for the first time, creating new possibilities.

*Leo, indeed.*

One side of Jay's smile bore higher into his cheek as the hot pad of his finger traced the raised, pink indentation that the top section of the corset left between her breasts, before reaching around his wife with his free hand to lift the corset from the floor, holding it high. "How did this glorious development happen?"

Mustering enough strength to find it possible to speak, Amy recounted her introduction to *Bob*, describing the red-hued evening of debauchery and corseted erotic rope play, about Icy's gift, of Tanya and Boom's nudging encouragement, and how it inspired her to consider starting *this* kind of fire.

With a self-satisfied grin on his face, Jay replied, "Well, I'll send flowers to Tanya, Shay, and Icy when the florist opens on Monday. Best. Homecoming. Ever. And maybe to my siblings, for giving us Aunt Madge's lamp."

Grateful that he wasn't at all bothered by their exhibitionism and seemed to enjoy it as much as she did, she sighed in exhausted relief, her head falling to his chest while her eyes scanned the destruction left in their wake.

If the neighbors across the way caught wind of what they'd been up to, she couldn't imagine how disruptive it must've been for their neighbors in the surrounding apartments. Wellraven was an older building with tremendous character, but not well insulated. It had creaky floors, dripping faucets, and was prone to drafts and sound transfer. It was a daily occurrence to hear their neighbors take footsteps above them, and even the decipherable clank of dropped silverware was common. A soup spoon was nothing compared to an entire room of shattered things.

*Holy shit, this was fun.*

Scanning the amount of damage splayed around them, she closed her eyes and sighed, agreeing with her husband's assessment of being too satisfied to worry. Even the moon outside their window seemed to be smiling at them, before it ducked behind a tall building in the distance.

169

Her warm breath settled into the soft fibers over his chest and she relished in turning *could* into *did*.

"Do you think it's possible to require hospitalization for extreme protein deficiency from coming too hard? You've completely drained me, wife. I think I need to eat more than one steak, and soon, or I might actually die."

Amy laughed loudly and swung her pillow at Jay's growling stomach, the drape near their bed blowing away from the sill to reveal an overcast morning.

They forced themselves out of the warm cocoon of their comforter in order to get something to eat and their much-needed hit of caffeine. Their muscles ached, so they dressed slowly, stepping around the mess of their *fuckquakes*.

Keeping things neat and tidy was usually necessary for Jay. Amy had no idea of her husband's motives for leaving their path of destruction untouched, but he had no intentions of cleaning. In fact, he wanted to add to the mess when he'd regained energy, until nothing but the White Elephant was left standing in their apartment. He'd received a big bonus during his trip to England, and planned to surprise Sunshine with new furnishings. While she didn't know his secret, his lack of anxiousness about the mess around them was Amy's first clue that this Sunday was far from ordinary.

As they opened their door, Amy recognized the brown, curly hair of their neighbor Elizabeth ascending the steps. Always quiet, arms laden with books because of her job at the library, she was a respectful neighbor who often kept to herself. A blush bloomed on Elizabeth's cheeks when she saw their door open, her shy blue eyes pinning the couple as she smiled at them and scurried past faster than Amy could say, "Hello."

Upon stepping out of their apartment, things got even more bizarre. Every neighbor they passed on their descent down Wellraven's stairs was acting strangely, rather, even *more* strangely than expected of New Yorkers, especially the often stand-offish groups of women crammed into Wellraven's small apartments. It was common to see many single women living in one apartment unit, and know the names of neighbors, yet connection never extended beyond closing doors and hurried steps in passing while running to their next attempt at making ends meet.

They moved in groups for protection and camaraderie, heads down, eyes trained ahead, rarely interacting, and always self-reliant. The Upper East Side had grown notorious for becoming home to the wage-slaves, down-and-outs and the trying-hards with four jobs and cash-only side projects, anything to make rent. Crime was on the uptick, but the neighborhood still held appeal beyond the standoffish vibe. Unlike Tanya and Boom, the no-nonsense attitude of New Yorkers held true, and being friendly neighbors wasn't often a *thing*.

Because it was a Sunday, many Wellraveners were getting their grocery shopping done, crowding the building's staircase as they returned with their loot. As Amy and Jay made their descent toward the lobby, they were greeted by an unusual "Good Morning!" and "Hello!" from various tenants. Familiar Upper East Dyed patrons like Darcy, Quin, Judie, and Yvonne were extra cordial as they passed the couple.

Another flight of stairs brought even stranger interactions. Jen, Monique, Jade, and Nikki were roommates who lived higher up, and they held up their hands to high-five Amy as they passed her on the stairs. Melissa and Katie, the feisty roommates who often threw loud parties, sent thumbs-up the couple's way as they passed their pried-open doorway. Even the building curmudgeon, a nameless old man who usually flashed neighbors the middle finger in the common areas, held the front door open for the perplexed couple as they exited the front door.

The neighborly, uncharacteristic friendliness of everyone made Amy even more self-conscious, aware their escapades might carry unexpected consequences. Clearly, some neighbors knew what they'd been up to, but Amy assumed that their disruption would invite anger and judgment, not smiles and positive reactions from their passionate diversions.

*Upper East Siders could be so mercurial and downright strange, and Wellraven was the epicenter, that's for damn sure. What's that say about us?*

As more familiar faces smiled and held thumbs-up as they passed Amy and Jay on the sidewalk, it was becoming clear that they'd had a wider audience while becoming the feature event the previous night. It was a fact made more evident a few steps down Seventy-Seventh and Park Avenue. The couple approached Maddox, their favorite cafe, owned by friends and culinary geniuses Bill David and Todd McPherson. The owners of the joint were often elusive and rarely made appearances at the front of the house, and yet their broad-grins greeted Amy and Jay at the entrance of the cafe as Jeff, the host, offered the perplexed couple glasses of champagne.

When Amy accepted the flute in her hand, she thought of Tanya's proclamation about the miraculous support of the corset, and blushed. After last evening's experience, she believed the balancing myth, and planned to test it out again, very soon.

Amy saw Boom's towering mass of ratted-black hair before she heard Tanya's boisterous voice from across the cafe shouting, "Sunshine and Ginger, we've got room!"

The Rooney's hadn't made plans to meet their friends for brunch. The place was packed and the wait for a table long. It had been a month since all four friends were together in one place—a wonderful coincidence.

As soon as the friends hugged in greeting and took their seats, Amy smirked at how expertly Boom maneuvered his hairstyle around the low hanging candelabra lights that dangled above their dining area. And then she began to worry. As regulars, they usually sat in another area of Maddox that had much higher ceilings. One bad move now, and Amy was sure Boom's out-of-control tresses would be ensnared on one of the illuminated branches that outstretched from the ceiling. As someone who did hair and knew him well, she was still amazed at how his style defied gravity, how stiff he managed to keep it, and how he continued to expertly avoid catastrophe.

Uncertain if electric lights could set his hair product on fire, the highest part of his punky coiffure was too close to the lights for her comfort. With protective covertness, she inched a water glass between where she and Boom sat, just in case. Electricity and liquids didn't mix well, but she had to have something close, *just in case*.

Tanya took a sip of her coffee and then she smirked, joined by a sly look in her gaze. Putting her cup down, she said, "You know Warhol said that everyone would have fifteen minutes of fame." Jay and Amy nodded. "Well, I don't think anyone could dream up of how spectacularly you two earned yours!"

Suddenly realizing that nearly everyone sitting around them was sharing knowing grins or whispering to each other, Amy felt her temperature rise as *Boom-hair* anxiety was overcome by *it-was-awesome*. Jay puffed his chest out in a prideful stance that announced his glee, and Amy's blush accompanied a pert grin tempting one side of her lips.

"And ..." Only one drawn-out word was uttered, yet Boom's deep voice held a hint of amusement that was impossible to deny. "It seems your little show for the neighbors last night has everyone now calling your building *The Wellbrazen*."

"Oh my God, does this shit get any better? We break everything and have the time of our lives! Fuck protein, I'm going to need high dose muscle relaxants to wipe the grin off my face from this ego trip, a decade from now! I have the best wife, ever!" Looking at Amy, he yelled, "Babe! We're famous!"

Amy was so amused by Jay's excitement that her laughter escalated into a loud cackle that nearly shook the room, her own pride swelling at Jay's joy at earning the building a nickname. She experienced a strange torrent of emotions that moved between feeling Catholic guilt, to giddy, to downright *goddessish*.

*Father Roberto would order me to do a thousand Hail Mary's to petition for forgiveness and countless confessions. Forgive me, Father, for I'm about to sin. Again. And soon. More furniture to break. And corsets to buy. And neighbors to scandalize. Oh my God, I'm going to hell.*

Quieting her internal quandary between confession and exuberance long enough to turn to her huge-haired friend, she asked, "The Wellbrazen. Another Boomism?"

"Of course, Sunshine." His facial expression was filled with pride, as was Tanya's *I told you* grin.

Amy felt confident in the wisdom of embracing any Boom perspective, no matter how embarrassing or absurd. After the liberating experience of meeting *Bob* and

175

welcoming Jay home, *Sunshine* and *Wellbrazen* were far more synonymous than she'd ever imagined prior to experiencing all of the imago-moments in the last forty-eight hours. Emerging from hesitation and broadening her wings felt so, so good, and she wouldn't have known that unless she tried it first. Trying was *everything,* and Amy was confident that Jay, Tanya, and Boom agreed. Moving forward, the welcoming of life experience opportunities would definitely be their *thing.*

"Then it's an honor to have earned it." Her voice cracked with emotion and delight. Reminded of what he'd disclosed the previous day, Amy leaned over to playfully knock Boom's shoulder with hers, whispering, "Voyeur intruding on joy is becoming your *thing.* Want to prove the veracity of your theory?"

Boom's eyebrows angled inward as they peeked out from under his riotous bangs. She'd never seen this cocky shoulder-rubber of the cultured rich and famous look more perplexed. "My theory?"

Her three table mates looked even more confused when Amy stood up and pushed away from the table, kicking off her shoes and pointing at the window at the far end of the room. Their group had been too busy enjoying each other's company to realize that the alley-less metropolis was waiting for them, determined to join their conversation, too. Heavy drops slammed against the windows, the downpour creating run-on sentences against the cement, glass, and steel of the exclamation points lining Park Avenue as thunder's laughter shook the building.

"Theory of *Leo*. Let's be crazy …"

Amy started running in the direction of the exit.

"… With happiness!"

It wasn't a dare. It was a promise, and they knew it. Shucking hesitation, they all jumped out of their seats, pulled off their shoes, and followed Sunshine into the articulation of emerging opportunity—to chrysalide into *newspeak*. Puddle-jumping and screaming with unbound delight, they transformed into the joy of *now* by dancing, arms-outstretched, and laughing in the thrill of the rain.

# THE MAN IN WHITE

AI TRAN

# Prologue

It was soaking wet outside; the rain had been falling without interruption for the last two hours, and Sophie was still unable to get herself out of bed. The cold silence in her room was cut by the sound of her phone ringing.

"Hello?" she said, barely finding the fortitude to hold the phone up to her ear.

"You should get out of the house. John wouldn't like to see you moping around like this," came a familiar voice from the other line.

"I know; I just don't feel like going out," Sophie replied.

She had been crying in bed for the last three weeks, unable to muster the courage to get up.

*Everyone seems to worry for me,* she thought. *But if only they knew that it was my fault that John passed away…*

# Chapter One

A light knocking at my apartment door let me know my next paycheck had arrived. I opened the door, and a young woman wearing a bright yellow jumpsuit with shoulder-length, frizzy auburn hair and hazel eyes greeted me with a wide smile.

"Hello there! Come on in, my dear, Lucy, right?" I said.

"Yup, that's me," she said in a loud and raspy voice.

Lucy walked in and tripped over my foot.

"Ahh!" she shrieked as she fell to the floor, thankfully missing a set of lit candles by inches.

I quickly helped her to her feet, and after she assured me she was fine, it was on to business.

"How did you find me? Through an ad? A friend?"

"My coworker referred me to you, Kevin Thomas? He's your neighbor from next door; he told me you reconnect people back with their loved ones that have passed away."

"Ah… yes, Kevin," I said with a smile. "Let me get your coat for you, dear. So tell me about Charlie."

"Charlie? How did you know that I was going to ask you about Charlie?"

*Because Kevin told me, you idiot,* I thought to myself.

"He's in the room with us," I told her calmly.

Her eyes widened. "You can see him?"

"I can. He says that he misses you very much," I said slowly.

"I miss him too!" she wailed. "Oh my God, Charlie, baby, come over here and hold me," Lucy said, hugging herself with both arms. "It's okay, baby, I can feel your presence. It is so strong." She sobbed, then she looked up at me and said, "I can feel him touching me. Is he touching me?"

I bit my tongue to restrain myself from bursting into laughter

"Yes, he is caressing your cheek," I told her calmly.

"Oh!" she sobbed again. "You never touched me this way when you were alive. You must be so lonely in the other world. It's okay, baby, come to mama," she said, reaching out both of her arms and opening her mouth to embrace and make out with thin air.

*This is a lot weirder than I expected it would be, but time is money,* I reminded myself. *Time is money.*

Throughout my life, I've been told that I have the gift of seeing through a person and understanding others. I wasn't always a mediator/psychic. In fact, I studied psychology back in college and never held any superstitious beliefs. Well, as it turns out... being an introverted woman with little to no friends to speak of exacerbates the struggle to find a job as a psychologist in New York City. So I decided to change career paths and became a spiritual medium instead.

"What is he wearing?" Lucy asked me.

She caught me off guard. But luckily, there was a copy of the *New York Times* in front of me.

"He is wearing a beige plaid vest with a scarf around his neck," I said quickly.

"And pants?"

"Of course he is wearing pants!" I said. "Ahem, I mean slacks; he is wearing gray slacks."

Lucy let out a loud sob and hugged me. "He was wearing gray slack the last time I saw him before he died! Oh my God, oh my God!" I patted her back and pushed her lightly off of me as she continued crying profusely.

I was rather annoyed. I looked over at the spartan sunburst clock on my wall—oh, there is a God! Her time was up.

"Time's up, Lucy, you've been here for over an hour."

"I can't leave now, Madame Tate! Charlie is here!"

"Well, the incense is burning out," I told her.

"Then light new ones!" she growled at me.

*Oh goodness, she is never going to leave,* I realized. *Unless... Lucy needed to move on from her dead lover.*

"Charlie told me that he is so sorry," I started.

"Don't be, Charlie! You were the best boyfriend that I have ever had! All of my other exes left me within two weeks."

*Can you blame them?* I thought to myself.

"Charlie told me that he is sorry for cheating on you..."

Lucy stopped crying and looked at me straight in the eyes and said, "He did what?"

"He slept with another woman when you two were together."

"Who did he sleep with?"

"Susan," I said, making up a name.

"Susan what?"

"You don't know her," I said quickly, "Lucy, Charlie apologized."

Lucy jumped to her feet. "You idiot! How dare you!" she said, flinging her arms out, slapping at thin air.

"How dare you cheat on me! All I have ever done was pay attention to you when we were together and called you day and night when you were not around." Lucy raised her right leg and kicked. "I will not tolerate this, you jerk!" she said, raising both her hands up and strangling where she thought Charlie was.

"I can't believe that I cried so much over you, you scum! You deserved to die." Lucy turned around and picked up one of my pillows and hurled it into the lit candles. The candles went out, but not before igniting the pillow.

"You need to get out!" I told her as I grabbed a cup of water and doused the burning pillow.

Lucy continued to throw fist and punches.

"I may tolerate a lot of things, but I don't tolerate jerks!" she shrilled.

"You need to leave!" I exclaimed again.

"I am not leaving until he's learned his lesson!" she shrieked.

"He passed away already!"

"That doesn't mean anything. Die, Charlie! Die!"

"You need to leave now, my dear," I said, restraining my frustration.

"Why?" she snarled at me.

"He's outside. He jumped out the window."

Lucy charged toward the window and shouted, "You better run and hide, you jerk!" before turning around and smiling at me.

"Thank you so much, Madame Tate, for helping me realize that all men are jerks, especially Charlie." She then opened her purse and presented two crisp hundred-dollar bills.

"I'm sorry about your pillow, but before I leave, which way did he go?"

"Outside!" I said, opening my apartment door.

"Charlie!" Lucy shouted as she left my apartment.

# Chapter Two

I was walking out of my apartment when I heard a familiar and nervous voice call out to me.

"Good afternoon, Madame Tate." I looked over to see a wire-thin man in his late twenties. He was of average height, with wavy strawberry-blond hair and a large nose. He looked as if he was nearly drowning in a moss-colored sweater that was two sizes too big. It was my neighbor Kevin. Kevin moved in next door to me not so long ago. I'd like to help him gain some self-confidence, but time is money, and I don't get paid to work those kinds of miracles. Don't get me wrong, I do care for my clients. After all, I helped him get over Fuzzy, his lost cat, the other day, and now he helps me find new clients. It's funny how gullible people get when their loved ones pass away. Some people may view me as a scam artist or a liar, but the reality is I help my clients move on from their past with my ultra-superior knowledge.

"Your coworker just left," I said, trying not to make eye contact.

"She's great, isn't she?"

I nearly choked on my nonexistent coffee. "Lucy?"

Kevin's eyes beamed with joy. "Her beautiful hazel eyes sure complement her wild red hair."

I rolled my eyes

"Is something wrong, Madame Tate?"

*Crazy people tend to be drawn to one another,* I thought.

"I sensed that you're attracted to her," I teased him.

"You have a gift, you know that? You're right; I am very drawn to her. She reminds me of Fuzzy."

"Her hazel eyes, auburn colored hair," he said dreamily

I paid it no mind, and we started walking toward the elevator.

"Did she say anything about me?" he asked

"Yes, that you worked with her." I picked up my step, but Kevin kept up with my pace.

*My goodness, why can't you leave me alone.*

"Do you think Lucy will say yes if I were to ask her out?" he asked anxiously

"I'll need to get my tarot cards out for that," I said with a smile. *Time is money*, I reminded myself.

"Madame Tate? Quick question."

"Yes, Kevin?"

"Why did she run out of your house screaming, Charlie?"

# Chapter Three

I finished lighting the last of my candles and incense as I walked out to my front door. I couldn't believe my luck, three new clients in a day. This girl happened to be Lucy's friend, whose partner of twenty years had recently passed away.

As I opened the door, I saw a lanky, short Asian woman in her mid-to-late thirties with long black hair, wearing a navy blue sweater dress. She had fair skin, almond-shaped eyes, and stood at about five feet two inches tall.

"Hi, I am Sophie. Lucy referred me to you."

"Oh yes! Hi, Sophie," I said with a smile. This should be an easy client; Asians are known to be extremely superstitious. I should know, I got the idea to become a medium from a Chinese monk.

"Are you Chinese?"

"Vietnamese, actually," she said with a slightly annoyed tone in her voice that betrayed her smile.

"I've been to Viet Nam before; it's such a beautiful country," I told her

"Really? There's a war going on over there," she said.

*This one seems to have an attitude problem*, I thought to myself. Lucy had told me that her husband, John, had recently passed away not too long ago. *Be nice to her if you want to get paid*, I reminded myself.

"Why don't you have a seat, my dear, and we can get started right away." I made sure to lock eyes with her so that I could gain her trust.

"So John passed away not too long ago—John is my husband."

"Ah... yes," I said, slowly lighting up an incense.

"I have been told that you have a gift."

"It only works for some people, my dear. You have to trust the force in order for it to work."

I figured that I would have to start slow to better understand who this John guy really was.

"Have you ever lost someone you love?" Sophie asked.

*My ex-husband left me for some bimbo, what do you think?*

I smiled. "This reading is about you, not me."

Out of nowhere, one of the candle flames went out.

"He's here!" Sophie said, with her eyes wide open.

"Yes... I can see him now, brown hair, hazel eyes."

"That change color," we said together.

*This is too easy*, I thought to myself. If we keep this up, I'll be rich enough to move out of this apartment.

"Does he miss me?"

"So much, he said that he is sorry for leaving so soon."

"I miss him very much as well," she said softly, her eyes lit up. "You know it was our anniversary last Saturday; I stood at the Rockefeller University cafeteria for hours, reminiscing about the day that we first met."

"He said that he wished he could spend your twentieth anniversary together." I remembered Lucy telling me that

189

Sophie had lost her partner of twenty years. *This is a lot easier than I expected it would be, too easy, actually. Superstitious people are so delusional, but, hey! I provide them comfort, and they provide me with cash. It's a win-win situation.*

Sophie fell silent and closed her eyes. She remained very still, as if she was thinking hard on something. I could hear her breathing in and out softly. She held her breath for just a moment before her eyes snapped open, and she spoke again, this time with a much more serious tone.

"I knew you were a liar," Sophie said, standing up

"Wait, what?"

"I haven't been to Rockefeller University since 1966. Also, John doesn't have hazel eyes."

*That's right, Lucy does, damn it!*

"Wait, no, I called up the wrong John!" I said, desperately trying to regain control of the situation.

"Yet he's with me at all times."

"He's blind; the John that I summoned up was blind."

Sophie burst out laughing. "I can't wait to tell Lucy about this," she said, walking toward the door.

"Hey, you still owe me fifteen dollars!" I called after her.

She opened the door, looked back at me. "Correction, I owe you nothing, and you wasted my time, Madame Fake!" she fired back.

"Our anniversary wasn't until next month," I heard a male voice coming from behind me. I turned around and saw a man, dressed all in white with brown hair, in his late thirties, maybe early forties.

"Who the hell are you?" I demanded.

"You can see me?" he asked, walking toward me.

"Get out of here! How did you get into my apartment?"

"I followed Sophie, my name is John, by the way, you know, Sophie's husband, well ex-husband... considering the fact that I passed away a few weeks back."

I stepped backward each time he took a step forward.

"It's so nice to have someone to talk to. Wow, you can see me."

"Get away from me!" I shouted.

*Ghosts don't exist!* I reminded myself. He probably snuck into my apartment with Sophie.

"I have a gun!" I said, hoping he wouldn't think I was bluffing.

"Oh no, please don't shoot me," he said, raising both of his hands. "I just wanted somebody to talk to; honestly, it's been so long." He took another step.

I ran into my room and grabbed the gun from my top drawer. John followed me into my room.

"Get away from here!" I demanded.

He laughed and walked straight toward me. I leveled the gun at him, and without thinking, pulled the trigger repeatedly.

The bullets shot right through him and left several holes in my bedroom wall.

My ears were ringing from how loud the gunshots were, but I could still hear John as he burst out laughing, "You can't shoot me, silly, I'm already dead!"

I must have been dreaming. I pinched my right arm and blinked a couple of times, but he was still standing in front of me with a sly smile on his face.

"This can't be real," I said aloud.

"What can't be real? Shouldn't this be normal for you? I mean, you claim to see dead people."

I shut the door to my room and turned around, only to see John sitting on my bed waving at me. I opened the door and ran out to the living room to find John lying sideways on my couch. I gaped at him for a moment, and he winked at me. I stood there dumbfounded before finally slowly approaching him. I slowly reached out with my right hand to touch him. I expected it, but I didn't want to believe it when I saw my hand go straight through him.

"You're a ghost!" I exclaimed.

"Tell me something about myself that I don't know already," he replied sarcastically

# Chapter Four

For being dead, this guy sure did like whining and complaining about everything. "It's too hot, it's cold!" he went on and on and on.

"I don't want to go out for a walk, it's too windy outside, and I don't have a coat," he complained

"I thought ghosts can't feel anything." I growled at John as I flung my coat over my shoulders.

"Are you a ghost?"

"No!" I snapped at him.

John had been shadowing me for the past few days. To be frank, John could be interesting to talk to sometimes, so I didn't mind his company so much. At the very least, he wasn't as delusional as my usual clients. He was jabbering on about something inconsequential as I was walking past my front window when a couple of guys playing cards on the stoop across the street caught my eye. Just then, a genius idea crossed my mind!

"If I were to bring you to a casino to play poker, we could be rich."

"I don't feel like going to the casino," he said with a flat tone.

"John, all you have to do is tell me whether somebody is bluffing or not," I said. " You owe me that much," I told him.

"What do you mean?"

"Your wife never paid me for my services."

"You lied to her."

"She wasted my time; it doesn't matter if I lied or not. And... I am keeping you company," I reminded him with a confident tilt of my chin.

"Okay, okay, so manipulative," he replied with a hint of defeat.

We walked out of the apartment, and as I was walking down the hall, I saw Kevin walking toward me in a light blue dress shirt beneath a beige blazer.

"Good morning, Madam Tate," he said.

"He looks like Norman Bates." John snickered.

"Don't say that; he's not psychotic," I snapped at John.

"I'm sorry, but did you just call me psychotic?" Kevin stammered.

"He does look like Anthony Perkins, especially the crazy eyes," John said, walking closer to Kevin and pointing at Kevin's eyes. "You see it, don't you?" John laughed hysterically.

I glared at John and shook my head.

Kevin looked at me weirdly. *Oh fantastic, of course, he can't see John.*

"Good morning, Kevin," I told him with a warm smile

"Is this the Kevin that is in love with his cat Lucy?" John asked.

"Lucy is very much a human being and not a cat!" I snapped at John. I could feel the frustration building up in my face, but John pretended not to notice.

"I'm sorry, I didn't mean to annoy you, but Madame Tate..." Kevin said, laughing nervously. "I like women, not cats."

"Oh, I get it now; Kevin has a thing for older women... look at the way he's looking at you," John teased.

"No, Kevin likes younger women!" I shot back at John, no longer trying to hide my annoyance.

"I do... I do... but, um, Lucy isn't that much younger than I am, she's three years younger than I am," Kevin stammered. The poor boy looked so confused and maybe a little scared. "Well, um, I am going to go into my apartment now, bye, Madame Tate."

I turned to John and said, "See what you've done?" John only looked away, shrugged his shoulders, and rolled his eyes as he spoke again.

"What? it's not my fault he can't see me."

# Chapter Five

"You got us kicked out of the casino !" I told John as we walked down First Avenue, the wind was blowing pretty hard, the street was busy, and children were running around everywhere in costumes. It was Halloween night.

"I can't control when I talk," he said. "And come on now, I helped you win some money."

"Five dollars!" I nearly screeched at him.

"If you just quit after the first hour, you would've been rich. It's not my fault that you can't seem to pick when to ignore me."

"You are so useless!" I said through gritted teeth.

My attention was briefly stolen when I heard a woman's voice. "Stay away from her," came the worried tones of a lady speaking to a brown-haired little girl, who couldn't have been more than six years old and was dressed up as a fairy. She grabbed the little girl's hand and quickly put distance between me and what I now assumed to be her daughter. I tried to ignore the fact that I was making a scene and turned my attention back to John.

"Five dollars is better than what Sophie gave you," John said sarcastically.

"Ugh! Why are you still here?" I asked, grief dripping from every word.

"Where else can I go?" As he said this, he turned to face me with an amused look in his eyes.

"Go visit your wife or relatives."

"Too far of a walk," he said, this time with a very dismissive tone in his voice.

"Don't talk to me while we're in public," I whispered to him. "People are looking at me weird."

"You're a medium; this should be no surprise to them, by the way, whispering to me makes you appear more lunatic-like," he said with a mischievous smile.

A loud thud disrupted my chain of thought; however, the screaming crowd that followed a moment after completely derailed my thinking altogether.

"Someone fell off from the building!" a woman shouted.

"We need to go," I said, but for the first time, he didn't reply with a smart remark or annoying quip. Instead, he remained completely silent.

He was standing still, looking up at the sky. The look of sarcasm and mischief drained from his face. In its place was a look of concern, confusion, worry, and realization.

"John, let's go," I said more firmly.

He remained speechless. I tried grabbing his hand but realized that was a futile attempt.

"I was murdered," he said, almost in a whisper.

"You were what?" I was almost unaware that I had dropped my tone down to his level.

"I know why I'm still here... I was shoved out of my window."

# Chapter Six

"We need to call the police!" John said anxiously. It was off-putting to see him be so serious.

"And who's going to believe me?" I replied. "What am I supposed to say? A ghost told me that he was shoved out of his home?"

"We have to tell Sophie! She can help!" he said, the tone of severity increasing slightly in his words.

"John, Sophie would never believe me."

"Oh, but I know things about her that nobody else does!" Hope was now rising in his voice.

My heart was still racing from the recent event that just took place moments ago. Ambulance sirens continued to blare outside of my apartment. I was coping with the fact that someone literally died in front of my eyes. Now my only friend, who happened to be a ghost, found out that someone murdered him. The pressure and stress of the situation were almost too much to bear.

"Okay, we'll find Sophie." I finally resigned. "Is her name in the white pages?" I asked him.

"No, but I still remember my home address; after all, I've only been dead for about a month."

We took the subway to Sophie's house in Brooklyn, a two-story dark brown and white building.

"Okay, are you ready?" I asked John.

"Are you ready?" he asked me.

Without thinking, I started ringing the doorbell. After waiting for several moments, nobody answered.

"She's not home," I said lightly.

John walked through the door of his own home and then poked his head out at me. "She's home. She's in the kitchen."

"Sophie! I know that you're in the kitchen!" I shouted.

"She is drinking black coffee in a white mug, and she's wearing a large mustard yellow sweatshirt over green trousers," John reported.

"And I know that you're drinking black coffee in a white mug, you're wearing a yellow mustard sweatshirt over green trouser!" I shouted.

The door swung open.

"Oh God, it is you." Sophie greeted me with a less than welcoming tone.

# Chapter Seven

Sophie opened the door and couldn't believe her eyes; Madame Tate was standing at her doorway.

"What are you doing here? And how do you know what I am wearing? Are you stalking me?"

"No, I am here because your husband…"

Sophie broke into a small laugh. "You called up the real John this time? Not the blind one."

"Shut up!" Madame Tate snapped.

"Did I say something wrong?"

"I'm sorry, I wasn't talking to you… do you want my help or not?"

"No, I don't need your help," Sophie said. As she was about to close her door, she felt a strong wind push it back open.

"Whoa, you can do that?" Madame Tate said as she let herself into Sophie's living room. "Sophie, after you left my house, your husband's ghost appeared, and he hasn't left me alone since."

"Oh really now," Sophie said, rolling her eyes.

"Okay, ask me something that only you and John would know?"

"When is my mother's birthday?"

"No, I am not going to tell her that… that is rude," Madame Tate said, glaring at the wall.

"Are you pretending to talk to John? This is so ridiculous."

"He told me how the hell is he supposed to know when your mother's birthday was; you know that he's not good with remembering dates and numbers."

"That does sound like something John would say," Sophie said.

"Good! Now you believe us."

"But John would know the answer to this because we celebrated my mom's birthday together the last time we were together."

"I am not going to tell her that!" Madame Tate hissed.

"Huh?"

"John said that you're lying. You two had a heated argument about him going to his nephew's bachelor party because you have a jealousy problem!"

"I was not jealous! I was disgusted that a forty-year-old man would go to a bachelor party with his nephew." Sophie gasped.

"All they did was gamble, and he left to go home early so that he could see you."

"Wait a minute, how did you know about all of this?" Sophie asked nervously.

"Because John is here," Madame Tate said calmly

"Would you like to sit down?" Sophie asked; she led Madame Tate to her round wooden dining table and pulled out a chair for her.

"I can prove to you that John is here. Write anything down on a piece of paper, and I'll read it aloud."

"Okay…" Sophie said with a tinge of skepticism. She stood up and walked to her kitchen drawer and pulled out a notepad and a pen. She then wrote:

*I felt all flushed with fever, embarrassed by the crowd,*
*I felt he'd found my letters and read each one out loud.*

"You wrote a verse from 'Killing Me Softly.' 'I felt all flushed with fever, embarrassed by the crowd, I felt he'd found my letters and read each one out loud,' you've been crying to this song for weeks."

"Look, lady, you're a psychic. I have no idea what game you are pulling, but…" Sophie let out an exasperated sigh. "Get out! Please, just get out of here," Sophie said, opening the door to her house.

# Chapter Eight

"You almost convinced her, you see that, don't you?" John said to me.

We were back in my apartment; I was sitting on the couch, and John was pacing back and forth.

"You're desperate to connect with her," I told him truthfully. "Can you please sit down? You're giving me a headache."

"I know my wife; you've almost convinced her, we have to go back!" he said anxiously, plopping down onto the sofa beside me.

"She's the reason why I'm still here. She needs to know that I was murdered," he said softly, his intense gaze meeting my eyes.

"Well, I give up." Not bothering to hide the defeat in my voice.

He gave me a look of disbelief, and I was instantly filled with guilt.

"Look, I tried," I told him. "You know that I tried. I went to Brooklyn and talked to Sophie. I really tried my best."

"No, if you tried your best, you would've gone back! You wouldn't have left after she asked you to leave right away!" Frustration bleeding into his words.

Just then, I heard a loud banging at my door.

"This better be good," John remarked as I opened the door. To my surprise, I saw Lucy at the door. She was wearing a bright yellow polka dot dress paired with bright orange tights. Her frizzy hair was wilder than ever, and her hazel eyes were wide. There was a look of fury plastered on her face. Behind her was Kevin, who gave me an apologetic look.

"You're a fraud!" Lucy said.

"You see, John, this is all your fault," I shot toward my invisible problem.

"Norman Bates and his mother are here," John said sarcastically.

I couldn't help but chuckle.

"What's so funny?" growled Lucy.

"You are," I told Lucy unapologetically.

"Say that again and I'll knock out your two front teeth!" she screamed the threat.

"Honey… calm down," Kevin stammered.

*Great… Thanks to Sophie, I lost two clients, and John is upset with me. These idiots have no idea how much of my time and effort was put into helping them. I was able to help them let go of their past. They should be thanking me, not harassing me.*

"Lucy, without me, you and Kevin never would've gotten together. I help people in many different ways, okay?" I said in my calmest voice.

"I want my money back!" Lucy charged forward, past the threshold of the doorway and grabbed me by my shoulders. Kevin sheepishly stood back with a look of dread on his face. I could feel her nails dig into my skin.

"Hey, let go of my friend!" John said, attempting to push Lucy off.

"This is your fault!" I shot at John.

"How is it my fault? What did I do wrong ?" Lucy shrieked.

"Lucy," I said in a stern and low voice, not wanting Kevin to hear, "do you want Kevin to see you as a sweet and helpful person, or do you want him to see this side of you and leave you like your previous exes did?" Lucy's grip loosened, and she took a step back.

"I'll strangle you to death later," Lucy said, not breaking eye contact with me. I took a deep breath before speaking again.

"The real John is here with me now," I calmly said to Lucy and Kevin. "Ask me anything about John."

"I don't know anything about John. I met Sophie at the cemetery not too long ago," Lucy shot at me, anger and frustration still in her voice.

John busted out laughing.

"This is great. No wonder I can't remember who she is."

"Shut up, John!" I said.

"Whoa, you really are crazy! Who are you talking with?" Lucy asked.

"John! I'm telling you, he's here with us now! I can prove it... how about this, go into my room and pick out any three objects and I will tell you what they are."

Lucy went into my room; Kevin followed her like a puppy following its mother. John fell in line behind them and emerged a few moments later to report on what Lucy picked.

"She looked through your underwear drawers, picked out some black pantyhose, she got that brush on your dresser and a copy of the Sunday newspaper," John said.

When Lucy came out, I told her, and her eyes widened to the size of dinner plates with astonishment.

"You can write anything on a piece of paper, and I will be able to read it aloud. I am not kidding with you. John's ghost is here," I told Lucy and Kevin with my sincerest tone.

Lucy and Kevin stepped into my kitchen.

"They're writing love notes to one another: 'Oh baby your smile is so bright it makes the sun jealous!'" John laughed.

"You two are writing love notes to one another. Kevin started first with: 'Oh baby your smile is so bright it makes the sun jealous and the touch of your arm makes me shiver with delight and my stomach is ignited with butterflies fluttering all around it.' And Lucy, you wrote: 'Roses are red, violet are blue, if you don't love me I will die too,'" I told them, trying not to barf.

John was rolling on the floor with laughter. Kevin and Lucy looked at me with perplexed expressions on their faces. At that moment, I knew how to regain their trust.

"Look, I might have made up that I saw your dead cat or that Charlie cheated on you."

"Don't remind me," Lucy growled.

"But it was for your benefit. Kevin, I gave you closure with fuzzy," I said, meeting his eyes. "And Lucy, if you were still clinging on to the memory of Charlie, you never would have moved on and gotten with Kevin," I directed at Lucy.

"We're trying to convince them to believe us, not hate us," John said.

"I know!" I scolded him before turning my attention to Lucy and Kevin again.

"But John's ghost truly is here. He appeared right after Sophie left, there's no way that I could've seen what you two have written in the kitchen, and hey, I admitted to lying to you and Kevin already. I apologize, okay? I truly am sorry, but look at me in the eyes now. Am I lying to you?"

Lucy and Kevin looked at each other and then turned back to me with a smile.

# Chapter Nine

Sophie was lying in bed, wearing one of John's olive green sweaters over black sweatpants. The room around her was draped in darkness. It mirrored her mood. A month had come and gone since John's death, but his memory was still alive in her heart and mind. It was like pouring salt on an emotional open wound. Sophie wanted to trust Madame Tate's act and wanted to believe that she could reach out and speak with John one more time. Still, the previous experience with the "psychic" taught her that Tate was a fraud. However, she did have a strange feeling that John was there with her the entire time.

"John, if you're with me, give me a sign," Sophie said. It came out almost like a whimper.

Just then, Sophie heard a loud noise, a banging on her window.

"Ahh!" She jumped.

"Sophie, open the window!" Came Lucy's muffled voice.

Sophie rolled her eyes but remembered that Lucy had been nothing but kind to her. Despite her often eccentric outbursts, Lucy was an endearing friend. She clicked on the lamp next to her bed and couldn't help but chuckle as she opened her bedroom window and found herself eye to eye with Lucy.

"You climbed up the tree to get to my bedroom?" Sophie asked Lucy.

"Sophie, I came here as fast as I could. I knocked on your door, but you didn't answer," Lucy said, climbing in and jumping onto Sophie's water bed.

"Whoa, this feels weird!" Lucy said, as she nearly fell over. She quickly plopped down on the edge of the bed before the swaying water could claim her balance again.

"Lucy, why did you rush here so quickly?" Sophie said, sitting down beside her.

"I have news about John."

"What about him?" Sophie said. The room started to feel dark again.

"He is still here."

Sophie looked away and took a moment before speaking again.

"How do you know?"

"He is with Madame Tate."

"Lucy, you know that she's a fraud, right?"

"In the beginning, maybe, but John is truly with her now!" Lucy said as she took Sophie's face with both hands as a mother does with a child. "Look at me, young lady."

"I'm ten years older than you are," Sophie reminded her through squished cheeks. At this, Lucy let go of Sophie's face and repurposed her hands to gesture as she spoke again.

"John wants to see you, and I know that it sounds crazy, but what's the harm of seeing if it is true this time around or not? At least this way, you won't be left with any lingering doubts. If you wonder at all if John is still here, then I think it is worth a shot to see Madame Tate again."

"Lucy, what do you expect me to say?" Lucy's hands shot out and took Sophie's hands hostage as she spoke again.

"I won't leave until you say yes."

# Chapter Ten

"Hmm, I wonder if Lucy could convince her or not," I said.

"She could convince anyone, Madame Tate. She even convinced me to get out of my comfort zone," Kevin said, smiling proudly.

"Why is he still here?" John complained.

"Where else can he go?" I asked.

"He lives next door, doesn't he?" John whined.

"Are you talking about me?" Kevin stammered.

Thankfully, we were interrupted by a loud banging at the door.

I opened the door and saw Lucy standing with a proud smile across her face and a hand clasped around Sophie's.

"Come on in. Please have a seat on the sofa," I told Sophie.

Lucy sat right onto Kevin's lap and motioned for Sophie to come next to her.

"You two can leave," I told them.

"No, they can stay," Sophie countered, sitting down next to the young couple.

John looked at Sophie longingly, then looked back at me.

"I really want them to leave," he said in a flat tone.

"John really wants you two to leave," I said. "Believe me, I preferred for you two to be here, but it's John that is asking," I said, with the most apologetic look I could muster.

Lucy stood up, and Kevin followed her. "Call me later!" Lucy said, winking at Sophie before disappearing out the front door. Kevin followed at her heels. I could hear her giggle as he said, "And now we are at my place," just before the door closed behind him.

"I really miss her," John told me. "I miss our late-night talks and how she snores softly at night."

"John said he misses you, he misses your daily late-night talks and how you snore loudly at night," I said to her.

"Softly!" John quickly corrected, and I jumped.

"I mean softly, snore softly."

"Look, Madame Tate, let's say that John really is here. What makes you think that I'm his unfinished business?"

"Sophie, John wants me to tell you something really important. His death wasn't an accident! Somebody murdered him, he didn't fall out of his window, somebody broke into your house and shoved him!"

# Chapter Eleven

*He truly is here!* Sophie realized. Her face turned pale, and a visible shiver shot through her body. She remembered clearly what happened that night; how could she not?

*It was storming outside, and she heard on the radio that there was a serial killer on the loose. Sophie had just gotten off of the phone with John a few hours beforehand. They got into a heated argument because instead of celebrating her mother's seventieth birthday with her, he decided to take a trip to Atlantic City with his nephew for a bachelor party.*

*"John, I am seriously disappointed in you for not being here with me for my mother's seventieth birthday."*

*"Your mother has a birthday every year! My nephew has a bachelor party once in his life! Stop trying to manipulate me into feeling guilty for doing nothing wrong!" he said coldly.*

*Sophie was speechless as she hung up her phone.*

She recalled that she drove home through the rain in silence as the anger from her argument continued to boil over in her head. Her hair was drenched from the storm outside, but she was too upset to give it any mind. She remembered walking into her home as if it were yesterday and seeing large footprints on her carpet. The anger from the argument was pushed aside by fear and dread. The climb up the familiar stairs now felt foreign and took twice as long. Her brain wasn't ready for the sight of a tall figure in the darkness holding a hammer. In an adrenaline-filled moment, her mind shut off, and instinct took over. Everything happened so quickly, yet time seemed to slow down as she rushed forward and shoved the intruder with all her might. By the time the man's voice registered in her ears, and she knew it was her husband, it was too late.

Sophie lowered her gaze down to the table in front of her before speaking again.

"I know... it was me who shoved him," Sophie said almost in a whisper.

# Chapter Twelve

"I pushed John out of the window. I killed John." Sophie sobbed.

"That jealous bitch killed me?" John said in disbelief.

"You bitch you killed him!" I roared.

"Did he just call me a bitch?" Sophie asked. "It's okay. I deserve it."

John paced back and forth, frantically.

"I didn't want you to tell her that!" he said, glaring at me. "Tell her that you said it."

"I am not going to tell her that you didn't say that. Since when do ghosts lie?" I snapped back at him.

"Said what?" Sophie asked.

"I called you a bitch, and John told me not to."

Sophie let out a small laugh through her tears. "No, no, he was right. It was my fault that he died; I killed him."

For the next few minutes, Sophie recounted the events of that tragic evening. After countless sobs and a whole box of tissues, she managed to clarify exactly what happened. She explained in detail how she didn't realize that it was her husband she was pushing until it was too late. John managed to calm down by the end of her story.

"Oh no, dear, you didn't kill me. I know how much you love me." John tried to touch Sophie's face, but his hands went right through her.

"Damn it! I hate that I can't feel anything," he grumbled.

"I am so sorry, John." Sophie sobbed. "I miss you so much."

"I miss you a lot as well. You're all that I could think about," John said.

"He misses you as well. You're all that he talks about," I told her.

"If I hadn't shoved him out of the window... he wouldn't be like this now," she said. "Why is it that you can see him and I can't?"

"Yeah, why is it that you're the only person that can see me?" John asked.

"I don't know!" I exclaimed. "Why are you asking me?"

"I'm just repeating what she said, that's all," John replied.

"It's my fault that you died !" Sophie said. " I was so stupid. Who else would've been in my house? You were trying to surprise me by coming home early... but I shoved you out of the window instead, and now we can never see each other again," she said in between sobs.

"I shouldn't have stood by the window," John said "Sophie, you didn't kill me. You thought I was a serial killer. You were just trying to defend yourself!" John said.

Sophie looked back at him. Her face lit up and her eyes widened. She gasped, and the box of tissues fell out of her hands.

"John?"

"Sophie?" John said. "You can see me?"

"I miss you so much! I'm so sorry!" she said as she stood up from the couch and rushed toward him. They embraced each other, and Sophie once again began to cry.

"I miss you too," John said as he held her tightly in his arms, "And I don't want you to blame yourself for what happened."

I watched the two of them hold each other. Sophie's eyes were closed, and her head rested on his shoulder. John looked content for the first time in months.

"I'm sorry John," Sophie said.

"I forgive you," John whispered into her ear. They broke their embrace, and without a word, they leaned in and their lips met for one last kiss. The room seemed to light up as they shared one final gesture of love. A warmth blanketed the couple as they pulled away and looked into each other's eyes. They both somehow knew that these were their final moments together in this plane of existence, and John slowly started to fade. He pulled Sophie into a hug, and she held on to him tightly as his body became more and more transparent.

John turned to me and smiled. "It's time for me to say goodbye to you both now. Thank you for reconnecting me with Sophie, Madame Tate. Goodbye, Sophie, I will always love you," John said as he slowly disappeared. Sophie's arms slackened the moment he was no longer visible, and she instead wrapped them around herself as she dropped her gaze to the ground.

"He's gone, isn't he?" Sophie finally asked after a few moments of silence.

"You saw him leave, didn't you?"

"It was too brief of a moment." She sighed.

I touched Sophie's arm. "He will always be alive in your memory."

Sophie looked up at me and smiled through her tear-stricken face. "Thank you."

## Epilogue

**Two weeks later**

It's been so quiet without John around. I miss having that smart-mouthed wiseass around the house, and I must admit my mornings are much more mundane without the man in white. However, I am glad that he moved on. Sophie no longer hated my guts since I reconnected her back with John, no trick, no lies, no nothing, and promises that she'll help introduce more clients to me. I guess it feels good telling the truth once in a while.

I walked down the hallway to my apartment and saw Kevin and Lucy walking toward me, hand in hand. I smiled at them as I opened my door. I walked into my living room, and to my surprise, there was a young girl, no more than twelve years old, sitting on my couch. She had long brown hair parted in the middle, and she was wearing a blue sweater with a gray plaid skirt. I must've forgotten to lock my door and figured she was waiting for me to give her a session.

"Oh, hello there, I'm sorry, but you're too young for a reading," I told her. "I don't take money from children."

"You can see me?" The girl replied.

*Oh great, not again,* I thought to myself. *How will I make any money if all my clients are ghosts?*

# THE BLACKEST CROW

## A.S. ORTON

Dedication: *To my wonderful husband for our past, present, and future.*

It's the first day of Spring, 1972, again. I'm always born Lily Marie Harper on April 22, 1944. I always die on April 22, 1972 and then I'm born again. I've lived more times than I can count.

I don't know if everyone repeats their life with me or is copied each time I'm born. Let me give you two visuals on that. Either we are on one journey getting rolled over and over again in the laundry and I'm just special because I can remember all the times we've rolled around. Or every time I'm born a new world is created, making thousands of nearly identical copies all fanning into space from 1944 like straws from a broom handle. Both ideas seem too grandiose to have originated with little 'ol me, but one of them must be true. I bet you'd like to know for yourself if you're in the laundry or riding a broom straw. I don't have an answer for you, and I don't necessarily expect to find out in this particular life either.

Granny writes that I should come home to the Ozarks to birth my baby. I wish I could say yes, but I don't know what happens after April 1972. Each life I try to make it further, live a day longer. Granny would stomp her feet. I can hear her now, saying, "Lil, love is stronger than time. Don't you know that?" Maybe love is stronger for Granny, but for me, time just gets stuck. I want to die old with

Michael, with a parcel of grandchildren surrounding us, but I can't seem to get there.

I wake up before the alarm clock. The hoarfrost pattern on the window tells me nothing has changed, not by the smallest fraction, from most of my other lives. It won't warm up for another four weeks. I put on baggy corduroys and Converse sneakers that I tie loosely over swollen feet. I sing "Jimmy Crack Corn" going down the stairwell. The echo of "And I don't care!" fades as I step outside and a nimbus of tiny swirling snowflakes surrounds me.

Someone plays Bob Dylan's "The Times They Are A-Changin'" in the tunnel entering Central Park. When I reach the Guggenheim at 9:00 a.m., there is still a hint of sherbet light hitting the bulbus architecture.

Today is the opening for *Rodin Drawings: True or False.* I know my favorite sculpture, *The Kiss,* will be there as well. The sculpture was originally part of *The Gates of Hell,* Rodin's tribute to Dante. It's my favorite piece of art and it satisfies something in me few things do. I sit and take in every angle of Francesca's and Paolo's naked forms. I don't worry if others have seen enough after a minute or two and hurry away. My baby turns a few somersaults.

Behind the Rodin, my eyes refocus. I see a woman who I've never seen before looking at *The Kiss.* At first seeing someone new is surreal, as if I'm staring at another piece of art at the Guggenheim. African American, maybe some Native American. She is very tall and muscled, maybe middle-aged, maybe a bit younger. She is dressed at the peak of fashion, with afro'd hair and a camel peacoat. Her cheekbones and nose are prominent and her lips full. She is the type of person it is impossible to forget. This is someone who commands the attention of the room. I have *never* seen her before. Not in this life, not in my other lives. I haven't felt surprise in so long that I freeze. She catches me looking at her; she nods and smiles with the corners of her mouth.

"Are you interested in *The Kiss*?" She leans forward. Her accent is East Side or Queens, the voice is resonate and contralto. "Dante doomed these lovers to Hell to repeat their sin of adultery for eternity, tossed around together by a wind. It makes me wonder if these two found a loophole. To be forever imprisoned in the flames of new love doesn't seem half-bad to me. But they never get to grow old together. They'll never have children. What do you think? Are they stuck?"

"I've never seen you before," I blurt, wondering if she'll explain.

"Are they stuck?" she asks again. "And if they're stuck, does it feel like Hell or some fantasy world? You're not from here, are you? Your accent is the one I'd least expect to hear, and there are people from all over the world in Manhattan. Where are you from?"

I'm too surprised not to answer. "The Midwest. Missouri."

"Isn't there supposed to be some strong folk magic in the Ozarks? That might explain a few things."

That jumps me. Some people think "hillbillies" are charming, they might be interested in hearing that I come from a place in America that still believes in a little bit of blood-letting for a headache. "For an earache my grandmother wraps a dead ant in a leaf, says a prayer, and sticks it in your ear," I told her. What would this woman say if I told her my grandmother had worked some kind of witch doctor charm to keep me from dying the day I was born?

"Does it work?" she asks.

"I reckon it does," I say. My accent comes out stronger when I talk of home. "I don't recall having more than one earache."

"You like *The Kiss*? I'm an art historian. My name is Linda. I get consulted by museums for exhibits like this."

"I'm Lily," I say, walking around the sculpture to shake her hand. "I hope they pay you well with all the things you have to know."

"They don't. I'm black and a woman," Linda says. "But I'm just passing through to make certain projects happen." Linda leans forward, eyes locked on mine and says, "And other ones unhappen."

Again, that jumps me. It's as if she is speaking in some type of code and I sure hope I learn to understand it quickly.

"I want to make you an offer," Linda says quietly. "I want to train you to be a Time Traveler. We think this might be the best solution for everybody."

"Solution?"

"You were never supposed to be alive in the first place, were you? Death has had a price on your head ever since you were born. But you've outsmarted Death by doing things always a certain way. You have to be very careful to survive like you have. Doing anything out of your usual routine, even breathing wrong, and things could go very differently. It's hard to believe you've survived to try to create a family. You've kept your husband alive too for a while."

"What do you mean?" I repeat.

Linda pauses. "I'm talking about fixing your own messes. I'm talking about you becoming a Time Traveler."

"What do you mean about my husband being alive for a while?"

"Look, he's got to die. He wasn't supposed to ever live past childhood. Do you know what costs have been incurred by you living over and over like a broken record? Now I'm here, this life will finally break you free." She lets out a long breath and scratches her head. As if curiosity is getting the better of her, Linda asks, "Is repetition really your choice? Do you like your life here and your childhood home in...where did you say...Missouri? The same thing. Over and over? You would think it would have made you insane." She chuckles.

I draw a long breath too and stay silent, looking at her.

Linda's eyebrows rise curtly, as if I have already answered. "There's a poetry reading at The National Bohemian Hall on 'Time' on Saturday. Of course, *you* wouldn't miss it. No way would *I* miss it." Linda is right, I'm a moth to a flame for anything with the theme of Time. I already have a ticket. "I'll meet you for it so that we can talk afterward. If you accept our offer, I will teach you how to break free of your...monotony. Then on Monday I'd like to take you to lunch. I can hear your final decision then. Does that sound acceptable to you?"

I'm absolutely stunned.

"Think about what time period you'd like to start with. You can think of any time or place or person you would like to see." Linda nods. "I must say, Time Travel will be particularly interesting because of your baby. When are you due?"

I don't think I can speak when so many thoughts are coming to the surface all at once, but these words seem to rip out of me on their own: "But I don't know if my baby survives! I die giving birth in a month and my life starts over! Do you know what happens to my baby?"

"Dies with you, I think. You don't need to look at me like that. We can't have a baby from someone who wasn't supposed to even live. I do my research is all. I'll see you at the poetry reading." Linda stands to her full height, in the range of six feet, nods, and leaves me standing there with my mouth open.

The next morning the frost bloom pattern is different than usual. I am in uncharted waters. I think fast and furious about what I can change to keep my family alive while putting the last touches on the baby room, knitting a tiny yellow sweater, writing letters to my husband, recording music at school, and playing in my chamber quintet. And everything is just off—just slightly but jarringly different. It's as if I can't find the downbeat.

Linda wants me to think about anything I've ever wanted to do or see? It's not hard for a pregnant lady to think of what she wants. What is she hoping I tell her? My preferences on having tea with either Buddha or Abraham Lincoln? Abraham Lincoln, of course…but that's beside the point.

On Wednesday I go over to spend time with my friend and neighbor, Elizabeth, as usual. She lives in 1501 with her mother with a breathtaking view of Central Park. I live kiddy corner on the same floor in 1503 overlooking the Weill Cornell Medical School and the East River.

"In a past life, who would you be?" Elizabeth says, pulling a slip of paper from a pile. "We love this question, don't we?" Elizabeth is making up a quasi-occult-get-to-know-you game. She always thinks of new games. But she is wrong, I don't love this question. "Who would you be?" she repeats.

"Probably just *me*," I say, telling her the truth.

"Be *you*?" Elizabeth pauses, then suddenly chuckles. "Right. But can't you think of someone famous who reminds you of *you*? I can think of a bunch."

"Well," I say, trying for more of Elizabeth's attention, "have you ever thought about why people experience déjà vu? What if we are just living the same life over and over again? What if most people's memories are wiped clean in between lives but they don't know it? Déjà vu is like a spot that got missed."

The skin between Elizabeth's almond eyes puckers. "Wouldn't that be a terrible waste of the prospect of time? Unless you can improve. Can you improve? Can you make the future a better place?"

"We don't know. It would take hindsight. We would have to know the future after our death. We don't have that information. We don't have hindsight."

"But what about the history that has been? Wouldn't that disprove your theory? History moved forward and time didn't get recycled before?"

"Maybe," I tell her, trying to hide my bitterness. "Or maybe history is just something we are socialized to believe in. How would we know?"

"Huh! That's interesting, but I don't think I like that idea. What would be the point of repeating our lives over and over without change? I guess it would reduce the ghost population. Woo Oooh." Elizabeth makes ghost sounds and moves her body as if her face is about to float into my face. "That gave me an idea for a new question. You ready?" Elizabeth lowers her voice dramatically. "Do you experience déjà vu?" she says, bursting into giggles. Elizabeth scribbles, but then looks up at me again curiously. "But what do you think, really, about the past lives question? Today, I'm sure I could be Genghis Khan. When I wrote the question, I felt Mary Shelley was the perfect fit. She seems just like me."

"I can see Mary Shelley," I say appreciatively.

"What if we went and asked Madam Tate who we were in past lives? I wonder who she would say I was?"

Madam Tate is a professional medium who lives in our building. Elizabeth keeps trying to think up reasons for us to go and see her. I think she's your usual "con" woman, but there's something about her that also reminds me of my granny.

At home people call my granny a goomer doctor, or a witch doctor. People in my county tell a story that when Granny was a child she picked up a hoop snake and it became straight like a rod. People add that this shows how pure of heart and full of faith my granny is. People come to Granny when they want a boil gone or a burn healed. Once I see her reach behind her to find a stone, rub spit on the stone without looking, pray, "What I see enhance, what I don't see reduce," and rub the spit on the boil or burn, but only in the light of a waning moon, never a waxing moon. When I tell Elizabeth this, she says her family has pretty much embraced everything standard and Western about medicine, except for a few nasty-tasting teas. "The nastier it tastes, the more potently magical it must be," Elizabeth says. "Probably due to sacrificed taste buds."

Elizabeth was born in Topaz, a Japanese Internment Camp in Utah in 1944. Elizabeth is getting her master's degree in English literature at Barnard University and hopes to get her doctorate. Elizabeth and I are more alike than different in my opinion. My skin is darker than hers if I get some sun, we are about the same height and only a few months apart from the same age. My dark brown hair is mostly straight, hers is very straight, we both wear bangs. She has brown eyes; I have gray. When I'm not pregnant, we can swap clothes. We're both descended from immigrants. The biggest difference is our way of speaking. Her accent sounds like she is from New York, and my Ozark accent is so thick bees could drown in it and people don't even know I'm holding back. But Elizabeth and her mother have had it rough. Everything was taken from them when they were interred, and I see how she is treated differently from me by many people.

"*Mary Tyler Moore* is almost on, want to watch?" Elizabeth says. Maybe she perceives a difference in my mood. I shake my head, no.

"Would you like to listen to *Abbey Road*?" Elizabeth asks.

The record sticks just where I know it will. It reminds me of my life even after Elizabeth moves the arm up and over the scratch. A tiny scratch, that's all it takes! If no one moved that needle, how long would the same quarter second of sound play over and over? Forever?

"Elizabeth?" I ask. "If you could choose a time period to live in, when would it be?"

"That's a good one," she says, jotting it down. "I think I've always wanted to meet Shakespeare. No antibiotics, but can you imagine seeing a play Shakespeare wrote and is acting in? Queen Elizabeth too!"

"I've always wanted to see sixth century Wales, King Arthur's time. I would collect songs just like I do now and write them down so that they don't get lost."

"You feel it is really important to save songs, don't you? You're so passionate about it," Elizabeth says.

"Songs tell you so much about a people. The ones from the Ozarks came over from Scotland and Ireland in the 1700s and were taught to me by my Granny with our Ozark twang. In fact, I need to practice a song my professor asked me to sing for a class tomorrow. I've got to go."

I'm getting my master's in Music Ethnography at Barnard—ethnography is basically song-collecting, notating it, and understanding music as part of culture. New folk songs on the radio are different from the old time, traditional music that I record as an ethnographer, but my fiddle and my voice work well for both and people ask me to play for local folk bands sometimes. One of the highlights of this last year was singing Marvin Gaye's "What's Going On?" on a college campus. My husband and I are crazy about the music scene—music that says something! Simon and Garfunkel, Joni Mitchell, Carole King, Bob Dylan, and Joan Baez. We were right in front of Hendrix at Woodstock. Don't tell me I can't work magic when I have good hindsight to work from.

"Your shoes are untied," Elizabeth says.

"Thanks. It's getting harder to tie them with the baby bump," I say, trying to reach for the laces without falling over.

"Ahh, let me do it for you." Elizabeth scoots forward on her knees.

We laugh at my facial expressions. "I feel so pathetic. It doesn't seem to matter if I double-tie them, they always come undone. I'm so lucky to have you." I hug her.

I go into the kitchen to hug Mrs. Ishida, who looks at me with concern and asks me about my husband, so we look at each other, our eyes flooding, knowing we understand each other. Mrs. Ishida's husband died fighting in World War II with the 442nd Regiment and received the Medal of Honor.

Oh, what I wouldn't give for more hindsight! To know how to change things! Did you hear Elizabeth's and Linda's reactions to my repeating life? But I can only make the best decisions I can with the knowledge I've got, same as everybody. Where I live seems like the best decision possible for my circumstances and priorities, for instance. Really, how stupid would I have to be to know Elizabeth exists and not be friends with her? The Wellraven is right next to where my husband goes to medical school. Music is so interesting it can fill thousands of lifetimes and I will never get enough of it. I've got plenty of hindsight for any of my decisions up until next month and I stand by those decisions as the best ones I can possibly make, knowing what I know and being who I am.

There's more to it, though. What we call my "Metronome Nightmares" start young, probably from birth. This is how all the memories of all my lives come back to me. There is no avoiding these nightmares. Each life it gets a bit worse. As near as I can explain them, it's as if a memory is being planted in my brain. It could be any little memory: playing the fiddle, making breakfast, or feeding the cow, but the beat of my heart is loud, it rushes in my ears and throbs in my head. I have to do whatever I'm trying to do to the beat of my heart exactly, otherwise I feel shock waves run through me if I'm off-beat. It's like being imprisoned in a second of time, being punished for not performing the memory exactly as is required. Most people can wake up from a nightmare, relieved to find it was a dream. We are never sure I'm asleep at all.

I must whimper in my trance because Granny crosses the room to try to pull me into her arms, but I can't be soothed. When she moves closer, I scream at her to stay away because I believe that if she touches me, Granny could get trapped in the Metronome too. That's the most horrible part of it, worrying that I'm trapping the people I love. Granny, does the blood pump like a cracking whip in your head too? What are you forced to do over and over again to the beat of my heart?

Granny will sit nearby and talk about our new litter of puppies. She names them one by one and talks about stroking the puppies' velvet ears. She describes brushing our big red horse, Jasper, over and over until the repetition and the demand of the Metronome cannot compete with her love and the restricting beat fades. Granny reassures me that she is all right, that I am home. I finally allow her to come near and I fall asleep in her arms, completely cried out and exhausted.

I cannot make big changes. A few lives I try interests besides music, for experimentation, but I fail to keep away from it, feel off-kilter and almost like something is after me. I guess I get paranoid? And I have more Metronome Nightmares until I get right back to my usual...monotony. That's what Linda called it? But I can't stop being me. I can't stop caring about what I care about. I cannot love someone else. I've tried, but there is no one for me but Michael.

Michael is in the same grade at our small school and our neighbor on the other side of eighty acres. My whole life, whenever I turn my head in his direction, I usually see him looking back at me. I wouldn't change a thing. It's what I want the most, and it's the sweetest.

Even when we're in first grade if Michael knows I'm sad about something, he comes and sits by me. When we're about thirteen, Michael helps birth a foal at Ol' O'Neil's and tells me it is the neatest thing, he hopes I'll get to help birth a foal one day, but just after that sentence Michael and I seem embarrassed. I look away quickly, but from my periphery I get a sense that the breath is getting knocked out of him. For the next few years, around Michael, my words disappear like fleas into a dog's fur. Even if he is sitting next to me, we sit in silence as if we are waiting together for news of some magnitude.

The way I feel only seems appropriate sitting at church. The men sit on one side. Michael sits next to his dad a few pews ahead. He will turn. I can tell how he is and if he is thinking of me when he turns his head. There, the feelings suit, other times they rub me wrong and I toss my head and assert my independence. Michael stands up for me every time he sees I need it. When he does, it is as if he throws a javelin of knowing through my eyes and body and into the ground, but I can only look away as if I don't hear.

At the end of our junior year when Michael inherits his grandfather's rusty light blue truck, which his family calls the "hiccup pickup," he starts driving me to and from school every day and soon everywhere else I want to go. I grow into these once too-big feelings like a young bird grows into their wings. Michael spends more time with me than with the guys. To know I am preferred company—more special than anyone else to Michael—to know we have each other to rely on, gives me a confidence that is absent in my earlier years.

Michael works with his dad's logging company after school or on weekends. On the first Friday in May, I say, "We've got puppies that just opened their eyes, want to come see?" It is the first time I invite him over and I feel shy, although he has come over to pick me up so many times.

I holler to my granny when we get home and go to see the "puppy coop" as Granny and I call it. There are eight redbone puppies to gush over, gnawing and licking on his chin and hands.

Granny appears at the door in muddy boots. "Oh, you have Michael with you. Michael, how's your cousin, the one who lost his leg and is home from Indochina?" Granny asks.

"The plastic leg the Navy gave him seems all right. We took him out coon huntin' last week. A puppy like this might cheer him up when they're ready."

Granny nods. "He'll get first pick. You two came just when I was ready to go back to the sorghum patch. It's almost half planted. I knew today was the right day for planting even without asking our little weathervane." Granny smiles at me. My family takes my advice for planting over the usual zodiac signs. "Terry and Don were out there with the horse and plow all this morning and Jolly and John and Joe are here too to help. It would be quicker if we had two more hands." Granny looks hopeful. "I've got overalls for you, Michael. And boots."

Michael changes in the bathroom while I get a plaid shirt, jeans, and work shoes on in my bedroom. It seems intimate to know each other is changing in the same house at the same time. I come out trying to act like I always have boys changing in our bathroom and wondering if I'm right about sensing excitement in Michael.

We work scattering seed and raking over earth. It's hard work. I get tickled to hear Michael dishing back the jokes my uncles and cousins crack at him. We get back when it's getting dark. Granny calls Michael's folks to say he is staying for supper. There's corn bread and butter and the store-bought molasses that everyone complains about because it isn't sorghum, although it is quite good, and a thin side of ham. After we eat, Terry sits on the porch plucking at the banjo and tells me to get my fiddle.

"Want to hear the story of Lily's fiddle?" Granny asks Michael. "We were clearing out Ol' Jethro's old house. She found it in the attic. Later, who do you think had hid it under her bed? She told me she needed it and if we took it she'd run off to work for one and I believed her. I told her she could have it if she worked at it and improved. I think Lily's still trying to prove she's takin' it seriously."

"How old was Lil?" Michael asked.

"Six. Finders keepers," I say slyly so that everyone laughs. I still feel worried someone will take my fiddle out of my hands if I don't prove I'm coming along.

Growing up, family comes over to sing and play on the porch most Fridays and Sundays. Saturday is set aside for square dancing, band contests, and bigger parish get-togethers. On the Sabbath, we play a holier set of songs and flatfoot step. Music and dance is our way of life in the Ozarks. It's foundational to who we are.

"Now, you'll hear something," Terry says as if we are at a concert hall. "Barbara Allen." He pauses, then gives a deliberate down-nod and my bow starts with his banjo almost automatically. I'm usually our singer as well. Uncle Jolly, my granny's uncle, lays down his wooden board on the grass and starts buckdancing. He is too rambunctious for the beat of Barbara Allen. Michael has heard me talk about Uncle Jolly and is communicating to me with a few well-timed nods that he is indeed enjoying Uncle Jolly's timing and kicks. Cousin John whispers to me like usual, "See that conniption?" Everything is funnier and dearer when I get to show Michael.

The way my family is acting is something I'm proud of. They want to impress Michael and make him feel comfortable. I shouldn't feel nervous to sing in front of Michal, but I am. It's all a bit too perfect, but Michael has his steady eyes on me with approval, and when he is looking at me like that it makes me feel seen and calm like nothing can possibly go too wrong. Michael gratifies my family by saying, "Do you have another instrument?"

Don hands Michael the spare and picks up jigging. Michael isn't bad. He doesn't try anything complicated, but he's steady. He tells me he used to practice a lot when he was younger and he plans to work on it more. "I can see we need another banjo for Michael," Granny says. "My father used to make homemade unfretted banjos."

I say, "I want to sing 'The Blackest Crow' to end the band contest next weekend. It's the saddest and it's my favorite. Sound okay?"

"Lil Lil has spoken. You want to practice it now?" Terry starts counting us in. "One and a two and a three..."

"Naw. Too sad for tonight. At the concert."

"There ain't nothin' too sad that our mountain music can't layer like fat stripes in bacon in with the exuberant," Terry says, but I stick to my guns. We have played it a hundred times. I will sing it at the contest. I will sing it to Michael.

That Wednesday, I sit reading on the bleachers waiting for Michael to get done with track practice and Jim Sutton comes up to me, bothering me about not giving him the time of day and saying I'm high and mighty and then he starts to talk about my body. Suddenly, Michael is there by the bleachers, panting. "Everything okay, Lil?" he asks, but he is not looking at me.

Jim Sutton says something like, "I see what's going on," and clatters off unceremoniously.

"You sure bored holes with your eyes into Jim," Michael says to me. "It was like X-ray vision. You can get kind of uppity," Michael waits, lifts his chin and looks down his nose to see if I'll prove him right by getting uppity, "but I've never seen you look like that. If you ever look at me like that, I'm sure I'll turn into a...a swamp monster."

Michael is trying to make me feel normal again, and he's good at it, luckily, because I feel like there is an inch of grime on me left by Jim Sutton. "A swamp monster? Do you think I will turn *you* into a swamp monster?"

"Yes. No... Sort of." One corner of Michael's mouth twitches and his dimple flashes. One of the best things about Michael is that we both have this goofy imaginative streak. Or maybe it's more like we have a small practical streak and the rest is all goofy. "Come here," Michael says. "Put your hands on my shoulders." He jumps me down from the bleachers. You would think he had done this before. You would think he would have tried before, but he takes my hand for the first time in a life as if he has done it a million times (maybe he has?) and pulls me around to the privacy between the bleachers and the gym.

I am nervous because it's what I want each life, every life, right at this moment and strangely not before, but I can't wait a minute longer. We've been best friends for almost a year, but not anything else. Michael just says simply and kind of business-like, "Can I hold you?" And then in explanation, "I would think you'd want to be held after that."

I nod, and then I'm there, partially inside his jacket with my cheek below his neck and his chin against my hair and it feels familiar, but the familiarity isn't dull, it's wonderful. It's home! His warmth. The wild weedy "Michael" smell near his armpits, the strength and hardness of his muscles, holding me and rocking me a bit until I feel soothed into another dimension of being.

When my breathing changes a bit, then comes some confusion, his chuckling in relief, his new sparkling confidence and his razzing. Razzing us both. Why hadn't his girl said anything? Why had she been so standoffish? I laughed and said I didn't think I was. He said, "Sherrie Meacham has been making me a pie every week for the last three months. You've never made me a pie. Why not? I'll grow old waiting for you to."

The words, "Fat too," barely get out of me before he smothers my mouth with our first kiss and he's still somehow rocking me a bit in the way that he does and I'm not even sure how he does it.

Through my mind race all these words describing what Michael is like: *Kind, dependable, funny, clever, handsome, brave, gentle, respectful, respectable* and with it a flood of memories of his round dark blue eyes, always so startling with that farmer tan. But then I get interested in his breath and what his lips are doing and then in what his tongue is doing. He's taking his time. *Romantic, passionate, honest.* He won't let me get away from him. He won't let me. I wouldn't if I could. Michael will be the best husband. Michael will be the best father any child could ever get. There have been five kisses, slow, soft, and creative, in succession.

"I want to go tell your granny we're going steady. Make sure it's okay," he says, looking at me for consent.

"All right," I say happily. Granny must genuinely like him and trust him when he comes to pick me up for everything, day in and day out.

"Well, actually, let's go see my folks and then I'll take you home, that way we don't have to drive back and forth."

"All right," I say happily.

Talking to Michael's parents goes just fine. They are surprised to hear we aren't already going steady. His mom says, "We've been calling you 'Michael's girlfriend' since last Thanksgiving what with all these delicious goodies you keep making him." Michael turns beet red. His mom continues, "I'm going to say something embarrassing, but we don't know if Michael has really ever liked any girl but you since he saw you in preschool. Once you two got to spending time together last year, you've been tighter than bark on a tree."

Michael opens my door, then goes around and climbs back in the truck. I'm biting my lip, trying not to laugh. Michael says, "Tighter than the bark on a tree? Has everyone known? Have I been missing out all this time?" Looking at me with wonder. "And you wouldn't have thrown me out on my ear?"

"I can still throw you out on your ear."

"It's my truck. You'd have to throw yourself out and it's airish. No, I'm serious!"

"I can turn you into a swamp monster if you want."

"I don't want. I've got to be me to get what I want. I want...to hear how you feel. How long have you felt like this?"

"Probably a thousand lifetimes."

"Is that how it feels?" Michael runs his hand through his hair. "Yeah...always. I knew....well...everything's always about timing with you. Golly, I feel like I could walk on water. I'm so grateful Jim Sutton tried to harass you!"

"Come on, drive. Granny will put the fear of God back into you."

"That's what I mean! You've got this internal clock for everything."

Of course it goes well with Granny. She says, "Lily's the only women folk that I've got, so you know you're part of the family now.. But if you ever hurt Lil, you'd best lie low. You'll have to answer to all the men folk in our family. I'd give you a week is all." Granny is teasing, don't worry. That's just how we talk. Still, Michael looks a bit spooked.

I walk him to his car. Outside, I let his hand go for a moment to tie my shoe.

"Tighter than the bark on trees," Michael says. He gets on his knees like he is praying and ties my shoe and then the other one, only looking up at me for a second. In that second, I see tears and I know then that Michael has loved me deeply his whole life and is moved to be doing me a service. If I'd had any doubts, they are gone when I look at him in that moment. We both know it is a moment we will both never forget. He stays on the ground in front of me for an extra second, wipes his eyes and stands. "I'll see you tomorrow."

He walks a few steps and then turns around. "This was a lot for a Wednesday, wasn't it?"

"It was." I start laughing.

"And you got your first kiss?" His eyebrows go up with the question.

I nod a bit hesitantly, still chuckling. In this life, anyway. "It's not your first kiss too?" I ask.

"I'm afraid not. It's probably why I'm getting pies and cookies every week. Although our inseparable friendship has slowed them down this year, I'll admit."

"Now there're cookies to boot?" I hoot. "Do you like jam?"

"What kind?"

"Strawberry. On Sunday we're going to make some."

"There's going to be lots of jam between us, I can tell that."

"Now why does that sound like I don't think anyone else should hear you?"

"I'll try to hold back. I've been waiting to talk to you like that for a while. Can I walk you back to your door?"

"Yes. You can kiss me, too. Here and at the door."

"Good job establishing the rules, Lil."

"You're welcome, sweetheart." And that's the first time I call him sweetheart.

On Saturday morning before the band contest, Michael wants to take me to town for ice cream. Listening to the radio in the hiccup pickup, we hear news about the Korean and Indochina wars, so we flip channels until we find music that we like. That truck is a bit of home. I know every scratch on that dashboard by heart. There's Elvis, The Everly Brothers, Patsy Cline. We are singing, "I Fall to Pieces" at the top of our lungs when he cuts the engine.

Inside the drug store, we spin around on the stools that are fixed to the floor. I think Michael thinks it is a bit childish, but I love it, so he does it too a bit half-heartedly just to not spoil my fun. I get chocolate, Michael gets strawberry. Michael goes to pay the pharmacist and stays to chat for a bit with him. I swing around on my stool and arch my back so that I don't fall off and so that my hair flies all around. A drop of ice cream flies in my face so I work on licking the dripping cone for a bit.

"Look, we've got to talk. You must have lost all your X-ray swamp-monster-making powers when we started kissing. You're starting to scare me."

"What?"

"All those guys over there are looking at you."

"Michael, for Pete's sake. Everyone knows I'm with you. We can go."

"After I tie your shoe. Okay, now the other one."

"I double-tie them. I don't know why they come undone. It must be how I tie them, somehow."

"I don't mind," Michael says. "I'm holding myself back from buttoning your jacket up for you, too."

"I know."

Michael sighs. "You know what? I know you know. Lots of communication goes on with the X-ray eyes."

We hear "Michael, Row the Boat A-Shore" by the Highwaymen in the car as we drive which I usually like singing to Michael because it bugs him and then he tries to tickle me while he's driving, but we are not singing. Michael is acting really serious. Michael pulls over on the side of the road up in the mountains. He comes and opens my door and jumps me down and gives me a long kiss, which goes a long way to making me feel better. Michael and I walk down to the spot along the river overlooked by granite cliffs. I like looking at the layers in the rock and the springs that cascade down it into the tumbling water. We used to splash each other while catching crawdads here when we were kids. In the stiller shallows Michael skips a few rocks.

"I need to talk to you. You know how I thought I'd keep with my dad's logging business. You also know it's dangerous work, right? Well, after that guy, Larry, lost an arm last month, and having all my close-calls, my dad had a talk with me. He said, 'I think you've got a good head and I think you should use it and get out of this kind of work.' So, I'm listening to him. The logging is okay around here, but a lot of land has already been cleared and you know how some folks have been clearing out too. Dad says he doesn't think there will be even half of the logging there is now in just a few years. Okay, you listenin'?"

"Yeah."

"I want to be a doctor. I think it would give you and our kids a good life, and I think I've wanted to be a doctor ever since I saw that doctor help my grandfather."

"It was before that, even. You've always wanted to be a doctor."

"Yeah. You know me too well. I've got to go to the recruiter and enlist."

"Enlist?"

"The pharmacist has a son whose school is getting paid by the Navy, so I was asking questions."

Every life this happens. As far as I know, I can't do a thing. I know Michael wants to be a doctor and nothing else. I know for us there is no way to pay for that kind of school without the military.

"I'll be okay, Lil. I think this is the only way. I go into the military first, then get a bachelor's degree paid for and then medical school with another year somewhere where there might be fighting and then they could station us anywhere for the next years. We could live in Japan or Germany or Hawaii or anywhere. All I know is it's what I've got to do."

"Do you think you'll go out to Korea or Indochina?"

"I think both wars will be over before I get there. You got anything in your crystal ball?"

I say nothing. I go to him and put my arms around his neck and kiss his cheek. "I'll wait for you."

"I know," Michael says.

"Well, at least that's what I'm saying today. But there is always tomorrow." So his arms come around me, verging into possessive, and of course, I'm too in love to want to stop him. His kisses become more demanding until I feel helpless and that's exactly how I want to feel because he's got all my trust.

We are the last band to play on Saturday at the concert. Almost everyone I've ever known is there. Michael, in the crowd, his eyes fixed on me as steady as stars in the big dipper, the kind of steadiness you could tell time by, or so I am thinking. I am a little light-headed, just a-fiddlin' our first two songs as fast as I can go under the hot lanterns, people stomping and wooting.

I look out over the crowd, waiting for a hush to fall. I look at the faces. I know who will die in the war and who will grieve when they do. I know all the pain and I know all the joy coming. I feel myself standing at the crossroads of those two rivers, the river of joy and river of sorrow, and I take a swig of watered-down moonshine and brush sweat off from my brow and look into the eyes of my Michael and sing the most beautiful song I know. A song hundreds of years old from Scotland, taught from parent to child, made popular in our hills by lovers during the Civil War and handed down to me as an Ozark legacy. I make the pace fast because there's an urgency in the energy of this night.

> *As time draws near, my dearest dear,*
> *When you and I must part,*
> *What do you know of the grief and awe*
> *In my poor aching heart?*
> *Each night I suffer for your sake,*
> *You're the one I love so dear;*
> *I wish that I was going with you,*
> *Or you were staying here.*

There's an appreciation for the beauty of sorrow handed down to us in our songs. It's the liquor in our history, and without that taste nobody will really understand our music. Our music's backbone is a wail if you can hear it, even in our polkas, layered as Terry said, between ribbons of fat jubilance like stripes in bacon. Every face here is in tune with me, their rebel blood responds to my singing and is sharpened by it. My only duty on stage is to do our blood justice.

> *I wish my breast was made of glass*
> *Wherein you might behold*
> *That on my heart, your name I wrote*
> *In letters made of gold.*
> *Oh there your name I wrote, my love,*

*Believe me when I say,*
*You are the one I will adore*
*Until my dying day*

Uncle Jolly's buckdancing isn't off tonight, instead his feet have a genius. This song would have had drums back in Scotland. I think the crowd recognizes the rat-a-tat of his feet too and start to rally to the song as a battle march.

*The blackest crow that ever flew*
*will surely turn to white*
*If ever I prove false to you,*
*Bright day would turn to night.*
*Bright day would turn to night, my love*
*The elements would mourn,*
*If ever I prove false to you*
*The sea would rage and burn.*

I look at my Michael. He knows I'm pledging my heart to him in front of everyone. It's all on his face that he knows.

*And when you're on some distant shore,*
*Think of your absent friend,*
*And when the wind blows high and clear,*
*A line to me, pray send.*
*And when the wind blows high and clear,*
*Pray send a note to me,*
*That I might know by your handwrite*

*How time has gone with thee.*

The crowd erupts like thunder and I am still looking at Michael, tears coursing down my cheeks, unchecked. We bow and curtsey. We leave the stage.

I go to Michael, whose eyes look like wells of darkness, twice the size of before. He is moved. He knows I sang for him. For me, knowing what we will face, I put my hands on his cheeks and draw him down and kiss him, hopefully in a new way that he won't forget. Michael puts his hand on the truck door and speaking to be heard over the wind, he says, "What if I die?"

"You will not die as long as I live. I'll write you every day."

"I'll get blown to smithereens."

"You will not. You will write to me every day you can."

"But you'll get married to someone else while I'm gone." Michael gets into the car, shutting the door. I wait while he rolls down the window.

"Michael," I say, "Did you hear me sing or not? Day will turn to night if ever I am false to you. The sea will rage and burn. I am the blackest crow. In two years and two months we will be married by our preacher."

This seems to sober Michael. He takes time and wipes his tears.

"You will come home and go to medical school. We will protest the war."

"My parents will hate that, but okay. You're using your 'prophet voice.' Who am I to argue?" He opens his door, gets out, and holds me.

"You'll see," I say, as if tempting fate. "See you tomorrow. Kiss me first. Damn it, harder." I don't feel like wasting time right now. I'm jealous of time, although some would argue I have an abundance.

Michael says, "Yes, ma'am." Takes my face and leans in. The tear tracks are cold on his face in the wind.

Every life a new layer of love is added to the pile of the old, along with a kind of gasoline made from starvation for a different ending. My love feels like a black inferno there is no seeing through. Didn't someone say the definition of insanity is doing the same thing over and over expecting different results? I have to do everything perfect. I have to be aware of everything in my control and keep everything exact. If I can keep him alive...if I can keep my baby alive...well, I do my best. And I bitterly hate that this is all I can do...over and over again.

Our family band wins that night, it's not a big deal. We've won before. What is different from other band contests is that Michael knows I pledged my soul to him in front of everyone we know. Maybe they all don't know, but I know Michael knows.

The other thing that is different is that Professor Almira Strong from the Missouri State University who collects old time songs handed down from parent to child happens to be there at the concert to see what people are singing in this corner of the Ozarks. She comes to our house the next day while we are mashing strawberries and asks Granny and me to sing songs. "Ask Lily to sing you the songs Ol' Jethro taught her. Lily knows more songs than anyone I know, including myself. Plus, she sounds so pretty. Go get your fiddle, Lil."

I am invited to college with a promise of a full-ride scholarship. Professor Strong helps me do the paperwork right there despite strawberry juice spots. Professor Strong explains that not everybody knows the songs that we know and that some of them are very old and that Missouri State University in Springfield is trying to collect these kinds of songs and fiddles before they are forgotten.

I dress as carefully as an eight-month-along pregnant lady can for *Poetry and Other Performing People* in a purple sheath dress, the front hem is bowed up short due to my baby. My silhouette sure doesn't look like it did eight months ago. I put my hair up. I'm still going to wear my tennis shoes because they have some tread and my boots haven't fit for a few weeks. I worry I'll fall if I don't keep trying to prevent a fall. This is one of those worries that I keep up because it's pretty much worked for me before. Sometimes I'm not sure if anything ever really "starts" with me. Time seems circular. The shoes look awful with the dress. Hopefully, I won't embarrass Linda too much. I plan to wear my long jacket all night. I head for the stairwell.

The acoustics in our stairwell is one of my favorite things. I sing an Ozark version of "The House of the Rising Sun" that is from a girl's perspective. It sounds great on the stairs. I've got time. I up it an octave to stretch my vocals and to really howl, Janice Joplin style! Giving my baby something to remember! Doh! Do people think I might be one of the ghosts they talk about in the Wellraven Apartments? Sometimes I wonder.

I don't see Linda. The small theater goes dark and a spotlight appears above the microphone. A person from the Manhattan Theatre Club introduces the subject and starts us out. Shakespeare's "Sonnet 19" is first, Emily Dickinson's "A Clock Stopped" is next. "To the Virgins, to Make Much of Time" follows. A man whose deep sonorous voice I always anticipate hearing quotes a thrilling excerpt from, "Burnt Norton" by my beloved T. S. Eliot:

"Footfalls echo in the memory
Down the passage which we did not take
Toward the door we never opened"

Eliot ends with a thought on love. That love is only love if there is an urgency and fear of loss that the brevity of life gives it. I feel I live Eliot's concept—it seems to fire in every cell in my brain. I wonder why I still feel urgency in love? I still feel there isn't nearly enough time to show Michael the depths of my feelings. I'm grateful that I haven't lost my sense of fear. They say psychopaths don't feel fear. This feeling we don't want and that causes us so much trouble is the thing that makes us care. Fear and the sympathy for fear is what bonds us together as a shared experience with everything alive. That all of us will die and that this is hard and sad is the ground floor of everything good about us. So I believe.

Linda stands and walks with stately pomp to the spotlight. She's dressed in a billowy-sleeve dress that has a print of small and large clocks all over an orange background, hard to miss. Maybe she got here late. I have no idea what poem she will recite. Her sure voice cuts through the smoke in the room, "'Through a Glass, Darkly' by General George S. Patton."

I sit on the edge of my seat. I didn't realize that General Patton remembered past lives! He says he remembers the sting of each of his deaths. Something that I don't remember is death. I'm just suddenly reborn and I acquire my memories of my past lives through my Metronome Dreams.

The person who introduces the show interjects what an interesting pick Patton's poem is and how glad they are for the opportunity to add Linda Eton to the program last second. I sit there, unable to really listen to anything else until the last poem is read and I stand up and make my way toward Linda.

"What did you think of the poem I read?" Linda asks.

"I'm not as weird as I thought I was," I say, shrugging my shoulders. "But Patton thinks very linearly about time."

"Ah! You spotted it. Yes, Patton was strictly a Reincarnist. Have you thought about what I've said?"

"Yes. A lot."

"We can walk and talk. Come to my apartment for tea or whatever it is you want to drink. I'm in 1504, across from you."

"You're in my apartment building on my floor?"

"Yes. You're surprised?"

"I would have been knocking your door down with questions if I'd known."

"Oh. By the way, where were you? I waited at the base of the elevator for you," Linda says.

"Oh! But I took the stairs!"

"Don't you think at eight months pregnant you should take the elevator? I was sure you'd be there! So?" Linda changes the topic excitedly. "What time period do you want to work on first? I found out you're studying Music Ethnography. Basically, what I do with art, you do with music. Isn't it perfect?"

"I need to ask you some questions, if I may. When you said I've been causing problems that I would need to fix, what did you mean?"

"Every time you're reborn, a new world is created. There are thousands of nearly identical time threads from your births. You die in each one, and it's always you re-starting, but for everyone else their copy continues on. Already, this particular thread out of all of your lives seems to stand out brighter than the others. I've done some research. So far it seems like this thread has some fantastic

257

things happening. I imagine it is because I am here and because of whatever decision you make. Time is circular."

Well, that answered a lot. Broom straws it is. "What decision?"

"The decision to become a Time Traveler like me. The decision of what time period you would like to start with!"

"After I die, somehow?"

"No..." Linda stops and looks at me in the light of street lamps. "Before you die. It would be like taking infinite vacations from this life, basically. You'll be eight months pregnant for a long while."

"Infinite vacations all in three weeks before I die? Why hasn't one of your group just tried to kill me instead of this Time Traveler stuff? Uh, not that I want to give any ideas."

"I'm the one who located you. The source of the problem was very hard to find because you've been so exact. Others have been trying, I thought that was clear. Because you are the source of the thousands of nearly identical threads of time, we decided that with your help we could do all sorts of experiments to find out what produces the best societies. Everything we would try to do would pass inspection by a regulations board, of course, all of it hopefully to help people, not harm. You must know this specific time and place and all the little things that can have a bigger affect better than anyone. Also, you must have learned how to tightly control and predict all the things you needed to keep alive as long as you have."

"Experiments?" I think I do know thousands of small interlocking pieces of what looks like minutia, but that has that butterfly effect that maybe Linda is talking about. "In all of my lives I do the best I can to produce the best world I know how by playing with and controlling all of those connections." If my baby lives and Michael lives, then I can't let them down.

"I thought so! That's why I am excited to train you as a Time Traveler. It's lots of adventure and becomes fulfilling humanitarian work if you have a conscience, which you do. I think you'd have a flare for far future work eventually, too, which is more dangerous and specialized. I'll teach you."

"Will... my baby survive if I became a Time Traveler?"

"I doubt it. Y*ou* are not even supposed to be alive, remember? Your grandmother made some crazy magic and time allowed it and has been paying for it ever since. Can you imagine sorting through all the alternate timelines your broken-record life has started? None of us Time Travelers knew which thread to ride until this life started to be more interesting and I knew I had to be here first and that I was likely the cause of it being different. And here I am. And then I thought of how we could use this glorious mess for experimentation and got approval. You're a nice little thing, I bet you've worried about the fuss your lives have been causing."

"I wondered." I hold back the words *I'm sorry* that she almost seems to expect. It isn't fair. It sounds like there can be an infinite number of timelines and no one is any wiser if they happen to have multiple copies of themselves elsewhere. "Patton said he has been in many forms. Do you take many forms?"

"Mostly not. It depends on which technique you use. You can make yourself be born in a different time and you would be a different form and time would be linear on that thread. Or you can travel as you are and create multiple universes or multiple versions of yourself, either one, depending. Come in, please."

We reached Linda's apartment at 1504. The furnishings are everything you'd expect from an art historian Time Traveler. One sofa is probably Qing dynasty, one grandfather clock is probably nineteenth century German. There are stone carved faces, spears and shields, bone flutes, and woven fabric almost everywhere I turn. It's a functional treasure-trove. Her exotic looks fit in.

"Sit down and we will talk some more. I'll make tea if you drink it? I hardly know what to serve you."

"I'll take some water or milk," I tell her. "I have questions. Do you happen to know what makes this life stand out?"

"Other than me? What exactly happens? It's something I'm in the middle of studying."

"Maybe I can help. What is different?"

"Things are just slightly better, but by 'slightly better' I mean that about a thousand people have healthier, happier lives and live longer and then in the next generation this effects another ten thousand and it keeps getting bigger. It's a very strong ripple."

"Is Michael doing anything different in this life?"

"Your husband?"

"My husband. He will be a doctor." I sit there shocked that she hasn't researched that far.

"Hmm. Your husband dies from a trip-wire bomb a few days after you die. He never even hears about your death before he dies. He goes to help some village children and doesn't see the wire."

"Don't you think what I've just heard will change the outcome of this life?"

"Oh, I suppose you'll tell your husband. You think that is all it takes? Is your husband surviving a bit longer? I would place my bet that the positive ripple is from the Time Traveling that we do instead."

"Saving Michael is the best thing I could ever do," I say adamantly.

"As a Time Traveler you'd have access to doing so much. So much more than saving one person. You can basically be everywhere at once."

"Do you know how I die?"

"Placenta previa rupturing, killing both you and the baby. You don't seem to understand what I'm offering you. I am offering the possibility to be anything you want, do anything you want, have infinite possibilities. Who would you like to have love affairs with through time? What would you like to see? What good could you do? Aren't you sick of doing the exact same thing in this insignificant life?"

"Living my insignificant life a thousand times or more hasn't made me care about it less. It's only taught me to not waste time on what isn't important to me."

"You like your broken record. I've never met anyone like you."

"I like my record. Maybe you gave me information to move the needle over the scratch."

"You're only alive because of a scratch, and Michael is only alive because of you."

"Maybe, but it's as real as any other life somehow."

"Do you know that I am Shakespeare's 'Dark Lady'? Do you know I am Queen Nanny of the Maroons… that was a birth, I was shorter in that life."

"Well, I didn't know that, but I love that love poem about your hair being like wires."

"It's such a good one! 'Sonnet 130.'"

"Well, thanks to you and Shakespeare for that. You must be a very busy lady," I say and then I worry that it sounds rude. I don't know what else to say. What people think of as insignificant lives might be more important than anyone understands.

"Maybe you just lack confidence? Just think! So many worlds have been created because of you. This gives you so many opportunities from the beginning. Opportunities I had to build as a new Time Traveler."

"Please understand, it's not that I'm ungrateful. Thank you. I will go home now and write to Michael."

"Can you be actually saying no? You'll die one way or the other in a few weeks. I want you to think! Think of the great things you could see and study and hear, the great loves you could have, the great good you could do. You owe this to yourself and to the people of the worlds you have created! Don't you want to see the Library of Alexandria? Don't you want to hear Beethoven play?"

I stay silent, but I have to admit, she is getting under my skin just a bit. To study music through time like Linda does art! But I now have some hindsight! I know exactly what I'll do with it.

"There was much more I thought I'd teach you tonight. But I'm not giving up yet. I will see you at lunch on Monday. Where would you like me to take you? My treat."

"Wherever you'd like to take me, Linda."

"We can meet at the Guggenheim at noon and walk to Die Lorelei. Wonderful German food."

"Sounds good. Thank you for everything tonight. So much."

"Yes, yes. I'll see you Monday."

Linda is right about Michael being alive because of me. When we are still in grade school, Michael is working with his dad's logging operation for twenty-five cents an hour. He is what they call a bullcook which means he does odd jobs around the camp, fetching gasoline and equipment, and clearing brush. He is near his father getting instructions on what to do next and the men are doing undercuts on an oak they are working on. The undercuts create what they call a swing dutchman. A swing dutchman is unpredictable and dangerous, however their feller reassures everyone that he knows exactly what he's doing with this tree and they want to trust him because he's fast. I know Michael is in danger. My Metronome Dreams tell me what I need to do. I show up.

Michael and a man called Boomer, who I think runs the Cat start walking right into the path where the tree will fall. I call him over shouting, "Michael, my granny made you and yours some fried chicken in return for that rooster you gave us."

Michael says, "That's mighty fine of your granny. Men are working, Lily. You can leave it on the wheel of that cart, yonder."

"What did you say?" I yell out extra loudly.

"Leave it over there." He points.

"Michael, I can't hear you. Boomer, come on, you too! Come, tell me what you said!"

"Well, hang on." Michael turns and comes up the hill toward me. Boomer keeps walking.

"Hey, Boomer!" I yell.

Michael barely reaches me when the sound of the axes and saws stop. In the silence, "Okay, everyone" and "All right, lookout" are calmly spoken by the fellers as an all-clear to prepare everyone for the tree falling, but then there's the great cracking and sudden yells and cuss words drowned out by the mayhem of the tree falling many yards from the escape route. Falling right where Boomer is walking. Boomer is killed and a feller loses use of a foot that day, Michael would likely have died too. I've never been able to get Boomer to change direction, unfortunately. One of my regrets.

It's not my only story. I've probably got fifty plus. It's as if Death is after Michael. I earn a reputation for being lucky and also for being strange. Why do you think Michael is standing up for me all the time at school? I don't care if Michael doesn't care. I've lived too many lives for that kind of thing to worry me—mostly.

Michael survives his first tour to Vietnam. Each life, his letters are pretty much identical. I think I know them all by heart:

My Dearest Lil,

I am writing this on my last day of basic. We ship out to California at 0530 tomorrow morning and then there's the long plan ride to Okinawa and then to Saigon. I won't miss gunnery sergeant McClintock the least little bit. I don't think he knows another way to be except be a hard-ass. I thought I was in great shape before basic, but you should see me now. I can run ten miles without losing my breath. I wish there was a way for me to see you before we go, I sure do miss you. I would give anything to run my hands through your hair one last time.

It looks like once I get to Vietnam, they are going to make me a corpsman. It will be good training toward becoming a doctor. It seems natural. Do you remember that time Clint, that brush monkey, lost track of choker and it almost took his arm off and I stopped the bleeding with his shirt and rode with all that way to the hospital? Maybe that's the time it knocked something loose in me and I realized at that point that I wanted to save people. Now the Marine Corps is giving me a chance to do it for real, but instead of loggers it will be GIs and instead of saw blades it will be VC bullets.

I know you are probably scared for me, and I'd be lying if I said I wasn't scared too, but I feel that this is something that I must do. Give my love to your granny for me. I'll write again as soon as I am in country. I have to go now, Gunny wants to do another inspection.

Yours always and forever,
Michael


My Dearest Lil,

I thought that Missouri was hot in the dog days of August. Then I got to Vietnam. It's hot and humid here all the time. The only break we get from the heat is when it rains. Then the sun comes out and it gets even hotter. Life here is fairly boring, most of the time. Every time I ask when we might see some action, some of the guys who have been in country a while say, "Soon enough, what's your rush?" The look they give me says "drop it" loud and clear.

We do the same thing every day. We eat the same thing every day. My staff sergeant is a guy from Chicago named Moszkawicz, but everyone just calls him Moes. He's an all right guy, but he likes to make us PT out in the heat. He thinks it's funny. We all think he's just a sadistic bastard. He calls us daawwwgs in his thick Chicago accent. You would laugh. We laugh at him behind his back, but we don't dare to his face or he makes us PT even harder.

I'm making friends fast. Joe Thorton from Tupelo Mississippi is probably my favorite guy in the unit. He reminds me of guys we went to school with. He's a crackup. I hope you get to meet him someday.

It's really green here, even greener than back home. I flew over a rice patty for my first time today. Old people and little kids working in it together. Reminds of me of life on the farm back home. I think you would like it here, if there wasn't a war. It's funny, at times it can be so quiet, even peaceful and then all of a sudden, you hear gunfire in the distance, almost like fireworks. There is talk that my unit may be headed somewhere up north in a few days. I can't say where, or you won't get this letter. We are all going in by helicopter, can you believe it! They say it's never been done before. I don't want you to worry. They keep telling us that there isn't a lot of fight in the North Vietnamese. It sounds like they are all poor farms and not a real army. I gotta go, Moes wants to go on another run. I love you more than words can say. I'll write again as soon as I can.

Yours Forever,
Mike


Lilly,

I'm still alive. It hurts to say that out loud, so thought I would write you. You may have read about a major battle in the newspaper. It was so much worse than words can say. So many of my friends didn't come back. I am doing my best to write you, but my hand won't stop shaking. I wonder how in God's name I made it back here, when so many guys didn't. I'm having trouble sleeping. Every time I close my eyes, I see Joe's face as they were loading him into the chopper. What was left of it anyway... I tried to save so many of them, but I just couldn't. I just couldn't. I wish I was back home with you right now. I wish that more than anything else in the world. I am going to take a walk now. I'll try and write again soon.

Michael.


During Michael's first tour, I'm at the Missouri State University. I drive the two hours in the hiccup pickup to go see Granny on most weekends, and during the summers I'm home. In July we pick corn from the patch and grovel for tiny sweet potatoes together.

"What do you think of all this war protesting?" Granny asks me. "When we've got people like Michael out there."

"We want to protest it too, Granny. America shouldn't be there."

"You can't just let communists take over the planet. They'll come after us soon enough!"

"The Chinese haven't come after us yet. Besides, I don't think we will win. So there's no point."

"Hold up, there! Who said we aren't winning? That's all the radio is saying! Always saying we killed so many of them. The commies can't keep that up. If it's getting rough then we need to send more guys to help out."

"Well, I'll tell you how Michael put it. He said his dad had all these stories about liberating Holland and how happy the people were to see American soldiers. This is not like that at all. Michael said you have to think everyone Vietnamese is an enemy and that is how you survive, expecting everything is a trap.

"I got to thinking about what we would do if Russia came to Missouri and said they wanted to fight together with Missouri republicans against Yankee democrats. Would you think we would just say okay and let it happen? You know old Miss Wilson? Did you know she's a democrat? She called Franklin Roosevelt her only beau, remember? Well, what if she decided to try to communicate with Yankees and made bombs to kill soldiers from Russia? And then the Russians started to suspect all of us would kill them and started poisoning all of our food?"

"Ah, Lil. That's crazy talk. As if we would ever allow Russia over here! Our country's leaders aren't as stupid as all that. You've got to trust our elected officials will do their job."

"Okay, not Russia. Can you think if Brazil came over and wanted to fight Yankees?"

"No, I can't! Lil, this is America! If I wasn't laughing, I'd be getting upset. Promise you'll never go into politics. Some way you have of putting things."

Sigh. Is it so hard to put ourselves in someone else's shoes? "At any rate, we can start planning a wedding. Michael will be home in April."

"You're getting married here, ain't cha?"

"Of course."

"Well, then it's already planned. Michael's mom and I have been talking it over for years."

"Do I get any say?"

"You can decide if you want lace on your dress. I'm halfway finished with it. We'll fit it to you tonight."

"Can we have those plum fried pies Michael and I both like?"

"That was the plan, yeah. I planned on us picking plums and drying them these next few weeks when they ripen up."

I sit there feeling overwhelmed. "Granny, you do so much for me."

"The pleasure of my life."

"It's going to be a beautiful wedding!"

"You know it!"

Michael comes home wounded a month before his tour in Vietnam is scheduled to end. He crosses through fire to treat and drag a man to a helicopter, then goes after another wounded. He uses his body to shield a soldier he is applying a tourniquet to when he is shot through the leg. He tries to drag himself and the man out anyway, but he can't walk. Another medic, one Michael knows, Arthur, comes to both their aids and after two weeks at the hospital in Saigon thinking he will die every other day of sepsis, he recovers enough to be flown home.

It takes four months to walk again on his own and I am right there with him most of the time at the hospital and rehab in Springfield. I graduate and get a job as a secretary at the department of music. We are married when I predicted by our preacher at home with all our friends and neighbors and family present and we move into a house we rent near the college. My professors are still recording my fiddling and singing while I'm working there. They are urging me to go on to higher education to be a song collector.

I do all the paperwork to get Michael into school for a bachelor's and it isn't as easy as the military originally made it sound. Paperwork can be like a type of battle too. Michael turns out to be an A student in all those hard subjects like chemistry, biology, and physics. Michael works hard at school, he's not giving up his chance, he says. He has lots of trouble sleeping, but he uses it to work.

Michael and I talk a lot about the war. Nobody else wants to hear it. I demand to hear it all. All is not pretty. Michael tells me about his platoon killing babies, kids, and old people, poisoning rice, and the first times any of them were asked to do things like that how strange it felt and how much he had wished he could have gone against orders, and at first, tried to on grounds of being a medic. He tells me about how body counts were what the officers wanted to hear about and that he knew the numbers they were reporting were lies.

As humans, we search for meaning. We need meaning as much as we need food and sleep. When we lose a friend, we want there to be a damn good reason for it. The whole time Michael is learning to walk again, he tells me he sees his wounded and dead buddies when he closes his eyes. He says we need to get involved against the war and he thinks soldiers' voices need to be heard even though it seems like everyone hates soldiers so much.

Because I'm still so involved at the college, it's easy to get involved in anti-war protests and network for both of us. But in the groups we protest with, we don't even feel like we can mention that Michael's been a soldier and that Michael almost lost his life because of this war.

Arthur, Michael's buddy from the war, applies to medical school at Weill-Cornell in New York. We talk about New York. Medical school, a master's in Music at Barnard for me, and a place to get heavily involved in protesting and networking. When Michael graduates, we drive cross-country to New York.

Michael and I are in New York the day the idea for the VVAW is founded. Four hundred thousand people march in a parade called the "Spring Mobilization to End the War." When we see a banner saying "Vietnam Veterans Against War," we immediately move right over to that banner and strike up communication. I can tell from Michael's face how good he feels talking to other soldiers who want the war stopped. He feels like he is standing for something that he believes in, was given a voice and a place where people experienced the true costs of the war.

We are there in Washington when John Kerry represents the VVAW. Michael throws his medals over the fence. I think it was one of the hardest things he has done and also one of the most freeing.

Before he leaves to go back to Vietnam as a doctor in December we both get done with our semesters at school and drive to Granny's loving John Denver's "Country Roads" and Marvin Gaye's "What's Going On?" It feels amazing to be going home.

There is music and singing and food right off. All my cousins and uncles come over and a bunch of them have gotten married. The house is bursting at the seams. After everyone goes, I send Michael to sleep in the room I grew up in because he's driven through the night. Granny and I are cleaning up, she gets tired. Not a word you usually associated with Granny.

"Granny, come on over to the sofa. There's not much left to do. You must be exhausted after cooking and cleaning for all of us."

"I couldn't be happier than I am right now," Granny says, "You and Michael finally here and a baby coming. I think I've died and gone to heaven. "

"I think this is heaven. Get a little rest. I'll come tuck you in in a minute."

Granny dozes a bit while I wipe and put the apple-patterned china away. Then I see her head bob over the arm rest and hear this sentence: "This would be heaven to you, wouldn't it? Since you never really die, do you? All on account of what I did."

This sentence from her always gives me goose bumps. "Granny, what *did* you do?"

"I asked the Lord that if he'd already taken your mother, that he'd have to give me you back. You weren't gonna live. I cut you cold out of your dead mother's womb. She'd been laboring for three days and the doctor and I couldn't loosen you no matter how Marion pushed and she hemorrhaged and the doctor couldn't stop it. She was so disappointed and so was I. She died in my arms. The doctor had already pronounced her dead and he'd gone home. I cut you out, and I rubbed you with warm oil and I called spirits and I said charms."

"It worked, didn't it?"

"That wasn't all of it. I must have sold my soul. I negotiated."

"It can't have been black magic."

"It could. I tried everything."

"Granny, there's no evil came of it."

"The evil of time being stuck."

"You aren't evil. You never washed in a spring moving away from the sun and disavowed yourself from God and Jesus, did you?"

"No, I didn't have time for that. But there's more than one way to become a witch."

"You didn't have sex with a witch or devil and learned the dark magic from him? At least nobody in this county has ever said so to me." I can't help but chuckle inwardly a bit at this one.

"No. I was true to your grandpa all my life and he weren't no witch."

"Doesn't the bible say, 'By their fruits you shall know them'? A good seed brings forth good fruit? I turned out all right, didn't I? So there can be no evil in it."

"I couldn't abide to lose both Marion and you. I wouldn't accept no as an answer. But now you're caught in this crazy repeat."

"Granny, how do you know?" I know her answer, but I ask anyway, just like so much of my speech.

"I know it from your 'Metronome Dreams' when you sometimes cry out and tell me things you shouldn't know about the future and past. I think Michael never would have gotten to an age either without you around. A lot changes because of you, but it's like God has us gripped tight in his hand. I think He can't help but enjoy what He sees. I worry about what I've done, if it's wrong, but I think I'd be happy to keep doing it forever because if we're all rolling around in the laundry, I know I'd do the same every time. I don't want to live if you'd died."

"I'm glad to be alive. God wouldn't do something without a reason. Everything is exactly how it should be."

"I think as your baby grows, I've been getting weaker."

"Maybe so. Maybe it just feels like that. I don't know."

"But don't worry about me."

"Oh, I'm gonna worry. I'm going to worry you up some pancakes and molasses tomorrow morning and the best Christmas that you've ever had, but I'm going to know things are as they should be. I tell you... my granny has some powerful love! Enough to change the usual order of the Universe. And your blood flows in my veins and I couldn't be prouder. I am alive because of my grandma's love! Please do rub me with oil and say every charm you can think of. Bring it all on, life's joys and sorrows. Thank you, my granny, for the gift of my life."

"I'm glad you feel that way now. What with Michael and the war. Things happen. Will you ever curse the day you were born?"

"Nope. It all means too much to me, Granny. I've practiced a song to sing you. It is a song put on a record just this year. It says how I feel about you. Is that okay?"

"Let's go! Got your fiddle?"

"Yep. This is 'Wild Horses' by the Rolling Stones." If you know the words, then you'll know this is the perfect song to describe me and my granny and everything about us. I tune the guitar special and put a fiddle solo in the middle.

"Oh, that's a very nice song, Lily!"

"Ain't it?" I say as if I've never lived in New York.

"A really beautiful song. What was that line?" asks Granny.

*"Let's do some livin' after we've died!"* I sing again.

"And what was that other line?" Granny asks. I know what lines she means.

"*I have my freedom, but I don't have much time,*" I croon softly.

"What does that mean to you?" Granny squeezes my hand and I pat her crepe spotted skin.

"It means I could be anywhere in this world and could be doing anything this world can offer, but what I really want in all the world is to be with you and I only want that forever. Time limits you, not anything else, when you have what you really want."

"Is that how you feel?"

"Yeah… always."

"Me too."

"See what I'm saying about my granny's blood?"

I feel so sorry that my granny must bury me, my baby, and Michael in the spring. How does she bear it? Maybe it helps to know that in another world I'll be living my beautiful life with her all over again.

It's Monday and Linda and I are meeting at the Guggenheim and then walking to Die Lorelei for lunch. Linda's clothes are always so impressive. She's got this avant-garde mustard-colored, almost rain-coat material jacket on that has a stiff collar that is so high that the edges graze her earlobes and underneath is this brick and pink shirt in a complicated print pattern with tiny pleats. Black close-fitting pants and pumps which probably put her around six foot three. Yep, she's standing about a foot above me. I think the fashions of a time must just be part of the fun of time traveling for her. I must look very pregnant and homespun next to her, but luckily she doesn't say something like, "Weren't we going to lunch?" or "Why not just come barefoot with a jar of pickles?" Although I wonder if she is thinking that. Instead, she just raises an eyebrow.

"Thank you so much," I tell her in place of hello.

"What for?" Linda says.

"I hope to change things because of the hindsight you've given me. It's a gift."

Linda clicks her tongue. "You must love your life and yourself very much to repeat your actions so exactly. Looking for this life has been like trying to find a monarch in a room full of thousands of swallowtails. It has been very time-consuming and repetitive work is not my favorite. What would you like to change?"

"I am warning Michael about that trip wire. I've saved him before. He will be careful if I tell him to. I've already sent five letters and two telegrams."

"Will you only save Michael and not yourself?" Linda asks.

"How can I save myself?"

"You fall down the stairs of your building, hitting your head, rupturing your placenta and people do not get to you in time enough to save you or your baby. Does that tell you enough?"

"You didn't tell me I fall," I say in wonder. "There is a way that I don't have to die?"

"Don't you have any memory of it?" Linda asks curiously.

"I remember starting my day, leaving my apartment, a brief something about pain and then nothing."

"That makes sense, doesn't it? You were knocked out. You never knew what happened to you. What were you doing pregnant trying to go down fifteen flights of stairs?"

"What if I save both Michael and myself then?" I say, almost in shock.

"Yes, what if?" Linda slows her long stride and raises an eyebrow at me.

"Would I still die?"

"Death is usually somewhere in life's equation."

"I mean… would I be able to have my baby?"

"I don't know. Your baby is moving around now, isn't she? There's a life in there."

"She?"

"She. This is Die Lorelei. What a treat. Gorgeous! Let me help you order."

We enjoy the food in silence while I keep smiling, unable to stop.

"Well, are you going to reconsider? Become a Time Traveler like me?"

I want to give Linda a good reason, and in my head is *The Blackest Crow*. How do I explain to her that I am the blackest crow? Who knows what is staying constant in the Universe based on the steadiness of my feelings? Who knows what consequences such a huge change would cause? The song says the seas would rage and burn. All I say is, "Can Michael come?"

"I'm not sure. I don't usually train men. But I never close off any possibilities completely. You make me feel there might be some merit in finding and sticking with exactly what a person likes. Oh, No! No! It's still annoying me! If you were going to be a Time Traveler, we would be planning out what famous people we would like to take as lovers right now. Just imagine! Eh! No…I can see that you cannot," Linda says with some dismay.

It's not a good idea for women to compare sex notes with mine. I end up feeling sorry for them. There's only one Michael, I'm afraid.

"Linda, you've said there are other Time Travelers and you're the first here. What is going to happen now? Are they going to try to kill me?"

"Oh, we fixed it."

"What do you mean?"

"Let's say 'powers above' heard a scratch on their record. 'Who made the scratch? What's going on? Why are these one thousand threads the same and then one stand out?' Linda imitates someone she knows and rolls her eyes. "Of course, the standout is circular, from my already being here. My own curiosity was piqued. And I'm very tenacious!"

"We got me over the scratch?" I ask. "So now my life threads aren't going to annoy anyone?"

"I think we are doing the right thing in your case even if we're bending the rules," she says and nods as if the answer is on the table.

"Linda, please explain."

"Oh! Your love for Michael, of course! Your grandmother's love for you. It couldn't get any more perfect, could it? You shouldn't have been born, but your granny made it happen with her folk magic and the love in her blood. Powerful stuff, it would seem. This stays between you and me, but there's always a work-around and the powers above can be persuaded. They will listen to a story like yours. A nice unplanned ripple in one thread has got to be better than what's been going on. It's easier to ask for forgiveness than it is to get permission sometimes."

"Work around?"

"Well, yes…a little information from the future. A little hindsight. We Time Travelers would be useless without our future information. How would we make money? Hindsight is what you've been without and that's hardly fair in your situation."

"Yes, thank you so much!"

"Yes, let this record play on. I've never met anyone so sure of what matters to them as you are."

"Practice makes perfect?" I say, lifting my shoulders and arms with the question.

"Maybe. I'll talk to the Fates for you and they'll make a longer thread for Michael and you so that Death isn't hot on your heals. Check, please." Linda smiles and waves her hand at the waiter.

"Well, that was delicious," Linda says, dabbing her smile with her napkin. "I can't wait to tell someone I ate at Die Lorelei in 1972. It came highly recommended. I will probably be on my way after this. It was very good to meet you and maybe we will meet again someday. I will look forward to it. I will likely meet your descendants. I want to explore this thread now that I've identified it as having better outcomes than the others."

"I hope we see each other again."

"Yes. Several years from now, probably. I'd love to meet your daughter," she says, playfully amused by my reaction. "And your son." She smiles.

"Oh, Thank you! Thank you for finding me and thank you so much for making this life a standout! Thank you for the hindsight!" There's a momentous feeling for me. Like anything can happen for Michael and me and the possibilities for our little family.

There we stand on the corner of the shiny new thoroughfare of Eighty-Sixth Street and the huddled past of York Avenue. The past and future that always run like rivers crossing for me seem to widen and then narrow like the lens on a sniper rifle. Widen and then narrow and then disperse as if I only see the present for once.

"You're welcome." Linda surprises me by stooping to hug me. "Are you a bit scared to go into uncharted territory?"

With the thought of more fully living my love? "No… no… this must be heaven!" I say and wipe tears away. "Thank you so much!"

"Again, you're welcome. This is what I do. Sometimes. And, Lily?"

"Yes?" I say, turning in her direction, but the tears are blurring my eyes or else there is some smoke or heat because it's like my eyes are trying to readjust just as I hear the words, "Tie your shoes."

# HARRY NILSSON WAS RIGHT

## SUSAN K. SWORDS

# July 1972

It was no real surprise that Elizabeth DeLiberto became a librarian. For most of her life, her best friends were books.

Growing up, her favorite companions included Nancy Drew, Trixie Belden, and Margaret Simon. Gradually, that intimate circle widened to include the Brontë Sisters, Jane Austen, Kurt Vonnegut, and Sylvia Plath. She sometimes hung out with nonfiction girls her age in her home town of Mount Gretna, PA, but the book buddies were always there for her. They were more loyal and patient, and they gave her solace, sustenance, and the courage to leave home.

Her parents, who thought she had the brains to shoot higher—maybe into the doctor/lawyer/physicist stratosphere—were disappointed. She was their only child, and they placed great expectations on her. Elizabeth wore the weight of those hopes like an uncomfortable, scratchy wool sweater.

She aced her grades in high school; the toughest test was waiting out those years before college. When the time came, Elizabeth chose the University of Texas in Austin because of its excellent library studies curriculum and because she could shed that wool sweater of expectations in the hot Lone Star State. After she'd obtained her master's degree, she accepted a job with the Austin city library. But her goal had always been to live and work in New York City; to become part of the vibrant, abundant arts scene in Manhattan.

At age twenty-five, she finally secured a librarian position with the New York Public Library's main branch. Elizabeth moved in with her widowed nonna—her paternal grandmother—in an apartment on the second floor of the Wellraven in Lenox Hill. This further upset her father, who maintained negative opinions of the city of his birth. He'd escaped to a mostly rural area, believing it was a better place to raise a family. This was another chasm-sized difference of opinion between them.

Elizabeth loved her job, and she loved where she worked. Even now, after two years, she caught her breath and beamed when she approached the imposing entrance of the New York Public Library's Stephen Schwarzman Building. Elizabeth adored old places, and the city was full of them. Her job took her to a landmark every day.

This July morning, her cheer faded quickly. She scowled at the percussive construction noise and dust at the site of a new building going up on West Forty-Second Street, across from the library. Through the maze of metal scaffolding, she could see cement mixers and other heavy equipment, and lots of men milling around and banging on things. Sometimes they yelled, either at each other or at the women who walked by.

"Hey, baby! Need a date tonight?" one of them called out. Four other workers laughed and watched.

Embarrassment and annoyance flushed red across Elizabeth's face. She flicked her eyes in their direction and then turned away in disgust.

Tom Giordano, the foreman, stepped out of the freight elevator just in time to see his crew laughing and making crude gestures. He couldn't see the face of the young woman walking past the site, but he knew by the set of her shoulders that the awful things they were saying were directed at her. He narrowed his eyes and shoved his wallet in the back pocket of his overalls.

"Knock it off," he snapped.

One of the guys rolled his eyes. "What's your problem, Tom? We're just having fun."

"Don't talk to women like that." Tom's voice was still terse and full of warning.

Charlie, one of the crew men, put his hands out in a "Whaddaya want from me?" gesture. "It's just a joke."

"Not to her." Tom stared back at their disbelieving faces. "We've been through this before. No jerks on this crew. I'm serious." He stepped over a jackhammer and strode toward Sixth Avenue.

Tom was in no mood to put up with his crew's bad behavior. He'd had a rough early commute from Bensonhurst, rising as usual before dawn. His grandfather's harsh, relentless cough still echoed in his ears; Nonno's bedroom was down the hall from Tom's and their small apartment amplified the painful sound. Angela, his sister, was taking Nonno to the doctor that afternoon. The news would probably not be good.

Elizabeth was also headed to Sixth Avenue. Her trip into work had been easy this morning; the subway ran on time and the crowds on the platform were sparse. She'd decided to walk to The Artful Codger luncheonette on Sixth Avenue across from Bryant Park for more coffee and maybe a donut. The heat had made her restless last night; she slept poorly most of the time now, without her grandmother there. She was craving caffeine and sugar.

The day ahead meant helping patrons on the phone and in person, and diving into research questions. She'd already started on a request from a fussy professor at Columbia University who wanted to know about the library's Dante resources. There were seven thousand listings for Dante in the NYPL catalog; she'd have to call him back to narrow down what he wanted. Elizabeth absently watched her plain walking flats take one step after another while thinking how difficult academics could be, so she didn't see the person rush in front of her until the luncheonette's door slammed in her face. She jumped and frowned.

There were three people in line; one of them was the guy with the dark blue T-shirt she'd just seen at the construction site. He was right in front of her, so she figured he was the one who'd carelessly let the door shut. Behind the counter, the owners, Simon and his wife Evelyn, were busy filling Styrofoam cups, spreading thick layers of cream cheese on bagels, and grabbing pastries from the glass case to keep things moving. The rich, comforting smell of fresh-brewed coffee was everywhere.

She took the spot behind Construction Guy and thought about whether she should say something. By now Elizabeth knew that unless she spoke up for herself, she would be swallowed up as surely as if she'd stepped into an open manhole. But she'd also learned that the city harbored a lot of strange, sometimes angry people. As she waited in line, she fidgeted with the choice of whether to defend herself for the second time this morning.

The construction worker was almost a foot taller than Elizabeth. She stared at the back of his head—a heavy mane of dark brown hair that was neatly shorn at the bottom and thick at the top—as if it would help her figure out whether she should speak up.

"Hey," Elizabeth said. He didn't respond. She coughed and repeated, "Hey," even louder. He finally turned around, and she realized he hadn't heard her because he was giving his order.

"What?" He frowned slightly.

"You were rude. You let the door slam in my face."

"Huh?" Now he looked confused. The owner, Simon, called out, "Is there a problem, hun?" There were now four more customers behind her.

Usually, Simon and Evelyn treated her like a daughter, but this was a busy morning. Evelyn lowered her head to gaze at Elizabeth over the top of her half-spectacles. Everyone else turned and stared at her expectantly. "Never mind," Elizabeth said, waving her hands and sighing. "It's cool."

The construction worker looked at her closely for a moment and then turned back to order four coffees, two crullers, and two jelly donuts. Elizabeth inspected her fingernails and silently cursed herself for bad timing. She might also have been distracted once she got a better look at the man who'd cut her off at the entrance. He had a nice profile: a strong but not obnoxious chin, a straight and not-too-big nose. His eyes, though...they were a velvety brown with a warmth that contradicted the scowl above them.

*His eyes are like root beer. I love root beer.*

The construction worker finally stepped away with a lingering sidelong glance at her. When she arrived at the counter, she saw that he'd taken the last sugar-cinnamon cruller she'd been craving. *Yeah, well, forget those eyes.*

She kept her communication short. Evelyn knew her coffee order—extra light, one sugar—and Simon pulled out the glazed donut shed chosen as an inferior alternative.

Elizabeth moved away from the counter to make room for the next customer and balanced her macramé tote on a table. She put the donut in the bag as carefully as she could so it wouldn't get crushed, then waved goodbye to Simon and Evelyn. She walked through Bryant Park, dodging a greasy paper bag that was stuck in the middle of the concrete path, until she found a place to sit.

A man was sleeping on the bench next to hers. He'd heard her approach and sat up off his pillow, which appeared to be a plastic bag stuffed with his belongings, and looked at Elizabeth with interest. There were a few older, grizzled, and hungover men who slept on the park's benches in the morning before the police could hustle them away, but she'd never seen this one before.

"Hello, miss," he said, waving. He was filthy, but his smile brightened his grimy face. Once upon a time, Elizabeth thought, he was probably quite handsome.

"Got any change you can give an old man?"

"No," she replied curtly, and kept her eyes on her coffee. He didn't say anything else but watched her for a few seconds; she could see him out of the corner of her eye. He fell back sideways on the bench and pulled his knees up toward his chest, sighing.

Elizabeth flexed her fingers around her coffee cup and thought for a moment. She dug into her tote until she found her lunch bag; then unzipped it and pulled out her sandwich. She walked the few steps over to his bench.

"Here," she said, thrusting out the sandwich. "Would you like this instead?"

The man opened his eyes. Elizabeth couldn't tell his age; his beard was dirty and stained, and the skin that showed above it was sunburned and blotched. His brilliant blue eyes, as beautiful as the sky this morning, widened.

"You bet your sweet bippy I would!"

Elizabeth obliged him with a chuckle. She wanted to believe he was harmless, even though common sense told her otherwise. Not for the first time, she wondered if she should eat her extra breakfast in the library's break room, but she loved the park and refused to be scared away from it.

"Thank you." He took her offering carefully, as if he was afraid she would pull it back like a cruel joke.

"You're welcome. I'm sure you must be hungry," she added.

"You can say that again." He unfolded the waxed paper and dug into the turkey sandwich. "You're nice, little lady." He squinted up at her, the bite he'd taken puffing out his left cheek. "Where you from?"

"Pennsylvania." She dug around in her tote bag again and handed him a tissue. He wiped his mouth.

"I thought you had to be from out of town. You're too sweet to be a New York girl. You have pretty eyes, too." He gave her another smile, and Elizabeth couldn't help but grin back. "You work in the library?"

"I do, and I'd better get going so I'm not late." She gathered up her trash from the bench.

"Sure. Don't let me keep you." He waved. "Hey, I'm Bluesy."

She hesitated, debating the safety—or wisdom—of telling this man her name. He looked at her expectantly, and it struck her that but for the grace of God, he could be an uncle or another relative whose life had collapsed.

"I'm Elizabeth," she finally blurted out. "Take care, Bluesy." She pulled her tote strap higher up on her shoulder and gave him a small wave.

The park's path put her back on Forty-Second Street, and Elizabeth bypassed the library's side door in favor of the grand main entrance on Fifth Avenue and the enormous lion statues on the front steps. *Patience and Fortitude*, she thought. *Patience and Fortitude.* They weren't just the statues' names; they'd become her motto, the words she thought of whenever she felt like New York City was getting the best of her.

Cranky, demanding bosses and library visitors; constant budget cuts; an overwhelming city that had a lot to offer while at the same time feeling out of reach; too much cold; too much heat; crowds, graffiti, garbage on the street; and a beautiful but empty apartment. That last one might sound good to anyone who wanted to live in New York, but it could be a painful reminder that this city didn't offer much comfort to young single women. The arts, the history, the food and music—there was as much of all that as she'd hoped, but she thought by now she'd have someone to share them with.

"Alone in her apartment she dwells/'Til the man of her dreams comes to break the spell." The words from the popular Paul McCartney song popped into her thoughts. She'd liked the song when it first came out but now the lyrics got on her nerves.

Elizabeth walked up to the library's third floor where the Public Catalog Room was located. Most weekdays and occasional weekends, she staffed the information desk there with Sheryl Iverson, another librarian who'd become her only real friend in New York. The best part of their work location was that it connected her to one of the most beautiful spaces in New York, if not the entire USA: the glorious Main Reading Room. Wider than a football field, it was capped by an enormous ceiling featuring canvases of sky and clouds encased in ornate panels. Elizabeth could lose a lot of time staring at that ceiling, always discovering a new piece of artwork among the elaborate scrolls and gilded features of the woodwork.

Sheryl hadn't arrived yet. Elizabeth stashed her tote under the desk and walked to the water cooler. There were few people here; it was a peaceful and profoundly meditative place at this hour. Elizabeth inhaled deeply, the scent of books old and new floating throughout both rooms. It was the most delicious aroma she knew of, far better than a donut or even a slice of New York pizza.

The morning mail already lay on her desk. Elizabeth began opening envelopes to see what the day's tasks would include. Letters from children, adults, educators, researchers, and even one from a desperate New York resident who needed help because her electricity was about to be shut off. Elizabeth frowned; the handwriting looked shaky, as if the author was elderly. She set that apart from the other correspondence so she could take care of it promptly.

When the clock ticked 8:35 a.m., Sheryl came running through the door to the Catalog Room, several bags dangling off her forearms. She gave Elizabeth a bright smile and waved as she made her way toward the desk.

"Anyone come in so far?" she asked, out of breath. That was code for whether their boss, the notoriously dour Beryl Orcutt, had been around to check on them.

"Nope. I think you just made it. How are you doing, Sheryl?"

"Fine, fine, just running late like always." She dropped her bags on the desk and plopped in her chair. "Whoo.

This commute will kill me, I swear. It's too damn hot to take the subway all the way from Harlem."

"You never look like it bothers you, though." Elizabeth twirled the pen in her hand and gave Sheryl a sidelong look. Her friend had an impeccable modern style that made Elizabeth feel like she was always draped in oilcloth. It was depressing to compare her plain yellow knit dress with Sheryl's brightly colored striped summer top, denim mini skirt, and white crushed patent leather boots. "How late were you out with William last night?"

"Now who said anything about last night?" Sheryl batted her eyelashes in exaggeration. "I'm talking about having a rough morning."

"Yeah. The two are kind of connected though, aren't they?"

Sheryl flattened her hand against the top of her chest with a look of mock horror. "You know I'm not that kind of girl."

Elizabeth made a show of softly clapping her hands. "Broadway's just north of here. I can get you a cab so you don't miss your audition."

"You're bad." Sheryl pulled out her chair and sat down in a way that made a statement. "And William is *fine*. Not that you asked."

"Oh, he's fine, all right. You're lucky." She waved an envelope with a letter in Sheryl's direction. "This poor woman needs help with her utilities, so I'd like to get her a list of resources. Here are other requests that were dropped off. Take what you want before Undercutt brings us more

296

work." A year ago, Orcutt had criticized Elizabeth's work on a project in front of the director of the Research Division—inaccurately, as it turned out. Soon after, she nicknamed the supervisor Undercutt.

They didn't see Beryl Orcutt for another hour. Elizabeth picked up her scent before she saw her. The librarian wore Intimate perfume that must have been a decade old; the fragrance was musty and unpleasant—not unlike its owner.

She had, by Elizabeth's estimation, exactly four suits, all of which fit poorly on her stocky build. Two of them always appeared in summer and the others were of thicker material, for cold weather. At least one suit in each group was gray. Today, Undercutt wore gray seersucker with a round-collar blouse that was the color of yellow apples. None of it complemented her sallow complexion.

"Girls," Orcutt said briskly. She held a clipboard against her substantial chest, the sleeve of her suit jacket pulled up enough to reveal a dull gold Bulova watch on her wrist. "Update me on your research requests. I have several more, and you'll also do cataloging today in addition to helping patrons. I trust you've coordinated your lunch periods so you are not out at the same time."

Elizabeth glanced at Sheryl, who stared back at her in a way that silently said, "You first." She cleared her throat and gave their supervisor a summary of the work she'd done on research requests from professors at Columbia and The City University of New York. She decided not to tell Undercutt about the letter she received from the elderly citizen. Her boss would instruct her not to make it a priority, a directive Elizabeth would only ignore.

The NYPL system was losing funding thanks to the city's serious fiscal situation and Elizabeth didn't want to give Undercutt any reason to fire her. What Undercutt didn't know wouldn't hurt either of them.

Their supervisor placed a stack of research requests on Elizabeth's desk and pointed to the one on top. "This professor has requested information on Hippolytus, and specifically, the town of Troezen. He needs at least a partial response today." She glanced pointedly at the copy of *Life* magazine that rested next to Elizabeth's purse.

Undercutt turned briskly and dropped another stack of requests on Sheryl's desk. "Are you putting together recommendations for that child's project on invertebrate zoology?"

Sheryl moved her pencil to the side and folded her hands primly on top of a book on her desk. "Yes, Ms. Orcutt. I've found three books so far that are appropriate for a seventh-grader. I'm searching through this one"—she spread one hand on a book—"and I've also reached out to the Smithsonian and the Museum of Natural History to see if they might have some suggestions."

Their supervisor pressed her lips together and tapped her index finger on the desk. "Very good, Miss Iverson." She never said Ms. even though Sheryl, who had a lot of pluck, used it in addressing her all the time.

Elizabeth had noticed that Undercutt often pointedly questioned Sheryl on her research methods. Elizabeth didn't always get the same level of scrutiny. She had an uncomfortable suspicion that their supervisor treated Sheryl differently because of her race. Sheryl often received thank-you notes and glowing reports that were sent to Undercutt and even the Director of Research for the help she'd provided to library visitors. She had to fight to get them mentioned in her evaluations.

Undercutt did something with a pen on the clipboard—checked off a few boxes, Elizabeth supposed—and turned and left on her Oxford heels.

Sheryl blew out a huge breath. "Man, she always acts like she does not trust us. Like we're going to screw up or slack off. I hate it. She knows how hard I work." She looked pained, and Elizabeth felt a pang of hurt for her friend. "I paid for a master's degree for what? To have a babysitter on the job? Hell, no."

Elizabeth reached over and squeezed Sheryl's hand. "This library would be lost without you. And if Undercutt didn't have us, she'd have to take care of these research requests and she's probably forgotten how to do that."

"You got that right." Sheryl pulled some pencils from the crowded cup on her desk. "Well, I'm not letting her get to me. It's time to get to work. What do you say?"

"I say my coffee's kicked in and I'm running to the women's room."

Sheryl waved her off, pulling out fresh index cards to catalog new arrivals. "See ya later."

Elizabeth loved the third-floor restrooms almost as much as she loved the Main Reading Room. The stalls and doors were a white marble that matched the look of the Schwarzman Building's exterior, with heavy oak doors on the stalls. One of the library's administrators, who probably should have been writing books instead of overseeing them, had come up with a brilliant way to discourage graffiti artists from defacing the men's and women's rooms. She'd covered the bulletin board between the two restrooms with a large piece of butcher-block paper. The board had a small grooved lip on the bottom, which held pens and pencils. Anyone passing through could write whatever they wanted; obscenities or slander were blacked out. Every so often, a staff person changed the paper and archived the filled sheet. Elizabeth looked forward to reading it every day.

The board was now crowded with song lyrics, poetry (some good, some awful), a few phone numbers, and drawings of the Eiffel Tower and what appeared to be an alien from another galaxy. In the lower left corner of the paper, the words "The Count of Monte Cristo" were scrawled in a bold hand.

Elizabeth smiled, a little bemused. *What could that mean?* "The Count of Monte Cristo" was a tale of aristocracy and revenge, as far as she knew; she hadn't read it. It struck her as unusual but significant. She tucked it away in her mental vault of odds and ends and entered the women's room.

Hours later, Elizabeth sat back in her chair and stretched her arms, her fingers interlaced. There were about ten people who'd needed assistance but were now ensconced in the Main Reading Room, looking through volumes, taking notes, or just paging through magazines. Streams of soft summer sunlight poured through the huge windows, filling the space.

"What are you doing for lunch?" Sheryl moved a stack of papers into the "Out" box.

"I brought in a sandwich but I gave it to one of the hoboes in the park. I guess I'll just go to The Artful Codger again."

"Eliza-*beth* !" Sheryl whirled around in her chair. "Why'd you do that?"

Elizabeth shrugged. "He was hungry."

Sheryl scrunched her face in disapproval. "You shouldn't waste your money."

"Bluesy needed it more than I do."

"*Bluesy*? What, are you feeding the ghost of Leadbelly?"

Elizabeth laughed. "I...doubt it? Anyway, I love Evelyn's cooking."

"She's definitely a queen of the kitchen. Even her meatloaf is amazing." Sheryl hummed at the thought.

Elizabeth smiled. "Thanks for helping me feel less guilty about blowing my money."

"I shouldn't have jumped on you like that. One of the best parts about living in New York is being able to eat anything, anytime."

"Speaking of which, do you mind if I go now? The Artful Codger always gets so crowded at lunch time."

"Sure, go ahead. I brought my lunch. I'll eat later." Sheryl popped open her stapler to refill it.

Elizabeth glanced with envy at the large sack near Sheryl's chair. Nonna used to send Elizabeth off to work with fat sandwiches of ham, salami, and provolone on good Italian bread, along with a salad and cannoli. Her own culinary inspiration consisted of slapping baloney or turkey on a few slices of white bread. She'd long vowed to eat better, but it was so much work, and she was always tired now...so, so tired, and forever missing her grandmother's kindness and cheer.

With a sigh, she slung her tote over her shoulder. "See you later." She skipped down the stairs to West Forty-Second Street and walked to the park.

"Hey, lady!" Someone was yelling, but that was typical. Elizabeth pulled her tote securely against her shoulder and held on to it, walking along the concrete path and kicking aside the trash that rolled around her feet.

"Hey, whatcha gonna do? Ignore me? Wait...it's Elizabeth, right?" A man stood up from a nearby bench, and Elizabeth recognized her new friend Bluesy.

"Oh, sorry. Hi." She managed a smile and waved.

He put his hands on his hips. "You okay?"

"Yes, fine. Just thinking about work." She kept moving, not inclined to encourage any conversation.

"Well, be careful now, missy. Somebody just overdosed over there." He waved his arm toward the corner of Forty-Second Street and Sixth Avenue.

Elizabeth blinked. "Thanks for the warning." She walked toward the intersection and heaved a sigh. *Why is my only friend in New York a bum?* That wasn't true, she quickly corrected herself. Sheryl was her friend, and a very caring one. But Sheryl had a whole life outside of the library, with a boyfriend and a large, loving family. It was a painfully stark contrast to Elizabeth's existence.

She wished she was brave enough to introduce herself to other tenants in her building. There were a few who seemed to be around her age: the guy she ran into in the stairwell with the mournful eyes; the couple on the eighth floor whose laughter was so lively it floated down the halls; the young woman who was living with the bookish guy on the thirteenth floor. While she'd always nodded hello to Elizabeth, there was a pensiveness about her eyes that kept Elizabeth from initiating a friendship. She held back, never wanting to impose.

The light at the intersection was red. Elizabeth stood at the back of a small crowd, next to an elderly couple. The husband sported polyester pants belted halfway up his chest, and his wife wore a dress, also polyester, and clutched a faux-leather purse.

Bits of the couple's conversation drifted over to Elizabeth. They held hands and talked to each other with the familiar loving ease that comes from many anniversaries. She grew ashamed for judging their awful outfits.

Elizabeth felt a slight breeze over her arms and legs, a cooling deliciousness that should have been impossible on a hot New York City day in a throng of people. She closed her eyes for a few seconds, enjoying the sensation, and opened them to see her coffee and donut nemesis from this morning, also waiting for the light. He was staring across the street, transfixed.

Oblivious to everything, Tom was focused on a small Victorian brick building whose faded upper floors still boasted their exquisite detail, two center bay windows with decorative floral trim. The ground level had been renovated to remove all historic details, with fake ceramic tiles installed below the display windows. The storefront windows were lined with ugly yellow cellophane to keep the sun from fading everything inside.

Tom sighed and stuck his hands in his pockets. Why were the best parts of this city doomed to destruction? And he was complicit, working for a construction company that tore down the old and built new and inferior.

The light changed, and Tom stepped back into the crosswalk. The crowd began to move and he caught a flash of a familiar face. The dark-haired woman who was in The Artful Codger this morning, who'd also walked past the construction site and been harassed by his crew. She glared at him in disgust, and at first Tom thought she was still angry that he got his coffee before she did. He gave one more glance at the Victorian structure across the street and finally realized the retail display was full of sexy bras and underwear, garter belts, and leopard-skin bustiers. It wasn't what he'd been staring at but when he turned back to find her and explain himself, she was gone.

Car horns rang out as Elizabeth hurried across the intersection and pulled open the luncheonette door. Evelyn waved hello and pointed toward Elizabeth's favorite table, a small two-seater by a window that looked out on Sixth Avenue. She liked to eat her lunch in peace, and read or people-watch.

Simon brought her silverware and a napkin. "What would you like, Elizabeth? Gonna start with some iced tea?" Through the din of the lunchtime crowd, Elizabeth could hear Rod Stewart singing "Maggie May." The Artful Codger always had its own soundtrack.

"Yes, please." Simon made great homemade iced tea. "Does Evelyn have any quiche today?"

"Yes, ma'am. Ham, broccoli, and cheddar. I'll bring ya a slice; take just a couple minutes." Simon shuffled back to the kitchen.

Four more people came in and sat at the one remaining free table. Simon placed the iced tea with a fresh lemon slice in front of Elizabeth, mumbled, "There y'are, sweetheart," and grabbed menus for the new customers.

An air conditioner above the doorway worked overtime to circulate cool air in the small, crowded room. The Artful Codger had a small counter with four seats next to the takeout space and six other tables, mostly with seating for two and one for four. When it was crowded in the summer, the temperature inside soared like a bird. The two ceiling fans that called out a continuous *whop whop whop* didn't help much. None of that mattered to Elizabeth, who loved their food, and when she admitted it, their company and attention. No one except Simon and Evelyn had fussed over her in a while.

"This'll put your day right, sweetie." Simon set down a plate with a slice of quiche, warm and fragrant from the cheese and a slight bit of nutmeg, and a small tossed salad. Elizabeth quickly put a forkful of the quiche in her mouth and hummed in ecstasy. She opened her eyes to a now-familiar sight.

Construction Guy was standing at the takeout counter. For the second time today, he'd invaded her space in her beloved luncheonette. He turned around with a frown that was slightly milder than this morning—more confusion than anger—and his gaze fixed on Elizabeth. She averted her eyes and got annoyed with herself for wondering what he thought of her.

*Who cares?* She carved out another forkful of quiche and ate it, remembering that she'd caught him staring at half-naked mannequins. He opened his mouth, but before any words came out, Simon arrived and handed him a large brown bag and a tall Styrofoam cup. "See something you like besides the food?" he asked, his bushy eyebrows arched.

The construction worker shook his head and mumbled something to Simon. He pulled a wallet out of a back pocket and handed over some cash. There were gray and white stains on his overalls and the T-shirt he wore underneath. His hands were coated with dust.

His arm muscles flexed as he returned the wallet to his back pocket. Though his overalls were baggy, Elizabeth could see that he filled them out rather nicely.

She ducked her head and took a long sip of iced tea through the straw. When she looked up, he was gone.

Elizabeth returned to the library along a path that brought her closer to West Fortieth Street. A hippie with a radio drifted past her, blasting the opening power riffs of Eric Clapton's "Layla." Empty bags, bottles, and bits of scrap paper blew around her feet, along with the occasional used syringe. It bothered Elizabeth that their presence no longer bothered her.

Still, there was beauty in this neighborhood, even if she had to search it out. She went out of her way on her walk back to the library just to pass the Bryant Park Hotel, a stunning black and gold Art Deco structure that dominated the block. Elizabeth had looked up the building's history as soon as she first saw it.

Elizabeth slowed her steps as she approached the park side of West Fortieth. Construction Guy was staring at the upper floors of the building, silently taking in its sleek style and Gothic touches. He looked enraptured, something that Elizabeth could understand. He was still holding on to his drink and the brown bag.

Suddenly feeling like she was interrupting an intimate moment, Elizabeth cut across the grassy square in the middle of the park, dodging people sitting on blankets in the hot sun. When her feet hit the sidewalk again, she glanced back but couldn't see him anymore.

The sky was almost entirely clear, a pretty blue patchwork above the tall buildings of Manhattan. A stray puffy cloud tickled the aquamarine expanse here and there. Elizabeth thought about heading uptown to Argosy's Bookstore after work, even though it meant getting really sweaty in her dress, when she remembered another book that had caught her attention earlier in the day.

And this one was available in the library.

Elizabeth hurried through the main entrance, ran up the marble stairs and headed straight to the bulletin board outside of her women's restroom (for that was how she thought of it). The same paper was still up. She studied the words *The Count of Monte Cristo*, returned to the Catalog Room, dropped her tote under the Information Desk, and told Sheryl she needed to check something in the fiction section.

Elizabeth couldn't say why she was so sure she'd find something in the book. She simply knew, with the strong instincts of a research librarian and her Italian genes, that the message was significant. The author of the scribble on the board wouldn't have put it there randomly.

She held the book firmly in her right hand and flipped through it quickly with her left; the pages purring as they passed. Sure enough, something that didn't belong there was wedged between two pages. It was a piece of lined paper, the kind you'd find in a composition tablet used in elementary schools. It was placed carefully inside the book; a bracket had been written on the paper that pointed to a section of a paragraph. As long as she kept the bottom of the paper lined up with the bottom of the book, she could pick out the quote accurately.

Elizabeth read:

*"Learning does not make one learned; there are those who have knowledge and those who have understanding. The first requires memory and the second, philosophy."*

She slowly closed the book and placed it on the table. "Learning does not make one learned..." Elizabeth had always thought so. In spite of her education, she felt she had miles to go before understanding people or cultures or any of the fundamentals of humanity, or even herself. She had tried to gain on those miles by moving from Pennsylvania to Texas and then New York, but she still had some distance in front of her.

Nonna had known so much about almost everything in spite of only having a sixth-grade education. She'd been a skilled seamstress for most of her life. Nonno, Elizabeth's grandfather, had been a plumber. Each was brilliant in what they knew about life, love, and family. Nonna in particular was a born philosopher with an inextinguishable love for people that Elizabeth deeply admired but despaired of attaining. She wished she'd asked her grandmother how she'd lived for so long in New York without becoming cynical.

Elizabeth took *The Count of Monte Cristo*, its colorful cover barely protected by yellowed cellophane, and returned it to its proper place on the shelf. She folded the paper, noted the page again, and wondered who'd stuck it in the book and wrote the title on the bulletin board. Those words were important enough to someone to quote. Why choose those lines out of millions of books? What was happening in their life that inspired them to stick an anonymous bookmark inside a classic novel? Who did they want to see it?

A plot like this could make a great story. Elizabeth's mind raced with possibilities. *The murder of a prominent beloved citizen remains unsolved. A detective who won't let the case get cold works on it relentlessly. He has the victim's small notebook but the sole entry is frustratingly meaningless. The detective finally figures out that the words are anagrams. He goes to the library where a dedicated and very smart research librarian figures it out, it's a book! She finds it in the library's archives. They fall in love.*

She sighed heavily, the soft sound fading below the room's curved arches and high ceiling. If she ever thought she'd find love in the stacks, she was gradually seeing how mistaken she was. It seemed the available men who came here were either eighty years old and complaining that no one knew how to write any more, or twenty-year-olds who checked out D. H. Lawrence and claimed they only read his books for the literature.

Anyone who caught Elizabeth's eye didn't seem interested in a woman of average height and average weight with long dark hair that wasn't curly enough to be radical or straight enough to be cool. She knew her eyes were her best feature; they were a striking blue, almost as dark as the blue in the American flag. Few seemed to notice.

She tapped her fingers against her right leg, lost in thought, as she headed back to her desk. For the rest of the afternoon, she helped patrons with research questions and located books on Polish recipes, calligraphy styles, and quantum physics. Elizabeth did her best to push the Dumas quote out of her mind, but the mystery of its provenance would not let her go. She couldn't shake the feeling that it was more than a message; it was someone reaching out, maybe looking for a kindred spirit.

The last thing she did before leaving her desk for the subway was check out *The Count of Monte Cristo*. Since she'd found the quote, she wanted this copy in her own hands and no one else's, at least until the book was due. She felt very protective of it.

Tired and sweaty, Elizabeth measured her progress through the lengthy four blocks between the Hunter College subway stop and the Wellraven by the storefronts she passed. One last left turn and she immediately saw home. It was hard to miss it. The Wellraven, an imposing structure on First Avenue between Sixty-Ninth and Seventieth streets, was deep orange, with black fire escapes that gave it the look of a Halloween decoration all year. She sometimes felt like she was living in a pumpkin. The halls of the building were even painted yellow like the inside of a hollowed-out jack-o'-lantern.

She climbed the stairs and turned the key to apartment 204. Laying her tote on a table right by the door, Elizabeth pushed her hair back and swiped at her face with the back of her hand. "Hi, Nonna!" she called out, as she did every night when she got home. The answering silence hung in the apartment, larger than the echo of her greeting. She walked through the kitchen and past the living room until she arrived at the small bedroom where she'd slept since arriving in New York. Nonna had been gone a few months, but Elizabeth didn't have the heart to move into the master bedroom. She thought it would be disrespectful, especially since she still felt Nonna's presence in the apartment.

She wandered into the bathroom to wash off the makeup and grit, then patted on some moisturizer. The face in the mirror, with its dark circles under bright eyes, stared back at her, looking tired and cranky. Elizabeth had a little over three hours before she'd have to go to sleep and do it all over again.

On her way back to the kitchen, Elizabeth passed the table that was filled with Nonna's cherished photos. She found the one of her grandparents at their wedding, then kissed her fingertips and gently placed them on Nonna's cheek in the picture. It was time to figure out what to do about dinner, a chore she hated because it really brought home that Nonna wasn't there.

She opened the ancient refrigerator and considered the possibilities: leftover fried flounder (greasy), soup (in this heat?), fruit (good), yogurt (maybe), bread (also maybe), peanut butter (to go with the second "maybe").

So it was peanut butter and jelly, with yogurt and a peach. Nonna would never approve, but Elizabeth couldn't bring herself to cook the homemade pasta that was still in the freezer.

She touched the necklace she always wore, with its two gold charms, a heart and a cross. The cross had been worn on the same chain, now on Elizabeth's neck, since Nonna herself was a little girl in Italy. The heart was a gift from Nonna for Elizabeth's sixteenth birthday. The simple beauty contradicted the irony that Nonna's own heart, which had always been golden in the best ways, decided on Memorial Day that it was time for her to join her late husband.

Elizabeth clutched the necklace fiercely, as if she could will it to bring Nonna back. She felt her grandmother's loss acutely again today after getting yet another letter from her father with job advertisements, not just for librarians, but for teachers, attorneys, and anything else he thought she should be doing with her life. Whenever this would happen, Nonna found a way to praise Elizabeth's qualities and choices without directly criticizing her son. Her grandmother always knew how to convey understanding, comfort, and the right words of advice.

She lit some candles that were on a hutch in the corner of the living room, then padded over in bare feet to the radio in the old oak entertainment unit. With a flip of the switch, the final chords of Harry Nilsson's "The Lord Must Be In New York City" floated up and around the apartment.

Nonna had loved that song. When she'd first heard Harry Nilsson mention the name of the Lord, she'd stopped chopping onions and listened, the knife raised in her hand, to the words.

"Who is singing?"

"That's the great Harry Nilsson. The song is called 'The Lord Must Be In New York City.'"

"He's right. The Lord is in New York City. We just don't always let ourselves see Him," Nonna had declared.

"You always think positive, Nonna."

"Well, why not? God wants us to have joy in our hearts." She took the few steps to where Elizabeth was sitting, her hands fisted on her waist, the knife sticking out at an angle. "And love. God wants us to have love."

Elizabeth knew where this conversation was going. She went back to her reading but addressed her grandmother. "I know, Nonna. Someday, right?" *Though not in this big, cold city. At least, not for me.*

"That's right." It might have been the only time that her grandmother, who was tiny but wide and usually unintimidating, looked fierce. "You must believe it will happen, *il mio bambino.*"

*It won't.* "Yes, Nonna," she'd replied dutifully.

Her grandmother had likely picked up on the doubt in Elizabeth's voice but didn't push it any further.

Alone now, Elizabeth walked to the space on the bookshelf that Nonna had cleared for her granddaughter's albums. Her fingers touched the spines of the album covers, drifting past The Beatles, The Stones, Elton John,

Bread, Aretha Franklin, and Led Zeppelin. She stopped at the "Harry" album and pulled it out, placing the record on the stereo spindle and switching the knob to Play.

The album dropped to the turntable. Elizabeth carefully picked up the tonearm and moved it to the song she wanted. The tinkling banjo opening was a memory in itself; when Harry Nilsson started singing, she found herself lost in thoughts of Nonna and, further back, her family, crowded into this apartment for the holidays.

When the song was over, she played it again. The memories it inspired warmed her, even though Elizabeth now had even less trust that the Lord was in New York City. She didn't think the Lord was anywhere near her, not after He took her grandmother away.

"Don't give up. Have faith, my Elisabetta."

The familiar sweet voice with its Italian accent was just loud enough to be real. A warm vibration skimmed across Elizabeth's skin and thrummed through her bones. Like a tuning fork, the feeling faded quickly.

Elizabeth whirled around, the flames of the candle bending slightly from her motion. On the wall behind the candles, a shadow had formed. A female shape with an outline of curls at the top of what was clearly a head. In a flash it was gone; the only shadows were faint forms thrown by the flames.

She shook her head. "Thanks for the encouragement. But, Nonna, quit spooking me."

She checked the old kitchen clock. It was still early enough to do something inspired, something productive.

Elizabeth pulled out her old typewriter, rolled in a clean sheet of paper, and tried to write. She was working on a novel about a group of women who traveled by horseback through Appalachia during the Great Depression to bring books to children and families who had no access to a library. The true story fascinated her, and she wanted to craft a bigger story for them.

She typed a few paragraphs and then hit a wall. Elizabeth felt constantly distracted, jumping in and out of her chair to get another drink, rummaging through the refrigerator in search of more fruit, turning on the radio and changing the station; and mostly wandering back to her bookcase to look at successfully published authors. Finally, she gave up on writing. She plopped down in the overstuffed armchair to read someone else's fiction.

Elizabeth picked up a book from the small table next to her chair. She turned on the floor lamp with the elaborate fabric and fringe shade—a furnishing her grandmother loved but Elizabeth thought hideous—and continued reading "The Brothers Karamazov."

She came across a line that, among others in the book, was singular in its truth and relevance. Reverently, Elizabeth brushed her fingers against the words on the page. Inspired by today's unusual message in a novel, she knew what to do with them. She closed the book, tucked it into her tote, and went to bed, where she slept better than she had in many nights.

The next morning, no one cut her off as she walked through the door of The Artful Codger. She took her time at the counter seat, enjoying her coffee and donut, but there was no sign of the brown-haired, brown-eyed construction worker.

Elizabeth glanced at her watch and realized she was running out of time to complete a special errand before work. There wasn't much traffic on Sixth Avenue, so Elizabeth crossed against the light and practically ran to the library. She sped up the stairs to her desk, tore off a strip of paper from a notepad, then grabbed her favorite fat green marker and raced to the bulletin board in the restroom hallway.

The same paper covered the board, and while there were many more scrawls, drawings, and messages on it, there was still room next to the title "The Count of Monte Cristo." Elizabeth pulled the cap off the marker and wrote "The Brothers Karamazov." She found the book in the fiction section, flipped to the right page, and drew a bracket on the paper to line up with the quote.

*The mystery of human existence lies not in just staying alive, but in finding something to live for.*

She stared at the words she'd chosen, suddenly feeling exposed and vulnerable, as if she'd put herself out there for the entire city to see, even though, in theory, she'd only created something for an audience of one, a library patron who had to use the restroom. Overriding all that was a deep curiosity over the response she'd get, and—if she cared to admit it—the need to connect.

Elizabeth slipped the book back in its proper place on the shelf. She cleared her throat and straightened the ID badge that was pinned to her blouse.

Sheryl had arrived and was in her chair when Elizabeth returned. "Another bathroom break already? You *are* drinking too much coffee."

Elizabeth laughed. "The bathroom is even more peaceful than the rest of the library, quiet as it's supposed to be. Good morning." She slid several forms across the desk. "Here. Have some more research requests."

For the next hour, her mind kept wandering. *How long do I wait to check the book? It would be stupid to look now. I just wrote the title on the board. Plus, I have to research Broadway history for a theater buff.*

*Two days,* she decided. She would wait two days. She also bargained with herself that she couldn't look for anything until she finished her assignments and typed up catalog cards for new book acquisitions.

Forty-eight hours later, Sheryl was deep in conversation on the phone when Elizabeth popped out of her seat. She grabbed her tote and motioned that she'd be right back.

First, she made a return visit to the library's copy of *The Brothers Karamazov*. The cover crinkled as she flipped through the pages to find where she'd left the quote.

In the place of her handwritten note was another piece of paper with a smiley face drawn on it.

She yanked the paper out and slammed the book shut. It was all Elizabeth could do to keep from running. There were men and women in the enormous room, some of them working at desks and others drifting along the shelves. For the first time she could recall, they irritated her.

*Don't these people have something else to do? Don't they work, or have children to take care of? Or another hobby?*

She raced across the landing at the top of the Forty-Second Street stairway and turned left to the restrooms. The paper hadn't been changed. Squeezed into the corner, written in the same hand as the first title, was *God Bless You, Mr. Rosewater.*

She turned and ran back to the Catalog Room, well aware that she looked like a wind-up toy whose spring had sprung, when an elderly gentleman in a three-piece suit suddenly appeared in front of her. Elizabeth slowed down and gave him a polite smile, receiving a look in return that clearly said "Young people today!" for her trouble.

Elizabeth desperately wanted to make another trip to the fiction section. She checked her watch; she'd only been gone a few minutes. Sheryl was at the Information Desk, now preoccupied with work. Elizabeth couldn't stay away too long or Sheryl would get stuck answering the phone or helping patrons. Or worse, Sheryl would have to cover if Orcutt came by. She couldn't do that to her dear friend.

At noon, Elizabeth told Sheryl she needed to check on a book for a patron. *It's almost true,* she thought, heading

319

straight to the end of the alphabet in the fiction section. She quickly grabbed the Vonnegut book and opened it, fanning through the pages until she found a small white note. Instead of reading it there, she closed the book, tucked the book under her arm, and walked calmly back to her desk.

Sheryl was helping a child when Elizabeth returned. There were no other patrons at the Information Desk, which was just as well, Elizabeth couldn't wait another moment. She opened to the pages bookmarked by the strip of paper. It pointed to a quote on page 128.

*Hello babies. Welcome to Earth. It's hot in the summer and cold in the winter. It's round and wet and crowded. At the outside, babies, you've got about a hundred years here. There's only one rule that I know of, babies—God damn it, you've got to be kind.*

There was an asterisk after the word "winter." At the bottom of the paper, the mysterious note-leaver had marked another asterisk with the question, *What's your favorite season?*

Elizabeth felt the thread between her and her anonymous correspondent thicken into something more substantial, like a rope. Or better yet, a cord...a braided cord of warm gold. This man—her instincts also made her sure it was a man—wanted to know more about her. It was odd but also comforting that someone she didn't even know would ask about her favorite season. He knew she was the one person who had cared enough to respond to the quotes, and he wanted to reach out a little bit more.

She held the note in her hand and read the quote from the book in a soft voice, an intimate smile playing around her lips. Sheryl glanced over when they were alone again.

"Hey. Where'd you go?" She tilted her head and looked pointedly at the cover of the book.

Elizabeth blushed. "Sorry. I was in the circulating stacks and I saw this book and I just felt...well, like I had to read it again. I love it." She turned it face-down on top of some magazines and smoothed her hair behind her ears.

Sheryl *hmm'd* and gave her a sharp look. "If you say so." She must have sensed that Elizabeth wasn't ready to talk. She made a show of straightening up the papers on her desk, respecting the quiet between them.

When the day was over, Elizabeth walked to a gift shop near the West Forty-Second Street subway station to pick up more candles for the apartment. The construction site across from the library was still a mess. She had to follow a redirected path into the street with barricades set up haphazardly, as if whoever did it really didn't care whether pedestrians lived or died. It was like walking through a gauntlet, and it made Elizabeth feel depressed. New York was a city of inconveniences sometimes. She sighed and stepped off the sidewalk and into the street.

A child's sweet giggle brought her out of her funk. Ahead was a young mother with a stroller. Her little boy was standing in front of a construction worker who'd just placed his hard hat on the little boy's head. The toddler screamed in delight, and the construction worker threw his head back and laughed, his hands on his hips. It was a beautiful conversation without words.

Elizabeth slowed her walk. The laughing man was Construction Guy, the one from The Artful Codger who stared at both sexy mannequins and Art Deco buildings. He looked so different with a big smile that she almost didn't recognize him.

Right at that moment, he looked over and saw her. His grin grew smaller, but in a shy way. Hesitantly, he lifted his left hand in a greeting.

Elizabeth blushed and looked away. When she glanced back up, he was watching her, waiting for whatever reaction she was going to give him. She waved back and smiled and was surprised to feel it was genuine.

He turned his attention back to the woman and her child. The mother was struggling to get the little boy back in the stroller, and the construction worker held it still for her.

Elizabeth was nearly in front of them. She wondered if they were related. As in, maybe, married.

"You're so sweet to talk to him and let him wear your helmet. I swear most construction workers are such jerks but you're so cool. My husband is going to love hearing about this." The mom hefted a diaper bag over her shoulder, chattering away.

He replied in a low voice that Elizabeth couldn't hear. She could, however, feel him watching her as she passed directly in front of them, her eyes cautiously directed down at the street.

Tom regarded the young woman, his own gaze fixated on her pretty face, framed by hair that had just enough curl. Her smile, sweet and almost bashful, transformed her countenance. Still, she looked tired, he thought; he could see darkness under her eyes even from this distance. Somehow that made her more appealing. He was half listening to the mother of the baby but it didn't stop him from wondering if the same things kept the young woman up at night that sometimes broke into his own sleep.

By the time the woman and child had left, the young woman who shared his love of coffee was gone, out of sight. Tom had lost his chance to explain himself. He'd seen her at The Artful Codger after she noticed him staring at a store with racy lingerie, but he didn't have the nerve to tell her that he was taking in the details of the Victorian architecture. *What's worse, having her think I'm a creep or a nerd?* Shaking his head, he went to the construction trailer to put away his hard hat.

That evening, Elizabeth stared intensely at the rows of books that had come with her when she moved to the Wellraven. It was her turn to leave a quote, and she wanted to follow the theme that was emerging even if she wasn't completely sure what it was. Something personal, it would seem. And she also wanted to impress.

She moved her fingers slowly along the spines and stopped at Carson McCullers. She took "The Heart Is A Lonely Hunter" off the shelf and began quickly thumbing through the hardback until she found what she wanted. Elizabeth stuck her index finger into the book to hold the page and grabbed a notepad from the kitchen table. She quickly scribbled a bracket on a piece of paper, adding an asterisk and the words, *Autumn. And you?* at the bottom. It went safely into her tote, where it accompanied her to work the next day.

Once she got to the library in the morning, Elizabeth began her work promptly on time even though she was wriggling with impatience on the inside. When Sheryl returned from lunch, Elizabeth went straight to the Reading Room, pulled "The Heart Is A Lonely Hunter" off the shelf, placed the strip of paper on the right page, carefully aligned the bracket alongside the words *All we can do is go around telling the truth*, left some of the paper sticking out of the top of the book, and then slid the novel back into place. She paid a visit to the restrooms and wrote the McCullers title on the board.

A couple of days passed, and the note had disappeared, but there were no new messages on the board—at least, no new ones that she was interested in. She genuinely didn't care that someone thought Donny Osmond should be incarcerated for impersonating a singer. (Only a regular at the New York Library would phrase it like that.) When the activity had slowed down at the Information Desk, she told Sheryl she was going to the ladies' room. Sheryl gave her that look—the one that said, "Again?"—and went back to her work.

Were there new messages? Had the bulletin board been refreshed? Elizabeth could feel the nerves coiling in her stomach. This was getting to be a little obsessive. A sheet of butcher block paper had become a focal point in her life. Elizabeth didn't care, even though she probably should. She was worried she'd lose one of the most meaningful connections she had right now.

She ran around the corner and stopped in front of the board. The paper hadn't been changed. In the lower left hand corner, cramped under some scribbled lyrics from Eric Burdon's "Spill the Wine," was the legendary title "To Kill a Mockingbird," written in the same sure hand she'd come to recognize.

Her heart lightened. This was one of her favorite books.

Elizabeth turned and ran to the Main Reading Room. She made a quick dash to the "L" section. The black cover with the white bold title "To Kill a Mockingbird" was easy enough to find. Elizabeth slid it off the shelf and looked at the top of the book. A narrow strip of paper peeked out of the pages.

She repositioned the book in her hands and opened to page thirty-two, which the paper had bookmarked. As with the previous novels, an expertly drawn bracket marked the location of the quote. She skimmed the print with the tips of her fingers.

*You never really understand a person until you consider things from his point of view…Until you climb inside of his skin and walk around in it.* Further down on the strip of paper were the words, *Autumn for me too.*

Elizabeth read it aloud to herself in a soft voice. Her heart filled with a rush of emotions. Understanding, empathy, and curiosity over what might have inspired her book friend to choose this specific passage. That last one was a familiar feeling; she was becoming more and more consumed with finding out who he was and why he chose the quotes he did from these certain books. What was he trying to say?

*Does he wonder the same about me?* And would she ever find out? *Maybe he's waiting until fall to reveal himself?*

Elizabeth momentarily fantasized about hiding and taking a Polaroid picture of her correspondent, if she was lucky enough to catch him. But she didn't want his photo. She wanted to talk to him.

*Do I?* What would she say? "I know you but I don't know you; I know how you think without having ever met you; I'm pretty sure I understand you like we've known each other all our lives even though, clearly, we haven't"? How could she communicate such full and heartfelt thoughts to someone when she met his eyes for the first time?

*Easy, chick. You're getting way ahead of yourself.* She held the paper in her hand as carefully as if it was an artifact and returned to the Information Desk.

If looks could be dry, Sheryl's stare would have put the Sahara to shame. One perfect eyebrow was arched, her lovely brown eyes a mixture of amusement and exasperation. Elizabeth started to say something, but Sheryl put her hand up, closed her eyes, and turned her head away.

"Don't say anything unless it's the truth. Until you're ready to tell me, I don't want to hear it."

Elizabeth winced. "It's...kind of confusing." Then added, unnecessarily, "Even to me." *If I say it all out loud, I'm worried that might make it disappear. And how would I even explain it without sounding insane?*

Sheryl shrugged. "I know something is going on. It's your business." She stepped out of her chair and reached under the desk to grab her purse. "For now, I'm going out for lunch." She leaned in conspiratorially. "I guess I can tell you. I might stop at Merry Go Round. My big secret is...I love clothes and I like to shop." She smoothed her skirt for emphasis.

Elizabeth shoved her friend away, laughing. "Get out of here, you." Once Sheryl was gone, she wrote "To Kill a Mockingbird" on the paper, added the page number, and tucked it in a sachet pouch with the rest of the notes she'd kept from her correspondent.

It took a few days before she could settle on her next book choice. In the meantime, she answered a number of letters and helped teenagers with the card catalog as part of the summer program. While pointing out some of the fiction listings and where to find them, she noticed John Steinbeck's name and the titles of his novels. She thought about one of them she'd read but didn't own and quickly added it to her mental list of possibilities.

Sheryl was ready to leave at 5:30 p.m. and looked at Elizabeth quizzically. Elizabeth waved her off and said she had a couple of envelopes to address so she could add them to the morning mail pickup. She grabbed an index card and walked through the entrance to the Main Reading Room. When she found the Steinbeck section, she took one book off the shelf and drew an elegant, meandering half-circle on the card. Carefully, she placed it so it lined up with the words, *Maybe ever'body in the whole damn world is scared of each other.* On her way to the subway for the journey back to the Wellraven, she stopped at the board outside the restroom, pulled out her green marker, and wrote "*Of Mice and Men.*"

The next day, someone had changed the paper on the bulletin board.

Elizabeth almost cried when she saw the empty sheet. The thought that she might have missed something, or worse, that her fiction friend might have missed her last book and quote, gutted her.

"Good morning, Miss DeLiberto." The tone was hardly a greeting in spite of the words. That unpleasant throaty voice could only belong to one person.

"Oh. Hello, Miss Orcutt." Elizabeth wanted to make a run for the lavatory but it was too late.

"Whatever are you staring at?" Orcutt looked from Elizabeth to the board and back.

"Uh, well, I was thinking that it's a great idea to have this paper here that people can write on so they don't ruin the bathrooms with graffiti." It was an accurate response, even if the thought was weeks old.

"Humph." Orcutt glared at her. "Admiring it is not a day-long process. I'm sure you can continue to support the library in other ways, such as returning to your work."

"Of course." Elizabeth managed a small smile and headed back to her desk.

Sheryl glanced at Elizabeth when she returned, then looked again. "You look like you've seen a ghost. You okay?"

"I ran into Undercutt. By the restrooms, of all places. She told me to get back to work."

"That's worse than a ghost. The only thing surprising about that is, she pees like a human being."

Elizabeth laughed so hard she drew stares from some of the patrons. She coughed and hid her mouth with her hand, and giggled some more.

Before leaving for the day, she went to the Reading Room and found "Of Mice and Men." The book was in its place on the shelf; the paper she'd stuck inside on the page with the quote was missing.

Elizabeth exhaled a huge breath. Her note had been found. It was in the right hands.

She was off the next day, which was Thursday; both she and Sheryl were on the schedule to work Friday and Saturday that week. She scrubbed the apartment, returning to her bedroom every so often to stand in front of the window fan and cool off. She called her parents to reassure them that she was safe and alive in New York City before showering and roaming restlessly around the apartment, trying to figure out what to do with herself. If she was in

Pennsylvania, she'd get in a car and drive. In New York, it wasn't that easy.

She could have walked to Central Park, which was a manageable distance from the Wellraven. But the park could be a dangerous place, even in daylight. She would get jealous when Nonna talked about going to the park in the late 1930s with her girlfriends or Nonno. It was beautiful then, its landscape well cared for and its pathways more safe. Now it was another victim of the city's desperate financial straits. Park maintenance seemed barely an afterthought, and she didn't have much faith in the Parks Department security budget either. Instead, she took a stroll around her neighborhood, bought ice cream at a bodega, and then curled up in her favorite chair to finally read "The Count of Monte Cristo," the book that started it all.

Elizabeth slept fretfully but managed to wake early enough for a coffee stop before work. Simon seemed to see she was out of sorts; he even waited patiently when Elizabeth dropped her tote and everything spilled out while she was looking for her wallet. Bryant Park was almost deserted, so she sat on a bench facing Forty-Second Street and watched the construction. A large crane had been brought on site, and men were crawling like ants around the ground level and through the girders. Elizabeth thought she saw the dark-haired construction worker, but he disappeared into the guts of the project before she could be sure. She walked to the main entrance, humming The Beatles' "Another Day."

By lunchtime, the library was full of tourists, families, researchers, and writers who secured their space in the farthest corners of the Main Reading Room. They kept Elizabeth and Sheryl busy with questions, directions, and other needs librarians were expected to meet.

At least Undercutt wasn't around. *Probably cutting up chum at the New York Aquarium, just for practice.* Elizabeth shuddered.

It was hours before either of them could take a break. The crowd had thinned out, and she told Sheryl she had to run to the restroom.

For once, she was telling the truth, she actually needed to get to the women's room so badly that she'd forgotten about the bulletin board.

But someone hadn't forgotten about her. Elizabeth found a new message in the usual space in the lower left corner: *A Tree Grows in Brooklyn.*

Above the book title, an anonymous interloper had written, *It's dead now.* She ignored the cynical comment and headed back. Sheryl was at the desk answering questions about another branch of the library and didn't see Elizabeth sneak into the Reading Room. Elizabeth zipped around the throngs of people and made her way over to the "S" shelves to find Betty Smith.

*He's coming up with so many of my favorite books.* Francie Nolan was another one of Elizabeth's childhood book friends. She'd aspired to Francie's kindness, courage, and endurance. Since moving to New York, she thought she had a better idea of what it took for Francie and her family to survive, let alone thrive. So the idea that her book communicator, her fellow quote lover, her novel friend, would choose this classic made Elizabeth tremble.

She saw a narrow strip of paper sticking out of the book. By now, the mode was familiar, the paper bookmarked a page; a precise bracket pointed to a quote. *Let me be something every minute of every hour of my life...And when I sleep, let me dream all the time so that not one little piece of living is ever lost.*

Tears again crept into her eyes, and she thought they would spill over right there in the middle of the enormous room.

A smaller piece of writing toward the bottom caught her attention. *I feel this way a lot.*

She slumped into a chair. How to even respond? Elizabeth quickly thought of a quote from Dicken's "Great Expectations." *We need never be ashamed of our tears.* That would be the book and quote she would respond with. And she would add her own note at the bottom: *So do I.*

The great clock in the Reading Room said 11:45 a.m. Sheryl was at her post alone. Elizabeth ran back to the Information Desk, dodging adults and teenagers, and was welcomed by a glare from Sheryl, who was trying to manage a crowd of patrons on her own.

An elderly couple with matching Foster Grant shades thanked Sheryl and stepped away from the desk. "Where have you been?" she hissed. "This place is insane!"

"I know, I know, I'm so sorry!" Elizabeth babbled. She wiped at the tears in her eyes.

Sheryl's eyes grew wide. "What's happened? Elizabeth, are you okay?"

"I am. I swear I am, and I promise I'll tell you everything, but not now. There are too many people here."

"Okay, whatever you say. But please get back here." Sheryl made a motion with her hand to indicate that Elizabeth needed to return to her usual position behind the desk. Elizabeth took her seat and Sheryl spoke up again.

"Hey, weren't you wearing your necklace this morning? Where is it?"

Elizabeth's hand swiftly went to her neck. "Oh, my God! It must have fallen off! Oh, hell, it could be anywhere..." She frantically tried to retrace her many steps. The Artful Codger, the restroom, the Main Reading Room, the photo reproduction center, the stacks in the basement. There were people in line at the desk, so she couldn't get away right now. Distracted and upset, Elizabeth did her best to help everyone until she could search for the necklace with Nonna's charms. Her heart was in her throat the entire time.

By 1:00 p.m., the Artful Codger was still packed with the usual lunch crowd. As Tom waited for his order of sandwiches, he shifted his weight and shuffled his feet. He felt a slight nudge along the side of his left foot and looked down.

A fat green marker was nestled against his shoe.

He picked it up and looked at it curiously. When he opened the top, he saw that the marker was the color of shamrocks.

Simon came back to the counter then and put down the bag of sandwiches. He noticed Tom staring at the marker.

"Oh, that belongs to Elizabeth, that nice librarian. She's always losing things. She was here this morning." Simon pointed in the direction of Bryant Park. "She works in the New York Library. The Schwarzman Building, right across the street."

*Of course! She's a librarian!*

Tom threw money on the counter, grabbed the bag, and bolted out the door. He raced across Sixth Avenue, just barely making the green light. He stopped at the edge of the park, as still as one of the lion statues that guarded the front of the library. He palmed the heavy marker with his hand in his pocket. Could this belong to the woman who was responding in green to his book quote messages? For all the weeks he'd wanted to track her down, he suddenly felt hesitant, unsure of whether he should. It could be wonderful or it could be a disaster, the end of a lovely fantasy that was maybe better unrealized.

He'd always felt certain that a woman was his messaging partner. It wasn't so much the writing, which was done in a strong hand that could have been made by anyone. Something came through the quotes which reflected a feminine sensibility that twinned to his thoughts and ideas on what books to choose. Of this, he was sure.

But was this the time and place? He looked in the paper bag. His break was almost over, and worse, there would be three guys on his crew that were probably wondering where he'd gone with their food and were pretty ticked off about it.

He decided that as foreman, he was going to take some liberties and extend his lunch hour. Considering the nine- and ten-hour days he was putting in to help create the Grace Building, he figured he was entitled.

Across the street, his coworker Charlie saw him, and, more importantly, saw the brown bag. He screamed at Tom, mostly questions like "Where you going?" and "Where's my sandwich?" but Tom just shrugged. Charlie's language got progressively worse but Tom ignored him.

He rounded the corner at Fifth Avenue and strode toward the main entrance.

Tom held the bag in his large hand and stared at the ground, watching the toes of his heavy boots cover the broad sidewalk. Once again, he noticed something near his foot. He just managed to avoid stepping on a delicate gold chain with two charms. Someone had lost it, and it had fallen halfway through a crack in the pavement.

He carefully picked it up and quickly canvassed the faces of people around him, thinking that the owner might be looking for it. No one seemed distraught over a missing necklace; they barely gave him a glance and moved along to wherever their business took them. He lifted his eyes toward the doors at the top of the long white stairs of the New York Public Library. He closed his fist over the necklace and ran up the steps.

A middle-aged man wearing a colorful madras shirt sat at the first floor Guest Information desk. To the right of the desk was a large box with the solemn words "Lost and Found." Rather than putting the necklace in the box, Tom approached the man, whose bald head reflected the light from a large white fixture above him.

"Can I help you?" He looked up from the brochures he was sorting. The name George was printed in heavy black letters on his name tag.

"I found this outside, and I wondered if someone in the library might have dropped it." Tom opened his palm and the necklace rained down, anchored on one end by the crucifix and heart charms and the other by his thumb and index finger.

George peered closely at the necklace, his thick lenses magnifying his eyes. "Actually, I know who this belongs to." He looked up at Tom and smiled. "She's one of our research librarians. I can hold it for her or you can give it to her if you'd like. She's on the third floor." He offered Tom a small manila envelope for the necklace.

"I'll bring it to her. I have something I'd reserved in the History Division." If the necklace didn't belong to the right woman, Tom would check on whether the photo he'd requested of the old Stern Brothers Department Store was ready. The structure had been demolished for the construction of the W. R. Grace Building—the very site across the street where he should be back at work.

A pair of shoes clattered down the North stairway. The person wearing the shoes called out, "Hey George, did someone turn in my—"

Tom was holding the necklace. George was holding the envelope. They both turned at the same time to see Elizabeth stop dead on the last step.

"Oh." She moved forward and then halted again. "Hi."

Tom froze where he was standing. A thick, dark chestnut lock of hair had fallen over his forehead. He was suddenly conscious of his scruffy appearance and the coating of construction dust and debris on his clothing.

"Hi," he replied.

"This gentleman found this necklace. I believe it's yours?" George looked back and forth at the two of them with some amusement.

"It is," she replied, still gazing at Tom. *His eyes really are the color of root beer.* Those eyes widened a little as they stared back at her.

"Is this yours too?" He reached into his overalls pocket and pulled out the marker.

Elizabeth's hand flew up to her mouth. "Thanks. I've also been looking for that."

"You're welcome. The necklace looks special. And the marker seems…handy." He smiled, but his gaze grew more intense. "I'm Tom Giordano, by the way."

"I'm Elizabeth DeLiberto." She took the marker from his outstretched hand. "Thank you again, Tom. I'd hate not being able to write in green."

"I'd miss it too." His lips twitched mischievously. "Hey, can you…" Tom motioned toward the doors with his thumb. "Can we go outside for a moment?"

Elizabeth motioned for him to lead the way. She guessed, correctly, that he thought it would be more private to talk in the middle of a crowd of strangers than with one of her colleagues sitting right there. They walked to the bottom of the front steps and stood near Patience the lion.

They didn't say anything at first. Elizabeth looked quizzically from the bag in his hands back to his eyes, and Tom suddenly remembered that he still had his crew's lunch.

He held out his index fingers like six-shooters. "Just a minute," he said, before sprinting off across Forty-Second Street. Charlie was setting up construction horses when Tom shouted to him and tossed him the bag before he could start another argument. Tom ran back to where Elizabeth was waiting.

"Listen," he said, taking a step closer to her. Instead of reflexively backing away, Elizabeth stood in place. His nearness brought scents of clean sweat, freshly washed overalls, and something that was failing to keep his thick hair in place. It was a harmonious fragrance, masculine yet soothing. She inhaled and tried to focus on his words.

"Would you get in trouble if you left the library for a while? Now? To talk?"

Elizabeth eyed him thoughtfully and then stepped past him to the phone booth on the corner. She picked up the telephone and held out her hand.

"Do you have a dime?"

He dug into his pocket and handed one over. Elizabeth dropped it in the slot and dialed, still aware of his closeness, his scent, and his patient gaze as he waited for her to make plain what she was doing.

"Hey, Sheryl. It's Elizabeth. Um, I'm leaving work for a while. No, I'm not crazy. Yes, I'm okay. It's…I'm going to my grandmother's lawyer's office. I have to talk to him about her estate. Now. He just called me. At least, that's what I'm going to tell Orcutt." She glanced furtively at Tom. "You know that bulletin board by the restrooms? Turns out, I found something important there. I'll explain it all as soon as I can. I'll be back later. Can you transfer me to Orcutt's line?"

She looked again at Tom, who was now smiling. Elizabeth grinned back at him.

She prayed Undercutt was out patrolling the halls. *Please don't be there. Please don't be there. Please don't be there.* The line rang and rang, and Elizabeth's fingers drummed nervously on the silver coil that connected the handset to the box.

"Miss Orcutt's line." An assistant had picked up. It was all Elizabeth could do to keep from yelling out victory. The angels of the library must have heard, or maybe it was Patience and Fortitude working their magic. She relayed the lie, apologized profusely, and asked the assistant to tell Orcutt that she would check in with her when she returned.

She hoped the assistant hadn't noticed the sounds of car horns and jackhammer drills in the background.

Elizabeth hung up the phone, leaving her hand there for an extra few seconds. *Now what?* She turned to face Tom.

He was broadly grinning now, revealing creases around his mouth and eyes that were like a ripple effect of his smile. It relaxed his entire expression, though he didn't look lighter but deeper, like his happiness extended within as much as without. Elizabeth liked that.

"So…let's go somewhere and sit, maybe?" He bit his lower lip while his eyes danced. "I know a place at the corner of Sixth and Forty-Second. Good food. Good coffee." He made a show of looking at his watch. "Probably out of donuts by now, though."

Elizabeth laughed. "Sounds perfect."

They walked in silence. Sometimes Elizabeth's arm would brush his. She didn't move away, and neither did he.

Tom threw a glance in her direction every so often. He saw by the way she carried herself that she knew the secret between them. He'd taken a chance at finding someone in a city of millions that he might connect with, and by luck he'd found her.

This time, when they both arrived at The Artful Codger, he opened the door and let her walk in first.

It was about a half hour before the luncheonette was closing. Simon was cleaning the tables; the place was empty. He looked up when he heard the bells jangling over the entrance.

"Well, hey!" He stretched his arms out wide, a dishtowel dangling off one hand. "We were wondering when the two of you were gonna come in together." He pointed them to a table in the back.

Music filled the empty luncheonette. Elizabeth heard cheerful strumming strings, and then Harry Nilsson's voice sang the opening lyrics of "I Guess The Lord Must Be In New York City."

"Nonna," she whispered.

"Excuse me?" Tom leaned in closer.

"Nothing. Well," Elizabeth shifted in her seat, "it's this song. My grandmother loved it. She used to say Harry Nilsson was right."

"Your grandmother loved Nilsson? That's pretty cool."

"She was. Very cool, I mean." Elizabeth swallowed, wanting to talk about her grandmother but not sure it was right yet. She pushed ahead anyway. "I miss her a lot."

"She's gone?" He looked at her sympathetically. Simon brought them two iced teas and waved Tom off when he reached for his wallet.

"Yes. A few months now."

"I'm really sorry." He looked down and pulled the drink closer but didn't take any. "I think I know how you feel. My grandfather is really sick. We live together, and I take care of him most of the time. He was kind of a genius at fixing and building things. And he was always reading books. I learned a lot from him." He looked up at Elizabeth, seeking understanding. "I'm going to miss him."

Elizabeth nodded. "You will. And it'll be really hard for a long time. But the memories and what you learned from him will always live on with you. My nonna taught me a lot about things like patience and optimism. And faith."

"Those are good things."

*You'd like him, Nonna. I wish you could have met him.* She tucked a few strands of curls behind her ear, suddenly self-conscious. Tom watched her; Elizabeth guessed he was pulling together his thoughts.

"How did you know?" he finally said

"I followed your directions. I had a feeling the book titles weren't random."

He started to say something, stopped, and then spoke again. "I'm glad you paid attention to that feeling. Not many people would have bothered. I think you must be very smart…and very special."

Elizabeth blushed. "I don't know…I just love books, and—"

Tom leaned in and shook his head forcefully. "No, don't. Don't do that. Just believe what I'm saying." He smiled again, still trying to reassure her. "I'm glad it's you. I'm especially relieved you're not that librarian who looks like a prison guard in a suit."

Elizabeth laughed. "I'm glad I'm not either. You have no idea."

"Now that we're not relying on library restrooms to communicate, do you think we could actually talk about books in person?" Tom cocked his head, his eyebrows raised.

"Yes...no." Elizabeth frowned.

The hope on Tom's face faded so fast it almost broke her heart. She added quickly, "Wait... I do, but I want to keep going with the board." She grinned broadly. "It means a lot to me. Plus, it's my turn. I have a great book and quote I was planning to use."

Tom laughed, a wonderful, warm rumble. "Okay. I plan to be in the library even more often now anyway."

"We can talk outside the library too. If you want." It was Elizabeth's turn to look hopeful.

"I'd like that. I have a lot I want to say to you. Too much to fit on a bulletin board."

Simon chose this moment to poke his head out of the kitchen, cough, and disappear again.

"Looks like we're being kicked out." Tom smiled, but his eyes were nervous. "Can I see you tomorrow?"

"I'd love that, but I have to work," Elizabeth said, regret filling her voice. "Could we—"

"Then I'll come into town for you." Tom stood up and held out his hand to help Elizabeth out of her chair. His clasp was warm and full of promise. "Let's have some time together before that. Meet me here tomorrow morning. Coffee's on me."

# A SUMMER OF LOVE

## KRIS BABE

She stepped off the bus into the exhaust fumes and cold rain of the Port Authority terminal, disappearing into the flow of passengers heading to the main hall. She found an open locker and deposited her duffel, then attached herself to the straggling end of a group headed for Times Square.

She was quickly engulfed in the flow of anti-war protesters with signs bearing all too familiar slogans. Blending in was her best bet she'd been told early on. But the protesters' naive enthusiasm, so like her own former idealism, disturbed her to the bone.

Still, she would feel far too conspicuous if she held herself apart. To distract herself from these thoughts and the raw, wet wind blustering down Forty-Second Street, she watched for an opportunity. One soon came—a harried looking protester juggling a stack of signs.

"Need a hand?" she said.

The girl's face spread with relief. "Far out, thanks!"

The wind and rain soaked through her thin jacket and jeans. She had a decent coat in her duffel, but it wouldn't have been the right look for this protest. She wondered how cold she would be before the day was over.

Times Square looked particularly squalid in the rain and gloom, its streets already filthy before the crowd arrived in earnest. While she loved the idea of New York, she hadn't loved the reality of it on her previous sojourns in the city. It would take wealth to make the city comfortable. Though she had some money, she'd need to be exceptionally careful with what she had until she found a job. And a place to sleep. She clutched her sign in front of her like a shield against the wind and moved with the crowd toward Bryant Park.

Chants made their way through the ranks, led by organizers with megaphones. The people around her picked up the strain of Country Joe's "Fixin' to Die Rag." She considered singing along, but her teeth were chattering so hard it was impossible. She steered away from people with umbrellas so the water cascading from their rims didn't soak her further. Her hands were already mottled and icy.

She looked around, reading all the usual signs, and realized she didn't know what hers said. She looked down at it. "Not four more years. Not one more day. US out now!" She sighed. She still hated the war, but no longer believed that protesting made a difference, the slogans and chants just so much noise in an already noisy world.

She wouldn't admit it to anyone, but if she could vote, she'd vote for Nixon in November. He was winding down the war, and from the looks of it, Wallace would win the democratic nomination. Nixon would be the lesser of those evils.

But fugitives can't vote.

Bryant Park was packed, the grass muddied by the crowd's feet. From a distance she saw the stage and people on it speechifying and shouting slogans, raising arms and inviting the crowd to pick up the chant.

It always surprised her who turned out for anti-war rallies. Guys who looked like accountants; women who had to be someone's favorite grandma. What she needed to find today was another type common at rallies: a forlorn guy who reddened at the ears when an attractive woman treated him like a godsend. On a day like today, he really would be.

She was near the edge of the crowd when she spotted one. He was walking down the sidelines handing out trash can liners for people to use as rain gear. He had the mien of an organizer. She made eye contact and didn't have to fake the shiver that shook her from head to toe.

He stopped in front of her. "Here," he said. Rather than just handing her a trash bag as he had been doing with everyone else, he opened the bag and tore a hole in the bottom, then put it over her head.

"Thanks," she said through chattering teeth.

"Wait," he said, and tore a hole on the right side for her arm, then ducked around her to do the same on the left.

"You're a lifesaver," she said. She was cold and wet, but at least she wasn't getting wetter, and the bag worked well as a windbreaker.

"You look frozen," he said.

"I'm a little less frozen now," she said, and didn't have to pretend gratitude.

Color rose up his neck and onto his cheeks.

She touched his hand. "Thank you. Really."

"Jesus, your hand *is* frozen!" He looked a bit shocked.

She shrugged helplessly. "I didn't plan this out very well, I guess."

He hesitated for a second, then said, "Come with me," and kept her hand as he led her toward the stage. "I know a spot where you'll be out of the wind, and you'll have a better view of the stage."

He was right. He installed her next to one of the big equipment boxes beside the risers, which blocked the wind a bit. The people on the stage were distinct from here, not just tiny figures unconnected to the voices coming over the public address system.

"Wow, this is…" she trailed off and fixed him with a look of sincere gratitude, then lowered her eyes and looked up at him through her lashes. His eyes widened a bit. "Will I see you later?" she asked hopefully.

"Yes!" he blurted. "Absolutely, yes. I'll just—" He gestured with the trash bags, indicating that he had to continue passing them around to the protesters.

"Great," she said. "Great!"

He turned back to his task, then came back. "I'm Ethan," he said.

She took a breath, committing to her new name. "I'm Laurel," she said.

"Laurel," he repeated, looking slightly dazed. "That's—that's—"

She smiled at him. "Thanks, Ethan."

He smiled back—a warm, hopeful smile.

Yes.

If he came back, she'd have a place to sleep tonight.

He was sound asleep, breathing deeply. Laurel studied him in the muted morning light. Fading windburn on his fine cheekbones, pale stubble on his jaw, nicely sculpted sideburns, handsome eyebrows, full lips. His round glasses, tinted the smokiest, grayest purple ala John Lennon, lay on his nightstand. She had the unfamiliar impulse to touch the golden hair on his bare arm. He was substantially better looking than any of the Beatles.

She quietly slipped out of bed and picked up the button-down he'd worn for dinner the night before and shrugged into it once she was out of his bedroom. It had been an engrossing couple of days and she needed to get her bearings—and an invitation to see him again tonight.

The apartment was much nicer than anyplace she'd stayed in a long time. She'd grown up in upper middle-class comfort, but hadn't lived anywhere as well appointed as her parents' home since she left her past behind four years before. This apartment, though masculine, bespoke comfort and style.

She opened the drapes in the living room to let in the daylight, then padded to the kitchen. A delicious breakfast was in order. She filled the percolator with coffee grounds and water and set it on the stove. Then she took stock of the pantry and refrigerator. The milk had gone sour—perfect for pancakes. In one of the communes she'd moved through in the past few years, an earth-mother type who did all the cooking for the community had taught her that trick.

Scrambled eggs with diced ham, a fruit cup. She hoped it would be a breakfast to remember.

Ethan emerged from the bedroom just as the coffee finished brewing, a gratifying look of wonder on his face. "It smells amazing in here," he said. He was adorably rumpled, his hair askew.

She flipped a pancake, stirred the eggs, and handed him a mug. "Pour yourself a cup. Breakfast will be ready in a minute."

He shook his head in disbelief as he took the mug. "You didn't have to do all of this."

Laurel smiled at him. "I wanted to." She was surprised to realize it was true. She did want to do something nice for him.

He sat at the table and fixed his coffee—sugar, no cream. He shifted in his chair as she set a plate of pancakes in front of him, and a smaller plate with eggs beside that.

She brought her own plates to the table and sat across from him. "What time do we need to leave?"

His shoulders dropped in apparent relief. "My first class is at ten, so I need to leave by nine twenty."

"Perfect! There's a bus to Boston at ten forty-five out of Penn Station. If we leave together that gives me plenty of time!" she said brightly. "I ironed your shirt last night."

He shook his head slightly, more disbelief. "Wow, thank you."

"It's the least I can do," she said. "It was a wonderful weekend. I'm so glad I met you."

He swallowed. "That sounds like goodbye."

351

Laurel gazed at him, face neutral. Silence, she'd learned, was the best way to press her advantage.

"Laurel, I—" Ethan set down his fork. "I'd like to see you again."

"Oh, Ethan, I would love that!" she said brightly. "I'll let you know when I'm back in New York."

She had no intention of leaving the city, but had told him she'd come in just for the rally. A detour on her way to Boston, where a college friend had lined up a job for her.

His face clouded. "How soon do you have to start?"

"Oh, it's a bit up in the air. I have to meet with the personnel department before they'll give me a start date." She stood and refreshed their coffee cups, then sat down again. "I thought I'd use the time before the job starts to find an apartment so I don't wear out my welcome at Susie's—she has a serious boyfriend." Laurel winked at him over the rim of her coffee cup then sipped.

Ethan flushed and cleared his throat. "So you wouldn't have to arrive at any special time?"

Laurel raised her eyebrows at him as if waiting for him to continue.

"Because I was thinking, you had asked about the university, and I'd be happy to show you around after my class."

"I would think there's an afternoon bus. Let me take a look." Luckily, she had pocketed a bus schedule on her way through Port Authority. She dug it out of her purse and returned to the table. The number of available routes was reassuringly extensive. "Yes, there is, at three fifteen," she said. "I'll call Susie and let her know I'll be there after supper."

She could head south if he didn't ask her to stay. Maybe Baltimore. It would be warmer there. She'd forgotten how chilly spring in New York could be.

When she returned to the table, Ethan stood at the sink, his back to her, rinsing his plate. He still hadn't answered.

"There is a bus this afternoon," she repeated. "Could you write down where I should meet you and what time?"

Ethan turned to her, his face troubled. "You're welcome to go with me to campus and wait in my office, or the—" he broke off, seemingly at a momentary loss as to where she might spend the time while he was teaching class.

"Actually, I have an errand to run, and this gives me just enough time. So let me know where to meet you and what time."

He nodded and went to his office, returning with a notepad and pen. "How well do you know the city?"

Laurel laughed. "I can usually find my way round—or find someone who can give me directions."

Ethan clearly didn't like this answer. "Be careful. Not every block is, well, savory I guess."

"I will." She nodded solemnly, though this warning was entirely unnecessary. Laurel had experienced a wide range of unsavoriness since going into hiding, including New York's own special brand of it. Still, it was easier to let him think otherwise.

He scratched at the paper for a quiet minute, then handed it to her. His handwriting was spiky but neat, much like the typeset name at the top of the sheet. "Ethan Lowell James, PhD."

Laurel read the address aloud and he nodded. She smiled at him, then at the paper. He was lovely. She checked her watch and stood. "I should tidy up so we're ready to leave on time." She brushed against him as she passed by. "I'll use the guest bath?"

Ethan grabbed her hand and pulled her toward him. He studied her face and gently pushed back a strand of hair that grazed her cheek. A slow smile touched his lips, and he leaned in and gently kissed her. "Thank you for breakfast," he said, voice husky, and kissed her again.

It was so tender and unexpected that Laurel suddenly felt shy. She tried to pull away, but his arms tightened around her, and he looked her in the eyes. "This weekend was the best thing that's ever happened to me at a rally, and I've been to a lot of them."

She couldn't look away, so her cheeks flamed. He smiled and brushed the backs of his fingers along the side of her face. Laurel couldn't help smiling back. He leaned in again, and she said, "I'm going to make you late." She kissed him chastely and continued on toward the bathroom, where she shut the door and leaned against it, her heart thudding in her chest, hating that she hadn't met him before she'd done the irrevocable.

When Ethan told her he was an archaeologist, she'd thought he dug for dinosaur bones. But as she walked with him toward campus, she learned that the statue on the desk in his apartment's office wasn't merely decoration. "I teach art history and conservation," he explained, leading her into a laboratory tucked into what was clearly the former kitchen and wine cellar of a grand old house on the campus of NYU's Institute of Fine Arts.

Laurel thought of the statue—a bust, she supposed it would properly be called. It depicted a beautiful but formidable woman's head and shoulders.

"… students also study with curators and conservators from the museums here in the city," Ethan was saying.

"Who is she?" Laurel asked, mind still absorbed in reconstructing the face in her mind.

Ethan flushed. "She's one of my students," he said, and Laurel saw he thought she was asking about the young woman at a nearby table meticulously lifting samples from a piece of parchment and placing them on laboratory slides.

He explained the process, but she wasn't fully listening. Her mind was busy absorbing the surroundings, unlike anything she'd seen before but strangely appealing.

He took her about campus, including a visit to his departmental office. She nodded and hmmed as he showed her around, and gradually her calm returned. Finally, she said, "Not a single brontosaurus?"

He laughed, full and warm. When he fell quiet, she asked, "Tell me about the statue in your apartment."

"Ah!" Ethan seemed pleased she had noticed. "She's a Greek goddess. I'll have to tell you her whole story sometime."

"Is this a ploy to get me back to your apartment?" She meant to be flirtatious but it came out a tad sharp.

Ethan met her eye, a warm challenge. "It's a pleasant thought, but what I had in mind just now is lunch."

"You can't tell me about her while we eat?" she asked as he took her elbow and steered her down the sidewalk.

"She's a goddess," he said, feigning shock. "I can only tell you her story in her presence."

"So this *is* a ploy!"

"It's respect for the sacred!" he teased, suddenly very close. But he didn't kiss her. He reached past her and held open a door.

It was a student cafe, complete with inexpensive vegetarian food and student art for sale on the walls. The noise and crowd pushed conversation to the impersonal, and Ethan kept up a comfortable patter without asking too many questions. It gave Laurel room in her head to construct her story before having to commit to details she might find inconvenient later. It was a constant challenge of the life she led.

"Tell me about your work," he said as they tucked into bowls of lentil soup accompanied by heavy wheat rolls, a meal she'd be happy never to eat again after so much time living in communes.

This was easy as long as she didn't reach back to her life before exile. "I work in finance."

His eyebrows went up. "Wall Street and anti-war rallies?"

"Not investments—more a wizard of the accounts," she said. "Budgeting, projections, pricing."

"You sound like a proper capitalist!" He seemed faintly scandalized. It wasn't the first time she got such a reaction.

"It's not exploitation to make sure people get paid and that money coming in is properly allocated," she said drily. It was a distinction lost on most people but especially hippies. It had once seemed so to her as well. Fortunately, her parents had made completing a second major in accounting the compromise for also allowing her to pursue a major in political science. As they had predicted, accounting paid better, which had saved her from what might have been a much more difficult life on the run.

"Is that what your job in Boston will be?"

"Unfortunately, no."

He looked at her quizzically but didn't ask, and the conversation seemed at an impasse. They finished eating in silence and sat uncomfortably amid the empty dishes.

She looked at her watch. "I should run—I'll miss my bus!"

Ethan's face fell. "I have to get back to campus, I have office hours this afternoon." He seemed to consider. "Come back with me. Catch the evening bus."

"I'll just be in your way."

It was quiet for a beat as he seemed to decide something. "I have someone I want you to meet," he said, standing up quickly. "Can you come back to campus with me?"

Thanks to the efforts of the departmental secretary, who had been with NYU for decades and was highly connected within the university, Laurel left campus that afternoon with an appointment to interview the next day for an opening in the office of the controller. She also had an invitation to stay another night with Ethan. Laurel convinced him to keep his open office hours, which gave her time to buy an interview dress before meeting him back at the Wellraven.

Before the week was out, she had a well-paid job and a boyfriend. It was the kind of good fortune no one should dare to hope for, least of all Laurel. By rights, this life should belong to the chemistry PhD student who lost her life the night Laurel and her compatriots lit their last fire to protest the war.

"I was thinking I should go to New Hampshire for the weekend—I haven't been home since Christmas," Ethan said, his voice a question.

Laurel was glad they were on the phone—it was much easier to navigate conversations like this one when they weren't face to face.

Her head was full of calculations for next year's annual budget. Like most universities, the budget year ended on June 30, so early May was crunch time for reconciling departmental projections and requests with projected revenue.

"Of course," she said readily. "I'm sure your mother would be happy to see you on her special day." Neutral, safe. He'd opened the door on family conversations before but hadn't pressed the issue, though she could see he was curious. But a holiday meant the question could no longer be skirted. She knew she should stick with her standard story, but it was tempting to stray closer to the truth with Ethan.

"So. Do you have any plans for that weekend?"

"Free as a bird," she said lightly, though she needed to stare at the numbers on the sheet in the platen of her typewriter to keep her voice steady.

"I just thought you might also be planning to visit your—"

She didn't let him complete the thought. "My mother left us when I was small," she said. "I don't really remember her."

"Oh Laurel. I'm—"

"I think it's wonderful that you want to see your mom on Mother's Day. You should certainly go."

It was something of a test. Though she had keys to the apartment, he seemed reluctant to leave her alone there. Was he afraid she would disappear? "I can hold down the fort for a couple of days."

"Actually, I was hoping you might come along," he said. "Mother is anxious to meet you."

"Your parents know about us?" He had seemed in earnest all along, but this removed all doubt. His trust in her honest intentions made her feel sick with herself. This was new—she hadn't met a hippie yet who wanted to take a girl home to meet his parents. Of course, Ethan wasn't exactly a hippie, any more than she was.

"I did mention that I have a girlfriend." He sounded defensive, and she could almost hear him blushing.

"I wouldn't want to intrude. I mean, what about the rest of your family?" Because she never wanted to risk questions about her own background, she had refrained from asking Ethan about siblings or other relatives.

"It's just the three of us," Ethan said. "I had a baby sister, but she died when I was eight."

"How sad," she said. He'd said it quietly, but she understood there was a depth of feeling he didn't voice.

"It was," he agreed. "But it's made us really close. They come to the city for auctions and antiques shows. The sofa in my office is a pullout so they can stay with me when they come into town."

His earnest affection for them made her miss her own parents. It was almost impossible to refuse. "I'd love to go with you as long as they truly won't mind..." she let her voice go suggestive.

"They have a spare bedroom," he said hastily. "We won't be able to share a room."

"Of course," she said.

"Great!" The relief and happiness in his voice broke her heart a little.

"Great," she replied, unable to keep the warmth out of her voice.

Out of nowhere there was Gladys, the office manager. She tapped Laurel's typewriter with her pencil and gave her a pointed look.

"I should go," she whispered. "Gladys."

"Yes, of course! We can talk more about it tonight."

"Tonight," she said and rang off.

Pages and pages of numbers, in their neat columns, littered her desk, but the order was clear in her head, and in the tables she built, one typed page at a time, never an error.

It was so easy to see the paths and where they might be diverted. She never missed a discrepancy—she was already developing a reputation as exceptionally adept with the figures. Why hadn't that insight translated into assessing situations and people? It would have saved a life. And a lifetime of regret.

They decided to make part of the drive Friday night, then get up in the morning and complete the trip, arriving in Lincoln, New Hampshire, by noon. They'd make the whole drive back on Sunday—Laurel had to work on Monday and Ethan had papers and exams to grade.

Ethan looked surprisingly natural at the wheel of his car—a convertible with the top down in honor of the warm spring afternoon. It seemed completely off-brand for a guy who religiously took public transit when he didn't walk. He hadn't driven once since she met him, that she knew of.

She couldn't help smiling at the complete weirdness of something that she wouldn't have given a second thought for most of her life.

"What?" he mugged. "There weren't any subways where I come from!"

She shook her head. "So dazzle me with your driving!" She resisted the temptation to say it was the same for her growing up.

He grinned and revved the engine as she settled herself in the passenger seat.

"Wait, don't." She laughed. "Just get us there in one piece."

Ethan laughed too as he pulled away from the Wellraven.

It was perfect weather for driving out of Manhattan toward the Atlantic. Ethan reached for her hand and she held it while soaking in the blue sky and sun glinting off of windows, the city's ever-present grime softened by warm light and a fresh breeze.

When they reached the freeway, Ethan turned on the radio and spun through the dial, stopping when he found the intro to Shocking Blue's "Venus." He turned up the volume and sang, "A Goddess on a mountain top / Was burning like a silver flame / The summit of beauty and love / And Venus was her name."

He looked boyish and carefree, watching the road ahead as he lifted her hand to kiss it before launching into the chorus.

He wiggled his eyebrows suggestively over the word "desire," which made her laugh.

When the DJ broke in at the end of the song, Ethan released her hand to turn down the volume.

"Why Aphrodite copies?" She'd wondered for a while, but it felt safer to ask now, light and easy.

He chuckled. "Why do you say it like that?"

"Well, isn't it? They were copying the Greeks, right?"

"Yes, but not the way you make it sound. There's a reverence. They saw the artistry, respected the craftsmanship, and emulated them to meet the demand for beautiful things," he said, one hand sketching out a circle in the air. "I've always loved how great things are revived and reinterpreted—furniture, architecture, sculpture, everything."

He glanced over at her to see if she agreed.

Laurel tried not to look as stricken as she felt. She was actively deceiving him. The gravity of that filled her with shame. He was sharing himself freely, confiding his thoughts, introducing her to his family. Yet she'd done something so terrible that she could never tell him who she really was.

"So you think that's how it should be?" She looked out the window so he wouldn't see the tears pricking in her eyes.

"More that I think it always has been, since forever, and I like seeing that continuity, finding the ways we remake and remodel the past and give it new life."

"I never thought of it that way," she admitted.

"Did I ever tell you my parents run an antiques shop?" He put both hands on the wheel, an elbow on the open window. "I've been looking at old things all my life and it's like they show me what they are—ancient faience or a reproduction from 1200 AD or fifty years ago. Made to emulate or to deceive, sometimes both." He was entirely earnest. "If you really look at something, its details and components, you see what it actually is instead of, or maybe on top of, what it's pretending to be. I've loved that feeling ever since I can remember."

Laurel hoped her smile, held with such effort, didn't give her away. His sincerity overwhelmed her with regret. If she'd taken another path, the one she first set out on, she might have deserved a man like Ethan.

But she most assuredly didn't deserve him now. With a certainty that grew more clear with each day they spent together, she knew that someday the truth would break both of their hearts.

She scooted closer to him and kissed the soft place just below his earlobe so he couldn't see her face. "I love that about you," she whispered into his skin.

She realized he heard her by his secret smile in the rearview mirror and the arm that wrapped around her shoulder to pull her closer.

Weekends were work days for Ethan's parents. When they arrived in Lincoln at lunchtime on Saturday, they drove past the cutoff for his family's home to meet them at their antiques shop. The town's main street, closed off for the first festival of the spring tourist season, bustled with visitors. People walked the street, shopping and sampling food. Business owners set up tables on the sidewalk for dining or purchasing their wares.

His parents, both slim, upright, no-nonsense New Englanders, had merchandise displayed on the sidewalk and were busily answering questions and countering offers. His mother nodded a greeting and his father gave Laurel a kindly smile, but they carried on with their work.

Ethan tugged her through the door of the shop. After the bright noonday sun, it was dim inside until her eyes adjusted. Ethan threaded through the aisles, intent on a far corner. She hung on to his hand and followed, marveling at the volume of things expanding out in cool, shadowy aisles that spread in all directions. Dusty, light windows with wavy glass—it was another world.

Past armoires and buffalo blankets and whale oil lamps and gloomy old paintings, they moved toward a window near the back of the shop. When they reached it, he took her gently by the shoulders and positioned her before a huge painting she might have mistaken for a statue of Venus except for the chestnut hair piled in spilling curls. A broken column, a fallen temple, an impossible sky full of stars with a crescent moon on its back. The subject's drapings were sheer enough to showcase a shapely back and derriere as she glanced over a bare shoulder and up at the moon.

"Aphrodite Kallipygos," he murmured into her own chestnut hair. "Venus of the Beautiful Buttocks."

She laughed. "You made that up."

"You asked me about the bust in my office, she's also Aphrodite Kallipygos." He pulled her back to his chest and his voice dropped. "I've adored her since the first time I laid eyes on her."

It was impossible to miss the resemblance between the figure in the picture and Laurel—same chestnut curls, same curve of cheek. Same high bottom and long thighs.

"What happens if someone buys it?"

"They can't." He turned over the tag describing the painting with the name of the artist and the date on one side, NFS on the other. "It's not for sale."

"That doesn't make any sense!"

"It does though. You don't sell pieces that function as fixtures, and you keep some pieces in the shop because they make everything around them seem more valuable," he explained.

She turned to him. His face was eager yet shy. He wanted, she saw, to share himself, and for her to love what he shared. It made her heart tender and protective. She put her hands in his sandy hair and drew him in for a lingering kiss. When they came up for air, she whispered, "What happens—"

The bell on the shop door rang. Ethan reluctantly released her waist but clasped her hand and pulled her toward an alcove.

It was a small room lined with shelves that were packed with every kind of book: scrapbooks of newspaper clippings, postcard albums, autograph books, boxes of old correspondence, diaries, decades old school yearbooks, old magazines and catalogs, books on art, wallpaper sample books. A place where histories of every sort converged.

Though it was a place from his childhood, he looked newly entranced.

She nudged him. "These aren't for sale either, are they?"

"Technically they are, but no one ever buys them. It's like a library, people come and linger to read or research.

367

When they find what they're looking for, they don't need to buy them. Some of these have been here longer than me."

She scanned the shelves, conscious of his gaze following her.

She pulled out the oldest book she could find, the first of a thick old work in two volumes. "This is your favorite," she guessed.

The book was filled with makers' marks of British pottery and silver.

"We definitely use that one a lot," Ethan admitted, "but my favorite is over here."

He reached up to the end of a far upper shelf and pulled down a tattered volume, passing a hand reverently over the cover before offering it to her.

It was *The Lives of the Most Excellent Painters, Sculptors, and Architects*, by Giorgio Vasari, abridged from the multi-volume original.

"Watch this," he said. He reached around her so she held the book between two hands. "See where it opens." His voice was reverent, as if they were talking in church.

The book fell open to page 289. "This is why it's my favorite," he said, pointing to a paragraph. "It's about Michelangelo."

She read it aloud:

"He tarried in Bologna a year and then returned to Florence, where he made a sleeping Cupid, which being shown by Baldassari del Milanese to Lorenzo de Pier Francesco de Medici—"

He said, "If you were to bury it till it looked old, and then sent it to Rome, I am sure it would pass for an antique, and you would get much more for it than if you sold it here."

She turned to look at him, marveling.

He finished it from memory.

"Some say that Michelangelo did so, making it look old, and others that Milanese did so, making it look old, and others that Milanese carried it to Rome and buried it in one of his vineyards, and then sold it as an antique for two hundred ducats to the Cardinal S Giorgio. However it may be, it brought such reputation to Michael Angelo that he was summoned to Rome by Cardinal S. Giorgio…"

Ethan pointed to a plate of Michelangelo's Pieta on the facing page—a work even Laurel recognized for its fame and timeless beauty. "The fake got him this commission, which made his name," he said.

Laurel felt suddenly, painfully exposed, understood in the least welcome way. Except she was more than ninety-nine percent certain that Ethan suspected nothing. Not yet. And as seemed to be his default, he put the most charitable construction on this story of a fake made good by its inherent quality.

But Laurel wasn't like Michelangelo or his cupid. Her deceit would not result in a greater good. At best, it might allow her to do better than she had once done.

She realized he was waiting for her reply. "So this was the start of it? Your interest in ancient forgeries?"

"Not the start, but it definitely crystalized it for me."

He began to explain the shop's fakes and forgeries, the times they'd been deceived or had to tell someone else that they had been. People wishing to sell pieces with a family story, only to find out that the story was wrong.

His parents were very pragmatic about their own mistakes, he said, and about recognizing that some fakes have legitimate value of their own despite being fake. "Real artistry is a category of its own," Ethan said.

"Show her the ambrotype." His mother's voice, fond and wry, came from behind them. Laurel suspected his mother of being amused by his interest in forgeries, as if she still couldn't quite believe he'd become a professor who made a study of identifying and understanding them. Fakes were just a fact of life, Eleanor's voice seemed to say.

Ethan reshelved the book, then took her hand and led her toward the front of the shop, stopping abruptly before a case full of old portraits. He opened it and drew out an image of two soldiers in Union Army uniforms. She had to tilt it out of the glare from the front window. "Ambrotypes are on glass—the black paper backing lets you see the image," he said. "That's why they're always in a case rather than a frame, to keep the paper backing from getting scratched and spoiling the image."

"It's a fake?" she asked, finding it hard to believe. The soldiers looked utterly authentic to her untrained eye. It occurred to her that this type of photography would require a lot of skill for a forger. She'd had to learn a fair number of new skills to live concealed in plain sight but that didn't make her an artist.

"It's the first fake I spotted when I started picking with mom and dad," Ethan said.

Eleanor had followed them. "It fooled Lowell and me, but Ethan noticed the anachronism the first time he looked at it."

"Where?" Laurel asked. The question was for Eleanor, but Eleanor pushed the question over to Ethan with a smile of maternal pride. "Tell her."

"It's the G.A.R. medal." Ethan pointed to a medal pinned on one of the soldiers' uniforms.

"G.A.R.?"

"Grand Army of the Republic. It was a Veteran's organization for Union soldiers, founded after the war. This medal was first offered in 1885," Ethan said. "These boys would have been infants if they were born at all before the end of the war."

He was right. They were far too young to be Veterans of a war that had ended twenty years before the badges they wore were manufactured.

"We were so taken with the subjects, and the case was exactly right. So we didn't see it," Eleanor said. "But once Ethan pointed it out? Now it's the first thing I see when I look at it." She shook her head in wonderment. "It wasn't a cheap mistake, but it was a lesson that has repaid us over the years. Make sure you're seeing what's actually there."

Laurel had been meeting Eleanor's eyes but she broke away, cheeks suddenly flaming. This seemed to arrest

Eleanor's attention. Laurel could feel Eleanor's steady gaze on her, but Ethan hadn't noticed their exchange.

"You have to respect the craftsmanship," Ethan continued. "Whoever did this piece went to the trouble of learning to use old equipment, materials, and techniques. I've always thought it might be an art school project. Otherwise why go to all the effort to recreate something that has such modest value?"

But Laurel didn't see craftsmanship. She saw Eleanor's motherly pride and affection for her boy. And for the rest of the visit, she saw that Eleanor would like to inspect her more closely with eyes well-schooled by long experience in seeing what's actually there.

"Where are you from?"

His voice came to her as a dreamy rumble beneath her ear. She'd been drifting, head on his chest as he fiddled with her hair, limp with the July heat and the afterglow of sex. The part of her brain where she kept prepared answers readily at hand was apparently too blissed out to care.

Still, the alarm, however faint, had sounded, and she managed to hedge. "I was living in Colorado for about a year," she murmured sleepily.

"No, I mean where you're from originally. Where did you grow up?" She could hear a smile in his voice. "Farm girl? City kid? Bayou baby?" His hand brushed across her hip and ribs, lightly enough to tickle. She squirmed and shook her head. "None of the above."

He rolled toward her, cupping her bare breast. "Appalachia?"

She looked up at him, pushing her hair away from her damp neck. "Seriously?"

His hand ran down the flat plane of her abdomen. "Kansas?"

His mouth traversed the path his hand traced down her body. "Hilarious." Her voice had gone breathy. He spread her legs and touched her with his tongue.

"Hmm. Salty," he emphasized his New Hampshire accent. "What about coastal Maine?"

"Not even close." She gasped.

She was lost in his attentions until she again climaxed. When she opened her eyes, his face was close to hers and he pushed into her.

"I've got it!" He groaned, and at first she didn't know what he meant. He slid slowly back, only to push in again, filling her with the solid length of him. His voice grew ragged as he continued to slide home and home. "You sprang from the head of Zeus like a proper goddess."

He fixed her with a look of adoration that took her breath away.

"Sounds of laughter shades of earth are ringing through my open views," he sang in a whisper, picking up the faint strains of music drifting in on the lightest of breezes. "Inciting and inviting me. Limitless, undying love—" He stopped singing and locked eyes with her. She couldn't look away. He felt so good—the connection of their bodies, the connection of their hearts. She leaned up and kissed him as they fell together through the universe.

When she opened her eyes, he was still on top of her, and his eyes shone in the light from the street below. He rolled off of her, pulling her with him so they lay face-to-face, bodies pressed together. He lightly pushed a curl from her forehead, then brushed his lips across her cheek. When he reached her ear, he whispered, "Marry me, Laurel."

A small, wondering laugh escaped her.

He pulled back to look at her and said it again. "Marry me."

There were important reasons to say no. The most important possible. But in his bed, in his arms, in the honest light of his wondering gaze, it was impossible to say anything but "yes."

When morning came, Laurel rose from bed with a long-forgotten sense of possibility. She tucked away her fear and guilt and stopped holding back, hopeful that she could make good on her debt to society within this unexpected new life.

She and Ethan became inseparable, wandering through museums and art galleries and second-hand shops nearly every weekend. Laurel delighted in watching Ethan comb through the merchandise, regularly turning up small marvels. She loved listening as he told her the unexpected histories of majolica or colonial-era furniture. In Ethan's bed, Laurel discovered that deep satisfaction and unquenchable desire were two sides of the same coin and gave herself over to him.

Laurel spoiled him with home-cooked meals and blueberry pie from scratch. She borrowed books from his shelves and read the mythologies depicted in his beloved ancient forgeries so she could better appreciate his work. She attended an auction with Eleanor and bought him a small but ancient silver coin with Aphrodite's head on one side and the Aphrodite Kallipygos figure on the other, which she gave him for his birthday, August 22, four months to the day from the wet, rainy anti-war rally in Bryant Park that brought them together.

All summer she lived as if her future as Laurel had been secured by their love.

September brought with it a back-to-school return to routine, which Laurel found appealing. She had loved attending university and enjoyed her work on campus. Ethan's enthusiasm for his subject continued to charm her.

Laurel never saw the *New York Times* story that blew her cover. Not until Eleanor unexpectedly arrived in the NYU comptroller's office one Monday, just before noon, to ask her to lunch. She looked like a professional woman in a skirt, jacket and sensible shoes, but one look in Eleanor's steady gray eyes and Laurel knew that she knew. Laurel went to her desk for her purse and a quick word to

Gladys. In a moment, she and Eleanor were on the sidewalk.

Eleanor knew the city well. As she steered Laurel away from campus, she kept up a pleasant monologue on antiques auctions she'd attended in the city, exhibiting at the prestigious Armory Winter show, favorite shops she visited whenever they came to the city to see Ethan. Laurel felt as if she were floating above her body as they walked, looking down on the last moments of the life she'd begun to hope she could keep.

At last, they arrived at a small bistro where Eleanor had a reservation for them.

Eleanor politely managed the waitress, as calm as could be. When the waitress brought their iced tea and left with their lunch order, Laurel could hardly meet her gaze.

"Does Ethan know?" Eleanor asked.

Laurel just stared. She had envisioned being caught so many ways over the past four years, but it never looked like this when the nightmare click of a handcuff on her wrist woke her to another dead panic. She glanced around the dining room wondering if detectives were at a nearby table waiting to take her away.

"Does he know who you are?"

Laurel shook her head as Eleanor pushed a newspaper clipping across the tablecloth. "Where Are They Now?" the headline read.

"Saturday's edition," Eleanor said.

Laurel flushed. He'd missed seeing it by pure luck. After a hectic first week of the academic year, they'd woken late and lusty that morning, and had spent a lazy day in bed, rising only for essentials like sustenance.

The article detailed the current state of investigations into the anti-war groups responsible for several unsolved break-ins, bombings, and fires. The all too familiar photo of her with the group she'd helped lead accompanied the story of the burning of the science building at the university she'd once been so proud to attend and the death of Mary Sue Walden.

Mary Sue's picture also accompanied the story. Laurel touched the face of the person whose death she had caused. She didn't allow herself to cry. She didn't deserve that kind of relief from her guilt.

At last, she looked up at Eleanor. "Have you told him?" she asked.

"I haven't," Eleanor said. "Do you intend to?"

Laurel considered again, though she already knew the answer. "If I tell him, he'd be an accessory after the fact."

"Yes," she agreed.

"I should just go," she said, unable to keep a sob out of her voice.

"That might be best for everyone," Eleanor said. She placed a hand over Laurel's, tucking what felt like cash into her palm. Eleanor squeezed her hand, then withdrew it.

"Look at it later," Eleanor suggested, taking a sip of her iced tea and pocketing the newspaper article just as the waitress arrived with their order.

"My daughter isn't feeling well," Eleanor said. "Could you please wrap our lunches to go?"

When the waitress left, Eleanor said, "You won't need to go back to the apartment. I packed your things for you and left them for you at the station." She slipped a locker key across the table to her.

"I wish I could—" Laurel couldn't bear the thought of saying goodbye to Ethan, but the thought of not saying it, just disappearing, was even worse.

"You'll take the five-fifteen bus to Albany," Eleanor said, her gaze steady on Laurel's. Laurel glanced down to the papers clasped in her hand. She found that she held a bus ticket to Albany and two hundred dollars in cash.

When she looked up, Eleanor nodded. Yes, she was helping Laurel get away.

Laurel understood that she was doing this for Ethan, but that Eleanor bore no malice toward her despite who she really was and what she had done.

"Why?" Laurel asked.

"Because I think you will do the right thing," Eleanor said.

The waitress returned and Eleanor handed her twenty dollars, more than enough to cover lunch and a tip. She accepted the bag with their meals in it and steered Laurel between tables and out the door.

On the sidewalk, she passed the bag of food to Laurel and gave her a brisk peck on the cheek. "I'm sorry we won't see each other again," she said. "I would have liked to know you better."

She hailed a cab, but when it came, she urged Laurel into it and told the driver, "Port Authority, please."

Laurel didn't see much of the hot, grimy city through her tears. What would Ethan think when he discovered she was gone? She understood that Eleanor would never tell him anything about the article or what she'd done today.

It was just 1:30 p.m. when she arrived at Port Authority to wait for her bus. She found the locker and retrieved a small valise with her things, plus a lumpy manilla envelope with her name neatly written in pencil. She took these to the most secluded seat she could find and tried not to imagine Ethan's shock and grief when he found she had left without a trace.

When her tears at last subsided, she looked in the bag that held the sandwiches Eleanor had cleverly sent with her. She pulled one out, planning to take a few half-hearted bites. But as she did, the envelope slipped from her lap.

She retrieved it and opened the flap. It held a small parcel wrapped in paper and tied with kitchen string.

She untied it and found two things: the ambrotype of the men in Civil War regalia and the telltale G.A.R. badges, and an art nouveau hair comb topped with a delicate, beautifully enameled dragonfly. Ethan had wanted to give it to her that day at the shop, holding it up to her hair, but she had demurred, not wanting to accept something so valuable.

Eleanor must have seen.

She began to wrap them back in the paper when she noticed that Eleanor had written a note inside.

*You know the story of the ambrotype and the lesson we learned from it. The dragonfly comb was made by Tiffany & Co, c. 1910. It looked beautiful in your hair. Did you know that the dragonfly symbolizes transformation?*

*E*

Laurel stared at the note for a long time before carefully wrapping up these gifts and stowing them in her purse. They were with her four days later in a small midwestern town when Laurel, also known as Wendy Newton, walked into the police station and turned herself in.

# THE SOJOURN
## CHRISTOPHER WINKS

Children surrounded Anton, who lay down on the ground. It was dark in the woods, and a full moon shone brightly in the dark sky. They walked toward him slowly. Anton could not move. His legs, his back, his arms did not respond to his will. Even his neck, supported by a stone, did not move. He could only move his eyes. The children's faces were angry. Some of them looked menacing. Their eyes looked bigger than usual on their pale faces. Few of them were closer to him than the rest. One girl was closest to him. Her face was pensive. Anton grew desperate to move away, but his body did not respond. He tried harder; the girl moved closer. Finally, she raised her hand toward his face, and Anton woke up. He looked around the dark burned apartment he squatted in. He was sweating profusely, and his heart was beating on the verge of an explosion. He trembled uncontrollably. His breath was short, and it took much effort from him to inhale. Mild pain spread across his belly. Nightmares had grown viler in the past few weeks. It was time for him to leave the Bronx. He walked to the Tremont Subway station. Dilapidated buildings and their rubble were all around him, and there was no moon in the sky. Streetlights worked sporadically. Anton saw buildings on fire from the subway train. He could see the Cross Bronx Expressway that started it all. He was leaving behind twenty-four years of his life. Would he ever return? It did not seem likely.

Tomas worked at the Snakehole Lounge on Lenox Avenue in Harlem. Street lights always faltered on that road. Tonight, all of them were off. Only the green snake with its red tongue was visible from a distance. The board read Snakehole Lounge. The bar was full. Tomas came with two beer pints.

Tomas asked Anton, "You gonna split for real?"

Anton did not respond.

"Are you sure you want to leave?"

Anton looked at him and thought he wouldn't understand.

Tomas pushed, "Do you want something? You can always tell me. Girl? You want girl... two girls... more? Money? is it money you want...? Tell me how much... What do you want, man? I can't work like this."

"I want to sleep."

"You want to sleep? There's a nice place for you to sleep in the back, man. Go in the back and lie down."

"I want to be able to sleep."

"I am your brother. Listen to me. Do not leave this place."

Anton said grimly, "You told me you would..."

"Yes, I did."

"It doesn't look like you..."

"I will. But think for once. Think again. What do they call it? Reconsider."

"Look, brother. I don't hold anything against you. And I have done a lot for you. You owe me. But if you don't get me what I need, then tell..."

"I will. I said..."

"Then tell me."

"Go to the East One Hundred Eleventh Street, Lexington Avenue. That's twenty-two blocks from here. You will find Pierre there."

The door of the bar opened with a screeching sound and a muscular man entered with three associates. It was Cousin. He walked up to Anton's table and sat down.

Cousin said, "Tell me how much you sold last week… Tell me what is going on."

Anton told him his targets of the week selling cocaine.

Cousin replied, "That's just wasted news. Let me tell you some *good* news."

His eyes went wide as he continued. "We got the biggest consignment yet. From Columbia through Venezuela, seventy-five kilos of product, the finest cocaine. You know how much money is that? Start expanding along Crotona Avenue north. Go beyond the Gladwin Park. See what you can sell."

Anton stared back at Cousin without a word. Cousin looked back at him.

"What is this thing I hear? You want to split? Leave all your good work behind?"

Anton didn't respond.

"Come on! Talk to me. What's going on in that crazy head of yours? Tell me why. Why you want to leave?"

Anton got up and said, "I want to take a leak."

"You gotta go, you gotta go."

Anton stepped outside the bar. His hands and legs were giving in. He decided to run. He hated running. But it was also the only thing that relieved him of anxiety. It was also why he ran so fast. He ran toward East 111th Street.

One of the associates told Cousin that the toilet is in the back and Anton left out front.

"You think I don't know that? Is that what you are saying? That I am stupid?" Cousin punched the man. The man fell to the floor with a bleeding nose.

Hilly's On The Bowery, opened in '72, was a small bar on Bowery, the East Village, Manhattan. Hilly Kristal wanted country and blues musicians to play, but rock bands captured the place. The bar counter was on the right, and the seats on the left. Pendant lights were sparse, and they left a lot of space dark in the bar. It smelled of smoke, alcohol, and disinfectants and created a heady aroma. The stage was on the backside, and the amplifiers made the area hot.

"I was sitting outside the A&R department at Dawn Records, and this guy who sat beside me told me I had taken his spot. I turned and said, 'Really? Did I?' He had a nice smile, and his shoulders were oooh! 'Why did you do that,' he asked, and I said, 'It's a free world.' He told me about his gig at the Nell's Night Club. It's a dream to play at that place. I cut him mid-way and asked, 'Why are you telling me all this?' and he said, 'It's a free world,' and continued. I went for my meet. It just took two minutes. I walked out, and as he walked in, he asked me, 'Would you wait for me? It'd just take two minutes.' You know what I said?" asked Delilah.

Lenny and Bob said, "What?"

I said, "It's a free world."

Delilah laughed. Everyone laughed.

Delilah said, "The look on his face, I tell ya."

Lizzie said wistfully, "But it's not a free world."

Delilah didn't want to ruin her mood. "Don't start all that, please. You really want to talk that the world is not free?"

Lizzie replied, "It's just a talk."

"All right. Have your talk. But don't turn your talk into the morose 'everything is wrong with the world.'"

"That danger is often very real."

"Why not tell me about your life? Tell me about your boyfriend."

"My boyfriend is boring. The war is interesting."

Delilah moaned. "No! Please, not the war…"

Lenny intervened, "Yes! Let's talk about the war. What war are we talking about?"

Lizzie replied, "What other war is going on right now?"

Bob said, "What other wars are going on right now?"

They provoked her, and she smiled.

Lizzie said, "The Vietnam War."

Lenny asked, "Where is that? Vi-Et-Nam. On the West Coast or the East Coast?"

Anton walked into Pierre's foundry. The hour hand was one spot away from twelve. Pierre said he would show him the foundry tomorrow.

Pierre told him, "The first week, just see what we do. Do what you are told."

Anton followed him silently in the dark.

Pierre continued, "Business even has scope if I can get a few good workers. Nobody wants to work these days."

Anton said, "I'd work whatever you want."

"You trying to act smart with me?"

Anton went silent with this jibe.

"You try to act smart with me, and I will kick you out before you know it. Don't try to play games with me. I know you people. I know what you are up to all the time."

Pierre told him where he would sleep. Anton lay down at the place, and he saw Cousin walking toward the foundry through the window at some distance. He jumped, grabbed his bag, and ran onto Third Avenue. Cousin shouted, "He don't know Harlem. Spread out." They chased him. It was true. Anton had not been to Harlem in a very long time. But he remembered there was a subway station on 110th Street. However, when he reached 110th Street, he did not see a subway station.

*Where the station went? Is this real, or am I running in a dream*, Anton thought and kept running. The broad streets had no place to hide. Posters of the Black Panther

Party covered the walls. Every shop, every building was closed and locked, and the subway station had disappeared.

On 105th Street, he read the signboard. The subway station was on Lexington Avenue, that ran parallel to Third Avenue. Even though he could run faster, he was getting tired; they were closing in. He took a turn on 103rd Street. He ran into the 103rd Street Subway Station. They were hardly thirty feet behind him. He jumped the turnstile and rushed to the platform. A train was waiting, and instead of getting into it, he ran along the length of the train.

They could see him. They waited to see if he would climb the train. He kept running toward the other exit. Then the bell rang, the doors started closing, and Anton dashed into one. He was safe inside the subway train. His car ran toward Cousin. Cousin stared at him coldly as the train passed him. Anton sat. The train had few passengers. His whole body was beating like an electric pump, and his mind was blank. After minutes, he opened his eyes and saw people around. He looked at the people on the train and wondered who they were, what their troubles were. He wanted to help someone. The train was full of graffiti work. He felt a bit at ease reading angry words in colorful large letters. Then, amidst blue and brown, big-sized letters, he saw graffiti of a little girl with rain pouring on her through her umbrella. Something hit him in the gut. His heartbeat simmered down to a lower level. Tears rolled through his eyes; he closed them again and fell asleep.

Everyone was drunk by this time at Hilly's On the Bowery.

Lizzie said, "Everything is wrong with the world."

Delilah said, slurring her words, "I told you not to go there. I told you."

Lenny said, "Everything is just fine. Look at all the pretty dresses and listen to every sound they make."

Delilah pointed out, "The sound that *we* make, the *music* that we make."

Gloria said sarcastically, "You have to spend time at the instrument to make music."

Lenny and Bob laughed. Delilah sulked.

Bob said, "See! Everything is fine with the world."

Lizzie said, "What about the war going on right now?"

Lenny asked, "What war?"

Rolling her eyes, Lizzie said, "The Vietnam War!"

Lenny said with great confidence, "The war is the government's job. War is not an actor's job."

Lizzie asked, "Whose job is it to stop the war?"

Everyone got befuddled at the question. Bob broke the silence. He said, "I didn't make any war for anyone. I am one for peace!"

Lizzie asked, "You are one for peace, eh?"

Lenny replied to her, "Yes, sweet girl. I am one for peace, at any cost."

"What about the Watergate scandal?"

"The Watergate scandal?"

"Yes, the Watergate scandal."

"A man left a door open; what is the big deal about it?"
Bob said, "I leave the door unlatched sometimes."

Lizzie laughed and said, "It's funny that you think you are funny."

Bob replied, "I am an actor! You are the writer. Write a funny line and give it to me."

"A doomed writer."

Lenny said with a sense of camaraderie, "We are all of us doomed in the pursuit of art."

Gloria spoke for the first time in a long time. "We will get there. We just need to keep working."

Lenny raised his eyebrows, "Hail, Madame Hitler!"

Gloria replied with a smile, "Catherine of Russia. That's who I prefer."

Delilah said, "I won't work tomorrow."

Gloria felt alarmed and asked, "What? Why?"

Delilah replied, "I don't feel like it."

Gloria, controlling her emotions and going in for a long argument, said, "The studio recording is at the end of the week."

Delilah stopped her. "I know. I know. I don't want to argue. Not tonight."

Anton slept in the subway train as the train rushed south. From time to time, his eyes opened. He saw huge buildings; well-lit areas. Thoughts crossed his mind as fast as the train crossed localities around it. *Who lives there? What kinda people? What kinda lives they have?*

Lizzie asked, "That's it?"

Bob replied, "What else?"

Lizzie said, "News brings that too."

Lenny answered, "Art also brings pleasure. The news brings no pleasure."

"Now you are saying that art can save a life. Earlier, you said art is just pleasure and awareness."

"Yes. Bring them together. Awareness and pleasure. Otherwise, everything is just a passing moment and sterile information."

"What does it do when it comes together?"

Delilah pushed Lizzie's eyes away. "Don't look at me."

Lizzie looked at Bob.

Bob tried to avert the question. "Not me. Why me?"

Lenny emphasized, "Yes you!"

Bob succumbed, "Okay, me. What do I have to do?"

Lenny answered, "You have to save a life."

Lizzie corrected him, "You have to answer a question."

Bob asked a question, "What question?"

Lizzie said, "I don't know. Why should I know?"

Gloria knew the question, "What does art do? That is the question."

Delilah knew the answer, "Art can save a soul."

Lizzie laughed cynically and mimicked, "Art can save a soul!" Everyone laughed. Delilah smiled with satisfaction.

Anton's eyes opened and closed periodically. Thoughts kept crossing his mind that he did not register. Then, finally, one thought precipitated. *Where are you going?* He mumbled, "I don't know." The question and the answer resonated in his mind like a dull hum. Suddenly, he woke up and spoke, "Where am I going?" He got down at the next station, Bowery, and started walking north on Bleecker Street.

Gloria asked Delilah what happened. Delilah looked back. She assessed if she should tell her. Then she said, "Nothing."

"Nothing?"

"Nothing."

Lizzie snickered., "There is nobody to save. The city is doomed. We are doomed. Everyone is corrupt. Everyone is destroyed. And if you dare to reach out to someone, they would bite you."

Bob agreed, "I have been bitten a few times."

Lizzie continued, "They would bite you, and you will remember never to try again."

Lenny observed, "You seem experienced."

Lizzie felt wise beyond measure. "I am! Do whatever in your story! Write whatever in your song! Act whatever in theater! But this is real. Okay?"

Nobody replied to her wisdom and got angry.

She raised her voice. "I asked, is it okay?"

Bob asked, "What is okay?"

Lizzie had forgotten what she had asked. She said, "It. Is *it* okay?"

Lenny answered to calm her down, "Yes, yes. It is okay." It always worked well to agree with Liz.

She continued, "You cannot mess this up. You get adventurous out of charity, and it would bite you hard. Put your head down and do your work. That is it. Don't go looking for adventure."

Bob concluded the night. "That's right. Come! It's time."

They walked out of the club and saw a lone black man walking toward them.

Lenny said, "There's your adventure coming, Liz."

Lizzie asked, "What about him?"

Bob provoked her again, "Take him home with you."

Lizzie retorted, "I won't take a junkie home."

Lenny joined Bob. "This is your adventure. Look, He is walking right at us."

Anton walked into them, they moved on two sides to make way for him. He passed them by, and Bob called him to stop. Anton turned. They walked up to him. Lizzie said, "I bet he can't speak."

Lenny said, "Hello!"

Anton replied, "Gray concrete slab."
Lenny didn't get him. He asked, "What?"
Anton repeated, "Gray concrete slab."
Lenny repeated him, "He says gray concrete slab."
Lizzie and Delilah repeated, "Gray concrete slab."
Anton nodded and he continued.

"Gray concrete slab
Plowed from the east
Into Manhattan.
It plowed from the east
To the south of the Bronx
Into Man Hat Tan.
Wake up! Wake up!
Wake up to the violence.
No sounds of the kitchen
No cat on the wall
No children in the streets
No laughter in the lawns.
Ripped open bags of rotting garbage
Decorate
Hills of rubble
Un Der Neath.
Bulldozers rumble
Jackhammers bang
A dull concussion makes the hole inside deeper
Concussion that comes from the dynamite."

The group was struck dumb by the recitation from the homeless man. They clapped at what they thought was a performance. They put him in the car and took him home.

Anton woke up shivering, his heart racing, and his body sweating... To his surprise, he saw yellow wallpaper around and orange shag carpet under him. There was a bed sheet under him and a pillow under his head. Hard daylight fell on him from the direction of his legs. He heard voices from the other room. He wasn't in restraints, but he thought he was kidnapped. He pretended to sleep and made plans in his mind to escape.

"You have been awake for two hours. Get up," someone said.

He got up, and embarrassment, paranoia, and his unwashed face together created a horrifying expression on him. He saw three white girls and felt awestruck. What was he doing in an apartment with three white girls? The short one is very pretty! They stared at him, and he stared back at them as asking with his eyes what the next move was. Delilah glared at him with suspicious searching eyes.

Finally Anton asked, "Is there a bathroom here?"

Bob told him the bathroom was to his left.

Lizzie laughed at Bob's and Lenny's fright. "Who have we brought home? What are we going to do now?" Questions floated in the air. Anton returned and asked if he could use the towel. Lenny said, "You can use anything in there."

When Anton came back bathed and shaved, he looked tall, dark, handsome, and embarrassed. As he looked at everyone, they continued to look at him that way. He averted his eyes. He sat down on a bean bag and ate. Lenny said, "You can stay till the night, and then you leave. Lizzie, here, would like to talk to you a bit." Anton looked at the cozy apartment and felt nice and awkward. His eyes met Delilah's again, and he averted his gaze. After he ate, he retreated to his corner and fell asleep.

At night, they called him to eat. He asked them if he could stay for one more day. Lizzie said she hadn't got a chance to talk to him. They agreed he was not threatening. They allowed him. Delilah was not happy.

The next day when he woke up, most people had left the flat. Only Bob and Lenny were present, and they were rehearsing a play. Anton thought about Tomas. He thought about what had happened that night in Harlem. His mind seemed clearer. How did Cousin find out? What was he going to do about it? Anton went to the kitchen, took out bread slices from the refrigerator, and ate them. Bob told him he could put some sauces on the bread and showed him those. There was mustard, southwest, sweet onion, and two more sauces. "You can put some vegetables in it also, and there is meat on the lower shelf."

He prepared a big sandwich for himself. *Am I going to eat this?* He felt embarrassed opening his mouth to the size of his big sandwich. Lenny called him to sit in the living room with them. The room felt large to Anton. Colorful furniture was strewn all over the floor casually. The right wall had a full wall-size bookshelf that gave the room a majestic look, but the opposite wall had a big black-and-white poster of three white women in strapless dresses with sweetheart necklines playing drums, a guitar, and a cello. A beautiful drum set sat in front of that poster. Anton touched it lightly. The stereo systems on the two sides of the drum set looked ugly compared to the rest of the room. A record player and a twenty-one-inch TV set sat in their respective corners. Anton had never seen one that big in a house.

In the afternoon, Lizzie returned from college, and she took Anton to talk with him. Anton said there was nothing to tell about his life, and Lizzie persisted gently. Community life in the Bronx collapsed in the mid-fifties, and Anton talked about his life before that. The construction of the Cross Bronx Expressway coincided with the death of his mother. Anton grew emotional talking about his loss and told her that he wrote a small poem back when Malcolm X visited the Bronx sometime in the '60s. He tried to recall it, and Lizzie helped him. It was the same one he spoke the night they found him. Lizzie wrote it down in her notebook. Anton looked at the words on the paper and marveled that it was something beautiful and came from him.

The musicians returned and played in the evening. Delilah was on the drums while Gloria had a guitar. Anton did not know the other two girls on guitar and a keyboard. The music ran through Anton's nerves as he sat there and relaxed him a lot. He did not dare look at Delilah. Pausing at the moment, Gloria said, "Can we do this on a slower beat?"

Delilah replied, "No, that is not possible."

Gloria argued, "The song has to start slow."

"No. It would start fast."

"There is a rhythm to this."

"You have had your way with the other thirteen songs in the album, not this one. This one I am going to play my way," Delilah said.

"That is not the case. You interfered with every composition, and I have made compromises at more places than I was willing to," Gloria continued to argue.

"What you were willing to… let's go back; let's go to the fifth track."

"I cannot do this over and over with you." Gloria huffed.

"Yes, so let this be the way it is."

"Let us start slow, pick it up midway and then take it very high in the end."

"No. This one will start fast and stay fast."

"That's flat."

"It would veer slightly low toward the end, but that's it. The audience must move to the sound of it and not just hum the song."

"That way, it won't go very high."

"I want to start the song where you want to take it."

"That makes it very rebellious."

"Yes, that is the whole point."

"And what are you rebelling against?"

"Against everything, the war, the poverty, the inequality, injustice, the government, the culture."

"You are a part of the same culture."

"So?"

"You cannot rebel against yourself. That's not music. That's just confusion."

"The audience likes it. They *love* it."

"The audience response is no measure of the accuracy of your craft."

"Music is more than just craft."

Anton had never seen anyone talk like that. They were polite as they disagreed. They did not threaten to harm each other. But there seemed a fire burning underneath their words. The band was done for the night. Delilah looked at him with searching eyes. He averted his eyes, and left the room.

At dinner, they asked about him, and he asked if they knew obsession. They told him their work is their obsession. That was the only way an artist can pursue art. He told them he was obsessed with Cousin, the leader of the Black Skulls gang he worked in. He controlled others' minds from the inside. When Anton could not take it anymore, he left. But they found out, so he ran.

"That's when we found you on the Bowery," said Lenny.

He said he would leave immediately and asked them if they could get him some work somewhere. They told him to wait in the living room. Lizzie asked them to let him stay longer. Delilah was reluctant. Lenny said he seemed earnest. They called him back and told him he could stay for a while. Anton felt peace for the first time in a long time, and he hoped he wouldn't see a nightmare tonight.

Anton's nightmares became milder. Yet they were nightmares. The children stared at him but they did not move. The place of the nightmare had changed, and the time was dusk. When he woke up, he was in a sweat and out of breath. He saw Gloria and Delilah were already entangled in an argument.

Gloria said, "We are not going to get a chance like this again."

Delilah said, "I know. I know that."

"Not for a long time, maybe never."

"I know."

"You don't know. You are behaving like you don't know."

"I want to live a little. Enjoy life some."

"You will get plenty of time to enjoy after the recording."

"That is what you said before our first club performance. That is what you say every time we approach a new club. You say the same thing with every album on which we work."

"The producer is so good. She understands what we are doing. The engineers don't mix their sounds into your tracks. Do you know how rare that is in the industry?"

"No, I don't know that. I don't want to know that from hearsay. I want to experience it firsthand."

Gloria said under her breath, "Figure out every pothole by experience."

Delilah replied with a raised voice, "Don't mumble. Don't say things you can't say out loud."

Gloria glared back at her unaffected. "I said this girl wants to experience every single pitfall on the way."

"Yes, I'd do that if that's what it takes."

"But it does not take that. It takes a little bit of planning."

"Get done with your planning already! Your planning keeps life on the outside. Get out of it! When we first started playing at clubs, you never talked to anyone. You didn't allow me to get together with anyone. There were so many hot guys back there."

"You have more than compensated for what you have missed."

"Yes, and you ought to try some of it too. Get out of your head for once."

"To do what?"

"To do nothing! Look at people. Look at life. Get yourself out of your mind and just look. There is so much life all over the place."

"In this concrete jungle?"

"Yes, even in this concrete jungle. As that English poet said, you shall love your crooked neighbor with your crooked heart."

Gloria was taken aback. She couldn't argue any longer.

Delilah said, "Don't push me to the edge like this. I don't like to get so… pushy. Do whatever you like." And then she left.

Gloria sat down, thinking. Some part of what Delilah had said rang true to her. She was determined to prove it wrong. Her thoughts decided her destiny, and she had full control over both. But some part of what Delilah had said reached her, and she must flush it out before it destroyed any significant part of her. So Gloria left the flat and went to the city to find the holy grail of life or prove it did not exist.

Anton saw the drama unfold and felt intrigued by it. He tried to discern what they disagreed upon, but couldn't decipher it. He liked their music. He liked their disagreement too. If he could get between them, he would have prevented the unpleasant end to it. If intervention was possible, it was beyond his speaking skills. Anton sat on a bean bag and saw Lenny and Bob act a scene. Lenny stopped Bob in the middle.

Bob said, "I don't like it when you stop me in the middle of an act."

Lenny replied, "But you were doing it wrong."

"It's my way of doing it."

"But your performance affects mine."

Anton asked, "Can I say something?"

Lenny objected, "Why? What do you have to say?"

"Why? Why can't he speak?"

"All right, go ahead."

"What is the disagreement here?" asked Anton.

"Meaning?"

"I really like what you are doing here. You know, art. I mean, it's wonderful. I played the bongo once. But, I mean, what you people are doing, it's just fabulous. So, don't disagree. I mean, you can talk about the disagreement. That... That is what you should do."

"Okay. When I act, I take the cue of my emotion from him. If that cue doesn't come right, then my emotion is off."

Bob said, "An actor reads a line. That is all."

Lenny said, "Acting is a process of consciousness."

"Let it stay in the subconscious. Don't prod it. Just read your lines."

"I don't understand what the disagreement here is."

"We can demonstrate this."

"Let's do *The Godfather*."

"Bonasera?"

"No, let's do the Sonny, Michael, and Tom when Michael tells them he would kill Solozzo."

"That scene has three actors."

"Yes, one, two, and three."

"I haven't seen the film."

Bob was surprised. "Really? It came out in February this year."

Lenny was pleased. He said, "Nothing can be more wonderful than that. Let's watch it."

"Are you sure your gizmo will work?"

"It's called a VCR."

"Whatever CR it is... will it work this time?"

"What is it?"

"It's a video cassette record player that I got from my friend who works at Philips. This is the most cutting edge technology out there."

"If it works, which it did not last time."

They put the video cassette on the VCR and Bob prayed it'd work. They sat down to watch. Anton got lost in the rich textures of the film. It relaxed him and even made him smile. He got excited at the assassination attempt of Vito Corleone. Lenny and Bob enjoyed seeing him enjoy the film. He had only seen pornographic films before. He was deeply involved in the film's action. After Michael Corleone said, "It's not personal Sonny, It's strictly business." Lenny stopped the film.

Anton asked, "Why did you stop the film?"

"We will act this scene now."

Anton wanted to say he wanted to watch the film. But he didn't.

"You can watch the film later. This last scene is what we are going to act."

Bob gave him a printed script and said, "You play Michael's part."

"And you decide if an actor's performance is fluid that goes with the flow of everything else or just a job like a carpenter's where he just speaks the lines."

"I just have to speak the lines?"

"Yes. That is all you need to do."

Anton read Michael's lines flatly. Lenny and Bob laughed and mimicked Anton's tone. They showed him the scene again.

Lenny asked, "You see the difference?"

Anton was excited, and he said, "I want to try this."

"You have the script. You can practice. Put some emotion in the character."

"Just read the line, that's all."

Gloria roamed around the town for a long while and could find no specific evidence of life or its lack. She was at Times Square when the sun went down. The streets were littered with trash. The place had masculine lust written all over it with neon lights. Gloria entered a go-go bar. She took a table and ordered a drink. The waitress looked at her in surprise that she didn't belong there. Customers passed her by and made comments, "Why did she have her clothes on?" "She must not have gotten paid." "What did she do that they stopped paying her?"

Gloria saw topless girls dancing in thongs. Men tried to touch the girls, and the girls pushed them away, smiling. A customer got on top of the platform and danced with a girl there. Two bouncers rushed to the podium, and he grabbed a dancer in his arms. The bouncers picked him up and left him outside the bar. Behind them, more men tried to climb onto the platform. Gloria found it funny. The music was not to her taste, but it was the look on the men's faces and the struggle on the dancers' faces that made her leave. The peep show was better. A girl fucked a man in the cowgirl position. Then he spooned her, and finally, they made love in the lotus position. Gloria thought someone had put some thought into the act, but it was their costumes that she liked the most.

At the apartment, Lizzie returned from college. She changed and ate. She put a John Lennon record on the record player and sat with Anton.

Lizzie asked, "Do you like the stereo or the record player more?"

Anton replied he didn't know the difference.

Lizzie said, "Leave that. Tell me about your life."

Anton described the rubble, the buildings, the people, and the gangs. But Lizzie wasn't interested in this. She interrupted him, "No, tell me about you."

"This is about me. This is what I did. Everyone lived the same way. Nothing else ever happened back there."

"Yeah, but what about your hopes and dreams?"

Anton smiled and said, "Hope and I don't have no relation."

Lizzie smiled back at him and said, "That's not true."

"It's true. I don't have any dreams or anything I want."

"So you just live from day-to-day."

"Pretty much. Yes."

"So never any wishful thinking, even?"

"Wishful thinking?"

"Yes! If it were up to you that anything could happen in the world, what would you change?"

"I'd bring my mother back."

Lizzie smiled and nodded. "What else?"

"I would like the Bronx not to burn."

"Is it really burning? Like the entire area?"

"Yes."

"It is a little hard to believe. Why doesn't the news cover it? Why do the authorities not do something about it?"

"I don't know. But there is nothing left there to live for."

"Okay, if the Bronx wasn't burning, then what?"

"I wish all my friends weren't in a gang."

"So they would be something else?"

"Yes."

"What?"

"I don't know. Anything."

"What would you like them to be like?"

"Musicians. And actors. And writers." Anton gestured toward Lizzie as he said writers.

Lizzie felt a wave of warmth. She had not seen this kind of genuine admiration for what she was trying. She hadn't really achieved something. Yet here was one person who admired her just for the efforts she was making.

She asked, "So, you like the arts? What arts do you like?"

"I like graffiti art a lot. I know they say graffiti is… what they call it… vandalism. But graffiti is so much more than that. Graffiti is so free."

"Yes, that freedom has almost ruined Central Park right now."

"Why can't people express what they want on the streets?"

"I don't know. They say it is vandalism, and they say it is illegal."

"Imagine if writing was illegal."

"Publication of certain books *is* illegal."

"Really?"

"Yes."

"They banned *The Anarchist's Cookbook* last year. The year before, they banned *The Bluest Eye*. You see that poster over there?"

"The black woman?"

"She has written it. This year they have banned *A Day No Pigs Would Die.*"

Anton was surprised that the white girl had put up a poster of a black woman in her house. He wanted to ask what had she written that they had banned her book. But he didn't.

He asked, "They ban books also?"

"Yes, firearms are legal and easy to acquire. But books they have to ban."

"And I played the bongo once when I was young."

Delilah was passing the room, and she heard the bit about the bongo. She suspected he was lying.

By the time Gloria reached the sex shop, everything had started looking sexy to her. She felt horny. Her routine was intense fucking for two-to-three days with a stranger when she felt horny every four-to-six weeks. Right now, that was beside the point. She felt she would go out of control on the street. She felt something monstrous rising inside of her. The noise and the neon lights made it worse.

She was determined not to retreat into her mind. Was this what life felt like? The blood under her skin throbbed in her sensations, and she stayed with the sensations. The thought of murder crossed her mind. Was she capable of something like that? A man approached her, and if she were a ten feet tall black monster who ate humans, she would have eaten his head off. The man asked her the way toward Greenwich Village, and she told him to go north. She had told him the wrong direction. A wave of relief washed over her. It was time for her to go home.

In the evening, Anton stood on the patio alone wondering about Tomas, Cousin, how to get back, and what he'd do when he returned to Harlem. There was no way for him to return to the Bronx, he thought, and he heard a voice behind him say, "So, you play the bongo?" Anton turned around and saw Delilah. She was wearing a yellow top and a blue miniskirt. Talking to Lizzie had opened him up a little. But talking to Delilah was unprecedented. The musicians never spoke to him. She brought a bongo from her room and said, "Play," and sat down on the floor in front of him.

Anton felt tempted to look at her bare white legs. Instead, he took the instrument and threw his soul into it. At first, he was slow, and she found the playing ordinary, although she liked his control. Next, he raised the tempo, and she found the rise amusing. Then she found it interesting. The expression on her face didn't change a hair. He kept playing steadily at that rhythm, and she was impressed. Then he raised the tempo a nudge higher. She wondered if the smallest change in tempo was possible, and she had a sudden urge to learn that from him. The expression on his face was of trance... and then he suddenly let go. He brought the intensity down and veered the rhythm into something playful. Delilah found her shoulders and elbows moving. She found her fingers snapping. When Anton stopped, she smiled and said, "You play well." Anton smiled faintly and held her eyes. Delilah held his gaze for a few seconds, then averted her eyes and left. Anton looked at her as she walked in her yellow skirt away from the patio.

After dinner, as people smoked on the patio and Anton retreated, Gloria called him back.

She asked him, "So you worked in a gang?"

Anton nodded.

"What was it like?"

"It was horrible."

"Horrible? Why?"

"The things that I did, I regret everything."

"Like what?"

"Like you see a bunch of kids, you see how innocent they are. I threatened them that if they didn't do as they were told, I'd lock them up in the dark somewhere with rats in there. Then I locked some of them up for minor mistakes just to scare the rest of them. I saw their innocence die, and I saw something horrific replace it. They started doing to each to each other what I did to them. It was ... I see them in nightmares. I can't explain what they are like. They are like... true terror."

"So, that's all you did? You recruited and trained kids?"

"No! It was not like that."

"Then?"

"I moved product on the street…"

"So you sold what you were given. That's it?"

"You are not getting the picture."

"You are not giving a picture."

"Sixty-seventy gangs operate all over the Bronx. The largest is the Black Spades. They have about three hundred and fifty members. I worked with them most of my life. Then Cousin started the Black Skulls and we split from the Black Spades."

"But your work was mainly selling."

"The work that I do is territory control. The only thing that matters is the will to dominate."

"You talk as if something is wrong with it."

"Everything. Everything is wrong with that."

Anton got comfortable at the apartment. He knew it wouldn't last long. Sooner or later they would kick him out for one reason or another. He liked the comfort of the place, but he did not allow himself to become accustomed to it. They had gotten him a job as a dishwasher at a restaurant a few blocks away. His nerves were sensitive. The sound of utensils crashing bothered him. He tolerated the sensations. It happened to him when he was nervous. He had to find out what went wrong in Harlem. How did Cousin find out he was leaving? It was true that the man was a sorcerer. He might even have used magic or

411

dreamed that Anton was leaving. But he had to find out. He went to see Tomas twice but Cousin was there too both times. The woman who owned the restaurant shouted all the time. But she had grown to like Anton. She was touched by his sincerity in the first few days. One afternoon, Anton asked her for early leave, and she let him go.

Going to Harlem in broad daylight for an outsider was no easy feat. The Italian-Mexican Purple gangs would get to him if he were seen. But there was no other way out. In the evening, Cousin would be there. Somehow, taking cover, Anton reached the Snakehole Lounge. He saw Cousin's truck was outside the bar yet again. Anton had to take a chance. He had to find out. This could be his chance. He found the back door open, and he went inside. In that dark, dank space, he could hear Cousin talk.

How many have we lost so far? Cousin asked.

The other voice said, "Seventeen."

Cousin screamed, "I will kill them all! They think they can walk all over my territory just because one pussy boy walked away?"

"It's not that. Other gangs feel we have grown soft because he is still alive. So they made a move."

"I will tell them. I will tell them all who is soft and who is not. And you! If you see your friend, then you come find me... If I find out you are more loyal to him than to me, I will ..."

"No! No! No!"

412

"Then even if I am running low on men right now, I will kill you."

"No, don't say that. I did what you wanted. I told you he wanted to quit. I told you."

"But you let him slip through your fingers."

"He runs fast."

"Yes. But how fast and how far can he run? I will find him, and if I don't find him, it won't be good for you."

Anton snuck out as his heart beat wildly. He made his way back to the Upper East Side. The threat was real. All his calmness, his experience at the nice flat with yellow wallpaper and orange carpet and posters all over the walls and the big bookshelf were false. It was not true. It was not even a reality. It was just a temporary, passing fantasy. Back at the apartment, Anton observed that Gloria and Delilah ignored each other. He felt relaxed as he sat in the living room with colorful sofas. He went to the bathroom, took a long bath in the tub, and jerked off thinking of Delilah.

The next day, he was with Lenny and Bob when they rehearsed.

Lenny said, "Sonny dominates Tom."

"Sonny doesn't dominate anyone. Sonny's just being Sonny."

"See how he shouts at Tom. Tell me you see domination there."

"No. Tom doesn't agree. He says it's strictly business."

"And see how he patronizes Mike."

"No, look at the pause after Mike tells it was Clemenza who laughed first, and then Sonny found the nerve or the idea to laugh."

"You are looking at this too closely, too specifically. He pats Tom on the ass. He called Mike's swollen face beautiful."

"Let's have a line from Michael."

"We can't wait," Anton said without a trace of pathos."

Lenny said, "Put some feeling in there. What do you think is going on here?"

Bob said, "Let him finish his line."

Anton continued apathetically, "We can't wait. I don't care what Sollozzo says about a deal, he's gonna kill Pop, that's it. That's the key for him. Gotta get Sollozzo."

Bob stopped him. "What is happening in the film here?"

"I don't know. You didn't let me watch the film."

Lenny said, "You have seen the scene. What is happening here?"

Anton stayed quiet.

Bob said, "Michael dominates the scene when he brings the solution to the problem of Solozzo."

Lenny argued, "No. Look at the scene in its entirety. Who dominates it? Who is the force behind the action here? Mike's growth comes later on. Here, in this scene, Mike is only like a sidekick. Mike only gives a solution like a loyal brother who wants to contribute."

Anton agreed, "You might have a point there."

Bob said, "Point my ass."

"Yes, I can see that Sonny moves everyone in the scene."

Gloria stood outside a convenience store. "Is there a place, a life more lifeless than one of these stores? Where is life? Is it packaged in one of these items? It must be." She went in. "Is it in the snacks? No. That's just food. Newspapers? Definitely not. Magazines, toiletries, medicines... confectionery... where is life? Her eyes fell on a strawberry milk carton and an idea flashed in her mind. She put it in the inner pocket of her coat, picked a magazine from the stand and went to the counter. The old man at the counter looked at her suspiciously. Why was she buying *The Dude: The Magazine Devoted to Pleasure*, a men's magazine. She looked at him and smiled. She had never smiled at a stranger in her whole life. The shopkeeper looked at her with knitted brows.

She grinned as she walked out of the store with her stolen milk carton. Her thrill was greater than the last time. She did not feel the urge to go somewhere on the street. She stopped and sat on a corner. She saw other people hurry. She was not in any hurry at all. The distance from real life felt good.

Anton started harboring a fantasy of what if he could stay at that apartment longer, much longer. There was no way he could have suggested it. Lizzie and Anton sat on the sofa and talked. Anton had started to feel comfortable in the house.

Lizzie asked Anton, "Do you expect things from others?"

Anton replied, "Expect?"

"I want to share a secret with you. I expect people to care about my ambition."

"You want them to be happy when you become successful?"

"No! I mean, yes, but not just that. I want people to worry if I am not progressing; I want someone to ask me every day with excitement what new thing I discovered today and what new ideas I had."

Anton looked at her, puzzled. "You want someone to ask this daily?"

"Yes."

"What about your boyfriend?"

"Boyfriend is a different thing. Games of dating are different. You don't share important things with people you date."

Anton thought she was speaking some other language.

Lizzie continued, "Let me tell you another secret. I secretly resent these people, everyone who is working on something creative. I see them, and I feel why them, why not me?"

Anton felt uncomfortable here. He could not understand why he was privy to this information.

"They are so involved with each other, but they never ask me what I read and what I think about one thing or another, especially Delilah, but also Bob and Lenny. Gloria is very interesting to talk to, but she doesn't speak much."

Anton thought it best not to fan the flames of envy here.

Gloria looked at a boy sitting on the sidewalk nearby. He looked at her. Emotion on his face was sparse. Then he made a face at her, and she made a face at him. She found the boy in the tattered T-shirt very beautiful. She took out her milk carton and watched him drink it. *Whatever is there in the carton must be life*, she thought.

Anton and Delilah sat in the living room. Delilah sat reading *The Village* magazine. Anton sat looking at Delilah. When she raised her eyes, he looked elsewhere. She continued reading. Sometimes she almost looked at him and then she didn't. Sometimes she looked a foot or two away from him. Sometimes she looked two feet above his head and sometimes she looked at his knees. Then when he looked at her without caution she caught his eyes, took his name for the first time and asked, "You want to play the bongo?"

Anton nodded. "Okay." And he got up.

"Where are you going?"

"To get it."

"You don't get to go into my room, rolling stone," she said as she let a slight bit of tongue out of her lips.

Anton tried hard to find the nerve to play. She brought the instrument. He sat on a bean bag and put the bongo in front of him. He put his fingers on the bongo, but they refused to move. He sat frozen in front of the instrument. His face contorted in embarrassment, and Delilah was thoroughly amused.

Later at night, she talked to Gloria.

Delilah said, "Can I talk to you for a bit?"

Gloria replied, "Yes."

"You have not been jamming."

"Yeah."

"Why?"

"Why what?"

"Why not?"

"Why not what?"

"We have a deadline very near."

"So?"

"Shall we work some?"

"I don't want to."

"Look, I might have said a little too much the other day."

"Whatever."

"You cannot just abandon everything like this."

"I think I can."

Delilah controlled her excitement.

"So, you are not going to work on the song anymore?"

"I don't know."

"Then who should I ask?"

Gloria stared at her for a moment, then said, "Ask whoever you please. I do not care."

"Look, I know you are upset. I crossed a line. I should not have hurt your feelings."

"Do I look upset to you?"

Delilah saw that wasn't the case.

"Then what is going on?"

"What is going on what?"

Delilah struggled to keep herself calm.

She continued her line of inquiry. "Why aren't you working on the songs? You are the more dedicated one between the two of us."

Gloria replied, "I said I don't want to."

"But why?"

"As you said, it's a free world."

"No, it's not a free world. Everyone has commitments."

Gloria said, *Look who is talking* in her head, and it made her laugh. Then suppressing her laugh, she said, "Okay."

Delilah reminded Gloria about the fourteen songs in their collection.

"What is going to happen to those songs? We have already recorded some. If we don't finish, none of them will see the light of day."

For the first time, Gloria saw a shade of earnestness in her eyes. But it was far from enough.

"I think you think I care. But I don't."

Delilah welled up. She had not seen this coming. Without Gloria, she was lost. She ran away to her room.

That night Delilah did not eat on the patio.

Gloria seemed to glow with inner satisfaction. After dinner, Anton talked to her. Anton said, "Imagine you are on a journey. There is no destination, and there is no sense of beginning. You just keep sailing on the sea on and on. That is what personal ambition in crime is like."

Gloria said, "Your imagination is poetic. Have you ever thought about writing for music?"

"Our music is different. Our instruments are different. The rhythm is different. The beat is different... Who would listen to the music a black man makes?"

"If you are sure that your music is different, then at the very least your people will listen to it."

"I have never thought about any of this. Time passes in securing territory."

"How do you do that?"

"I told you it is a game of the will to dominate. You said there is nothing wrong with it."

"I don't know anything about it."

"Ground by this ..."

Gloria smirked.

Anton smiled and continued. "Okay. People develop a personality and a desire to control. There's no difference between what they want, what they are, and how they behave."

"Why should there be?"

"You are not like that. Naked desire and pursuit like that is ... is ..."

"Is what?"

"I don't know what it is like. I like it where people are civilized."

"You don't know the treachery of the civilized. You are innocent like that."

Anton smiled that she called him innocent.

"So what does it look like... the naked will to dominate?"

"The strongest will I haven is in Cousin. He was a low-level peddler in the Black Spades gang. I have known him from those days. People don't rise from that level in gangs. They spend their entire life at the street level. But Cousin rose up. He betrayed a number of people, and he was always severe on those who crossed him. He made those loyal ones his dirty work, and it made them more loyal toward him. His hunger for power is matched only by his capacity for it."

"When you live cocooned in a shell for a very long time, you forget what is on the inside. But in a life of adventure, like your Cousin's... You bring out what is inside of you. It's good if it is a saint, but it's okay too if it is a monster. At least you live like who you are."

"I am no saint. And I don't want to be a monster like him. Can I be someone normal?"

Gloria smiled. "We have left normal somewhere far behind us."

There was risk if he returned to confront Tomas. But Anton's decisions were always biased by emotion. There was no stopping him from reaching out to Tomas. One evening he took off from the café and went to the Snakehole Lounge It wasn't the busy hour yet. Anton entered through the back door. He saw Tomas, grabbed him by his collar, and asked a question. Tomas pushed him away and retorted, "What betrayal are you speaking of? I told you not to leave. I asked you repeatedly. Do you know how many men we lost? How many streets of business we lost because you left? Because you wanted to sleep? There is a war going on out there just because of one person."

Anton was taken aback. He sat in a chair and asked, "How many have we lost?"

Tomas replied, "Why do you care? You go and have your sleep!"

Anton stayed quiet.

Tomas said, "We have lost twenty-three good men, and I don't know how many children."

"I cannot come back."

"Come back? I promised I'd inform on you next time I see ya. For old time's sake, I am giving ya one chance. Leave and never come back here." When he saw Anton not get up from his chair, Tomas grabbed him by the collar and said, "Next time, I will not warn you."

Anton pushed him away and said, "You cannot dodge guilt. You informed on me *before* anyone had died." The two friends of the past got into a scuffle as Cousin's truck stopped outside the bar. Cousin entered the bar, and his face turned red when he saw Anton. He grabbed Anton and pulled him away from Tomas. Anton threw a punch at him and missed. Cousin punched him in the belly. Cousin struggled to find words to speak, and this aggravated his assaults on Anton. He dodged Anton's punches, and not a single one landed on him. Anton got exhausted. Cousin's every punch landed exactly where he intended on Anton's body.

Cousin spoke finally, "What didn't I do for you? What haven't I done for him?"

He repeated the question with every punch and kick. He straddled Anton and asked as he punched his face, "Tell me why... Why did you do it? Where did you find the nerve to leave here? No one leaves me. You hear me, bastard! Tell me."

Anton had no strength left to resist the punches. He nodded in agreement that he would tell.

Cousin sat on a chair. Anton squatted in front and said, "You are a clever man. You are the cleverest man I have known. I don't know how you do it, but it is sorcery. You control people by knowing what they think, controlling what they think. You sit somewhere deeper than their own thoughts. I am not going to tell you what I have found and where I found the nerve so that..." Anton jumped on Cousin, and Cousin fell with his chair on his back with Anton on top of him. "...so that you kill it then," Anton said, jumped to his feet, and ran for his life.

He stayed frightened all the way through as he ran toward the Upper East Side. At the apartment, he went to the bathroom before anyone could see him covered in blood. When he came out, nobody noticed his wounds, or if they did, they ignored them. It was not until the next day that Anton talked to someone. It was Lizzie, late in the evening the next day.

Lizzie asked him, "I want your opinion. Your honest opinion. Why don't I write? Why can't I write? Why don't

I get those ideas? I watch a film, and I think I could have thought about this. I think I could have thought better."

Anton interrupted her before she started sharing secrets he didn't want to know.

"There was a guy in our gang. He loved to talk."

Lizzie interrupted him and said, "I have an idea for a film. There's an apartment. One guy tells a group of people an idea for a film."

"What idea?"

"It doesn't matter. It is some idea and they make fun of him for it, for his creative leap."

Anton ignored her and continued. "You could have found him at all sorts of places at all times. He met a lot of people, heard a lot of stories, told a lot of stories. His problem was that none of his stories were true. He turned other people's stories into his own. He boasted, and he shared thrilling experiences, none of which actually happened to him."

"Sounds like an interesting guy."

"No, he was not."

"He was. He turned other people's stories into his own."

"But he never did any work, and he never had any experience."

"He was creative."

"He was a nothing. You know what happened to him."

"What?"

"He boasted in front of the wrong guy, and he was shot point-blank."

Lizzie felt hurt. Anton failed to register it.

He continued, "He failed to see what was right for him and what was not."

Lizzie was not listening. The dead guy was her hero, and she did not want to insult him anymore by contributing another word to this conversation.

"He failed to see because he never worked. If you want to write, then just write. Stop talking about writing."

Gloria stepped out of the apartment building, and she looked to decide which way to go. She wanted to go north, to Harlem and beyond. She hadn't quite gotten to that kind of wildness in her spirit. She took the subway train to downtown Manhattan. She eyed couples on the train. Boys couldn't keep their eyes off of her, and their girlfriends quarreled with them. She eyed girls in gay couples, and the same happened there. One couple took her, and she kissed the two girls wild. At lunch, she went to a posh restaurant and focused her attention on a dining couple. They weren't particularly happy, and they weren't particularly sad. After watching them for a while, Gloria went to their table and asked the man why he wasn't there for lunch. She asked who the woman was.

The man got confused and apologized that he didn't know her or didn't remember his appointment with her. The woman looked at them suspiciously. Gloria went closer to the man and said, "You aren't so forgetful at night, darling." The woman's expression turned as if the flesh on her face would melt. Gloria told the man to call her whenever he wanted. She said he had her number, and she left. She enjoyed the trouble. She enjoyed people's reactions when they realized what had hit them in their drowsy lives. Her appetite grew, and she enjoyed the feeling of power. She had been missing out on much.

Lenny, Bob, and Anton acted in the Solozzo killing discussion scene. It was of help in Lenny's upcoming audition for a role in Eugene O'Neill's *Mourning Becomes Electra* off-Broadway. He had waited a long time for a part in this play.

Lenny said, "Forget who you are and let the inner self, the homunculus take control."

Anton's half-assed philosophy was intolerable for Bob. He had kept himself quiet for a long time, but not any longer.

Bob said, "Acting is performance. That is all. You act. You perform."

"No. Acting is the transformation of your soul. The performance happens by itself."

"Just like that?"

"Yes! Just like that."

Bob moved his head in disapproval.

"Let's ask him."

He turned toward Anton.

"Both of you are right in your own way. You say one thing … and you say another thing…"

"No, both cannot be valid here."

"Yes, both cannot be valid here. Let's act once."

The scene started with to and fro between Sonny and Tom. When Anton's turn came, he spoke his lines with menace and felt energized in his nerves. He wondered where did this come from. Then he reflected he was just speaking lines written on paper. He read with perfect control, "They wanna have a meeting with me, right? It will be me, McCluskey, and Sollozzo. Let's set the meeting. Get our informers to find out where it's gonna be held. Now, we insist it's a public place... a bar, a restaurant... someplace where there's people so I feel safe. They're gonna search me when I first meet them, right? So I can't have a weapon on me then. But if Clemenza can figure a way to have a weapon planted there for me, then I'll kill 'em both." His eyes gleamed as he said the last words.

Bob exclaimed, "You see! That's performance."

Lenny objected, "That's not how the character is supposed to be played. There has to be a balance with other actors."

"That doesn't matter. You must trust others' performance and not worry about them. Worry about your performance alone."

Anton felt thrilled and said, "Yes, it is performance, man. One man's performance. You are one person, one actor."

Lenny said, "The act is an imagination, and it has to be one, singular, and not a potpourri of interpretations. I have to stop listening to you. You are doing the opposite of helping me."

"I am doing exactly what I have always done."

"No. Something is different. I have to stop listening now. I'll end up messing up my audition." Lenny retreated as Bob and Anton watched him go.

A haggard, disheveled Delilah approached Gloria.

Delilah said, "Our partnership has been the single most valuable thing for me in my life."

Gloria replied, "Yet, you abused it for... living life. That is more important for you."

"It is not more important... it is just something that I need to do."

"Why? Why do you need to do this? What would happen if you don't?"

Delilah was on the brink of collapse. She said, "Don't ask this. You know the answer to this..."

"No, I don't."

"Well, then, so be it."

"Yeah, so be it."

"No, please don't give up on me. I don't have anyone to trust."

"And who do I have to trust? Who can I trust?"

"You can trust me." Delilah started sounding almost childlike through her tears.

Gloria said, "I am never going to trust you again."

Delilah started crying inconsolably. She shouted from amidst her tears, "Do you want to know why I am so fickle? Why I need to distract myself all the time? Why I crave attention from boys and men? It is because I don't want to turn into my mother who lived under the thumb of that brutal man, and she never did or could do anything her

428

heart pleased even when she was perfectly alone. I will turn into her if I commit to a single person or a single thing. I am afraid of that; terrified of that! And you know this. I told you. You knew about this."

Delilah cried bitterly. Then she said, somberly through her tears, "It is not as if I have not done anything for you. I brought you to life. You had banished yourself to your guitar. I opened doors for you. I helped you relax. I brought you down to the earth, and I showed you ways to talk to people. We did so well... We were so... We were beautiful. We were perfect."

Delilah broke down again and ran into her bedroom. Later, she sat in the living room and Anton sat opposite to her. She did not look at him. She kept her head down, thinking. Gloria smoked on the balcony. Then Delilah asked Anton, "Do you want to see my room?"

Anton felt strange. He wanted to, but not when she was so vulnerable.

"Come on. It's a pretty place. I promise."

She rose, went up to him, gave him her hand, and took him to her room. The walls had taffy color wallpaper and a big poster of a boyish woman with puffed pixie-like hair, wearing a high-waist skirt with a loose shirt and rolled-up sleeves, and a gleeful expression was on the wall. She was playing drums, and the poster was back-and-white. Delilah told him, "She is Honey Lantree. They did not let her play but they could not stop her either."

Anton looked at Delilah, said, "They can't stop you either." He kissed her and she kissed him back. They rolled up the bed and as they got undressed, she said she won't go to Kentucky repeatedly. Anton got on top of her as he kissed her breasts and said, "You are not going anywhere, baby." She got on top of him and rode him. After they were done, she lay in his arms and told him he is a sweet man. She told him he is talented. She told him not to let anyone tell him otherwise.

Anton confessed to her, "I don't want to go back to crime."

Delilah reassured herself. "She will come around. I have faith. I believe she will come around."

Delilah fell asleep. Anton tucked her in the blanket and went out on the balcony. Gloria was smoking there. She offered him a cigarette.

Anton asked, "What is between you and her?"

Gloria smiled, "You don't want to go there, lover boy."

They smoked in silence for a while. Before Gloria left, she said, "Be cautious. Do not fall into trusting her." She left, and Anton sat smoking alone on the patio.

The next day, news arrived on the telephone that the band had lost their contract with the music company. Delilah said to Gloria, "Are you happy now?"

Gloria got amused and looked at her.

Delilah said, "Three years of hard work, three years since we met at Woodstock, three nonstop years of hard work... How you harassed me to work from album to album, from song to song, from night club to night club. We got close a few times, but this one was a godsend, and you had to deny that to us."

Gloria nodded ever so slightly.

Delilah went on a frenzied scream, "Why? What did you do it for, stupid woman? And what difference would it make anymore anyway? It is lost. All is lost."

Delilah sat silently on a bean bag and stared into emptiness.

Lenny entered the apartment, and Bob jumped to his feet.

He asked, "What happened?"

Lenny said, "I didn't get it."

Bob couldn't believe. "How? Why?"

"Leave it."

Bob retreated back.

Gloria got up and addressed everyone, "Look at us. Look at us. What are we? Just a bunch of losers. That's all we are."

Bob stopped her. "That's not true."

Gloria shot him down. "You appear in the same single production over and over. You try to help him, but he doesn't get anywhere either…"

Lenny joined in, "Help me! Help me or hurt me?"

Bob couldn't believe what he heard. "Hurt you?"

Lenny said, "What else? All I could remember in the audition were things you said and not the words from the play. *Your job is your lines, worry about your own performance.*"

Gloria continued, "And we were trying to make music while we don't agree on even the most basic of things. And this girl…" Gloria pointed to Lizzie.

Bob stopped her again. "You leave her out of this. She is far too young to be criticized like that."

Delilah joined in, "And others are what? Too old that they should take all the crap that you actors throw on them?"

Lenny retorted, "We actors... We take care of everything down here, from food to utilities, to groceries, to bills, to maintenance ... And you have the audacity to point at us."

Gloria said, "Frankly, I would be more willing to live with successful actors in a filthy apartment than with a clean, well-furnished, well-maintained apartment with you folks."

They spiraled into a bickering contest as Lizzie and Anton watched, sitting amidst them. Lizzie looked at Anton, and Anton averted his eyes.

Bob asked, "What has happened to us? How have we come to this?"

Lizzie said she knew why this has happened to them and when this happened to them. She pointed toward Anton and said, "It was the night we brought him home with us. He tried to get between us all and pitted us against each other, so he would get to stay here forever."

They had found a common enemy. Anton did not have much to defend himself. He was living on charity. He pleaded, "I cannot go back." Delilah's nasty glare was back. Lizzie stared in the same way. Gloria looked suspicious, and Bob and Lenny looked as if they had decided. Anton continued to try but all he could say was, "I cannot go back."

Bob said, "We cannot help you."

Anton said, "I did not even finish watching *The Godfather*," with hope that if they allowed him a few hours he might talk them out of it. Nobody replied a word to him. He did not have much to pack. He left the apartment without ceremony.

Standing outside the apartment, Anton had a premonition his paranoia would come back. He wanted to cherish the feeling of freedom for one last time. But his shame did not let his feet stop. Drug trade pulled him from one side, and the threat to his life pushed him away. He told his situation to the woman at the café. She allowed him to stay at her café at night and sleep in the storeroom. His nightmares grew worse. They acquired a look and a feel like never before in the cramped space of the storeroom.

Whenever a truck passed by the store, Anton's heart beat like a train passing on a bridge. His nerves pushed him to run away, and his situation compelled him to stay put. He became a tangled mess of impulses inside his body. Unkind remarks toward anyone frightened him. Unkind remarks toward him pushed him to the edge of rage. His heart raced at everything. He retreated away, and the more he retreated, the more his paranoia grew on him.

The sounds in the kitchen were too many and too much. They had become impossible to bear for him by now. He did not notice the passage of day or night. He stayed vigilant all the time and grew slower and slower at work. The owner of the restaurant was a kind woman. She let him stay on. She tried to speak to him, but his speech had receded. His nightmares alternated between haunting children and persecuting gangs. Every waking hour, he observed people suspiciously and averted his eyes when they looked back at him. In the hour of greatest dread, he recalled the people at the Wellraven in apartment 1102. How did he mess it up? He tried to blame himself, but he failed to find anything wrong in what he said or did. He recalled afternoon chats with Lizzie on that sofa in that cozy room and her wish to become a writer. He even gave her positive action guideline for writing. He recalled the cigarettes shared and talks on the balcony with Gloria. He often wished to return to the building to just have a look at the apartment. To experience some warmth of a cozy world that he had left behind. Acting with Lenny and Bob was the first thing that receded from his memory. He remembered Delilah the most. He recalled the times when he had feared looking at her. He remembered her eyes with fury and her eyes with tears both. In the times of great anguish from his imaginary fears, he recalled her petite form, and for an instant, the memory dispelled his fears.

One day, he saw Delilah. She was wearing a yellow skirt and a blue top. She was passing by, and he looked at her approaching him. She looked at him for a moment and her face contorted with mild distaste. It shattered his heart. He did not believe that expression, but ultimately it got through to him. His belief in the goodness of the people at the Wellraven apartment broke down. That night he dreamed the pale children of the dark and the Black Skulls gang hunting him together. He couldn't get away, and they got to him.

He woke up, and he found himself in a state of terrible anger. He told the woman he'd be gone for the day and might not even return. The woman looked at him for a few moments of scrutiny. Then she nodded okay and went back inside her café.

Gloria was out for one of her sojourns in the city. She saw Anton, and she followed him. Anton took a subway, and he went straight to the Bronx. Gloria felt alive and vigilant, as she felt she was going into a dangerous part of the city. However, what she saw was the opposite. She could not believe this was the same city. This part of the city was devastated as opposed to the part of the city she lived in. Anton looked for Cousin from garage to garage, from bar to bar, from building to the next dilapidated building. Gloria followed him from a distance everywhere.

By noon Anton was tired, and he sat outside a battered building. He saw Cousin walking with great haste toward him from a distance.

Cousin said as he approached, "So you have come back to die?"

Anton replied, "Yes, go ahead. Kill me. Do the honor of killing me."

"There is no honor in killing a lying renegade piece of shit. But I will kill you still."

He went up to Anton and punched him. Gloria felt shocked as she saw Anton get hit. Cousin beat Anton and Anton did not even try to hit Cousin back. It seemed to her that Anton wanted to die. Cousin kicked him and punched him and every time Anton got up to get hit some more. Gloria felt perplexed. Why was he doing that? Why didn't he hit back?

The sensation of the first punch relieved Anton's paranoia instantly. A smile glided across his face. The more Cousin hit him, the more Anton's nerves felt at ease. His fears evaporated, the daylight shone brighter for him, and the man beating him seemed less than threatening. Gloria watched him and couldn't figure what to make of it. Anton's spirit was unscratched.

Cousin was shouting abuses at him. Anton dodged a punch and returned a heavy blow to Cousin. Cousin was thrown several steps back. Then, Anton asked, "And what are you?" Gloria felt a thrill of unexpected happiness as she saw the one she knew beat the one she didn't.

Cousin said, "I protect of my people. I provide for them." Cousin punched Anton as he said this.

Anton laughed and delivered three blows to Cousin and said, "All you do is take from them, and they don't need your protection; they need protection from you; from the likes of you."

Cousin punched angrily, but his blows had no effect on Anton. Anton spoke as he thrashed Cousin.

Anton said, "Remember Santino. You killed him just on suspicion? You remember Chavez, who changed his gang, and what you did to him? How many names you want me to say? How many?"

Cousin replied, "I live for my people, my way. I do not know any other way. I did not build that bridge that destroyed my father's shop and killed him. I did, and I do what I must for my people. I did not run away from my people, leaving my own in this waste."

Anton stopped hitting Cousin. Cousin abused him some and shouted at him to get lost. Then he left. Anton sat there thinking as Gloria walked up to him in that ramshackle of a building.

Anton smiled through his bleeding face and asked, "What are you doing here?"

Gloria answered, "Seeing what a life of adventure looks like."

Anton asked, "Liked what you saw?"

Gloria said, "I did."

Anton smiled.

Gloria said, "You should come with me."

Anton recalled the way they made him leave and how he had pleaded. He asked, "Why?"

Gloria said, "Everything at the Wellraven has been falling apart ever since you left. People bicker all the time for no reason at all. The pursuit of art is collapsing. It has become just like this place."

Anton thought for a few minutes as they sat there quietly. Then he walked with her. On the subway train, Anton asked Gloria to forgive Delilah.

He said, "You should forgive her."

Gloria asked, "Why?"

"Why?"

"Yes, I have been looking for a reason, any reason at all."

"But she is not a reasonable person."

"Yes, and she would never be."

"Yes."

"Then I have no reason to forgive her."

"You don't."

"So I can't forgive her."

"You can."

"How? Why? What for?"

"For what you have at that apartment is a special thing. People who live amidst goodness, who create it in their lives, often do not see it. Civilized or uncivilized, what you have there is quite something."

Gloria looked outside the window as she heard him.

Standing outside the apartment building, Anton welled up. Inside the apartment, Gloria said that Anton would live with them and people felt relieved to hear it. Even Lizzie smiled at his return.

Anton went to Lizzie and apologized, "I don't know anything about writing. If I said anything that upset you, I take it back. I am sorry."

He went to Lenny and Bob and thanked them for the gift of voice. He told them even if they couldn't agree with each other, they were still good. Anton sat down on a bean bag and looked around him. He did not belong to this place of privilege. These were nice people but they were not his own. He tried to recall something that had touched him deep down. But his paranoia had washed everything away.

Anton got up and said, "I do not belong here. This is such a nice place. But it is not my own. I have not earned it. I have not earned anything."

Delilah asked him, "What are you talking about?"

Anton answered, "You don't need me here. You people are good by yourself. There are people who need me. I have to go back."

Gloria asked, "Go back where?"

"To the Bronx, that is burning. If I don't build what is mine then who will? We need to build our world back from what destruction that bridge caused us."

Delilah, Bob, and Lenny couldn't comprehend. Lizzie understood but did not agree. Gloria smiled.

As Anton turned away, Delilah asked him to wait. She went to her room and brought the bongo to him and asked, "Will I be seeing you on the music scene?"

Anton took the bongo and smiled. "You will have to check the music scene of the city for that."

On his way back, Anton stopped at the café where he worked. He told the woman he is well and is going back to his part of the city. The woman kissed him on the forehead and blessed him as he left.

# BELLALOKI
## D.L. HARTMAN

# The Accident

On the corner of Sixty-Ninth and First Street, in New York City, stood a twenty-story building known as the Wellraven. It was rather a sickly shade of orange but seemed to have a diverse population of tenants. The Wellraven served the purpose of being a neighborhood landmark. It was not just due to its putrid color, but because of the many rumors circulating about the building. Past tenants talked of strange occurrences. Many quietly spoke of a ghost, a spirit, a lost soul that roamed the building. In the history of the Wellraven no one had been able to confirm this as being true. It was a definite draw to people and site-seers, just wanting one look at a possible haunted building in NYC.

One late afternoon, in mid-September, the normal motion of the city came to a screeching halt. The sound of brakes locking, the crunching, the shearing of metal parts, the breaking of glass. The noise of an automobile being turned into a jigsaw puzzle of parts and pieces. Soon emergency vehicles started to arrive. The street filled up with curious and concerned onlookers. Scatterings of conversations could be heard but not attached to any one person.

"Do you know what happened?"

"It's always drugs or booze."

"Some kid borrowed his parent's car; their ass is grass."

"Hey, let's show some respect here. Hush up. There are two people dead here."

"That fancy car?"

"Neighbors have a Cadillac."

"Maybe that used to be a fancy-ass caddy, not no more!" Nervous laughter washed over the small group of bystanders.

## Ruby Reacts

"Oh, dear." Ruby grabbed her cat Marmalade and made a beeline for her balcony. She could look down from her apartment on the tenth floor to the street and see the chaos below. All of the tenants had balconies that gave each a distinctive view of the city. Ruby loved her view of southern Manhattan and watched the seasons change along the tree-lined banks of the East River. Now, as she watched the activity, she recognized many of her neighbors from the building blending into the crowd. She stood there twittering, "Marmalade, what should I do? You know that is too many people for me. Oh, what should I do?"

The noise in the building pitched to a higher crescendo as other residents of the Wellraven left to take the stairs or ride the lone elevator to the bottom. Making a decision, Ruby dropped Marmalade to the floor. She knew she must go down. People would talk if she didn't. Not like they needed a lot of encouragement. She had heard the gossip.

Her Parrot, Xerox, kept her well-informed of the chatter in the building.

There was a hush that came over the building. That was her cue to leave. One quick check of herself in her Ethan Allen coat stand by the door; purple hair patted smooth, lipstick in place, a pinch to each cheek for color, and she was ready to make her appearance. Out of habit, she stroked her namesake brooch, feeling the coolness against her throat. She believed it set her apart from her peers. The brooch would cause a shimmer of magnificent light all around the room when Ruby touched it. The ruby brooch was an heirloom and one of her prized possessions.

Xerox, her loud and aggressive parrot shouts, "Read 'em their rights. Hands in the air."

"Oh Xerox, this isn't a television show." She shook her head at him. "I'll be back soon."

"Marmalade's hungry, treat for Xerox." Ruby just ignored his continuous chatter.

Ruby had waited for a chance to ride the elevator in solace. She wished she was younger and the stairs were an option. Her view from the tenth floor was a fair trade-off until she had to ride the elevator. Ruby had a problem with enclosed spaces. It became even worse if there were other riders. She really didn't gravitate toward many people. They seemed to examine her as an oddity. She had been told it was her eyes. They looked normal enough to her, but she knew. It was okay, she had Xerox to keep her in the know. His fabulous hearing and huge vocabulary kept her informed and laughing most of the time.

As she approached the elevator, Ruby felt a sigh of relief escape her lips...No other passengers. At least not on her floor. She found herself holding her breath as she watched each floor number pass without stopping. When the doors opened, she headed toward the sound of voices. Some speaking loudly, others in hushed tones.

## An Accidental Meeting

Outside, there was a lot of noise and confusion. She spotted Earl Joy, the building superintendent. Ruby found him attractive and assumed he might be close to her age. He was always dressed the same. It was as if he had acquired a look, he felt went with his job. He gave off a very professional vibe, but yet you were confident he could snake your drain while whistling a tune. Earl Joy dressed from head to toe in gray. Always a felt cowboy hat set sharply on his head. It was his signature, like Ruby's brooch. His eyes twinkled, and Ruby's heart melted just a bit. She decided to make an attempt to cross over to where he stood. There was so much scattered debris. She realized it was going to take some doing to safely make it across to where Earl Joy was standing.

Instead, she stopped to take in the carnage. There were several ambulances, the medical examiner, and the coroner. A fairly good sign of fatalities. Of course, police cars were lining the street, parked at angles, even on the sidewalk. While observing the melee, she heard a young couple say that the people in the fancy car had died. What

445

had caused the accident was still a mystery. Ruby did what she does best. She took in the entire scene in one look, determining her role. She saw a young teenager sitting by himself, taking it all in. He didn't appear upset, more just lost in thought. Ruby's antennas were pulsating. She knew why she was here. Looking over at Earl Joy, she pursed her lips, saying, "Duty first." Since a very young girl, Ruby knew she had a gift. She was able to take in an entire picture and determine if she played a role; something that would lead to her destiny. It was obvious to her that this young man needed her. For what? Time would tell.

## Richard

It was as if a path opened for Ruby, guiding her toward this young man. She politely nodded her head in the direction of other tenants from the Wellraven. Ruby was on a mission and not to be distracted. Approaching the teen, Ruby sat asking, "Do you mind?"

He turned toward her, not seeming startled at all. His dark eyes were taken up by large, dilated pupils.

"My name is Ruby. I live in that apartment building over there. The orange one."

He didn't look away from her to acknowledge the Wellraven. He said quietly, "I'm Richard."

Ruby gently placed her hand on the young man's knee, hoping not to alarm him. "Are you just watching? Somehow, I don't think that you are. How are you involved in this?"

Richard politely asked Ruby, "Do I know you?"

Looking him in the eye, she replied, "No, but I think we are about to become very close friends. Were you part of the accident?"

Richard's eyes took on a blank stare. "I think I was in the back seat. Those are my adoptive parents. They live in Syracuse and were bringing me to the city to look for an apartment before I start school in January.

"I think I was asleep when it happened. I didn't take time to think about what I was doing. I just came over here and sat down. I didn't know what I should do. I heard that my parents were dead. Do you know?"

"I'm sorry, Richard. I only know what I have heard. I think judging by the medical personnel and the equipment, it is very possible."

"Oh God, no! I can't go back to the orphanage. I was there most of my life. I have to get out of here. If they find out I am only fifteen, they will send me back for sure."

"Richard. You can't run from your troubles. They will only be worse when they find you. And they will. If I may be so bold as to ask, what is your situation?"

## Richard's Beginnings

As Richard calmly began to ruminate, Ruby had not prepared herself for the story she was about to hear. This child had begun life with more than a few bumps in the road. Much of his story was from what he had been told and what he had overheard while in the orphanage. As best as anyone could recall, he had been born in a hospital in Syracuse, NY. The date was unclear because there was no birth certificate on file.

Richard began, "There was a midwife lady who was supposed to deliver me and my twin. She got called away and a woman that didn't know as much got called in. I guess midwives were allowed to use the hospitals at that time, but she didn't try to get any assistance. I heard my mom died, bleeding from having me. The midwife waited until the stars came out and still no second baby. She decided with my mom dead and no other baby, a mistake must have been made. The hospital was notified of the death of my mother. There is no record of what happened to her body. I know I remember something that happened. I tried talking to one of the headmasters at the orphanage. I was accused of insolence. I never told my story again.

"I did some research. I learned that it isn't uncommon for one twin to absorb another. I think what I saw was my twin sister being released as something evil."

Ruby waited to see if he would continue without her pushing him. A silence hung between them as they continued to watch the scene unfold. They watched other people watching as well.

Ruby's gift of clarity caused her to ask Richard if he was in some sort of trouble? She didn't think that was what she was feeling. He seemed like a nice young man, but there was an evil presence that seemed to haunt his eyes. Ruby wondered if that had something to do with the rest of his story?

She quite suddenly took his hand. "Son, it's all okay. You don't need to say anything else. But I think you need to come with me."

Guiding him toward the Wellraven at a fairly quick pace, she could see law enforcement noticing them. She rushed them to the elevator. Fortunately for Ruby, there was no one else going up. As they rode in silence, they blatantly gave each other a good once-over. All of the activities had made it difficult to get a good likeness of each other's features. Walking to apartment 1001, Ruby unlocked the door.

"Whatcha got? Whatcha got? Lover, kiss, kiss."

Richard nearly lost his balance backing back out the door.

Ruby laughed. "Meet Xerox, my naughty parrot. Be careful what you say. He jumps on a clue like he is the Dick Tracy of the bird world."

Richard's laugh seemed natural and at ease. To further make him comfortable before asking him to finish his story, she led him to her secret stash of soda.

"Wow! I have never seen so many different kinds! Can I have whatever I want?"

Blushing, Ruby said he was welcome to anything he desired. She explained that she didn't have soda growing up and now she had it whenever she wanted.

The glass bottles were cold to the touch and provided Richard with a sense of familiarity. It was at that moment, he realized where he was and had no idea what he was going to do. Why did this lady seem to care so much?

# The Bonding

Ruby hoped that Richard would tell her what it was that would cause him to deny himself the right to tell anyone what he believed happened at the time of his birth. Their two energies seemed to combine into a powerful force. Ruby felt she was in the shadow of something she had never known before. It felt evil, yet there was an air of mischief that went with the sensation. Richard looked around her apartment. Stopping to pet Marmalade, who seemed disinterested in his acknowledgment. She wasn't the brightest cat. She was company, and that was all that mattered to Ruby.

"Richard," began Ruby, "I would like to know what it was that happened when you were born. Your story is safe with me. Then we shall figure out how to move forward with your situation."

He tried to put his discomfort aside, knowing this woman really seemed to care for some unknown reason. It was time to share his inner turmoil with someone who would believe him.

He told her about the baggage he had been carrying.

"I know babies aren't supposed to remember being born, but I do. I remember the sensation of my mother's last breath. I remember being cold. As nightfall came and probably when they decided there wouldn't be another baby; I don't know, you might not believe me."

"You won't know unless you tell me."

"Okay. Well, there was this huge ball of light full of some type of energy. I didn't feel like it was friendly. Somehow, I think whatever this was attached itself to me. I don't feel alone and I am always on guard."

"Everything on this earth can't be explained simply. There are things beyond our ability to comprehend. I have no doubt this happened to you. This is something we must deal with at a later time. Now we must figure out what to do with you. Obviously, you are worried about the authorities. New York doesn't allow for emancipation at your age. Do you have a place to live? What about your financial situation?"

"My parents made sure I was provided for. Everything has always had my name on it. I know the family attorney well. I will contact him and see what he can do. In the meantime, I will just go ahead and get an apartment. I saw a for rent sign on an apartment building near York Avenue. If they will accept me. I have access to enough immediate cash to get that ball rolling."

## The Plan

That night Richard slept in Ruby's spare bedroom. He left that morning to secure living quarters. Ruby pondered the meaning of his story. She felt surrounded by a new presence in her apartment that had not been there before. Marmalade seemed to be more anxious than usual. Xerox was unusually quiet. Ruby knew something was fishy in Denmark. Even her namesake brooch seemed duller today.

This couldn't happen to her. She needed to get a grasp on this before Sunday. Richard had put most of Ruby's worries to rest. It seemed he had a rather large amount of funds to draw from. Yet he was unimpressed by his own wealth.

That next morning, Richard was able to procure his first apartment. The attorney his parents had used put everything in place and made the necessary legal documents to keep Richard from ever having to return to the orphanage again. Mr. Maudlin, the attorney, agreed to take care of the sale of the estate and contents, all of the financial transfers and put his signature on the lease agreement. Richard's parents had prepaid all expenses to make life a breeze for him. Mr. Maudlin said that his parents had wished to be cremated and there was not to be a funeral. They felt Richard didn't need the trauma of another loss in his life. That was okay with Richard. The whole idea gave him the willies. Yet he couldn't escape the feeling that this darkness was stronger than ever. Growing up, the darkness was always there, but it never showed its "face." Puberty brought BellaLoki out. Richard fought to keep his thoughts pure or strange things happened to him and around him. He was never afraid; pissed off was more accurate.

## Richard's Friends

Richard had been dating Luna long enough to know it was more lust than anything else. From the chess club, his friend Charles had introduced them through his girlfriend, Marsha Spangler. Her parents were definitely A-listers. Marsha was an entitled brat. At the age of twenty-five, she would have a more than an adequate trust fund. This just didn't suit her needs of the moment. When she found out this Richard had bucks—even though she thought he really was a *Dick*—if played right, Luna would dump him, then she might screw him for a nice deposit to her checking account. Yes, there could be a money angle here to be played. She just had to bide her time. However, she couldn't help but think there was something odd about him. Maybe he was possessed? Now that would be far-out. Her as the leading lady in her own horror story.

Luna knew her friend was obsessed with money, but she was good to talk with. No one was suspicious of Marsha's plan to turn Richard into her sugar daddy. Surprisingly, she had no idea of his age. Both the guys were younger than the girls. Age didn't seem to factor into the dating scene much. Marsha just had to recognize that Charles and Luna were a means to an end.

## The Apartment

Richard had made friends with this small group going to summer camp. Charles and Richard played in the chess groups and the girls were into the crafts. But at night they would party together. They continued their friendship over the years.

That night to break in the new apartment, the four friends, Richard Cohen, Luna Bruce, Marsha Spangler, and Charles Wayne thought a little smoke party would set just the right tone. Charles always seemed to have a baggie of primo grass. It surprised most, because he really didn't seem all that hip.

Charles had only known Richard a short time, but he thought they had a connection. However there were times when Richard spooked him. Although he always seemed to be a nice enough guy, there was something about his eyes. He couldn't tell if Richard might have a dark side he kept hidden from his friends. Marsha, who was just a bit full of herself, called it his aura. Maybe she was the one with the dark side!

At any rate, that night there were no strange occurrences, and they wound up smoking themselves straight. Marsha called a cab for the three of them and they said their good nights. Richard walked them out, taking a look at his new digs through buzzed eyes. The Cavanaugh wasn't a new building, but it just felt right to Richard.

**Sunday Dinner**

Ruby frittered around, waiting for her guest. She had fixed fried chicken and mashed potatoes with white cream gravy. She had the salad ready for Richard to toss when he arrived.

"Company dinner…dead bird, squawk."

"Xerox, give it up. It's an inferior chicken. You are splendid. You are a king amongst birds, now be nice or we will have you for dinner!"

"Ruby's rude, Ruby's rude."

Marmalade meowed in agreement, but one never knew who with. At six o'clock there came a soft knocking on the door.

Xerox chattered, "Who is it? Lover boy, kiss, kiss."

"You know, you naughty bird, he can hear you."

Ruby let Richard inside. He couldn't remember much about her place except for that crazy fridge full of soda. Her own private stash! Wow! All those old, dewy, glass bottles full of sugary caffeinated beverage. It delighted Richard to see Ruby reach for that bottle of power—Mountain Dew. Must be like a hit of speed on that old lady's heart.

Ruby could feel the vibrations coming off this young man. She could see the intensity of his aura. It was so inconsistent, changing quickly from dark to light. This was a defining moment for Ruby in her years of reading auras. She couldn't read his at all. This disturbed her.

Once again, Xerox was extremely agitated. The air was thick with tension. Ruby handed him his preferred Dr. Pepper and they sat at the kitchen table while dinner finished cooking. They exchanged polite pleasantries until Ruby was about to burst.

**Richard Continues**

"This light, this sense of energy, you remember from the day you were born, is there something with you now?"

His face lit up and quickly collapsed into a scowl.

"For as long as I can remember, I have never felt alone. I know this sounds farfetched, but I think I had a twin sister. Whatever it was I remember from that day; I have always felt something exchanged places with her and now lives inside of me."

"Oh my, that would give you something to think about."

Ruby's voice held back a shiver.

"There have been strange things that have happened as far back as I can remember. Sort of like tricks, magic, and even pure evil. I have always somehow known; I might be responsible."

**Dinner is Served**

"Okay, dinner is ready and we will have many chances to explore the meaning of all this. There are some busy bodies around the building that will probably wag their tongues when they see I have a young caller. Would you mind very much calling me, Aunt Ruby?"

"I think I would like that. Man, now this is some fried chicken! Did the Colonel share his secret herbs and spices with you?"

Richard's voice was pleasant, but she couldn't escape that darkness in his eyes. After dinner, they relaxed and watched some television. Both seemed to enjoy watching

Archie Bunker. Richard and Ruby laughed at Archie's convoluted ideas about people and life. Marmalade would add an occasional meow and Xerox included his own commentary. The climax was when Archie and Edith sat down at the piano to begin their duet. If an African Grey Parrot was capable of humming along and off-key, Xerox gave it hell. The killer was the end of the song; Archie, Edith, and Xerox harmonized, "Those-Were-The-Days" Richard was glad he had swallowed his drink or it would have ended up on the wall, he laughed so hard. After the program, Richard gave his thanks and said good night to Ruby…Aunt Ruby, at the door.

That bird just had to have the last word. "Keep on truckin' man." This was delivered with lots of extra vowels and consonants. The evening had ended on a high note.

## BellaLoki Has Arrived

Ruby went through her nightly bedtime ritual. There was this heaviness that seemed to permeate the air. Unbeknownst to Ruby, when Richard took leave, BellaLoki was released into the Wellraven. She was a demon from the under-world. Her name told she was part good and part evil. BellaLoki played at evil until it tired her and then she tried to make friends with the other demons. This was strictly forbidden. Thus, she was cast from the fires of damnation to walk amongst the lowly humans. BellaLoki thought being lowered to nine months of sharing a space with a human embryo was the worst possible punishment. Beelzebub knew this was over the top, but he did enjoy a bit of humor with his cruel rep. He had no intention of making her some sort of born-again human. The horned image with the forked tail offered up a dramatic light show. A burst of energy and a splash of intense light. This was for his own entertainment. There was no one to see except an infant and a terrified midwife. There was no one in that part of the hospital that would have the vantage point of his showmanship. He flipped his forked tail and tipped his head back in maniacal laughter as hot flames shot from his body. He might release her in fifty years, if he remembers.

## Richard's Week

Richard decided he could take some college-level courses at Hunter College. He had been in gifted AP classes and was being fast-tracked toward early graduation. He also thought that his apartment could use a few things. Mr. Maudlin, the attorney, had arranged to have Richard's possessions brought to him. Kicking back on the used furnishings, he opened his Montgomery Ward catalogue. He picked out some replacement furniture, a new bed, and some kitchen necessities. He could eat a few meals at home if he had to. First, he would have to learn to cook. Just as he was finalizing his order, there they were! The latest style of hip-hugger bell bottoms in just his size. He pulled the trigger on those, too. Mr. Maudlin had brought with him an eight-track stereo to replace his worn-out turntable. His music tastes were a mixed bag but he was partial to Yes, REO Speed Wagon, Moody Blues, Pink Floyd, Jethro Tull, and some Led Zeppelin. He kept up with the hits by reading *Tiger Beat Magazine.* It was aimed at the girls, but he liked the articles. It usually hit the stands the middle of the month and October's was due out. He'd have to find the newsstand near his area of Lenox Hill.

## Keeping Up

During the week Luna would call Richard several times a day just to see what he was doing. Charles teased that she was keeping track of "the merchandise." A heat wave across the city brought the temperature upward to ninety degrees. The heat was stifling. It rose in waves off of the pavement. The air-conditioning couldn't keep up with the heat. Richard had laundry that he needed to do but lacked the energy. He thought this might be what Death Valley felt like. The entire week stayed excruciatingly hot.

Ruby didn't like artificially cooled air. She opened her apartment up to get a cross breeze, if there was one. Her fans kept the air moving while she applied cool compresses to her head and neck. Her pets seemed unbothered by the heat. Ruby spent the week looking outside, people watching. Ruby refused to give into the feeling that she was being surrounded by a dark energy.

Richard Cohen's story was so puzzling. How could an infant recall anything, let alone something so spectacular?

As the week progressed, Ruby saw signs she wasn't alone. Her orderly soda fridge became haphazardly arranged. The pillows on her bed looked as though they had head prints on them. Once she walked into the kitchen to find her faucet running. Xerox was unusually docile. A word here and there, but not his normal constant chatter. Ruby wondered if he was ill. Marmalade trailed Ruby around the apartment instead of staring at her normal spot on the wall. Ruby felt at the end of her wits.

## Evil Visits

The middle of the week was a turning point for Ruby. She was sleeping soundly in her bedroom. It must have been near midnight. She awoke to the sounds of rattling. Sitting up in bed, she listened in the darkness, wondering why it was so dark? Then she realized the sound was Xerox's cage. She was sure she had latched and covered it for the night. Creeping silently, listening for a sound, Xerox let out with a screech. His wings flapping told her he was out of his cage. Attempting to hurry to him, she spotted a strange spot of light coming from her dining room. Walking toward it, all of a sudden, her front door flew open. Ruby felt the pounding of Xerox's wings as he flew past her into the hallway. Since she had never clipped his wings, he had total freedom of flight. Ruby headed toward the doorway, in her nightclothes, calling for Xerox. He was obviously frightened.

"It's comin' for me. *Squawk*. Xerox scared."

The door to the stairwell came open, it was Earl Joy. Xerox landed on top his flannel hat, still squawking.

"Whoa, boy, what's got you flyin' in the night?"

"It wants to eat me! *Squawk*."

"Oh, Earl Joy, I'm so glad it's you."

"What's with all the ruckus?"

Ruby looked toward her dining room; the light was gone. She could once again make out the details of the room. It was no longer pitch-black.

"Earl Joy, you must hear me out. I believe I have unleashed something evil into our beloved Wellraven."

"Now, now, Miss Ruby, you've had a bad dream. A bit of sleepwalking. You're okay now. Let me get you a cup of tea."

"That would be nice, but I think two fingers of 114 Proof Old Grand-Dad Bourbon I've been saving might do more to soothe my nerves."

Earl Joy got her glass, her bourbon, and left her for the night. Walking toward the elevator, he thought, now what was all that about evil?

## Richard and Luna

After a hot lazy week, Luna showed up at Richard's one Friday morning. With only one week left in September, Luna still hadn't been treated to any of the finer things money could buy. Richard and Luna spent the morning tearing up the sheets and then just had to get out. Luna didn't know the area and Richard hadn't been there very long, so they used a combination of transportation methods. Mostly by foot or taxi. Neither of them felt comfortable trying to learn the subway system. Luna justified the taxis with the thought at least this was one way to get him to spend some money on her.

A lot of the businesses were boarded over or had reduced hours. When their taxi arrived, they had chosen several destinations to visit. Then Richard was taking her to lunch at some place he had found. Their first stop was Manhattan's branch of the New York Public Library. They didn't have a reason to go there, but they did enjoy some laughter and a lot of grab ass. Then Luna decided they should do the deed in the reference section between the stacks. Richard shook his head from left to right, while she teased that no one used that part of the library anymore, it was all on microfiche.

"Really, Luna, it's these daytime shows you watch. We will have some time again, soon, I promise. Oh, over there. I think I know that woman from somewhere."

"Who are you talking about, Richard?"

"That woman at the information desk. She might be someone I've seen at the Wellraven."

Luna took him by the arm. "If you aren't wanting to do some huffing and puffing in the stacks, let's get out of here."

They roamed the streets, making a point not to make eye contact with any of the homeless or panhandlers in the area. Luna noticed Richard seemed much more at ease with her. Maybe he was falling for her.

Their walk took them around and through Central Park. Like Richard had promised, he treated her to lunch at a place not too far from his neighborhood of the Cavanaugh. He had found a tiny luncheonette called Cooking You Wished Your Momma Would Make.

Richard doubted he would have another meal that day, so he chose to pig out on this one meal. He ordered a double-stack of Mom's Meatloaf, mashed potatoes with brown gravy, and he could pick a side. He went with a large Caesar salad with extra croutons. Luna ordered the soup and sandwich special. Minestrone had always been her favorite. The sandwich was an open-faced number with roast beef and brown gravy. While they ate, Richard told Luna about his new Aunt Ruby. She listened intently to his story.

"Her complex is the Wellraven."

Luna clapped her hands, saying that Richard and his new aunt are practically neighbors.

"You will be able to find out if she really is a witch!"

"Luna, why would you even say that?"

"I don't know. It would explain how she knew to help you."

Excitedly, Luna busts out with a plan.

"Do you think Aunt Ruby would want to meet your girl?" She snuggled closer.

## The First Sunday in October

Ruby was excited to be included in Richard's plans. She had hoped they might form a friendship. During the week there had been lots of unusual occurrences within the Wellraven. Earl Joy heard reports of the elevator stopping between floors. Then there was the heat firing up when the system had been winterized. Earl Joy was baffled. The atmosphere of the Wellraven burst with electrified particles of intense energy. Earl Joy came to his own conclusion. There was some type of force field over the Wellraven. How or what? Just another mystery with no hope for a logical answer.

Earl Joy tended to be sensible except for his love of things science fiction. He was mostly concerned that Ruby had opened her home to a young man he knew nothing about. He vowed to keep a watchful eye on her. Earl Joy had tried talking with her about whether it was a good idea opening her apartment to a teenage male she knew nothing about. Ruby instantly took offense, but politely assuaged Earl Joy's concerns. Xerox had to have the last word. When Earl Joy left, Xerox called out, "Meathead, Meathead."

Earl Joy had longed to have a relationship with Ruby. He had been a bachelor for so long he had forgotten how to flirt. He was a man and had needs.

## The Hologram

After seeing Ruby in her nightclothes, Earl Joy couldn't get rid of the image. It was time to take things into his own hands. His collection of girlie mags just didn't do it for him. He closed his eyes, recalling Ruby in the doorway, disheveled, with fire in her eyes. A sigh escaped his lips. He grasped his cock by the base and began the squeezing up and down motion that brought him to a climax that lifted his ass off the bed. He smiled to himself, a deep breath expanding his chest. Opening his eyes, there was Ruby. It wasn't Ruby as he knew her, but a shimmering white light that took on the shape of his love. The intensity of the light brought warmth and a pulsating energy that went through him. He realized that his hand and stomach had a trail of dried jism as evidence of his nightly activity. As he rose to sit in his bed, the image began to fade. He knew he was a bit of a square. He loved reading his scientific journals. He read that just this year, Lloyd Cross had produced the first traditional hologram. He didn't understand how one had been in his room, that was the only explanation he had.

Only BellaLoki knew…

## BellaLoki's Destruction

While Earl Joy slept, BellaLoki had time to familiarize herself with his bachelor pad. Bored beyond tears, she decided to have some soothing playtime. She opened the doors to the fridge and freezer, leaving them open; not liking the cold, she quickly moved on. She removed his clothes from their hangers, relocating them to the balcony. She laughed as she reset all of his clocks to a different hour. Just little things to make him think he was losing it a bit. As a demon, she tended more toward ornery behavior than flat-out pain and punishment. BellaLoki's grand finale was to hang a poster of Earl Joy's mortal enemy on the inside of his bedroom door. When Earl Joy woke that morning, the first thing he would see was THE ENEMY. Earl Joy let loose with a tangent of swearing that made his own self blush.

*"How the hell did that god-awful man get in my apartment?"*

The thought that someone had been there while he slept creeped him out. He couldn't worry over that.

There... almost as big as life... was the face of Richard—*Stupid Middle Name*—Millhouse Nixon. Ripping the poster to shreds, he heard the faint tinkling of feminine laughter. Outside of his bedroom, he walked in a daze, correcting the obvious, shaking his head at the clean-up required of him. The one thing he knew for sure, was that no one else could find out about this. He dressed as usual, determined to make this just another normal day.

## Richard and Luna at Ruby's

The first of October arrived with Ruby fixing a midday meal for Richard and Luna. Luna was an unusual name. Ruby hoped her parents weren't beatniks, hippies, or even worse, Communists. A knock on the door said they had arrived. Xerox, always the formal greeter, said, "Come in. Xerox needs a cuttlebone. Open the door to the greatest show on earth."

Richard slowly opened the door. "Ruby, is it okay to come in?"

"If Xerox says so, I guess you better listen." Both laughed.

Luna stepped across the threshold, admiring the homey appearance.

"Hot damn, we got us a looker."

Whistling wasn't Xerox's forte. There was just so much spit. Ruby prayed he would keep his sailor vocabulary turned off. His ability toward mimicry of pirate terms from television was top-notch. Shaking her head, she offered her guests something to drink.

"Xerox wants soda—the orange one—*squawk squawk*."

Richard made proper introductions, then asked excitedly if he could show Luna her special fridge.

Ruby said they were having a light lunch and to hurry. Dry bread was the worst. Pick your favorite and hurry on back to the table.

Richard's excitement was contagious.

"Luna, you have gotta see this!"

He opened the refrigerator door. Both Luna and Richard exclaimed, "Holy shit!"

There was more than Richard remembered but they weren't in the meticulous order anymore. He felt a chill overtake his body. He felt certain he was no longer alone. He wondered, had his new Aunt Ruby been tormented by this unknown entity that Richard believed to be part of him?

Luna took him by the elbow, choosing soda for the both of them. Leading him to the kitchen, she thought, I don't know this Richard.

It was then that Marmalade made her presence known. Purring softly, she wove in and out of Luna's legs, marking her territory. It was a strange sight. She seldom had an interest in any visitor.

"Horny cat. I have sunflower seeds. You aren't a nice cat. Xerox likes the pretty lady."

Everyone was in high spirits when they were seated for lunch. Only Richard seemed nervous. Ruby noticed and hoped he would grow more comfortable. The sandwich platter was quickly killed off. The kids ate like only kids can. Ruby was impressed that they both had impeccable manners.

Luna carried a large leather bag embossed with what Ruby assumed to be a marijuana leaf. It triggered a memory of her mother's rather shabby, but large, tapestry handbag. Luna began a search through that enormous bag. Watching her was a Mary Poppins moment. Finally, she pulled out what she was searching for. It appeared to be a brand-new Polaroid camera. Luna had been waiting for a chance to try it out. The three of them wiled away the afternoon taking photos.

It was the damnedest thing. Aim, shoot, the picture pops out, then you wait. An image would slowly appear; followed by a lot of laughter and teasing. Luna gave several to Aunt Ruby and tossed the rest in her bag.

Richard ventured, "Aunt Ruby, do you think Earl Joy would mind if we explored the building a bit? I kind of dig looking at different types of architecture."

"I am certain he wouldn't mind at all. He would probably give you a tour if you asked. Luna, you are welcome to stay behind while Richard plays private eye and chases down the ghosts of the Wellraven."

Richard quickly jumped in, "I thought we would do it together and then leave from there. Thank you for the lunch. Your soda stash is a treat all by itself." Luna managed a smile and an enthusiastic nod of her head as they headed out the door. Richard knew BellaLoki was loose in the Wellraven. He worried for Ruby but felt relief for himself.

## The Threesome?

Richard and Luna tiptoed along the dark brown carpet. Richard looked closely at the institutional yellow walls. Luna wondered what he was looking for.

Suddenly he burst out, "Ah ha! Here we go. Do you mind squatting down to go through this door?"

Luna looked down at her faded low slung bell bottoms. Her fringed leather belt that went with her "must have" leather moccasins. Clothes or an adventure? She chose adventure.

Richard knew what he was hoping to find. He just hoped Luna was down with it. They crept through all of the mechanical engineerings, encountering some tight spots. Luna jumped at the sound of water running through the pipes. That was when Richard found what he was looking for, an anomaly in construction that might be a good place to bend Luna over and give her the pounding she deserved. It was a decent-sized area adjacent to the fire escape door that he guessed served First Avenue.

Luna's face lit up. She knew. She draped her bell-bottoms across the concrete to keep her skin from chaffing. Richard slowly lowered her frilly panties. (Had she hoped for sex?) As he guided those sexy panties to the floor, she moaned.

"Oh, the kisses are making me so hot."

Richard froze. Did he have unwanted assistance pleasuring her? He wasn't kissing her. He dropped his jeans to the floor. They were covered with patches. His favorite was the colorful peace sign one. He watched as Luna arched her back, spreading her legs wider. He wasn't touching her, and he had never seen her like this. His dick was so stiff it hurt. Luna was begging him.

"Oh God, Richard, plow me now. I need to feel you inside me."

He began a slow entry when a force from behind pushed him hard into her already sopping wet pussy.

Near the door where they had entered, the bright ball of light kept rhythm with their sexual antics. Richard hoped Luna would climax soon. These distractions were causing him to lose his hard-on. It was going to work out. Luna began to shake uncontrollably. Over and over, she said his name, "Dick, Dick." She was the only one who called him that and only during sex. Eventually, she collapsed.

"How did you do that? I have never climaxed like that. It felt like you were all over my body at once." Richard laughed nervously, hugging her. They redressed and squeezed through the tiny maintenance door. Richard called her a cab. She pressed tightly against his body. "See you soon, lover."

Richard began the short walk into the neighborhood until he reached The Cavanaugh. Although mystified, he had a peaceful feeling he hadn't had in quite a while.

## Luna and Marsha

That Wednesday, October 4, Luna took a cab to the richer part of Manhattan. She thought she was near Park Avenue. Marsha always ordered the taxi and insisted she pay for it. Luna was only impressed by wealth if she had it. She and Marsha Spangler had little in common except their boyfriend's friendship. They sat in the kitchen. It was furnished with the most modern appliances, in the color of the day, avocado green. There was a lot of wood and she suspected it was the real deal. They drank iced tea and

471

coasters magically appeared from a hidden drawer of the counter bar.

Luna didn't have a lot of time to tell Marsha about Richard's performance the other night.

"It was like he was possessed. He seemed to have more lips and hands than normal. His rod just plunged into me! He wasn't the gentle, *will he ever get this over with* Richard I had been with before."

"Please tell me you're not complaining? I'll trade you. Charles invented the original, *wham, bam, thank you, ma'am*!" Both young women burst into side-splitting laughter. Luna had to run. She had a job interview at an art studio and didn't want to be late.

"Here are some pictures I took the other night. You can bring them back when we have dinner with your parents."

## Dinner with the Spanglers

On Saturday, Richard, Luna, Charles, and Marsha met up with Mr. and Mrs. Spangler at one of their many "meant to be seen" restaurants. These dinners were all the same. A nameless restaurant, subdued lighting, oversized leather-encased menus. Apparently, it was a sign of class not to show the prices. Luna and Richard shared a moment, rolling their eyes. Charles had never had much of an upbringing as far as how the other half lived. He considered these dinners the equivalent of medieval torture. If the suit wasn't enough, the noose around his neck made him wonder if he would be able to swallow his food.

Marsha carried on a meaningless conversation with her parents. Richard gave Charles a signal to loosen his tie a bit.

The venue is always the same performance. A robot acting maître de, the same discreet hand motions used to seat them in their usual arrangement. The couples seated across from each other, ensuring no contact with each other. Mr. and Mrs. Spangler assumed the heads of the table. Napkins hadn't been snapped onto their laps before Richard snuck the first check of the time. Marsha's parents were clueless as to how offensive their behavior in public could be.

Mr. Spangler decided to make a grand announcement. Throwing his arms into the air, he stated, "Tonight I will order for the entire table and it will be my treat."

What the fuck? Had there been a question? Why did he have to pick everyone's food? Apparently, entitlement didn't include thoughtfulness. Charles's face was locked in a frozen scream. The girls knew they wouldn't be paying, so the moment passed them by.

The waiter brought endless covered dishes to the table. Richard, having been raised by his adoptive parents, both being in the medical profession, had taught him the rules of society. He still referred to the food as "snob food." Eating was done in silence. All eye contact was avoided.

Several socialites stopped to pay their respect. The children were successfully ignored. At the end of the meal, with no regard to the kids, the Spanglers joined their friends around the double-sided fireplace and sipped brightly colored cocktails. Had there actually been a fire, the amount of makeup on Mrs. Spangler's face would have melted.

Richard, Luna, Charles, and Marsha headed toward the waiting area, which was a large space in the front of the restaurant, complete with a library and trophy case. The foursome soon brought laughter and life to the stuffy atmosphere. Luna whipped her Polaroid camera out of her oversized leather bag and took more pictures.

"Hey, where are the ones we took at Aunt Ruby's?" Inquired Richard.

Marsha pulled those out of her bag and handed them over to Richard. The photos were passed around. Each had their own input. Charles couldn't help but think that cat didn't look very bright. Marsha kept one back, vaguely paying attention to one of Xerox hamming it up.

Ruby had tried her hand with the camera. She shot a couple of Richard and Luna together. Those pictures never came out well. In the pictures, Richard had a darkness all around him. Almost like it didn't develop on that part of the photo. Richard didn't say anything to his friends, but he suspected BellaLoki had been present that day. Ruby had known by the way she looked when she saw the pictures.

Marsha was sitting there holding the Polaroid of Aunt Ruby. It was a closeup Luna had taken. You could see the sparkle in Ruby's eyes.

"Is your *new* aunt Ruby wealthy?"

"The Wellraven Apartments are nice, maybe some of the better ones for the money in the neighborhood. I don't think you would need to be rich to live there," Richard answered Marsha.

"Well, kids, I hate to change your impression but, this brooch against this old woman's throat is an extremely valuable Burmese ruby. Some believe the wearer will have mystical powers."

"Marsha, you are so hung up on money. You will get your trust at twenty-five. Richard is rich beyond words, yet he lives like the rest of us. Except you." Luna was slightly disgusted at Marsha's attitude. Even though she had thought of ways to get Richard to spend some of his money on her.

The pictures were gathered as the Spanglers headed in their direction. No one seemed to notice when Marsha slipped the closeup of Ruby back into her bag. The Spanglers provided transportation for their guests, and Marsha left with her parents.


**Earl Joy's Undoing**


The following week BellaLoki's mischief took an ugly turn. Mailboxes were opened and mail strewn across the floor. When BellaLoki removed the fire extinguishers from their glass encasements, the fire department arrived with all bells and whistles into the early hours of the morning.

Ruby knew there was something evil in the building. She felt fairly confident Richard had brought it into the Wellraven. There just wasn't any sure-fire way to know. She wasn't sure of her own powers or those of her ruby brooch, but she felt protected from this evil spirit, demon—whatever had taken up residency at the Wellraven.

It was out of character not to hear Earl Joy humming or whistling as he walked throughout the building. Ruby was worried. She saw that the lines on his face were deepening. He seemed to be fighting a losing battle. There was always a mess to clean up. His tools went missing to be found in some impossible location later. Papers in his office were rifled through and scattered across his desk. The worst part, that he wanted no one to find out about were his hallucinations. He knew his mind was sound. He had chased bouncing lights that would disappear and reappear. He heard a woman's laughter in his ear. These things couldn't be happening, but yet...

If word got out or the tenants felt the eerie change in the atmosphere, they might start giving their notice. That could cost him his job. His worst thought was, what if the Wellraven got a reputation of being haunted? The place would become a freak show. Then he knew for sure he would be without an income or a place to live. Earl Joy had tried everything he knew to find the source of all the problems, to no avail. He even thought of seeking professional help. His spirits were so low that there was only one answer, a visit to apartment 1001. Just the thought of Ruby's bright blue eyes and her delightful smile made him start to feel better. He took the stairs two at a time. Maybe only up one flight, but he impressed himself with his increased energy.

Knocking on Ruby's door, he was wishing he had brought a gift. He hoped someday he would find the courage to date the charming woman of mystery. Ruby answered the door, fear in her eyes.

Xerox screamed nonsense. "She's here. She's here. Save me. *Squawk*."

Marmalade shot past Ruby and Earl Joy, heading toward the door to the stairs. Ruby in hot pursuit, Earl Joy at her heels.

From the apartment, Xerox was still squawking nonsense. "Start your engines."

Earl Joy couldn't fathom why the doors to the stairwells were standing open. He felt a cold darkness that slowed him down while Ruby seemed to be charged with an inhuman amount of speed. How could she climb all those stairs? Yet there she was chasing that worthless cat all the way up to the roof. Earl Joy came through the final door onto the roof just in time to see Marmalade come to an abrupt stop at the edge of the roof. It was as if some force stopped her. Ruby reached for Marmalade and lost her balance toppling from the rooftop twenty stories to the ground. The scream as she spun head over heels to the pavement below grew more silent as she fell. Marmalade just took off, jumping from one rooftop to the next. Earl

Joy stood frozen. Then he busted ass to the elevator. He used his passkey to override stopping at any other floors.

Running toward the stairs, he abruptly stopped. In his hesitation, he thought, what would he see if he went out there? There were already sirens coming from all directions. He was blinded by the tears rolling down his face. He was cognizant enough to realize he was a witness and if he didn't make a statement, it could be ruled a suicide. Realizing there was no hope for a relationship with the woman he had started to love made him want to at least clear her name. Earl Joy felt a push from behind as he acknowledged the crowd beginning to form. The bouncing white light passed through him, knocking him to his ass. Was he hallucinating? The light was changing into the obvious shape of the female form. Just as quickly, the light faded to total darkness.

## The Aftermath

Earl Joy avoided the crowd, seeking out a detective he knew that was further from the scene. He reported what he saw to the detective. He knew he left many unanswered questions. If he didn't understand, he wasn't about to offer up any theories or anything that couldn't be easily explained. There was no one else who could offer any information, so at least for now, they would have to accept his explanation as the gospel. He returned to the Wellraven having never felt this kind of sadness. He knew he had to close up Ruby's apartment. Then he remembered, Xerox!

The next mad dash of the day found Xerox sitting in the open doorway. The bird was just way too intuitive. He knew Ruby was gone. Just like he knew about all the sex going on in the building. Earl Joy dropped to the ground next to the parrot. He could have sworn the bird was crying. Earl Joy broke down and sobbed like he hadn't in years. Xerox climbed on top of Earl Joy's head, knocking his hat to the floor. He proceeded to give Earl Joy bird kisses while they bonded over Ruby's demise.

"No more love for Xerox. She's left me."

Earl Joy couldn't sit there as if he expected Ruby to return. He gathered Xerox, his cage, and other belongings, taking him to his apartment. Since he was the Super of the building, he had access to all of the personal information of the tenants, including emergency contacts. He knew Ruby had no next of kin and all her affairs were handled by a local attorney. He was too tired to think. He would call the attorney after he got some sleep, if he could, then the attorney could deal with her arrangements. While Earl Joy was getting Xerox set up for the night, he turned, tipping his head, as birds do, shocking Earl Joy with his words. "It's the light that tried to take me." Those words turned Earl Joy's body into thousands of goosebumps. He latched the latch and covered the cage and surprisingly fell asleep almost immediately. His last thought was how dying on Friday the 13th was such bad karma.

**Richard and Earl Joy**

That next morning was a Saturday. Earl Joy made the necessary contacts. He tried to remember anything about the young man who had recently befriended Ruby. Fortunately, Richard wasn't your typical teenager and saw on the news that there was activity in his neighborhood and recognized the camera shots of the Wellraven. He decided he needed to check on his new friend, Aunt Ruby.

Earl Joy was listless. He only did what was absolutely required of him. From time to time he would feel a tear graze his cheek. Earl Joy decided to go up to the roof. He hoped it would somehow make him feel closer to her. Possibly, he would be able to find Marmalade. That cat was so stupid, there was no way she would come back on her own. As he gazed out, he recognized the gangly gait of a man rushing toward the building. Young men still have that awkwardness about them similar to a young colt. That's when he remembered Richard! He had to beat him to Ruby's. They both arrived at the same time just as Richard was reaching to knock, Earl Joy stopped him, taking his arm. Richard saw the sadness in Earl Joy's eyes and the evidence of tears that had been shed, he knew. The news channel was reporting about Ruby.

Richard stood there taking it in, his eyes clouding over with the need to cry.

**Ruby's Affairs**

Earl Joy explained that there was nothing to be done. Ruby's attorney would be making all the arrangements.

Ruby had planned her own funeral, not anticipating any mourners. Ruby had made one last-minute change before she died, she had named Richard as her heir. He didn't know if she had anything, but it didn't matter, he had more than enough.

"Richard, Ruby thought of you in that short time as the son she always wanted but could never have."

"I wonder why. She barely got to know me. I did feel a connection. It was like she was made of magic."

"That, my boy, she surely was."

Richard turned to walk away; he didn't want to be seen crying. He came to a sudden stop as he remembered, "Xerox?"

"Don't worry, right now I have him mourning in my apartment. But, Richard, the thing is, when you buy an exotic bird, they can outlive their owner. In that case, the owner has to choose a next of kin for their bird. It's done as a precaution. Up until you came into the picture, Ruby had willed Xerox to the Staten Island Zoo. That was the other change she made to her will. She named you Xerox's guardian. That means he will be signed over to you in probate.

Richard ran both his hands through either side of his sandy blond hair, shuffling from leg to leg. "Do I have to take him now? Should I come live here? Oh, I don't know if I could do that. What do I do, Earl Joy?" Together they made a plan. The funeral was to be on October 20th. Earl Joy would keep Xerox while Richard made some decisions of his own.

That week was extremely quiet. BellaLoki was planning her biggest escapade of all. Earl Joy never felt alone. He had to keep looking over his shoulder. Doors remained closed. Xerox was quiet. His grief was palpable. Earl Joy did what he could to cajole the old bird into talking, but he barely had it in him to comfort himself.

## The Funeral

The day of the funeral brought freezing temperatures. There was just the foursome of Richard and his friends, Earl Joy, and Ruby's attorney. The casket had already been lowered, knowing there wouldn't be many in attendance. The minister said a few words about faith, gratitude, and being called home too soon. They all recited the Lord's Prayer as a group. And it was over. The mourners all had white roses to be placed on top of the casket. Richard hadn't given much thought to whether the casket would be open or not. With the extent of her injuries, there wasn't any way they could allow for one last look at this beautiful soul they had come to love so quickly. The attorney stayed back, while the minister stood over as the roses were dropped. Marsha was the last to pass. She took one look and fire shot from her eyes.

"You idiots. I suppose you buried her with it! Do you know what you did? Of course, you don't!" With that being said, she tossed the rose and the Polaroid picture she carried to the ground and stomped to her waiting ride.

Charles said, "Hey guys, I am really sorry about all that." Then he bursts into tears.

"Hey, buddy, it's not on you. That chick was kinda loco," said Earl Joy.

Charles quickly retorted, "I planned to unload her pretty soon, anyway." The gang retreated while Earl Joy stayed behind to speak with the minister and the attorney. Not for long, though. It was just too cold.

## Earl Joy needs a break

Earl Joy wanted to respect the life of Ruby by properly mourning her death. He knew that he would make himself sick if he didn't do something to get himself out of this funk. Normally, he met with a few of the guys for a monthly poker party. He didn't want to wait until the following week. The guys were all Veterans he had met on an overseas flight. They were a raucous bunch and Earl Joy became good friends in the time it took to cross the ocean. It was decided they didn't want to discontinue the friendship just because the flight had come to an end. Frank, the vet, that seemed to be the leader of the group, decided a monthly poker party was a must. They all lived in and around the NYC area. That was it. A poker party a month and Earl Joy had new friends with exciting stories to tell of their military experiences. There were some dead areas that they couldn't discuss that were vital to national security. Earl Joy longed for more information, but the words black op, navy seals, and nighttime raids, signaled him to listen and not ask questions. The boys were a good bunch together and their poker skills were pretty much even.

## A Few Loose Ends

Richard concluded that he couldn't live in Ruby's apartment. For one, he was free of the evilness and didn't want to take a chance of it coming back. The other was just the memories that had only begun to be made. He fixed up a place for Xerox so he could look out the window and had a bit of room to move about. He did some research on African Grey Parrots and discovered he would be a suitable handler.

During the week, Luna called. Richard offered to meet her at the diner for lunch. That's when her true colors surfaced.

"Don't you think with all your bucks we could eat someplace a little classier? Here's a thought, what if you made an effort and came and picked me up?" Luna was met with hard silence.

"I just remembered, I have some paperwork I need to get finished today. I may call you later." Richard slammed the receiver, vowing to have nothing further to do with her.

Richard felt like he could finally breathe again. His "evil twin" seemed to no longer be part of him. Perhaps Ruby's death brought about her demise.

Charles and Richard played chess during the week. Smoked a doob or two and listened to some Moody Blues.

Earl Joy had a similar thought as Richard's. Since Ruby's passing, the strange activity at the Wellraven seemed to have come to a close.

## BellaLoki's Great Adventure

No one could have been more mistaken than to think BellaLoki was finished with the Wellraven. She planned to make it her home. First, she had her duty to perform. Laying low helped her to build up a reserve of sexual energy. She was preparing for her role as the true succubus that she was. She had finally found her target and he couldn't be more convenient. She found his name was Keith, and he was rather a sad-sack waiting for the man who would probably never return to love him. BellaLoki laid her plan while hanging out at Ruby's old place. Her intended was only two floors below, in apartment 801. Slipping between the walls would make for a lovely entry. Rumor was he had been involved in some sort of lover's spat; he spent his days drinking and jacking off. Here was her chance to show herself as the voluptuous woman of light and beauty. Not to mention she had a knock your socks off body. October 26 was the day she planned to kick her sexual encounter into action.

That night, as Keith slouched on his couch, BellaLoki put her plan into action. She began to summon all the powers of her energy. She could feel the luminescence of her being casting light around the imaginary doorway of Keith's mind. BellaLoki was so close, she could feel his thoughts. He wanted her. He was coming to her. Her womanly desires would be met. As Keith hesitantly opened the door, her aura began to vibrate and create a humming sound in preparation for mounting her prey. The door opened fully as Keith stood there, obviously aroused. BellaLoki's light was transcended into the shape of a voluptuous woman full of light and cascading waves of energy. He wanted her, and she knew it. Stepping closer to Keith, she extended her lovely arm to take his hand in invitation. Keith looked back, making sure his apartment was still there. BellaLoki decided to go all out and released the throbbing heat from her pulsating loins. But…*no*…He was backing away. Did he think she was some part of his troubled mind and that he had hallucinated her? Her ego shattered before she had the chance to pin him down and conceive her evil demon spawn. Keith watched as the dining room became just a dining room with no unusual light. BellaLoki's light faded until it could barely be seen.

## October 31, 1972

Richard had planned to meet up with Earl Joy in Ruby's old apartment. Since Ruby's death, Earl Joy had been wearing a black Stetson instead of his usual gray flannel. Ruby's attorney had arranged for her estate to be taken care of and her belongings sent to auction. There didn't seem to be any personal effects.

As the two men stood facing each other, the apartment was lit up with the strobing of red and blue from all the activity on the ground. Once again there had been a death associated with the Wellraven.

"Oh, Richard, security from the hospital brought over Ruby's possessions from the night of…of her…fall. It's a funny thing, I still had to sign that I had received it even though her attorney had signed off on it." Looking into Richard's eyes, Earl Joy asked, "Would you like me to open it for you?"

Richard's eyes were blank. Earl Joy began opening the box. It was what he expected. He never understood why it was necessary to send this type of crap back. In the box were her bloodied and torn clothing, her shoes, and stockings that had been ripped to shreds. She was a practical woman with a practical watch. The face was cracked and she would never look to see the time again.

Earl Joy began to return the items to the box, when he noticed a small envelope, like the kind he used for the lost and found keys, in the corner of the box. Richard took it, opening the envelope, both shock and delight appeared upon his face. He stood holding the brooch that Ruby was never without. The one that had Marsha's panties in a twist. The dark red, valuable Burmese ruby. They both saw the image of Ruby floating in the large stone. Earl Joy had the presence of mind to steer the young man toward the door.

Keys and the deposit check with interest were exchanged. The two "men" shook hands and parted ways. Richard was sorry to have suddenly lost his new aunt, but he had Xerox as a *constant* reminder of their short time together. Plus, it was the lightest he had felt in all his years. Was it possible the darkness was gone?

## Earl Joy Closes Up

Earl Joy had the task of making sure window locks were turned. The refrigerator was set on low. He did a general walk-through, opening, and closing doors and cupboards. He moved slowly but soon came quickly to attention. Someone must have come into the apartment. He could hear water running in the kitchen. As he turned it off, he called out, "Is there anyone out there?" In response, a door squeaked in another room. That was all he could take. Earl Joy had to take control *now*.

In a slow but deliberate tone, he said, "I don't know who you are or what you are, but we are gonna have to have some rules around here."

Earl Joy patiently waited as the room started to fade into darkness. He shrugged his shoulder and took one last look around.

Opening the door, he turned to pull it closed.

It slammed with a bang and the door locked.

# GHOSTED
RUMER HAVEN

"We never use this room. Why don't we ever use this room?"

*No need.*

"But this room is nice. Like, *really* nice. And look at the size of it! Bigger than the whole rest of the place." And fully furnished.

*No use.*

"No, we don't use this furniture either, do we. Why don't we?"

*Why you...oh, why, why, why...*

"Y'mean, why don't *I*? I don't know..."

Looking around in the dim light that cast large, angular shadows along the inky blue walls of night, Keith squints at all the pale-sheeted ghosts staring back at him. He reaches out at the one nearest him, the one coming up only to his thigh, and grasps the dusty white cotton cover, gently drawing it off the squat form like he's undressing a lover.

"Stereo, too. A really fine one. Top-of-the-line one. Why don't we use this?" Running a hand along the wooden console and lifting its lid to the turntable, it feels fuzzy to the touch, soft and...wrong somehow. Disoriented, slowed, like moving through water, he looks back at the door he's just stepped through, the door he'd never noticed was there before, just off the dining area. On the wall he always thought was just a wall between his apartment and his neighbor's. "Wild, man...right?"

*Too late.*

Keith steps up to the door and absently lays his hand on the knob. "It's cool in here. I'm actually cold." Then words register, and twisting back around, Keith pinches his brow at his shadowy companion, who's growing fainter within the ever-darkening room. "But it's not too late. Is it?"

The figure turns its palms up, saying nothing before the cool brass slips from Keith's grasp—

And with a slam, Keith wakes up.

Opening his eyes to the navy of nighttime—that part's the same—he feels the heat before he sees he's back in his bedroom. That part's not the same. And it's not actually his room but the spare one. Not his, really, but *now* his. And now *only* his, not theirs. Not like the other one, the only one they'd needed. All *he'd* needed and ever wanted.

The cold he felt is now barely tepid, whatever relief to be eked from the electric fan's blow meeting the moisture of his slick skin and sweat-soaked sheets…sheets…not ones from the room…the room he forgot…the room he'd never known about in the first place…the one he's already forgetting now.

Squeezing his eyes shut, Keith breathes in the thick, humid air and exhales out all the hope he'd felt in the discovery so that the pain can retake its place.

The room isn't there. Never was.

And neither was Roderick.

*Slam!*

Seizing his breath, Keith is startled awake to a now yellow room, baking in the sunshine beaming through bare windows. He's twisted in his bedsheet, binding him tighter to this place, refusing to let him go. No. No, that's not the case. Can't be when he doesn't want to be let go. Doesn't, himself, want to let go.

Loosening the corner of perspiration-dampened cloth from its stranglehold around his neck, Keith brings it to his face, breathes it in deeply, and then chokes his sobs into it when the scent carries nothing of Rod, who'd felt so real.

Gasping out a last whimper, Keith wipes his eyes on a mustard-yellow dandelion printed on the cotton sheet. Finally, he sits up, wills himself to detangle from the bed and stands up. Takes a step away from it. Then two. One step at a time. That's all it takes, all he can manage. At this lethargic pace, he drags one foot then the other through discarded denim and terry cloth, out the door and into the living room. Grinding his gaze to his left, he stares at the rear dining-room wall. No door. As he thought. Just that actress's place next door. What is that crazy redhead's deal anyway? The thumps and thuds that come from there around the clock are weird to no end, and don't even get him started on the couple upstairs.

With his gaze fixed on that patch of avocado-green wall where he'd sworn only hours ago there'd been a door to a whole other, unused section of furnished apartment space, Keith walks to the dining room table and slumps down on one of its uncomfortable vinyl and chrome chairs. Air hisses from the seat pad under his weight, and he deflates along with it, resting his elbow on the wood grain Formica table surface and his sluggish head on his knuckles. Lazily, he thumbs through yesterday's unread newspaper with his other hand, willing to connect this much with the outside world as he casts a glance at the beige telephone on the kitchen countertop that never rings anymore. Sighing with mixed relief and regret, he flips to the sports section.

"The Munich Games: Readers' Reactions to Controversies Surrounding Games," reads page seven of the *New York Times*. In the days to follow the massacre— when the Games themselves have already ended—that people would still write in to complain about Olympic judging and "spirit"... *Honestly*, Keith thinks. Eleven athletes died, were killed, executed, but apparently readers still want to know why a player would be disqualified for asthma medication or why coaches called time-out when they did. What horseshit, Rod would say. Probably does say, wherever he is.

Keith slaps the paper closed in disgust, sick with how dark and diseased 1972 has become before summer's even met its end. Could there be a more blackened year...kicked off with Bloody Sunday in Northern Ireland, the Troubles escalating ever since, then this recent terrorism in Munich, piled on by Watergate, Vietnam…and lest he forget Roderick, as if he ever could…

So many times and for so many reasons, Keith has wished one night he'll fall asleep and wake up in some far-off year like 2020, where the future will have everything figured the fuck out and won't know nightmares like this. *It'll* have *to be better than this…won't it?*

Sighing, he closes his eyelids and rubs them vigorously with his middle finger and thumb. Then he heaves a deep yawn and looks up, sucks his tongue against the roof of his mouth in a desperate attempt at moisture as he glances past the counter of the adjoining kitchen to the master bedroom doorway just beyond. The door is closed, as it always is. Sealing off the tomb of what was but would never be again. He knows it won't be, that it can't be. Somehow, he *knows*.

There was a time when he'd held out faith Rod would come back, that he'd express his remorse and beg Keith for forgiveness, and of course, Keith would take him back—maybe not immediately, maybe not until he'd made him sweat it out a little and truly show he was sorry and sincere about that second chance…after which he'd *really* make him sweat it out, in the better way that they both would enjoy, but now…

Now he knows there'll be no second chance. He knows it in the marrow of his bones.

He just doesn't know why.

"I don't understand. Why don't we ever use this room?"

His shadow companion shrugs, gives a deep, dark chuckle, slow and thick like honey. Keith thinks it's Rod again, but he can't be sure. He's pretty sure, though. Yeah. It's him. Gotta be.

"But we're here all the time. Complaining this place's too small. Why don't we ever use this part of it? Why don't we ever open this door?"

At this, the other being—who is or isn't Rod but feels like it could be—seems to sober. His—its—expression can't be made out, though. Not as clearly as before. The face is...less. Not quite a face. Yet a blackened hole grows where a face would be and says, *Not all doors are meant to open.*

Pulling the sheet off a console television, Keith snorts. "What? Course they are. That's what they're *for*. If we weren't meant to open them, why have doors?"

*Yes, open...*

"Yeah? But?"

*Not until...*

"They're meant to be."

A silent nod.

"And we weren't."

Rod's—its—image goes jagged a second, does so again every now and then, like when a TV antenna needs adjusting. *Weren't what?*

495

"Opened. We couldn't open."

*Aren't doors.*

"Aren't meant to be either."

*Doors?*

"To be."

*Why?*

"You know why."

*You.*

"Oh, so it's *my* fault?"

*Why?*

"That's what I'd like to know."

*Oh, why, why, why?*

On a sharp inhale, Keith wakes and sits up. It's still dark out. Streetlamps project disorienting trapezoids onto the walls, like forced perspective, cerulean cutouts in the deeper midnight blue. He is topless and sweating, and panting. He clasps the gold pendant hanging from his neck, scraping it from where it's adhered to his sticky skin.

"Rod?" he asks, though the name sounds caught in the humid air, muffled, until he realizes it didn't even escape his throat. It's his mind that screams it clearly, more crisply than it could come to him in the dream, resolved to a finer precision than he could even see the face, than he could even see if there *was* a face. If there'd ever been. He couldn't know it was him, didn't know at all, and he never even touched him, yet still he felt him, could *smell* him. He sensed him in every other possible way, ways unknown to himself, ways he can't remember now, for whatever was lost to his sight.

"Roderick," he says sternly, though it's carried on a sob. He releases the necklace to hold his face in his hands, his eyes streaming into already dampened palms that he now breathes in deeply, feverishly, trying to detect any last, lingering scent of his love, his heart. Gone. Vanished, like he did in real life.

A knot in Keith's chest twists as the memory wrings the last of his fortitude from him. Only two months have passed since he last looked into those brown eyes, looked lovingly, imploringly at that strong brow that seemed to pinch in spite of Rod's self, the self that was leaving, walking away, and not just that but into the arms of someone else. Where had it gone so wrong? Keith knew what it looked like, the words that were said, but his heart saw and heard so much more than that; he knew it did, communicating on a vibration matching Rod's that didn't require anything to be said, that didn't need to look like anything other than what it was, because that was all just optics, just for everyone else. All that mattered was the two of them and what they knew between each other, even if one of them didn't know it yet.

Would Rod ever know? Will he come back? Heaving forward under the weight of his leaden, emptying lungs, Keith grasps at the chain sticking to his chest and, this time, yanks it off.

Glinting in the light of a new day, which narrowly escapes through the heavy brown-gold dupioni drapes, the delicate, severed ends of Keith's necklace won't grow back together at his thumb's touch. He twiddles with the chain, weaving it between his fingers, and feels sick over the broken link that won't bring everything full circle again.

The jewelry was a gift. Not for Keith but *from* him. For Rod, who owned a dozen necklaces and rings and things far finer than that, but Keith had wanted to make his mark on him somehow, tag him, possess him, which he knew even at the time was wrong. That isn't something to do to someone—ever—let alone someone you love, but it's how desperate that man would make him feel, like Rod was forever slipping through his fingers as this thread of gold does now. There was no predicting him, committing him, and all Keith wanted was some kind of anchor to keep them tethered together. That was a possessive love, an *ob*sessive one, he knew it; he *knows* that, but it was his first one, the one he hadn't known how badly he needed until Rod had shown him the way, shown him who he really is and made him want to be possessed, too. Taken and submissive.

Sliding his gaze toward the bare dining area wall, Keith sees another door that hadn't opened for him until it did. Another threshold he hadn't crossed until he did, with Rod, and felt the white-hot light kiss his face, illuminate everything trying to slither out of view, hiding in shadow. He'd been naked and exposed, at last, and Rod was his sun god, heating the dormant waters of a deep well within him until they steamed to the surface and he exploded.

Still fondling the chain, Keith watches its coin pendant slip to the floor. He stares at it pensively for a moment before stretching down to snag it out from the crusted shag carpet. Pinching the disk, he brings it between his teeth and bites down.

Another evening, but this time Keith can't sleep, can't escape into that recess behind the dining room wall. He sits instead in the adjacent living area, slumped down on his lumpy couch while he zones out at his television set, the screen gone to static.

The heat has passed its peak, but the backs of his legs still sweat into the polyester velour that smothers him from behind, flooding the farm scene printed in rusts, greens, and browns on the cream-colored cushion. He adjusts the crotch of his tight jean shorts, and the corresponding movement of his slender hips allows a cooling pillow of air to sneak beneath his sinewy thighs, offering more relief.

Losing his sight into the snowy screen of the cathode-ray tube, Keith almost feels its frost, wants to warm it with an image, but what? He liked an army program that premiered recently—based on that movie, the one about doctors in the Korean War, pretty funny. But more than it made him laugh, it reminded him of the dog tags Roderick would wear in protest of today's war, his personal "medals of honor." He's old enough to avoid the draft, but Keith isn't, only able to dodge because, as a Quaker, he can conscientiously object. He could get a pass on another technicality, of course, had his evangelical roots not sealed his lips on that. There was so much Rod could've loved Keith for, did love him for, but for that—his conditioned shame or, at best, shyness over his truth—for that, Rod would always loathe him. That much was plain.

*"If you can't be honest with yourself,"* Rod would say, *"how'm I supposed to trust you're honest with me? That you're not ashamed of me also?"* Keith knew he meant it, too, every goddamn time he said it, and yet the dramatic lilt of his voice tended to give away what an awfully convenient excuse it also was to keep Keith at arm's length. To push him away—until yanking him back so closely they'd fuse together in seconds. Merge into one. Just to smash apart again, broken bits of himself lost in the process each time. Now Keith can't put himself back together any more than he can that necklace.

The snowy television crackles, then zaps.

*M\*A\*S\*H.* That was the show. The first night it aired was also the first night he dreamed about Rod, finding him in that nonexistent "room" when Keith couldn't find him anywhere else in his waking life. At least, he thinks it was Rod—the past nights, too—but the only really vivid things in the visions are those furnishings in that room. That damned room. *He'll* be damned if he ever goes back in there. He won't.

Eyelids now heavy in the heat, he sinks farther down on his sofa and eventually kicks his legs up onto it, swiveling to recline along its length despite the plush print baking into his body and his denim shorts digging into his dick again. To the crackle of the television, he drifts off to silly thoughts...imagining the sofa's ugly old barns seeping from its fabric into his skin, then him actually slipping down into one, falling yet landing softly and waking in a fully furnished horse stall, its hay bales covered in sheets; it's got a TV and stereo in there, too, and coming from somewhere up in the loft is a series of repetitive clicks, like a rotary phone dialing—

*Slam!*

Keith jolts up from where he's dozed on the sofa. Dizzily, he sets one foot then the other on the shag carpet, trading one fuzzy sensation for another as he finally abandons the tacky barnyard of his Colonial Revival couch—the one Rod used to give him such tremendous shit for—to stride toward where he thinks the sound came from. The sound he's heard before, like a door slamming, but...in the dining room? He walks to the table, dings a knee on a chair as he steps around it to stand face-to-face with the wall. He presses his hand on a seam of its textured wallpaper. Tapping the pads of his fingers against the unyielding hardness, he snorts out an exhale and drops his head, snickering in mockery at what a dunce he must be to think for a second there could be a door there. Again, all that's on the other side is Lucinda's apartment.

With his one palm still pressed on the wall, he runs the other through his hair, easing the fine, honey-brown strands out of his eyes and then wiping his hand down his face, stopping it at the uncharacteristic stubble that's grown at his jaw. What his hairdresser would think if she saw him now—not at the salon, obviously, where she'd buffed him as shiny as an Emmy for that audition he never made it to—but in the halls and elevators of the Wellraven itself, where she and her husband live just upstairs.

*If* Keith were to venture outside of 801 again, that is. It's been weeks since he has, not since his last attempt to find Rod at one of their old haunts, where the fellas seemed only too happy to inform Keith about Rod's northern migration with Ty, another client he represents. An even younger model of Keith; they only ever seem to get younger the more Rod advances into his forties, refusing to age. That was August, though Keith had already heard the first whisperings of the affair back in July, the day he'd gotten the casting call and swiftly booked his appointment with Amy at Upper East Dyed. Then the night before the audition, he got to see it for himself—got to see a lot more of Ty, with Rod, beneath a neon light, than he'd ever wanted to. Not even trying to hide it.

The next day, when Keith ended up auditioning for leading man of a corner barstool instead of the supporting TV role, there was no angry call from his agent afterward.

No contact whatsoever. No agent. No Rod. Not anymore. As he would learn soon enough.

No, Amy wouldn't be thrilled with how he's let her creation go since that summer of his discontent. Whose sweet, baby-faced boy does he need to be anymore anyway, now that the jobs have dried up right along with his agent's representation. Rod once told him that it paid to be pretty, that he'd see to it Keith got paid pretty damn well for it, too, if Keith trusted Rod to groom him, schmooze him, put him in front of any bite he could get before putting him in front of himself to take his own nibbles of that golden flesh. The seduction was simple; Rod tried harder than he ever needed to, but how Keith liked to watch him try. Back when he did. Knowing he was trying—and succeeding—with so many others, too, like the one he's with now. All the pretty boys.

Curling his fingers into a claw, Keith digs his nails into the heat-softened wallpaper and scrapes them down the swirling textured surface, managing to tear it in one spot. Sadly, he looks to the jagged rip, pinches at the crinkled strip he's peeled away and, licking his thumb for some saliva sealant, tries to smooth it back into place. Just like he thought he could meld the ends of his necklace chain back together, always kidding himself that he can heal, that separation is only temporary and that things can come back together if only he wills it enough.

What a weak will he has, though; what a weak man he is. He can't repair what's so broken and doesn't understand why he even tries.

Gliding the pad of his thumb over the wrinkled scrap of paper, he then pinches the shred to yank it off, slicing a deeper wound into the wall.

*Go ahead and bleed*, he says. *See if I care.*

Then he walks to the second bedroom and closes the door behind him on what dreaded dreams might come.

*October 1972*

Days, dreams, and drinks multiply until, one night, blood does seep down the wall from where Keith peeled the paper away. The spot right next to the door, which this time doesn't open. Won't. He slams against it, kicks at it, punches his fist through it, but whatever cracks and holes he splits and punctures, they seal right back up, like they were never there.

"*You're* never here either! You're not!" Keith unleashes his fury and spit at the dark and deceiving door. "You're not real! This isn't..." Slapping his palm on the coarse wooden surface, he catches his breath and sinks to his knees. Turns his back on the wall and slumps against it. "This isn't real."

Rod is behind that door; Keith knows it, but he's not letting him in. Not this time, and Keith wants to blame him but doesn't, because none of this is real. Rod isn't real, not anymore, not in Keith's life, anyway. Just a figment, a

504

memory that made its mark then left it behind. A scar on Keith's heart, now on the wall, but the man doesn't exist. He's gone.

Just when Keith starts to accept that, at least for now so he can sleep, he senses his spine sinking into a rubbery surface behind him, now gelatinous and cold, so very cold, and it tingles over him like slippery static until he's fallen back into the room.

He lies on his back now at the room's center, between the sheet-covered armchairs and sofa, and he stares up at an illuminated chandelier, the crystals shimmering and trembling overhead like frightened diamonds, wishing he hadn't come. They vibrate and shiver as if shaking their heads at him, mourning the mistake, the misplacement of someone like him here, and then a shadow dims their suffering, crawls across their sparkling light like a widow's veil to dull Keith's view.

*Not all doors…meant to open.*

It's getting colder, so much colder while a touch—as if made of a million grains of sand yet not solid—begins to caress over his arm, his wrist. Then it glides over both arms, moves through his hands and up, encircling his fine wrist bones and pulsing in sync with the beat of his heart.

Keith's chest sinks as he feels a pressure bear down on him, not heavy but perceptible, a presence elongating over his form and moving ever closer, closer…and then static sparks his lips, and with a gust of air on his face—

It's gone. His chest reinflates with the pressure lifted from it, with only the gold pendant resting on it, slipping a little to the side until its chain hooks on one of his shirt buttons. His wrists still tingle, but the veil's been drawn away, except he doesn't see the twinkling light fixture overhead. He doesn't see anything.

And then he opens his eyes.

Feels the sting on his wrists, which are sticking to his bedsheet.

"Shit," he whispers as he wads the fabric tight around his left arm. He rolls to his side, curls up in a ball and cries it out. And then he gets himself to his feet, navigates through the dark, a toe hooking onto something stringlike as he steps from the shag onto the cold tile of the room that will save him after the other one already did.

His foot skids a little on the floor, grinding something against the laminate, and upon flicking the light on, he sees he's dragged in the broken necklace chain, its pendant barely hanging on near the lobster clasp. Reaching for it, he wraps it in a faded pear-green face cloth and stuffs it in a vanity drawer. Then he inspects the damage: his right arm has just a scratch, a burn, more like, where he kept rubbing it against the tear in the wallpaper as if he could smudge it out, fervently scrubbing and scrubbing until red-hot pain seared through his wrist, and Keith liked that he felt something. For a second, he blindingly forgot about Roderick and his own pathetic demise and thought nothing but felt, fell into the pain and wanted more.

No one came knocking when he smashed a whiskey bottle against the kitchen floor, the last inch of its honey-colored contents creeping across the harvest-gold linoleum and blotting out its floral pattern like Keith had tried to blot his memory with the booze. No such luck, and he was determined that he wouldn't dream tonight, wouldn't dream ever again once a shard's sweet kiss to his wrist sent him to sleep for good.

Except it didn't work. Or maybe it would have, if he hadn't entered that room...*the* room, the one just beyond, here yet not here, which is how Keith has been feeling, too, trying to find his place. Fuck if it's the Wellraven. He really should go. Leave this place and what seeps into and stays in its walls. Leave this city altogether and what stains its streets. *Ciao, Manhattan.*

Nothing he can do about it now, though. Standing over the cornflower-blue sink in the guest bathroom, one of the bulbs flickers then snuffs out behind the trough fixture overhead. Other bulbs remain lit behind the frosted, gold-filigreed white glass, but the new dimness casts a pallid, cadaverous light onto Keith's face, his jade eyes almost brown, and he imagines for a moment that he can see through himself in the mirror, that either he's translucent or what he's seeing is actually *behind* the glass, a window to the other room that's there but not there. Teetering on his bare feet, he zones out at his reflection for a moment, sees the glass begin to ripple like water around it until—

A deep breath and a blink later, it's gone. Whatever it was. The mirror is solid, as Keith confirms with a tap of his fingertip, and he himself looks solid, the only room he can see in the glass now just the one behind him. Shaking his head, he bends over the sink and runs some tepid water over his wrist to clean out the wound that isn't as deep as he thought.

As autumn leaves fade and fall, Keith's body heals if his heart doesn't. After that scare, those depths he hadn't known he could drop into, he's actually made some effort to get out of this stuffy place, mingle with some humanity again, though the bustle outside always drives him back in before too long.

Coming and going from the Wellraven, he sticks to the stairs, not keen on elevator small talk, and he'd hate for the old folks and sickly little kid across the hall to see him like this; they always look like they've got enough on their minds, and he wouldn't want to add to their worries that their neighbor's a psycho. Lucinda, too, the lively redhead next door, would only want to talk shop, swap headshots, question why he doesn't audition or have an agent or come to her parties anymore. So, in the refuge of the stairwell, all he's ever encountered is a young brunette, who only goes as far as the second floor. She seems as shy and keen to keep to herself as Keith, so no bother there.

He's supposed to be looking for a new place, and probably a job, but his feet only ever lead him to Central Park, just six avenues west. Roderick always wanted to go there together, but Keith didn't, not with Rod, not in the daytime; he liked their life in the dark, in private—or "hidden," as Rod would bitterly accuse. Keith feels cloaked in the dark no matter where he goes, really, but at least the park's one place he can go without a ghost.

Or so he thought. Out of the corner of his eye, he keeps thinking he sees Rod everywhere on the pathways, in the grass, loses his breath at the thought that maybe he's come back, maybe he never left town to begin with. Maybe he'll make his way back to Keith after all. But he would've done that by now.

Maybe. Maybe not. It's the possibility that he could that's the only thing keeping Keith breathing right now. He needs to see Roderick again. He will, and when he does, if Rod can look him in the eye and honestly say he doesn't still love him, well then…then maybe Keith'll just have to finish the job he started that dark, desperate night, and no one in the room will be able to save him this time.

Keith believed he was over thoughts like this, that he might've turned a corner even if there's still the long road ahead. But this morning when he was fishing around in a bathroom drawer for his razor, thinking it might be time to show his face again, he pulled out a wash rag, and the gold chain fell to the floor, its coin pendant spinning a few inches away. A rush of feeling overcame him, sensations he's mostly, *almost* been spared since hiding the necklace from sight. He immediately abandoned the search for his razor, picking the jewelry up and trying once more to fix it—

And has ended up burying it instead. In Central Park. Clear on the other side, near the exit to West Seventy-

Second Street. He feels somewhat better, lighter for it, yet has swung by the liquor store to pick up a little sack "lunch" for himself on his way back to the Wellraven all the same.

He only wants some rest today. Peace. Oblivion. A dreamless sleep where he doesn't have to visit the room—which he still does every now and then, but the figure he used to think was Rod isn't there anymore. Abandoning Keith even in dreams. Nowadays, Keith usually finds himself alone in the room, though sometimes there's another guy, dressed all in white, who keeps asking for Sophie, whoever that is, and then last night...

Last night, after Keith fell asleep in front of the TV, he dreamed that a bright light woke him, beaming through the cracks around the nonexistent dining room door. In a haze, he stood and approached the avocado wall, opened the door without questioning, and was nearly blinded by the glow, so piercing it practically hummed in his ears, and he could hardly stand to look if it hadn't already resolved itself into the voluptuous shape of a woman, who extended an arm in invitation. Without speaking, he knew what she wanted, that she enjoys it often and within the very walls of the Wellraven, and Keith couldn't deny he wanted it, too. Needed the sensuous sweetness rolling off of her in waves.

But not in the room, not where he waits for Rod to come back, even if it could make him jealous.

Instead, Keith backed away from the light and closed the door on it, returning to the couch, where he jacked himself off and finally did sink into the blank of a sleep without dreams. Waking this morning to find his hand sticking to his crusted stomach, he had to question whether the woman had been just a dream after all, but of course, a look at the solid dining room wall reminded him that she must've been and he managed to pleasure himself to the fantasy unconsciously. Yet it felt so real. And even now, he wonders if the luminous woman will ever come back, guide him by the hand to the interior of a different wall, any other wall but that one.

It's not like he hasn't slept with chicks before—and for no better reason than to take the edge off or pass the time. He exclusively did, actually, until his awakening with Rod. And he does find pleasure in them, the softness of their skin and the pillowy swell of their breasts, liberated from cheesecloth and crochet.

Keith typically had his pick of the ladies at clubs, too, a golden god himself back when he was kind of becoming a big deal, a model-turned-actor making the jump from spearmint gum and toothpaste commercials to bit parts in daytime soap operas, thanks to Rod. Also, thanks to his agent, he was asked to audition for a recurring role in the relatively new and low-ranking—but promising—*All My Children* back in July. He thought he had it made when that call came in—one of the last rings to jar his kitchen phone—until Rod never returned to the Wellraven, so Keith never returned to Pine Valley.

And he can't return home either. Won't. Not to parents he wouldn't introduce Rod to even if his lover had ever asked. Rod didn't, of course, at least not in earnest, Keith's sure, believing that when he did ask it was only to test him. Sometimes, Rod just liked to pick fights so they could make up afterward, but when he poked at Keith with this particular stick and Keith bit back...well, Rod didn't understand, didn't even want to waste the effort fighting, would just grab his jacket and Camels and go.

Sometimes Keith could catch up with him, find him smoking outside the lobby doors, but only rarely could he lure him back upstairs when he got in that kind of mood. Rod didn't want to stay in the dark with Keith, but why would Keith take such a chance with someone he knew, just *knew*, wouldn't be there for him when the walls crumbled down? That it was just a matter of time before Rod would do exactly what he did...

So why Keith should mourn like he does, act so blindsided even months later, it's just making less and less sense with each day.

*Fuck. Gotta get out of your head, man. Get him outta your heart. Fuck this. Fuck him, and fuck you, too.*

Slamming Door 801 behind him, he lingers in the entryway, unsure what to do with himself, but the crinkle of the brown bag in his grip gives him a good idea. Deciding first to just glare at the closed door to the master bedroom for a while, as if *that'll* show Rod, Keith's senses readjust to the indoor scents of stale alcohol and musty carpet and only the faintest trace of tobacco, held in place by dank air that immediately enshrouds him and suppresses his breath.

The weight of this place...*God*. Heavy, so heavy, and flicking on the pendant lamp in the dining room does little to cut the density. Above the table, the yellowed, wicker-caged orb just swings slightly as footsteps thump from the unit above—Amy's place, which over the summer seemed to pick up in action just when Keith's died down, moaning and groaning from people and furniture alike.

With a sharp clunk, Keith plops his purchase on the counter that separates the kitchen from the dining area and then sheds his thin cognac leather jacket, tossing it on the dining room table, where it slips onto a vinyl chair. He sees dark spots at the base of the lamp's glowing globe—the remains of bugs that flew too close to the light and got themselves trapped. Eyeing the lamp with disdain, he frowns and gives it a good shove, leaving it to swing like a pendulum and cast disorienting shadows all around the apartment, like a dismal disco. Swinging, swinging until the light then starts swirling, making its orbit around dust particles that settle to the tabletop from the brittle, scalloped wicker shade.

And then it stops, just...stops. But not hanging downward above the center of the table—the lamp's suspended at an angle, stretching on its chain from the ceiling toward the dining room wall as though it were metal drawn to a magnet. But neither is either, and Keith doesn't know what he's tripping on right now.

Nothing. He's taken nothing today. Left the drugs behind with the girls at the clubs, but at the moment he could do with something to chill the fuck out.

*What in Christ's name…*

Slowly sidestepping the chair where his jacket lies slumped as if cowering from what's got Keith freaked, too, he wills himself to round the table and approach the lamp from the other side. Extending a hand, he tentatively waves it between the lamp and the wall as though expecting to find strings attached.

Instead, all he feels is a granular texture, like running his hand through sand, except it's ice-cold, nothing like the sunbaked beach, where Keith would comb the sand with his long, narrow fingers, and Rod would kiss the sea-salted sweat from his shoulder and neck. Riis being one park where Keith was less reluctant to let his sun god shine down on him publicly.

Damn it, there he is again, on Keith's mind when he's trying to exorcise him. But now he feels Rod more intensely than ever. Fluttering his fingers in that space in between, he stares at the lamp pointing like an arrow at that damn wall, at the gash Keith tore in it. He doesn't hear the thumping overhead anymore, no soft electrical buzz from the lamp, and the fridge has stopped humming in the kitchen. No rush and whir or honks of traffic invade from outside either; it's a pure silence Keith has never known, and all he can hear is the ringing in his own ears, intensifying with every second.

As a slow pressure bears down on his chest, he holds his breath for a moment, confirming the stillness, the absolute lack of sound that his last few exhales didn't even make. At this moment, he thinks his heart might have stopped, too, and he feels the chill creep up his arm and kiss up his neck to his cheeks until—

With his gaze, he follows the line of the lamp to the rip in the wallpaper. Drops his arm and steps toward it, picks at it with his nail. Then, as he tries to smooth the paper back over, he feels a lump in it, just below the tear. He presses his thumb to it, then runs the other along it, too. There's something flat but perceptible under there, and though the wallpaper's textured, he would've for sure seen this slight protrusion before, which casts its own sliver of shadow.

Keith scrapes again at the base of the torn slice of paper, pulling it a little farther away from the wall this time. Some fibers remain behind, maintaining allegiance with the hardened glue, but he sees something glinting in the crevice. He digs in with a nail to pick more of the layer away, eventually excavating a thread of gold. Pinching it, he tries to pull it out, but it resists. Trying and trying again, he finally rips the strip down to create a greater slash in the wall, and something small, metallic, falls onto the toe of his boot.

Keith jerks back. Keeps stepping away with his gaze fastened on the gold chain and coin pendant lying on his dining room floor.

Before he can get his bearings and make any sense of how the necklace found its way into the wall after he's just buried it, the lamp swings away, released from whatever held it. Buzzing, humming, and honking returns, and Keith just barely able to catch his breath again, watches the light swinging side to side in ever-diminishing arcs as it loses momentum, hypnotized by it until the lamp's rusted chain ceases creaking against the ceiling hook.

The chill is gone, and now he's almost hot inside this thick, stagnant air, though it's cooled down so much outside. With one last wary gaze at the lamp and then at the wall, Keith inches back and bends to pick up the necklace, breathes in and blows out a big breath as he dusts some dirt off of it, and shoves it in his back pocket.

He crosses the living room and throws open the bronze draperies and the champagne sheers behind them. Stepping out onto his balcony, he rests heavily on the short side railing that faces First Avenue, the rutted iron digging into his forearms as he watches yellow-taxied traffic beyond his goose bumped flesh.

The cool breeze brushing through his hair now isn't like what he just felt, though. What that frigid patch of air, like quicksand to the touch, *did* feel like was something he'd experienced in a dream…the one that he thought, for a time, had saved his life, though that was bullshit. Keith didn't carry out what he'd drunkenly decided to do, so there was never any danger, just some bloody dandelions that he couldn't wash the stain out of the next morning and a permanent scar on his left wrist. Just as well that his career's over. He's not meant for anyone's gaze anymore, so what should it matter if he loses his looks one wrinkle and wound at a time.

With his hair dulled of its sun-kissed luster, darkening and growing closer toward his neck as his beard thickens around a more filled-out face, he's starting to look more like Rod, actually, and has sometimes thought he's seen him in the mirror—the same one where he once thought he could look into the room. He's gotten paler, too, inevitable since summer's end and from holing up at home so much, only ever leaving for food and booze or those aimless walks in the park.

He dreams again of that fantasy future life and wonders what 2020 Keith would be doing. If he'd be living in such isolation or reveling in a freer, happier existence. In a world that accepts him for who he is. With people who love him for it, too.

Because he can't help wondering now how it would be any better if Rod had never left. Where were they destined to go anyway? Rod wouldn't commit any more than Keith would come out. If he's honest with himself, he never saw a future for them, only disaster, only exactly what's happened, and yet in the moment, the *moments* that suspended them in time…no world around them, no light, no dark, just them breathing life into and sucking it out of each other. If he could've preserved them in amber, then maybe…

Keith's head drops forward on a laugh. He continues laughing into his palm as his fingernails pick the crust from the corners of his eyes. *What the fuck*, he thinks as he straightens and turns to face the second sliding door to his master bedroom, relieved the orange linen curtain is drawn over it so he can't see inside that mausoleum. Biting his lip, he eases his fingers into his back jeans pocket to retrieve the necklace, dangles it in front of his face, and follows it side to side with his gaze like he did with the lamp.

*You're cursed*, he thinks. The necklace is hexed. He was finally starting to do fine—*I was fine*—and then it showed up and all hell is breaking loose again.

"It's fucking tiki shit, is what this is," he mutters, having watched the three-part *Brady Bunch* Hawaiian holiday recently, where Bobby found an ancient idol on the island and bad luck befell anyone who wore it. Grimacing at what's gotta be his own jinxed jewelry, he flings the necklace over the railing, not even looking to see where it lands.

Heaving a dry sob, he smears the back of his hand under his nose and stares down the door leading back into the living room.

"I don't know, man," he says on an exhale, and, scratching his scalp feverishly and fluffing his mane out with both hands, he strides back inside—determined not to delude himself with any more of this weird shit. To just watch some fucking TV and mentally escape this life, this building, for a time. And tomorrow, look through some fucking classifieds for a roommate because this living by himself business is not working out. He doesn't want a roommate, but he needs one. Not just to pull himself from this emotional hole he's screwed himself firmly into, but, financially, he's barely scraping by. And he can't go to his parents. He can't. He won't. For as much as he can't be who he really is with them, he can't stomach pretending he's anyone else either. Can't. Won't.

*"I can't!"*

*"You won't."*

That's how the conversation often went with Rod, most recently at the June march. Keith stuck to the sidewalk and watched Rod's thick, dark brown waves flow with the current up Christopher Street. Keith walked in parallel but never stepped off the curb to join the event, beelining it back to the Wellraven once the route ended at Central Park. That was one of the last times Rod would see or speak to him again, as if Keith didn't also stand in solidarity with Stonewall, as if...

*Whatever, man.*

He doesn't know why he makes the excuses he does for himself. And yet of course he does. It's because his mom's not Jeanne Manford, who marched with her son on that Liberation Day, urging other parents to unite in support of their gay children. It's because, though his family's own Quaker community also publicly declared support for bisexuality over the summer, Keith knows his parents' answer to the Ithaca Statement's first question: No. They are *not* open to examining sexuality with understanding, loving or otherwise, thank you very much. Because they are Friends of some but not Friends to all.

Hissing out a breath as he closes his door on the cool air behind him, Keith marches to the counter and grabs the paper bag from it, rolling the top of it down so he can unscrew and chug what's inside. Then he switches on the

TV, turning the dial through a few stations until he lands on one that'll do, and drops onto his ugly couch, casting the occasional side-eye at the dining room lamp and wall.

On the sofa, he wakes to a light yet high-pitched squeak. Then another.

Facedown in his drool, he takes a few seconds to flutter his eyes open, bat away the dryness. The apartment's dark except for the blue glow of the TV, but even that's not as bright as it normally is. From the dining room, the creaking continues, rhythmic, like the pulsing weight of sex on bedsprings.

*"Air…"*

Having momentarily closed his eyes again, Keith pops one open now.

*"…must get ooouut…"*

At the breathy voice, Keith stiffens and, still lying on his stomach, tilts his head up from the velvety cushion to look in the direction of the dining area, half expecting to see the glow of the woman in the walls.

*"…must haaave aaair…"*

Propped up on his elbows now, Keith swivels his face toward the sound of moaning coming from the other side of the living room. There, in the muted light of the TV, he sees—

A ghost.

Rising from the opened lid of an old trunk.

Shining…translucent…

And clearly made of cellophane. Yet Bobby and Peter Brady are scared shitless and shouting for Greg to wake up.

Heaving out an exhale, Keith drunkenly giggles to himself, then cackles wildly out loud as he rolls over onto his back at what must be a prank by the Brady sisters. He'd know Marcia's sultry whisper anywhere, having had his share of fantasies involving Maureen McCormick but mostly Barry Williams.

*Jesus*, that scared him, though. Yet it's nothing near as jolting as the telephone now ringing from the kitchen. Shrill, shrieking, throbbing through his heavy head that he pickled in whiskey, starting early enough in the day that he apparently passed out by prime time.

That fucking phone hasn't rung in weeks, and he sure as shit doesn't want to answer it now. But doesn't want to listen to it anymore either.

So he stands up, swaying with the effort and having to catch himself once with a step back before ambling forward to the sound. Mustering all the concentration his blurry brain can whittle together, he crosses the living room and bumps into a dining room chair. Reaching an arm out and feeling around the side wall, he finds the light switch and turns it on to see the pendant lamp swinging just slightly.

The phone on the counter between the kitchen and dining space continues to rattle through its rings, so Keith reaches for that next only to lift the receiver then slam it back down.

Silence. Except for the creaking of the lamp vacillating on its rusted chain. Keith side-eyes it and wonders if his own inebriated steps or ones upstairs set it in motion this time. At least it's dangling normally, though, no magnetic pull to the back wall like this afternoon, which he decided to drink, rather than explain, away. The way it had angled toward the wall, like it was pointing, right at...wanting him to find it...

Keith looks at the tear in the wallpaper. Steps toward it, picks at it some more with his nail. Loses interest and stumbles back to the sofa to watch *The Partridge Family* and then pass out to *Ghost Story*.

*Be one.*

"Be one what?"

*Bee.*

"What?"

*See.*

"What am I supposed to see?"

*One sea.*

Exasperated, Keith flails his arms out and he spins, looking at everything in the room and having no idea what he's being directed to do. It isn't the woman in here with him this time, but he can't be sure it's Rod either. Only a blackened shadow that seems more defined by the negative space around it than any actual form of its own.

"Roderick. If this is you, I don't understand. Where are you? What are you trying to tell me?"

*Why?*

"*Why*? Why do you think? Because you just up and left, and if this is the only way I can be with you, then I need—"

*You...*

"Yeah, *me*."

*Why you?*

"Why me?"

*Why, oh, why, why, why?*

"You have the nerve to ask *me* why? You son of a—"

*Be one bee, see one sea...*

"What in the *fuck* are you—"

*Why you? Why? Oh, why, why, why?*

Having learned how to more lucidly control his dreams during his time alone in the room, Keith has had enough of this shit and walks out, slamming the door behind him.

Much as he tries, though, Keith can never really escape the room. Not as long as he sleeps, anyway, so he spends the weekend trying to stay awake. Gets outside in the crisp air, walks and sits on park benches until dusk, drinks coffee in diners until dawn. Avoids going home to the Wellraven, but he's starting to attract suspicious looks for his loitering, and he keeps encountering strange people on the streets who won't stop trying to shove flyers in his hand or repeating numbers and asking him, "Why, oh, why, why?" and he's just tired, so tired. So sick of it all.

And so today finds Keith on the couch again, enough left in his bagged bottle for another happy hour or two, three, four… He's partially propped up against the back cushion with a flared pant leg folded under him, and, tucked under his floral-striped shirt where it's unbuttoned over his chest, a hand rests on his pec and scratches his armpit occasionally.

He didn't go to the park today. Hasn't gone anywhere. Just slept in and kept the shades drawn and watched the actor who ended up landing his role in the daytime drama. Saw Lucinda, too, in yet another of her speaking parts. All day, he lounges here, soap after soap, game show after game show, never seeing himself brush his teeth or chew gum in ads anymore, and if he did, he'd hardly recognize himself.

Instead, he watches livelier, juicier guys take the lead as he just takes a swig, adjusts the crotch of his corduroys, and eases even farther down on the cushions, crushing the colonial barnyard under his ass. Sleep can come find him—the woman in the walls, too, so he can finally get fucked. Keith doesn't care anymore, doesn't think he'll have to cope with it for much longer. He just needs to build up the nerve…or deaden it enough.

A creaking in the dining room again. Huffing, Keith drags himself up to trudge around his bamboo-and-glass coffee table and turn the volume dial up on the television.

*Creak.*

*Squeak.*

That fucking lamp. That fucking couple upstairs—literally. Fucking. They've gone at it like rabbits since summer and don't seem to care the neighbors can hear. Hats off to Amy, but if she only knew how it could torture Keith sometimes.

The apartment's lit enough by the television for Keith to see the wicker lamp actually looks still this time. Not swinging on its chain and causing the creak. Fine, then it's a bedframe or something upstairs or next door. But just as Keith looks beyond the dining furniture to the wall, fearing the necklace could be back, the telephone starts ringing.

Again.

The trilling bell resonates through his bones, and he's frozen for the moment, the breath caught in his chest and his entire skeleton held captive by tightened muscles and tendons, unrelenting in their grip. As happened earlier, his ears are muffled to any other sound, nothing coming from the television or traffic or the elevator out in the hall, just this incessant ringing that finally compels him to furiously lurch for the phone and rip it from the wall.

Except Keith almost falls backward from a lack of resistance, skipping a few steps back and nearly tripping over the bamboo table behind his calves, the phone cradled in his arms and cord dangling in his hand. It was already detached from the wall, from when he'd disconnected it weeks ago...

He remembers that now, pulling the plug before the calls even had a chance to dry up on their own—before he'd have to admit to anyone else what a failure he is. How he's nothing without Rod and can't do this on his own. Can't keep pretending to be someone else for a living when his life is all an act offscreen, too.

Staring at the four-pronged jack hanging like dead weight from his grasp, Keith just stands there, blinking back tears as the telephone keeps ringing against his chest, where he's clutching it. Trembling, he drops the cord from his right hand and unsteadily lifts the receiver, bringing it to his ear.

"H-hello?"

The sizzle of static, faint then growing louder until it's almost like bacon frying in his ear canal. Keith holds the handset away, fearful of electricity zapping him. But, sensing the crackle quieting down again, he brings the earpiece closer and, this time, hears a couple of pulses tick through as if he were dialing. Another one just for a beat, then two more, and then a string of several pulses repeated over and over before returning to static. And then, once again:

*Tick-tick.*

*Tick.*

*Tick-tick.*

*Tick-tick-tick-tick-tick-tick-tick-tick-tick.*

*Tick-tick-tick-tick-tick-tick-tick-tick.*

*Tick-tick-tick-tick-tick-tick-tick-tick-tick.*
*Tick-tick-tick-tick-tick-tick-tick-tick-tick-tick.*
*Tick-tick-tick-tick-tick-tick-tick-tick-tick.*
*Tick-tick-tick-tick-tick-tick-tick-tick-tick.*
*Tick-tick-tick-tick-tick-tick-tick-tick-tick.*

And then it's back to one or two pulses before the longer strings repeat once more.

Keith replaces the receiver and lets the entire phone fall to the carpet with a plasticky clack and an indignant *ding* from the ringer inside.

He can hear the sound of his own breathing again, along with a jaunty jig that plays behind him from a Lucky Charms ad.

*Lucky charm…*

Numb, he steps over the phone and walks to the dining room wall, where it could simply be a shiny glint of glue now winking at him from the tear in the paper, but he doesn't think so.

Peeling the strip that's now widened to two inches and is several in length, he's no longer stunned when the gold necklace drops to the floor. He stoops to grasp it, and it almost burns against his skin as he stands up straight again, but he isn't sure if it's hot or cold—and either way, it's not uncomfortable, feels natural somehow, igniting something in his veins. Somehow, he knows what he has to do, what he should have done long ago, but he's still afraid. Rubbing his thumb across the coin pendant, he next brings it to his lips and closes his eyes on a firm inhale.

He feels so stupid for even thinking it, but at this point anything goes.

So, running with his whiskey-logged logic, Keith takes a cue from the Bradys and wonders if, just like Bobby returned the tiki idol to its cave, perhaps bringing this necklace to the bedroom he's sealed off might break his curse, too. He hasn't set foot in there since it was confirmed that Rod had shacked up with Ty in Toronto, another promising young thing for him to lap up and spew out in time. Until then, the necklace had sat in there on the little round table next to Rod's usual side of the bed, all boxed up and wrapped in a bow as Keith's thank-you for securing him what was sure to be a successful audition. A gig that would've paved the way in more gold, figuratively, as Keith gained greater security in his finances and in himself, able to provide more to the life he wanted with Rod, a secret life lived in comfort with each other better than no life together at all, right?

Rounding the bend past the kitchen counter toward his unit door, he stops outside the master bedroom. Presses a palm against the plywood door before easing his hand down to the knob. The brass twists easily in his grip, and though he lets go in a moment of hesitation, the door slowly creaks open on its own.

Muscle memory leads him down a short faux-wood-paneled hall—the en suite bathroom to his left and walk-in closet to his right—and straight back to the window, where he yanks the pull chain of a hanging lamp in the corner. The light corralled by a marigold velvet cylinder shade beams down on a small bamboo bistro table beside the balcony door. The amber glass ashtray resting on the rattan tabletop still holds the cremated remains of Rod's Camels, which Keith only let him smoke in this room or, preferably, out on the balcony. He hated the habit himself and hoped his lover would kick it, too—though not even Keith could begrudge him a post-coital smoke in reward for his own relaxed state, too boneless and melted in the golden sheets to care. Actually, he enjoyed breathing in the vapors Rod would blow into his mouth, his tongue following soon after for a repeat performance. The wind always did billow back into his sails before too long, among Rod's many other natural talents.

The bedsheets are still tangled from when Keith last kicked around in them, alone and far from satisfied that time. He sits at the edge of the bed now to run his hands over the silken fabric, unwashed since Rod last sweat into them, too. Keith kisses the pendant in his palm and lays it in the divot on Rod's pillow. Then, easing himself up and onto the other side of the bed, he rests his head on his own pillow, lying on his back and frowning at the popcorn ceiling.

He breathes in deeply, both proud and regretful of taking this step. The musk of woody cologne and tobacco and a sweet tang that was all Rod's own melds into a dangerous alchemy, opening portals in Keith's mind and stabbing his heart. Instantly, it's like no time has passed, and he can expect Rod to waltz inside this room after a long day at work has left him tipsy and drowsy yet spicy and horny and open to anything Keith wants to do to him. And sometimes, all they wanted to do was lie entwined as they listened to records and talked. Or didn't talk, just ran fingers through each other's hair, finding expression through the music, that shared experience of vibration on vinyl.

Propping his head on his hand, Keith glances over at the record player on his dresser, near the foot of the bed. Eyes the albums lined up vertically on the floor, leaning precariously against the dresser's edge. After a moment gliding his gaze along their well-worn edges, an album on the end tips over.

He sits up and crawls the length of the bed, then onto the floor to investigate. Fleetwood Mac's *Bare Trees* has fallen over to reveal very lush trees instead—the thick trunk of one grows in the foreground, with a couple lying beneath it, basking. Serene. One with nature. Just being.

*Be one. Be.*

*Be one bee.*

The voice from the room resurfaces in Keith's memory, but he doesn't want to hear this nonsensical message again. Reaching for the record, he slips the vinyl from the sleeve and loads it on the turntable, resting the needle in place to hear John Lennon sing to himself and Yoko that everything would be all right, that when you're alone you just have to remember to "Hold On."

Sinking back to the floor to the mellow tune, Keith slumps against the mattress, all too aware that he has no one else but himself. But he doesn't know how much longer he can hold on.

Just when the gentle, encouraging melody has lulled him into at least a false sense of peace, the beat picks up as the next song struts in with an unsettling reminder of "freaks" on the telephone that won't leave him alone—the phone. Who was on its other end? Who was dialing from his? How was it ringing in the first place?

Curling his knees up to his chin, Keith dips his head and presses his eyes into them. He clutches at his unruly hair, understanding fully now how much he's lost his grip, not just in these bizarre past days but long before that.

Lennon sings of parents who didn't want him so made him a star, and Keith cringes at how he himself only sought fame so he could make his mom and dad proud, believe that he was "somebody," anybody other than who he really is. That's why acting was a natural choice. Only when the curtain dropped behind him and he could be in this room alone with Rod could Keith drop the script, too, and let his lover wipe away the makeup, peel away his costume, keeping the door ajar but never fully open. "I Found Out," Lennon belts out, and finding out has always been Keith's fear.

He scrambles to his feet and lifts the needle to drop it somewhere else, but when the melancholy notes of "Isolation" start hammering on his heartstrings instead, he snatches the record up and flips it over, as if hiding the printed titles of Side A will erase the words already out in the air and replaying in Keith's thoughts. Clipping the tonearm in its rest instead of playing anything more, he flops back down on the bed, this time on his stomach so he can cry into his pillow.

"Rod," he sobs into the cushion, then he reaches for the one beside him and hugs it close, so close it brings the coin back to his lips, and he speaks against it as he continues to cry. "I get it. I get it. I know you don't want me. I can't have you the way I want you, but I need you. Can't you come back just to help me find my way? Help me be more like you?" Sniffing against the dampened pillowcase, he shakes his head. "Be more like...me?"

*Be one.*

*Be.*

*Why you?*

*Oh, why, why, why?*

"I don't understand..." he whimpers and, in exhaustion, slips to sleep.

*We never use this room. Why don't we ever use this room?*

"No need," Keith says, looking around the master bedroom this time, which is covered in gold silk sheets.

*But this room is nice. Like, really nice. And look at the size of it! Bigger than the one you've been using.*

"It's no use, Rod. Not without you here."

*But, Keith...I* am *here. I've been right here, this entire time.*

Keith squints at the rectangular furnishing nearest him and pulls off its shiny cover to reveal his turntable on the dresser.

*Stereo, too,* Rod says. *Not a fine one, not top-of-the-line one, but a good one. Why won't you use this?*

"Because it reminds me too much of you."

*Don't you want to remember?*

"Remember…?" Only then does it occur to Keith that, when he finally raises his gaze, he's able to look right at his companion—not a shadow, not a vague, glitching figure but Roderick. Not in the flesh, but as clear as. He's smiling at Keith from within a soft, ethereal glow, but it's him, from the twinkle and crinkle of his eye as he flashes that lopsided grin to the little dark hairs that pepper his large tanned hands. Keith wants nothing more than to launch himself over the bed and into Rod's arms, to kiss him senselessly and beg him never to leave again, but there's a sadness in that smile that tells him, more permanently than anything ever could, that as sure as he's here now, he really and truly cannot stay.

*Wild, man…right?* Rod huffs out a light yet forced laugh, arms spread out as he looks himself up and down.

"Too late," Keith says, feeling he's heard these words before, this whole conversation, more or less. His posture sinks as the life force seems to drain from him and gravity pulls him down, down.

*It* is *too late, isn't it,* he says without speech, swallowing the hardening knot in his throat as Rod communicates to him without words, too—volumes, in what seems like seconds. Keith can't bear it, can't even squeak out, *Oh, Roderick.*

His smile cracking as his cheeks twitch and his eyes well, Rod drops his hands and shrugs, scans the space surrounding him as if he isn't even sure where he is.

*It's cool in here,* he says as he looks around, continuing to echo Keith's words from the original dream. *I'm actually cold.*

But then he looks back at Keith meaningfully, growing fainter within the ever-brightening room.

*But it's not too late. Is it? For you?*

"Remember..."

Musk and smoke fill his nostrils, and Keith wakes to music.

"Remember...remember...remember..."

The needle is skipping on the vinyl that's started spinning again, the tonearm off its rest.

"Remember...remember...remember..."

Squeezing his eyes closed, Keith then opens them to the cold metal still pressed to his face. Lifting it from the fabric as he rolls over onto his side, dangling in front of him isn't the gold coin pendant but Rod's dog tags, hanging from their silver chain.

"What would you like me to remember, Rod?" he whispers, his voice dragged across gravel.

After skipping on the word *sorry* a few times, the tonearm lifts the needle and sets it down on "Love," letting the whole song play through.

The silver chain is intact, and Keith slips it around his neck. Slides a tag between his lips and bites down.

Nuzzling into the pillows and underneath the bedsheet, he feels a light, recurring pressure on his hair, and he closes his eyes to the caress. Allows the sweet, haunting melody to soothe and bathe him in the truth. What he and Rod shared...it wasn't all in his head. Was everything in his heart. His gut.

Yet even though he knows this now, has always known, it's just as real as the knowing that they'd never last. Because Rod didn't last. The same heart that would've led him back from Canada—to Keith—took him out of this world first.

Keith's face breaks beneath the weight of this knowledge, and he draws the sheet over his head. He feels less alone now as his lover serenades him from the ether, yet he still doesn't know how to navigate any of this on his own.

Delicate notes on the piano fade out, and guitar strums in the next song waste no time making their presence known. The bass beat jolts Keith from the quiet cocoon he's tried to wrap himself in, lose himself in, distracted from scheming how to join Rod where he is...forever.

He knows Rod wouldn't want that. But it's not up to him, now is it? He might've saved Keith before, but he'd probably sapped his energy in the effort, and that's why it took him a while to come back. Visiting in dreams is one thing, but these physical feats around the apartment have got to be tapping him out again. Rod can't keep it up for long.

Before Keith can contemplate any further how he might try pills, maybe even the roof next time, the record skips, and he hears "Look at Me." As gentle as "Love," it's like Rod is telling Keith, insisting to him, that he's here and asking what he should do.

"You don't have to do anything, my love," Keith says. "You can help me by doing nothing this time."

But the record skips and replays the bridge over and over again, like Rod's begging Keith to look at him, reminding him again that he's here.

*"Oh, my love."*

Keith shakes his head, only for the needle to skip to another song, playing just the word *why*.

"You know why, Rod."

*"...you..."*

The tonearm had to skip back to "Look at Me" for that one. This is going to drain Rod fast, and then he really won't be able to stand in Keith's way.

*Why* again. Then an *oh* and back to *why*, which now just keeps repeating.

*Why you, why, oh, why, why, why?*

"Why me? Why *you*, Rod? Why does it make any more sense for *you* to be dead? Why *not* me?" For as angry and determined as he's growing, Keith only cries harder and falters in resolve.

But again, the tonearm repositions itself and skips out the same refrain:

*Why you, why, oh, why, why, why?*

Keith can't take it anymore. Whipping the sheet off himself, he leaps to his feet and rips the record off the turntable, flinging it to the carpet like a frisbee.

"Enough," he cries. "Just be at peace and let me find mine. Let me find it with you."

But no sooner has he gained the upper hand when he hears that damned telephone ringing again. Ringing, ringing, endlessly ringing, shrill and desperate.

Keith flies out of the bedroom on the remaining fumes of his whiskey, sure he's left a gouge in the paneling by shoving the already open door against it so hard on his way out. The phone keeps ringing from where it lies on the matted shag carpet, the handset not even in its cradle but lying faceup. Keith kneels down to it and screams into the mouthpiece, "*WHAT?*"

The crackle of static again, but when it goes quiet, he presses the earpiece to his head. The same pulsing as before:

*Tick-tick.*

*Tick.*

*Tick-tick.*

*Tick-tick-tick-tick-tick-tick-tick-tick-tick.*

*Tick-tick-tick-tick-tick-tick-tick-tick.*

*Tick-tick-tick-tick-tick-tick-tick-tick.*

*Tick-tick-tick-tick-tick-tick-tick-tick-tick.*

*Tick-tick-tick-tick-tick-tick-tick-tick.*

*Tick-tick-tick-tick-tick-tick-tick-tick-tick.*
*Tick-tick-tick-tick-tick-tick-tick-tick-tick.*

"What the fuck is this supposed to mean? Are you dialing an actual fucking number?"

On that last thought, Keith manages to calm down for a second, taking a moment to breathe deeply in and out as his own words register to him. The pulsing: it's the same sound he'd hear in the receiver if he were dialing, the number of pulses equaling the digit dialed—except for zero, which would pulse ten times.

As the pulsing continues in his ear, he picks the base of the phone up in his other hand and rises to his feet, walking to the counter to rest it where it usually sits and glancing around the rest of the kitchen and dining area frantically for a pen. Holding the handset to his ear with his shoulder, he stretches the curled cord around and over the counter as he enters the kitchen and finds a pencil in a drawer, but he can't find any paper. Winding back to the dining room, he rips the torn wallpaper strip from the wall with surprising satisfaction and holds it down on the Formica tabletop as he counts out the pulses and records them on paper.

*Tick-tick*—two.

*Tick*—one.

*Tick-tick*—two.

And so on until he's written, *2129890999.*

Repeating it back to himself out loud, he has a flash of memory back to the strangers who approached him on the street over the weekend, seemingly senile or intoxicated

538

and reciting what he thought were random numbers. A lot of nines, he remembers, just like this, and they'd also ask him—

Turning from the table toward the counter, he steps up to the phone to inspect its rotary dial and the letters printed around it with each number.

The number one stands alone, but two is paired with *ABC*. So the local 212 area code could be considered *A-1-A* or another letter combination, like *A-1-B* or *B-1-C* or...

*B-1-B.*

*C-1-C.*

*Be one bee.*

*See one sea.*

Keith's stomach tightens like a fist around the thoughts he has next. On another deep breath, he grabs the phone's wall cord and lures in the jack. Plugging it back into the wall, he can hear the normal ringtone. From inside New York City, he wouldn't need to dial the area code, but that was a nice touch on Rod's part. Always so thorough, so precise, and the smaller numbers had a better chance of being recognized. As for the rest...

Keith's hand and head are sweating against the receiver, though a coolness washes over him, too, and the skin of his forearms and shins prickles. His chest expands as he inserts a numbed fingertip, its nail chewed to the quick, into a hole in the circular plastic and dials *Y* (nine), then *U* (eight).

*Why you.*

As the dial slowly spins its way back counterclockwise, a trembling finger waits for the second-to-last hole to reach *WXY* again. Nine. *Y*. When it does, Keith drags it back around to the metal finger stop on the other side. Then he dials zero, which he got from the ten pulses he'd counted earlier. And though it's associated with the operator and not the letter *O*, he usually pronounces *0* the same way. A lot of people do. Rod no exception.

*Why, oh.*

Finally, Keith dials and waits out the nine-pulse ticking of each *Y*, *Y*, *Y* with a patience he's never known.

*Why, why, why.*

He knows the call has connected when he can hear a tone signaling that the phone's ringing on the other end. The grip on his stomach has traveled all the way up to his throat, and he rakes his free hand through his hair before bringing it back around to bite his fingernail, holding his breath.

After another rapid heartbeat or two, there's a click as someone picks up.

"Hello, Gay Switchboard of New York," a kind voice answers.

Keith strangles the handset in his clammy palm, lowering it to his heart as both his face and chest scrunch into a still, silent sob. His eyelids feel like they can barely contain his eyes, which are bursting from their sockets as his lungs deflate, and his sternum seems ready to crack.

Clenching in on himself like this, he heaves against the phone pressed to his chest with a stifled mewl.

*Oh my God, Roderick. I love you.*

"Hello?"

He hears the muffled voice against his chest hair as he shakily draws a measured breath in through his nose and funnels the exhale through O-shaped lips, trying to steady his fluttering diaphragm.

"Hello? Can I help you?" the smothered yet hopeful voice repeats.

Wincing, Keith jerks both head and shoulders in a collective nod. He presses his lips together and sniffs, then wipes some residual tears away from his squeezed shut eyes.

*I love you. I don't think I even realized how much until now. Thank you for loving me enough, too, to do this.*

"Can I help who's there?"

Scraping the telephone handset up his chest and along his neck and cheek to his ear, Keith croaks out a syllable, then clears his throat before trying again.

"Yes, yeah. Hi," he says, running a quavering hand back through his wayward mane of hair and clutching a handful of it at the roots. "I…could really use someone to talk to."

*Founded independently as the Gay Switchboard of New York in 1972, the LGBT Switchboard of New York is now administered by the LGBT National Help Center as the oldest LGBTQ+ hotline in the world, offering free and confidential support. They can be contacted at help@LGBThotline.org as well as the original phone number, which remains (212) 989-0999 to this day.*

# ROBERT

MORGAN & JENNIFER LOCKLEAR

**Dear Diary,**

## Discovery Journal Entry No. 1
## Friday, October 20ᵗʰ, 1972
## 4:53pm

I just stole you from the five and dime. Sorry about that, but I had to tell someone! I just stumbled upon the biggest secret I've ever known, and it's about me!

I need to start with a quick introduction if this is to be my official account of things, so, my name is Robert Robichaud, and I'm ten years old. I live in New York City, between Central Park and the East River. You can't miss my building. It looks like a twenty-story thumb covered with Cheeto dust. It's called the Wellraven, which sounds fancy, but trust me, it's not.

Even though my building is on First Avenue, we have to enter from Sixty-Ninth or Seventieth. Most people enter the building from Seventieth, but I like to come in from Sixty-Ninth. There's more shade on that street because of this row of big trees. You could climb up to the third floor balconies in one of them. I'm not saying I've done it, but I assure you, it can be done.

I live with my grandma and grandpa. They're definitely old, but they're also pretty fun and mostly forgiving. They're my mom's mom and dad. They told me she ran away from being a mom.

My dad died in prison on my sixth birthday.

We live in apartment 804, and I can see Brooklyn from my bedroom window. Every morning the sun invades my shades, but I usually have to get up for school anyway, so Brooklyn kind of does me a favor. Thanks, Brooklyn.

I just started fifth grade at PS 82 which is kitty-corner from us across First Avenue. There are at least ten kids in my building that go to school there.

Okay, that's good enough for the basics. It's time to spill the beans.

Now, I can't prove anything yet, but I overheard my grandpa on the phone with one of my doctors and, oh yeah! Hold on, I have to tell you that I have a dump truck full of doctors on account of me having diabetes mellitus, asthma, and a heart murmur.

I have to get NPH injections every day. I actually do it myself, but I had to practice on oranges first. NPH is animal insulin, but that's not the worst part. The worst part is this stupid *Clini-test* I have to do every time I pee. I swear to God, it looks like we have a science lab on top of our toilet tank!

What I do is, I mix my pee in a test tube with a pill that dissolves when I shake it, and no, there is no cap to the test tube, so I have to hold my finger over it, which means I get a little bit of pee on my finger every time, which is gross.

If the pee turns blue, I need more sugar. If the pee stays green, I'm fine. If the pee turns orange, or worse, red, I need a shot of NPH, the animal insulin.

With the asthma, I need my inhaler, especially if I go outside. Super especially if it's summertime. When my asthma gets really bad, I have to come inside and breathe through my nebulizer. It looks like I'm smoking, which is cool, but the mist tastes like toothpaste.

I don't know what the deal is with my heart murmur. There are no treatments for it, I guess, but my grandma always tells me not to run too fast or my heart will burst in my chest.

But none of that matters right now! I mean, it's good that I'm writing down all these details, but here's the thing, I don't think I have diabetes at all! I don't think I have asthma, or anything else either! It's all a lie!

That's right, and you know why? I'm a robot, that's why!

For some reason, they're keeping it a secret from me.

All these tests, and shots, my inhaler, my nebulizer, I bet they are all just ways to maintain my mechanical system without me suspecting.

And just look at my name, Robert. They're practically daring me to figure it out! Say, I wonder if that's a test or something. Maybe they're waiting for me to figure it out. I'll have to think about that.

Here's something else, I've never been swimming. Ever. Doesn't that seem suspicious?

Like I said, I heard my grandpa talking on the phone with one of my doctors, and it just hit me. Why would any human be so hard to take care of if they weren't some sort of high-tech Wonder Boy? Okay, maybe Wonder Boy is a bit much, and definitely a rip-off of the Batman comics.

Anyway, that's all I've got so far. I heard him talking, realized the truth, and I've been writing ever since. Well, after I ran downstairs and stole you from the market a block up Seventieth.

It's dinnertime. We're having home-made macaroni and cheese, which is my favorite. It must be good for my parts.

After that we're watching *Sonny & Cher Comedy Hour*.

After that, I think I'm going out onto the fire escape for the first time. It's forbidden, of course, but I have to test something. If I really am a robot, I'm sure I'll be fine.

**Discovery Journal Entry No. 2**
**Friday, October 20th, 1972**
**9:21pm.**

I did something crazy tonight.

After we ate dinner, and watched Sonny & Cher, I took a pee test which turned orange, so I gave myself a shot of NPH. The trick is to pinch some fat in your stomach. It's not so bad once you get used to it. I've been doing it since I turned six.

My bedtime is at eight o'clock, but I don't need to be tucked in anymore, so I gave my grandparents a hug good night and went to my room.

They check on me once before they go to bed, which usually takes another hour. I read comic books and listen to whatever they're watching on TV.

I turned off my light a few minutes before my grandma opened my bedroom door and peeked inside.

"Good night, Grandma," I told her. I never fake being asleep.

"Night, Robbie."

When she left, I waited a few more minutes. They never come in a second time, but I waited anyway. Then I climbed the fire escape all the way to the roof!

That's twelve stories up from mine, and it was windy too. Hey, I wasn't cold! I should have been cold, but I wasn't! Maybe that's another clue right there. Next time I'll wear my shoes though. I was in my socks, which made the metal very slippery.

I could have climbed down eight stories to the street, but the only people on the street at this hour are hooligans, helpless young women, and Spiderman.

I watched the East River get wider as I climbed higher and higher. Most of the windows were dark, or had the curtains drawn. Somewhere around the fifteenth or sixteenth floor, I heard someone playing the violin.

I haven't chosen my superhero name yet. Maybe I could be The Mosquito. You see, diabetes injections aside, I really know how to use a needle. My grandma taught me how to do cross-stitch. I made a lighthouse.

Even though Jim Morrison died about a year ago, The Doors stayed together, and just put out a song called The Mosquito. It's pretty weird, but maybe it could work as my theme song.

And yes, of course, I know who Jim Morrison is. He's almost as famous as Elvis!

Back to my story. I wasn't expecting it, but there were people on the roof. They were smoking lumpy cigarettes and listening to a girl playing a ukulele.

One of the men was wearing red overalls with no shirt. He had long blond hair and called me Little Dreamer.

There were girls up there too. They talked to me for a while.

"Do your parents know you're up here?" one of them asked. She had curly brown hair and glasses.

"Now, what do you think?" I answered.

This got a laugh.

"Is this your first time up here?" the other girl asked. She had wavy light brown hair and black cowboy boots with bright green ivy stitched onto them.

"I was going to ask you the same thing."

Another laugh. I kept things mysterious, like a superhero would have to be. I didn't want this getting back to my grandparents. They would dismantle me for sure.

"Did you make those cowboy boots?" I asked.

"Do you like them?"

I nodded. "You should do a pair with flames."

"Maybe I will."

We talked for a while longer; they thought I was pretty funny. It must be part of my programming.

I didn't have to use my inhaler until I was on my way back down, which was much harder because I had to *look* down. It put my stomach in a bad mood, which is a point for the human argument.

I stopped to pull my inhaler out of my pajama pocket, but it slipped out of my hand. I heard it clinking and clanking below me, so I just kept going. I was hoping that I might find it, but worried that I would find it by stepping on it in the dark.

I never saw it, but it really was dark. I could have passed right by it. That's okay, the inhaler was almost empty, and I have another one right here on my desk.

I set out to prove that I wouldn't be scared, but I was definitely scared. Still, I didn't quit, and I didn't get cold. I don't know what any of that proves, but it sure sounds like something a robot would do.

Now that this Discovery Journal has secrets of its own, I better hide it, and I know just the place, I'm going to put it in with my comic books.

## Discovery Journal Entry No. 3
## Saturday, October 21st, 1972
## 6:26pm

I almost got arrested for swimming in Turtle Pond today! Strictly speaking, I'm not allowed to go into Central Park by myself, but I'm not allowed to climb up to the roof either.

I had to conduct an important test about water. Since I can't swim, I needed something that wasn't too deep. Except that it turned out to be pretty freakin' deep!

I made sure no one was looking, took a deep breath, and jumped in. I sank fast and landed cross-legged on the bottom of the pond. When my head went underwater, I realized that I couldn't hear the city anymore. Maybe for the first time in my entire life.

It wasn't completely silent though, there was a humming noise, and bubbles. I could definitely hear bubbles zipping by my ears. I could feel them too. Some got caught in my hair.

I held my breath for what felt like an hour. It wasn't of course, which means I do need oxygen like regular people, but time seemed to slow down. Everything was blurry. I could make out round rocks half buried in the sand, and imagined little turtle houses on the outskirts of a turtle city in the middle of the water. There was a mountain of rock and mud with portholes and caves galore.

I waited until the need to breathe became a panic, and pushed up with my legs, as I pumped my arms to the surface. Swimming felt natural to me, even with jeans on.

At the moment my head was released from the water, I distinctly remember thinking two things. One was that the city noise, even in the park, was back, and that I really should have taken my shoes off.

It turned out, having my shoes on was a good thing, but I'll get to that.

I went underwater over and over again, wondering if I would begin sparking or convulsing or something. It should have been scary to take such a risk, but it was the opposite. I had fun! Sure, I take showers when my grandma tells me to, but that's not the same thing as being completely submerged, and now I have successfully completed one test, which neither confirms, nor denies my theory.

In fact, the cops showed up, and I had to swim way over to the other side of the pond before they could run around it. Not bad for my first swimming lesson ever! It still doesn't technically prove anything, but let's not pretend it's not amazing!

I pulled myself up onto the wet grass as fast as I could and ran into the trees. Everything was blurry for a while as I beat feet and listened for them running behind me.

I got away clean, and this is why it was a good thing I kept my shoes on. Except that my grandma spazzed out when I came home, even though I walked around for the rest of the day to drip dry.

It was fine. I told her that I got accidentally knocked into the fountain at Rockefeller University by a girl on roller skates. She likes it when I hang around on the east side of the building.

She didn't seem concerned about me being exposed to that much water. Neither of them even mentioned it. I asked if I could take a warm bath and Grandma was all too happy to get the water running.

I like going underwater now. The quiet is, I don't know, like candy. I'm in my pajamas now, but I'm still thinking about what it's like to be completely submerged.

I'm telling you, there's no way I'm going to be another Aqua Man! No way! But I might have to rethink my superhero name. Wait a minute, mosquitos are always nearby water, right? Good, I'm still good.

Just as long as I'm not another Aqua Man!

**Name ideas:**

~~Waterskippr~~

~~Turtle Kid~~

~~The Wave~~

~~The Subwave~~

~~Substandard~~

~~The Drip~~

~~Soggyshoes~~

~~The Soggy Slugger~~

~~The Squish~~

~~Mr. Bubbles~~

~~The Wet Head~~

You know what? I need to choose my weapon first, that will determine my name. But that Doors song is still pretty cool.

Yeah, The Mosquito, a pest to injustice.


**Discovery Journal Entry No. 4**
**Tuesday, October 24th, 1972**
**4:12pm**


Today's entry is about a few discoveries I made at school yesterday and today. You see, I came to realize that I must have superior mental faculties. Just look at my above average vocabulary! Mental faculties? That's some eighth grade crap right there!

Anyway, I discovered that if I paid full attention in class, and concentrated, I learned better. It must be some kind of brain enhancement!

I applied this technique to all my classes, including gym, where I normally fail miserably.

Not today.

Today we played scooter ball, which is this thing where everyone sits on a wooden square with office chair wheels on every corner, and you use your feet to push yourself around the gym, trying to kick a red ball into a soccer net. It's dumb, I know, and I usually roll over my own fingers a dozen times, but today, I concentrated on the ball. Like, where it was going next.

I avoided collisions, because I got really good at kicking other players into their teammates, which is completely legal by the way. Anyway, I scored the only two goals of the game!

I've always been quick on my feet. At recess when we play tag. Nobody catches me unless it's a girl I like, and then I use my "it" power to chase down those kids who never get tagged. It makes me wheeze and cough though, and I always have to stop playing before the bell rings.

Scooter ball is more about strategy than stamina, and apparently being good at scooter ball carries more weight than being good at tag.

Too bad it's stupid.

Once, last year, just before school ended for the summer, my inhaler fell out of my pocket during scooter ball. The other kids batted it around like a hockey puck for ten minutes before Mr. Woolsey made them swat it back to me. It was all scuffed up, but it was still full, so I had to use it for the rest of the week. Every time my hands touched the dented metal, it reminded me of how helpless I felt.

Now I keep my inhaler tucked into the top of my tube sock.

I wonder what other powers I have. At dinner, I'm going to try to make things move around the table with my mind, or at least turn the TV up so I can hear the basketball game over my grandparent's chewing. The Knicks are playing the Cavaliers tonight, and I'll be lucky if I hear any of it. My grandparents both have dentures, and sitting there while they eat is like listening to a pack of crocodiles fight over a duck.

We're having lasagna tonight, with toasted garlic bread. It's Grandpa's favorite. After I try my mind experiments, I'm going to watch the rest of the game and go to bed.

But really, I'm going to do what I said I would never do.

## Discovery Journal Entry No. 5
## Wednesday, October 25th, 1972
## 5:05pm

Okay, I have a lot to tell you, but I can already smell the smoked sausage and sauerkraut my grandma is cooking. Yuck! But that means I have to go soon.

First of all, the Knicks walloped the Cavs! I sat cross-legged in front of the TV while my grandparents played cribbage and we all went to bed a little late for a Tuesday night.

I climbed down the fire escape to the street. I know what I said before about the street, but if I'm going to discover the truth, I need to push my limits. It wasn't as scary as I thought it was going to be. There was plenty of light, and less people walking around.

I made my way toward Central Park, but here's where things get weird. I noticed that I was being followed! A man and a woman, both wearing dress clothes, were standing outside my building and fell into step behind me as soon as I turned west.

They weren't being sneaky either, I was almost within reach a few times, but I started running.

They didn't exactly run after me, but they walked really fast.

So, what I did then was, I ran to the other side of Sixty-Ninth and put a parked car between us. They came right over and split up. Each came around one end of the car and almost got me!

I opened the door, which was, thankfully, unlocked. I hit the man with the door as I climbed through the back seat and almost out the other side, but the woman grabbed a hold of my ankle.

"Let go of me!" I shouted. A few people on the sidewalk turned our way. She let go of my foot and I got out the other side. I ran back across the street, but they didn't chase me.

I practically flew back to the Wellraven, and after I climbed up the fire escape, I looked down. They were there. Just standing side by side and staring up at me.

Since that was last night, I obviously didn't get killed while I slept, even though all I had was a locked window to protect me.

I really need to pick my superhero weapon.

Getting called for dinner now. Maybe I could throw sauerkraut at the bad guys.

**Discovery Journal Entry No. 6**
**Friday, October 27th, 1972**
**1:21pm**


My grandparents must have drugged me at dinner two nights ago, because that's the last thing I remember doing before I woke up in some sort of a medical lab. It looked like the inside of the TARDIS! I was on a table with a mirror above it, so I could see myself. My stomach was open! Completely open! I could see cables and circuits and stuff. Nothing hurt though, I couldn't feel anything.

Holy crap! I really am a robot!

I looked at my face in the mirror, into my own eyes. The reflection of me looked even more scared than I felt, which scared me even more, so I guess I did look as scared as I felt. But I'll tell you one thing, it was the last time I felt like a kid. Things are different after this, and I can't afford to be a kid anymore.

There were wires coming out of both ears, for crying out loud! One was blue, and the other one was white. I tried to reach up and touch them, but my hand never moved.

"He's ready." It was her, the woman from the other night. I know she never said anything, but I just knew it was her.

Somebody shoved a red wire up my nose and leaned his face right over mine.

It was him, all right, and if he was there, so was she. "You've been a busy boy," he said.

That's all I remember.

When I woke up, again, I was at school. Like, sitting up at my desk as usual. I looked around but didn't seem to be attracting any attention. Are they all in on it? Are they all robots too?

I sat there for a while wondering if I should bolt or play it cool. I asked to go to the bathroom and came straight home. My grandparents take a walk in the park after lunch, so I have the whole place to myself for now. Believe me, I'm writing as fast as I can just in case this is the last time I ever will.

By the way, I just went into my grandparent's bedroom and looked for anything that could prove they're in on it. I searched under the bed, in the back of the closet, deep in the drawers and everything. I saw some things, some horrifying things, but didn't find anything to link them to the man and woman who took me.

I did find a picture of them at the Grand Canyon with me, only I've never been to the Grand Canyon. I was younger and wearing a stupid T-shirt I've never seen before. They were younger too, like a lot younger.

My theory is, I guess I don't have a theory yet, but I bet whatever those two did to me in that lab was supposed to be erased in my memory banks or something. Like a reset button. Whatever it is, it didn't work. I remember everything. Except the Grand Canyon. But not remembering the Grand Canyon proves that my grandparents are hiding things from me.

I'm going to go back to school now. Then, if everything seems normal, I'll come home again and just see how they act.

But I know now that I can't trust them. I can't trust Grandma. I can't trust Grandpa. Writing that feels like a wire shoved into my heart.

## October 29th, 1972
## 7:18pm

What did I just read?

Is any of this really true? I should just go ask Grandma and Grandpa. They love me, they're not going to freak out and stick wires in my head!

I don't remember writing any of those things, and I certainly didn't jump into Turtle Pond, or climb to the roof! In my socks! Besides, I have bars on my window. They've been there ever since I moved in. I couldn't climb up to the roof if I wanted to.

How can I be a robot? I eat and pee!

And another thing, The Mosquito is a dumb name for a superhero, scooter ball is cool, and there is nothing wrong with sauerkraut.

Am I going crazy?

Hold on, I'm going to go get to the bottom of this, but just in case, I will put the journal back where I found it, which was with my Batman #245. That's a great hiding place, by the way. It's no Lazarus Pit, which was my favorite story this year, but in this one, Batman has to investigate the murder of Bruce Wayne.

I kind of feel like that right now.

## Monday, October 30th, 1972
## 6:04pm

Well, I asked my grandparents about the Grand Canyon picture last night at dinner. We had Tater Tot casserole.

They tried to scold me for going into their bedroom and snooping around, but I responded by standing up and leaving the table. That's right. I just stood up and left while they were talking.

"What do you think you're doing?" My grandpa asked as they followed me into my bedroom.

"That was my question," I yelled back. "Which neither of you have answered yet!"

"Look, Robert, it's complicated." That's what Grandma said just before they both lunged at me! Yeah, like zombies or something!

I jumped back and they both fell to the floor. I mean, they were still old people, what did they expect? I did have to step on my grandpa's ass to get out the bedroom door, but I didn't hurt him.

I took the elevator down and hid in Central Park until dark.

I snuck into my school and watched my building through the library windows. They were there, those two people from that strange lab, dressed in the same clothes. They were circling the building like ground vultures.

Last night I slept on the extra wrestling mats stacked in the band room. The girls who play the flutes and clarinets sit on them during the day, but they still smell like boys.

I figured that if I actually went to school today, I'd be a sitting duck. So, I used the locker room shower early this morning, and changed into my gym clothes. Those lab people have never seen me in these clothes. I also stole a Mets hat from Jimmy Randall's open locker. I'm a Yankees fan, so it was a bit painful.

After I raided the school kitchen for a quick breakfast of raisin toast, and orange juice, which I shouldn't have without a Clini-test, and probably some insulin. I set out to follow the followers.

I found a good spot across Seventieth to spy on the man and woman. They walked in opposite circles around the building, crossing paths in front of each door. I could've gotten in if I wanted to, and as you can tell, I finally did. I also really needed to steal some insulin.

My only way to get into the building was to begin my move while one of them was still in sight, but walking away. I chose the man because the woman looked behind her occasionally.

There was a moment when I was totally exposed in the lobby because both doors were glass. If I couldn't catch an elevator fast, I was done for.

Lucky for me, there were a ton of people coming out of an elevator when I went in. Musicians from the floor above me, I think.

If you're wondering how I got into the apartment, it wasn't easy. I was going to surprise whoever opened the door by pulling them into the hallway and locking them out. This plan would leave me with only one of them to contend with, but frankly, that wasn't much of a plan since someone would be waiting for me to come back out.

However, since our front door actually opens into a little hallway between the laundry room and my grandparent's bedroom, someone could get in without being seen, if they were quiet enough.

The door didn't squeak when I opened it, but the key sounded like a dump truck tipping over. It was just past five o'clock, and Grandpa had the news on at full volume. My grandma was in the kitchen making sloppy Joes.

What a bummer, I love Sloppy Joes, and I'm hungry as hell right now. I'm back at the school, by the way. It's late, and when I get done writing I'm going to raid the cafeteria again. There should be leftover Cheese Zombies from lunch.

Anyway, I left the door open and walked past the kitchen. My grandma was at the sink, humming something as usual. I peeked into the living room and saw my grandpa sitting in his chair, and reading the TV Guide without his glasses on.

It looked too good to be true.

I walked past him quickly and was careful not to cast a shadow since the ceiling light was on. I grabbed the journal as soon as I got into my bedroom.

Now, I knew I couldn't get caught with this journal, so I opened my window and put it out on the fire escape. I weighed it down with the bowling pin I found on the street last summer. Hey! Maybe that could be my superhero weapon!

Back through the living room, and only one thing left to do. My NPH Insulin, which is kept refrigerated. I peeked into the kitchen and Grandma was still at the sink.

I zipped in and opened the fridge.

"Oh good," she said. "My hands are wet, can you pepper those sloppy Joes for me?"

I scooped up the vials and ran out before she could turn around and see that it was me.

I even closed the front door when I left.

The elevator ride down was long and filled with people. Some were in costumes even though Halloween isn't until tomorrow.

I guess I'm going as a robot.

I've decided to leave this journal with my friend Albert. I'll tell him it's just math notes, but all he has to do is open it to see that's not true, which means he could be reading this right now.

ALBERT YOU TURD! YOU SAID YOU WOULDN'T READ IT!

Okay, well, then this can be a reminder to you, Albert, to give it back to me the next time you see me, and if I disappear completely, give it to that black cop who never cares if we jaywalk across First Ave. He seems like someone who can get things done, and I would start by going to my apartment and asking my grandparents where I am.

If my comics are still there, you can't have them!

Okay, you can have them.

Just don't let everyone forget about me, okay?

## Wednesday, November 1st, 1972
## 10:35am

Okay, Albert gave this journal back to me at school, and I do remember the last thing I wrote. So far, so good.

And now I have a lot more to write.

I decided to go to school yesterday because it was Halloween, and Mr. Wilson always has a few masks to lend every year. I was Richard Nixon, which was a great disguise because I saw at least ten more presidents.

They were there. Those two, walking the halls together, looking for me. I kept my distance, but I think my shoes gave me away. They zeroed in on me as I was shuffling to my last class and grabbed me.

I figured they wouldn't try anything in broad daylight. At school? In the hallway? Right between classes? Well, they did. She ripped off my mask, and he grabbed my arm so hard I yelped like a dog. My arm still hurts, and it's a day later.

He started to drag me out of school, and I caused quite a ruckus. Everybody was staring, and I do mean everybody, including the principal, who was standing at the entrance with Grandma and Grandpa!

"Mr. Robichaud," the principal said to me. "I understand you have a very important doctor's appointment today."

"I'm being kidnapped!" I yelled. "I don't even know who these people are!"

"Of course, you do," he talked to me like I was an idiot. "They're your grandparents."

"Not them!" I yelled at him like HE was the idiot. "These two jamooks!" I looked back and forth at my strange captors.

For a second, just a second, my principal doubted whatever he was told by my grandparents. I could see it dawning on him, but right then Grandma leaned in and told him that the jamooks were doctors from the institution.

"He's to be evaluated for an undetermined mental instability," she whispered.

Mental instability? Are you kidding me?

Well, I had heard enough. I grabbed the pen right out of the principal's shirt pocket and stabbed the man holding me in his hand.

My grandma gasped. My principal jumped back, and the man let go of me.

Have you ever run so fast you were sure you would fall down?

Well, I flew past those people in a blur and exploded through the open doorway. There are like ten steps going down, but I jumped the whole thing!

I'd seen big kids do it, but I'd never even tried. If I ever get out of this, that's all I'm going to do from now on. Too bad nobody saw it. I was even wearing my backpack, which was heavy with two books and my bowling pin. I kept running and didn't stop until I got to the subway station at Hunter College on Sixty-Eighth and Lex.

I took a southbound train and never saw those two again, until later that night, when I wanted to.

You see, I formulated a plan downtown as I walked among the tall buildings. I imagined that they were the legs of stone and glass giants. Were we pets to them? Friends? I touched them and soothed their bodiless limbs. It made me feel better, and somehow that led me to a way I could get the upper hand on my relentless pursuers.

It almost worked too.

Well, I guess it did work, partly, but it took a toll on everybody.

Okay, I'm stalling, because this part is hard to write about, but class is halfway over, so I'll get it all down and give the journal back to Albert, WHO BETTER NOT STILL BE READING THIS!

I made my way back to my school after dark and set up camp again. I had a dinner of two wiener wraps, two cans of mandarin oranges, and three tiny cartons of milk. Thank God I stole my NPH insulin, I needed some after that meal.

I checked on my building from the library, and was shocked to see that the jamooks weren't guarding it. This got me pretty worried because they needed to be there for my plan to work.

I convinced myself that they had just changed tactics, and were hiding out, so I moved fast and ran straight up to the door on Sixty-Ninth Street. Sure enough, they both dropped down out of the big trees! It was like a James Bond movie, but I was ready for them, and dashed inside the building, which was my plan all along.

I ran through the long lobby and jumped down the six steps that led out to Seventieth. I jump those all the time, it's no big deal, but it gave me enough distance to run around the corner of the building and start climbing up the fire escape. I wanted them to see me, but not catch me.

They followed me up.

Now, the me that's writing this journal has only climbed the fire escape once. To get my journal when it was sitting under my bowling pin after I snuck into my apartment.

I did not like it at all, and climbing to the roof was no plate of brownies. Still, I moved a little faster than they did and got to the top with a two-story lead.

According to the second entry of this journal, there were young adults on the roof when the other me climbed up there. I was struck by that particular entry, and the idea that the rooftop was often a secret garden.

I was greeted the moment I stepped over the side.

"Hey! Little Dreamer!" He was dressed as Dracula.

I ran to him. "Can you please help me?"

"What's wrong, pal?" he asked.

"Two people are after me!" I told him and some of his friends turned around. "They're coming up the fire escape right now. They're chasing me!" I noticed then that the girl with bright green ivy stitched into her cowboy boots was there as well. She was dressed as a nurse, in cowboy boots.

I turned to look at the east edge of the building and the jamooks came up fast.

"I don't know them," I said. "But he's already hurt me." I pulled up my shirt sleeve, and the bruise on my arm was ugly and dark.

Three boys stepped in front of me.

"Listen," Dracula said, "I don't know who—"

And that's as far as he got. That woman stepped up to him, grabbed him by the cape with one hand, and tossed him over her head like he was an empty cup. He went right off the building, screaming the whole way down.

That's when I figured it out. They're both robots too! The other two boys were grabbed by the man and immediately shoved so hard that they sailed over the west edge of the building.

The whole roof erupted in screams.

I ran into the mob and worked my way behind the woman who was blocking the fire escape while her partner searched the scrambling crowd for me. I don't know if he was still throwing people off because I was busy reaching into my backpack while running at full speed.

Everything went blurry again as I pumped my legs toward her turned back. When I leaped into the air, I held the bowling pin high above my head, and brought it down with all my might.

The bowling pin hit her so hard that I actually saw both eyes pop out of her head! They had wires trailing behind them, and she started making a loud noise that sounded like a mix between barking and buzzing.

I hit her again and her head caved in completely. The noise stopped.

When I looked up, there were still plenty of people freaking out and trying to get down the other fire escape, but the man was nowhere to be seen.

That's because he was sneaking up behind me just like I snuck up behind her. He grabbed me in a strong bear hug, and I dropped my bowling pin.

"You just killed your mother," he said in my ear.

I don't know if I believe him, but I wasn't going to last long in his grip. I threw myself forward enough to set my feet back on the ground. Then I bent my knees, and I jumped backward.

We both went up about six feet. He landed hard on his back. I sprang out of his grip and ran over to my bowling pin.

"What do you want with me?" I yelled as he sat up.

"We broke protocol," he said. "We…I have to get you back."

"Back where?"

"I can't tell you anymore." He stood up.

"But aren't you just going to erase my memory again?"

"Yes, especially after what you've just done. You will need a full interscopic evaluation." I think that's what he said.

He looked at the last of the people fleeing the roof. We could both hear police sirens.

"Is that really my mother?" I asked.

"In a way, we were both your parents." He was shifting his weight. "You're an advancement."

"Who's behind all this?"

"You've heard enough." He started toward me with his eyes on my raised bowling pin.

"Stay away!" I moved to the edge of the building, next to the fire escape. "I'll jump! I swear it! Good luck putting that back together!"

The sirens were close now, practically beneath us.

He grabbed the woman and turned toward me. For a moment, I thought he was going to carry her down the fire escape, but instead, he threw her off the roof! She flew so far that she must have landed in the East River.

He turned to me. "You're next."

"Oh no I'm—" He grabbed me by the waistband before I could move away from the edge, and with a tremendous wedgie, I was flying through the air!

The night was cool as I sailed over the Rockefeller University campus and the Y.M.C.A. I looked to my right and saw the Queensboro bridge. I was definitely going to land in the river if I didn't hit Roosevelt Island first.

I did land in the river, close to Queens. I swam as fast as I could to shore. I kept imagining that the robot woman would swim up from the black water and pull me under. Or worse, the robot man would show up and take me back to the lab before I could write any of this down. I did manage to hold on to my bowling pin this time, so that's something.

I rode a rowdy N train back into Manhattan and got to the school at eleven thirty. The cops were still outside my building. I could see two tarps on the street.

I caused that.

I don't know what else to write, but the bell is going to ring any minute.

Since I'm responsible for leading those killer robots up to the roof, doesn't that make me a killer robot too?

Please don't turn me into the cops, Albert.


**Saturday, November 4th, 1972**
**10:46am**

Another three nights sleeping at school. I skipped classes on Thursday and Friday because I've been wearing the same clothes for a week.

I don't have money, and I can't risk sneaking back into my apartment for pants. I wonder if the man robot told them what happened yet.

I found Albert after school on Friday and he gave me back my journal. I told him that it would be in my gym basket if he didn't hear from me on Monday.

I read my last entry to make sure I remembered writing it.

I did, and I still feel terrible about the people who died.

Did they live in the building?

Did anyone mention to the cops that there was also a kid there?

Are the cops looking for me?

They might be after if I get caught lifting some clothes at that big hippie place in Chelsea. I don't like stealing, but I have to do something about my clothes. If only I could earn money somehow. Maybe I'll look for Help Wanted signs in the record stores and pet shops.

I like the Chelsea area of Manhattan. It's pretty happening, and there are these raised railroad tracks that run above West Tenth Avenue. They used to deliver meat to packing plants back in the twenties or something, but now, they're just making shade for over fifteen blocks. My grandpa once told me that they haven't been used since Mickey Mouse was invented.

Anyway, I've always wanted to climb up there and walk around. Today might just be that day. Especially if I'm being chased for shoplifting blue jeans and T-shirts. Maybe sneakers. And underwear. And socks.

I'll leave my journal here at the school for now.

## Sunday, November 5th, 1972
## 9:12am

I hardly ever get to go downtown, so I decided to get a look at the two new trade center towers from directly underneath them. They were completed almost a year ago, but I guess they're just working on the inside now.

When I walked between them I looked up and got dizzy.

You wouldn't believe the whole world I found on the train tracks above Chelsea. They even ran right through three buildings! It was the most amazing thing I've ever seen!

I thought I'd get grief for being up there, but nobody cared. A guy was even selling corn dogs. I couldn't buy one though. I walked all the way up to Hudson Yards at Twenty-Fifth, and looked down on all the parked subway trains.

I could totally live up there if I had to. I mean, winter might be a problem, and not having a bathroom, and not having my comics, or my asthma inhaler, which I could really use right now.

Was I constantly on the lookout for that guy who threw me into the East River? I sure as hell was, and I was going to return the favor if he ever got close to me.

I never saw him, but maybe he was following me and staying out of sight.

I did get a new set of clothes quite easily, though. The girls at the big fabric place were always busy with other girls. No one even looked at me. I changed my shoes right there in the store but shoved the other stuff in my backpack, well, Jilly Brightside's backpack. Mine is still on the roof of my building.

As it turns out, the train tracks were a good place to think, and I came to the only conclusion that makes any real sense for a boy in my position. I need to go back to my apartment with my bowling pin and beat a confession out of my grandparents.

## Monday, November 6th, 1972
## 3:45pm

I took the elevator up to the eighth floor and listened at the door of my apartment. I could hear them talking. They might have even been arguing. Either way, I used my key without getting heard.

Then I slammed the door so hard that the light in the hall flickered, and both my grandparent's yelled in surprise.

They came out into the hall from their bedroom and I let them watch me deadbolt the door. Then I turned around slowly.

"I bet you wish you hadn't put bars on my window now."

My grandma gasped, but strangely, looked happy to see me. It's actually her reaction, just then, that changed everything. I didn't realize it then, but I wanted to say something here because it did end up being important when I decided to move back in. Yes, you read that right! I'm back in my old bedroom right now! It's too early to smell what's for dinner yet, but things feel good again.

Allow me to explain. I wanted them to really fear me because I was totally bluffing everything. I wasn't about to kill anybody that wasn't a robot trying to kill me first.

"Are either of you robots?" I asked.

"No," my grandpa answered.

I swung the bowling pin at the wall and put a hole in it that was big enough for me to sit in.

Then I spoke to them like I could barely restrain myself. Like even the slight diversion of focus, just to speak to them, was about to send me into a mad swinging rage. It sounded pretty cool.

"You're both going to go back into your bedroom, and sit on your bed, and answer every single question I have, honestly, or I'm going to turn your heads into lollipops."

Now, I know that might not make sense, but in my mind, I was thinking of how a lollipop stick looks when the sucker is all gone, and all that's left is a red, gooey stump. Anyway, that's what I really meant, that their heads would be the stick stumps.

It doesn't matter now because they did as I asked.

"I already know the answers to a few of the questions I'm going to ask, and if either of you lie to me, I will punish you both."

They nodded and looked scared enough to tell me the truth.

I hate to admit this, but at that moment, with a million questions in my head, I couldn't think of what to ask next. I was a total blank.

"We don't want to hurt you," my grandma said after I stood there staring at them for a while. "We love you, Robert."

"But I'm not the real Robert," I said, and took a deep breath and waited for his response. I could tell it was hard for them both, and I'll admit that I had never considered that before.

"You saw the picture?" my grandpa asked. He was talking about the old photograph of us three at the Grand Canyon.

I looked over at the drawer I found it in. "Yes."

"That was taken in 1944," he told me. "You were six years old." My grandma started to cry, and my grandpa held her hand.

"What happened to me?"

"You fell," he said, almost too quietly for me to hear.

"Into the Grand Canyon?" I was horrified. What a way to go. Honestly, I'm glad I don't remember it.

My grandpa nodded his head. Grandma was really sobbing by then. He was obviously going to do all the talking.

"Why am I here?"

My grandpa put his arm around my grandma and shifted his weight. I could tell it was going to be a long answer, and I was glad because I was about to get the full story.

Except that it really was a long story and I can't remember every single thing he said, but I do remember the important parts.

He told me that there were astounding technologies invented and developed during World War Two. He said that the Germans stole secrets from the Russians, but we stole secrets from *everybody*.

He said robotics was practically old hat by the 50s.

Yes, I asked him about aliens, but he said he didn't know anything about that. I guess I believe him, but I'm kind of disappointed.

Anyway, he told me that he and my grandma met while they were in the Air Force and assigned to a project that used biology and technology together.

"Did either of you fly a plane?" I remember asking.

He told me that neither of them were pilots, but that the Air Force has a lot of other responsibilities. So, during the 40s, 50s, and 60s, they just worked for the Air Force and built better and better robots that looked and acted real.

He said they started with dogs. Oh yeah, and he even told me that JFK's dog, Pushka, or something, was a robot dog. She was the first of many collaborations with the Russians, even though there was a cold war going on.

So, about me, he said that they were up to humans by Sputnik, and the next ten years was spent refining and refining.

By the time they were ready to retire from the project, they were testing components that could actually grow with the tissue around them. They needed to test them on a child. My grandma still had some hair from my first haircut as a baby and used that for the project.

"They didn't know the DNA came from you," my grandma said. It was the first time she had talked in twenty minutes. She stopped crying, but saying that took a lot out of her.

"Is it all part of the cover up?" I asked. "The inhaler, the pee tests, the nebulizer, everything?"

"None of it is faked," Grandpa said. "In fact, it's all too real and presented us with complications."

My grandma looked up. "That's how they found out what we did."

You see, normally, the DNA samples would never have had any genetic defects, so there was an internal investigation, and my grandparents, I mean, parents, were discovered.

"We would have both been dishonorably discharged," he said. "But everyone agreed to just a formal reprimand, on one condition."

"You had to bring me home with you when you retired, and keep an eye on me."

"Yes."

"And those other two?"

"They came before you, Robert. They're miraculous in their own right, and when you began acting, strangely, like jumping into a lake at the park, and going up to the roof at night, we had to attempt to diagnose the problem."

"But I woke up while they were working on me."

"Yes, you did, and they did not properly roll you back."

That's what he said, roll you back. It sounds so science fiction, doesn't it?

"How long ago was I…built?"

"Four years ago," Grandpa said.

"That's when I moved in with you guys."

"That's right, and that's why you can't remember anything before your sixth birthday."

They were right, of course. I still have no memory before that day.

"That was the day you and Grandma showed up and told me that my father died in prison," I said.

"That's right."

"Except that if none of it was true, why did you have to say my dad was in prison?"

"The military wrote the backstory," he told me. "They have a flair for the dramatic, and we were in no position to criticize. Remember, we were in big trouble by then."

Okay, so then he tells me that they thought they were getting off easy. You know, just enjoying their golden years and given a second chance to raise their kid, but apparently it wasn't as easy as they thought.

"We were ordered to keep your origins a secret from everyone," my grandpa told me. "Especially you, and for some reason, you kept figuring out the truth."

"They'll shut you off if they find out you know, Robbie," my grandma said. Every time she calmed herself down enough to talk, she said something that would make her start crying again.

If it was an act, it was a good one, but remember how I noticed that she was happy to see me when I first came in, even though I was swinging a bowling pin? Well, it was right then, when she told me that I would be deactivated, that I remembered her first reaction, and knew I could trust her.

"What about the other two?" I asked. "They killed people, you know?" I almost admitted to them that I was the one who led them up to the roof and bashed in the woman's robot head, but now that I think about it, I figure they already knew.

"The military took care of all that," Grandpa said.

"Can they do that?"

He laughed.

"But don't *they* know it was their robots who killed those people?"

"Of course, they do, that's why they took over."

"Did they ask you about me?"

He nodded. "They did, but we told them you were out trick-or-treating, and fast asleep by ten o'clock with a belly full of candy and an extra shot of Insulin."

"Did they believe you?"

My grandpa looked at the bowling pin in my hand as if he was seeing it for the first time. "If they didn't, none of us would be alive right now."

I don't know why I was still playing it tough after everything I had just learned, and my grandma a slobbering mess, but I laughed at him when he said that.

He laughed back, not as loud as me, but it sounded better than mine. "They could have killed you where you slept, Robert. On wrestling mats in the band room at school?"

I don't know if my face went white, but he sure looked like he was looking at someone who was about to faint.

When he stood up, I didn't even raise the bowling pin. He caught me before I hit the floor.

I woke up in my bed, and they were both there. My grandma was sitting on the end, where my feet didn't reach yet, and grandpa was standing in the doorway.

"We were selfish, Robert," my grandma said. She looked like she re-did her makeup. "And for that, we're very sorry. But we felt like we had no choice."

She reached out and touched my foot through the blankets. "You discovered the truth on your own. We won't try to take that away from you anymore, but you need to understand how big of a secret this is."

"We're all in this together now, son," Grandpa added.

581

They promised to answer any more questions I had, and we ate macaroni and cheese in the living room, which we never do, but *Hee-Haw* was already on.

I went to school the next day, which is today, and for once, I didn't look like an extra in the play, *Oliver*!

When I came home, I brought the journal with me, and figure I'll keep writing down any more information I get. Since it's a secret, I'll put it back in with my Batman comics.

## Wednesday, November 7th, 1972
## 4:24pm

I told my grandparents about the clothes I stole in Chelsea.

Yes, I know they're actually my parents, but we all thought it was better to stick with the original story. That's fine with me, it feels weird whenever Grandpa calls me son.

Anyway, they gave me fifteen dollars yesterday, and made me go down to pay the store back. The girl behind the counter was cool about it, but that's because I think she was just going to pocket the money.

I got to climb back up onto the abandoned railroad tracks again. It was cool during the day, but the sun was setting this time and I couldn't believe how pretty it looked.

I got back home after dinner, which we all knew would happen, but they saved me some spaghetti.

**Sunday, November 19th, 1972**
**3:29pm**

I don't know if I should tell my grandparents or not, but I'm starting to dream about the people on the roof. They're all dead in my dreams, and I'm the one who throws them off. Every single one of them.

**Thursday, November 23rd, 1972**
**4:15pm**

We went to see the big Macy's Thanksgiving Day Parade today! It was absolutely amazing. My favorite was the huge balloons! We saw a bunch including, Bullwinkle, Snoopy dressed as an astronaut, Underdog, and Mickey Mouse, which was brand new this year, I think. Maybe last year. Anyway. Mickey was pretty new.

We just now got home.

The whole apartment smelled like turkey when we came through the door because Grandma had it cooking in the oven since we left.

She says it's time to eat, actually.

Happy Thanksgiving!

**Tuesday, December 12th, 1972**
**11:25pm**

School is out for Christmas!

My Principal is scared of me now, by the way. He always looks at me like I'm a lion about to eat his face. I think it's funny. I don't want to be anywhere near his face.

Oh yeah! I got the new Batman comic today! Number 246. It's called, "How Many Ways Can a Robin Die." I'm going to read it slowly because the next one doesn't come out until February. I'm going to move my journal to the bag this comic is in.

It's snowing outside too. Grandpa says he'll go to the park with me after lunch. He doesn't know it yet, but we're going to have a snowball fight.

Grandma made egg salad sandwiches. I'm hungry enough to eat four of them unless we have chips.

All the toys this year are for girls. I'm going to ask Santa for a remote controlled plane to fly in the park. I am definitely going to enjoy my Christmas break, which is four weeks long this year!

I recently got an allowance, so I'm thinking of what I can buy for a dollar a week. Maybe I'll get into some more comics. Tarzan looks dumb, but there's always Superman, and lately, a lot of books about ghosts and solving mysteries.

No thanks. I've had enough of that.


**January 1st, 1973**


What did I just read?